ACROSS THE DESPERATE MILES

Patrick Michael Murphy

Edited by Jan Takac

Project support: a list of others I will not name here, but you know who you are and that you are loved.

Cover Photograph © Peng Guang Chen / Dreamstime.com

Additional photoshop artwork by Dick The Walking Man Rinehart

This is a work of fiction and any resemblance to person or event is coincidental.

To my mother, Jeni, and my father, Bill
For their unconditional love
and support
and for the freedom
to truly live.

Part One

Chapter 1

Rand lay there shivering, leg muscles seizing painfully, his side flaming again like it had when he'd been stabbed. *How many times now have I thought I would die as I fought my way along? Three? Five? Sooner or later it will be true. Don't the odds make it so?* If he couldn't get this journey behind him, if he couldn't reach his children and find his wife, wouldn't it be best to die anyway? *What the hell is anything for?* What the hell would life be like, living and knowing how he had lost everything, *EVERYTHING!*

Three Weeks Earlier...

Black as a moonlight shadow the Ferrari F-355 bolted down the Avenue of the Americas in the heart of Manhattan. It boasted a glossy sheen, wide Pirelli tires, and personalized license plates that read LENSMAN. Past sky-high concrete, glass, and steel the streamlined profile cut through traffic like a rabid dog on the run.

Six speakers pumped out *The Good Life* by Three Days Grace on the radio as thirty-two-year-old Rand Priven maneuvered his newest obsession in and out of traffic. When the song ended, and a morning show newscaster started blabbing about the nationwide rise in terrorist activities, he set down his to-go cup of hot syrupy latte and changed stations with a flick of his clipped and clean finger. *Let's have some MUSIC!* Unfortunately, the next station started in on political gridlock—*Damn!*—forcing him to again jab the buttons as he slipped the Ferrari around a corner and past a streetlight more red than yellow. Its fender brushed the pant leg of a bum in tattered blue jeans who then screamed some red-faced obscenity and shook his fist. Rand glanced at his rearview mirror and held up his middle finger, "Get a fucking JOB!" He shifted hard into second, tailgated a motorcycle doing the speed limit, and cut off a taxi as he accelerated into the outer lane. He checked the time on his gold Rolex wristwatch.

In short time he veered west off the avenue, raced down a couple side streets, an alley, and skidded to a stop in front of a renovated red brick warehouse turned Priven Photography Studio. He guzzled the last of the coffee, checked his hair and teeth in the rearview mirror, then grandly rose, khaki slacks and black tee-shirt, out of the car. At the front door he paused to gaze back at the exquisite Italian machine. *Damn, she's HOT!*

Smiling, he entered the finely decorated office portion of the studio— a French glass chandelier, South American wood trim and floors.

Setting his briefcase onto a mahogany work table, he said, "Good morning, Claris."

A college-aged young woman sat behind a desk, tapping the keys on the latest Mac. She had glossy blonde, shoulder-length hair and a face made for the camera. "Rand, Marla Pole is here, she's—"

"I know." He pressed his index finger to his lips and stepped over to the door where he peered into the larger open body of the dimly lit studio.

About thirty feet away, wearing two-inch heels and a thick, stiff pants suit, Marla Pole, chief art director for *Lady Professional* magazine, paced the ancient and restored plank floor of the great space. Despite her agitated state, her sprayed-stiff hair held precise shape, parted down the side to a sheer cut at the earlobes. Rand could smell her over-sweet perfume from where he stood; it nearly gagged him. Blaire, her anxious assistant, stood by her side and leafed through their monthly scheduling calendar—for her a perpetual act. Two other women stood behind them. Rand knew the make-up artist; the other he wasn't certain of, but presumed her to be Marla's client. They all looked testy to him.

Two lithe, female models—one wearing a transparent, low-cut body stocking, the other a dress-suit—sat on a blanket with their long legs stretched out before them on the floor of a two-sided backdrop. One half of the set celebrated femininity with rosy colors and immense overstuffed pillows, and the other side, the working life, with hard-edged office decor. The models picked purple grapes out of a prop bowl, pulled them off the stems and popped them into their moist mouths, spitting the seeds off to the side. Other than the echoes of Ms. Pole pacing, and the "ptew" of the two lovely ladies spitting seeds, the place maintained a heavy, anticipatory silence.

Two Hasselblad cameras sat on tripods in front of the models and several portable light boxes stood in varied locations around the set. Jimmy, the camera assistant, came into view and started nervously sweeping up the grape seeds.

"My God! Jimmy, have you no idea where he is?" Ms. Pole reprimanded the assistant.

The erratic whisk of Jimmy's sweeping increased. "Yes, ma'am, he's on his way, traffic, you know, but he'll be here soon." At that moment he glanced toward the office and Rand signaled him with a quick nod, then shifted back inside.

Claris rose and approached Rand. He noticed a bit of moisture on her forehead and that her eyes seemed larger than usual. She said, "The Gretten account called this morning and canceled the shoot for next week."

He could see this worried her and he paused, but then blew it off. After working his rear off for many years, he was on a roll with top name clients. Teasing her, he scrunched his eyes and puckered his mouth, concentrating theatrically. He had lush, impenetrable, chocolate brown hair with cinnamon strands neatly out of place over the forehead, kept it short and lightly moussed. "We have Cosmetica and Barque Clothier next week, right?"

"Yes...." But she continued to hold her hands clasped before her, questioning eyes fixed on Rand, waiting for more.

He smiled, let her stand, and went to a small table full of fresh cut flowers, poured himself a cup of Kenyan coffee, then opened a refrigerator and added creme. "Where's Rachel?"

"She ran to check out the location permits for next week."

Jimmy came in and stood with fists crammed into back pockets, shoulder blades pressed to the wall. He wore baggy jeans and tennis shoes, a baseball cap with *Shoot Me!* and the outline of a camera printed on the front.

"Hi," Rand said. He looked at Jimmy's attire. "We've agreed to wear nicer clothes on shoot days, right?"

"Sorry. You won't see these again." He sounded tense, out of breath.

Rand studied the two of them as he sipped from the cup. "You two look freaked."

Claris turned to him again. "Gretten was going to pay for that last shoot when they got here next week. Now they're not coming and they never pay unless they come in for another shoot. You know how they are."

He sipped the coffee again and smirked as he swallowed. "Relax. They'll pay and they'll be back for more."

Claris's eyes fluttered frenetically as she over enunciated each word, "But we are not going to make the loan payment at the beginning of the month if we don't bring in something substantial!"

Rand chuckled. "We will, we will. Just do what you're doing. Call Gretten and ask them again if they can send us payment." He turned to

Jimmy. "We ready?"

"Yes." Jimmy said, with his eyes on Rand, but his face tilted toward the floor. "She's really pissed."

Rand swallowed the rest of the coffee, refilled, then strode past Jimmy. "Well, then," he smiled and cut a glance toward the younger man, "let's make art she can't help but love."

They moved together into the airiness of the studio. Ms. Pole saw them coming, flipped closed her cell phone, slapped shut her personal appointment book, pushed back her sleeve and looked at her watch. The two models smiled openly at Rand and he allowed one side of his mouth—the side away from Ms. Pole—to give a little smile back.

"Marla," he said, "I know you'll love what we have in mind today."

***

Kera Priven drove an over-priced and elephantine Ford Excursion four-by-four through Mount Vernon, New York, a city with avenues named after the likes of Lincoln and Columbus. She knew that on this ground Glover's Brigade played a part in the Revolutionary War that may have saved General George Washington's army from defeat, but for her, living more than two hundred years later, the rat-a-tat of British drums had been replaced by the constant grind of automobile traffic. In little more than three months the Excursion had nearly six thousand city miles on the odometer and creases worn into its leather seats.

Radio news reported militia activities in Montana and Louisiana. Kera wanted to listen, but couldn't, harried as she was keeping the lumbering SUV in the center of her lane, trying to appease an older man in a BMW who was veering over at her, shouting angrily and shaking his fist. She hated driving the thing and had entered the roadway too slowly to blend with traffic. The guy in the BMW was forced to take his foot off his accelerator and now seemed bent on running her off the road. She cringed and shrank behind the wheel. *Oh, please!* It seemed to her that anger and tension on the road—everywhere in the city—had reached boiling point.

At 7:48 a.m. she was already biting her soft, pouty lower lip, feeling shredded and consumed by the city—by life itself. Small dark bags underscored her big brown eyes and jaw-length chestnut-colored hair had been hastily rubber banded into a chopped ponytail. Loose wisps fell across her forehead, partially camouflaging her right eye. She had the look of an overwhelmed child in need of a hug.

Turning right toward the grade school she glanced sideways and saw the BMW continue on, then took a deep breath and wiped her eyes with the sleeve of her sweatshirt. *Thank you!* She dug another chocolate-chip cookie from the bag in her lap. It had evolved, with all she had to do, that the concept of a decent breakfast had faded into her past. *De-evolved*, Kera thought. *What was the word for that?*

Pulling up to a three-story hundred-year-old school building, quarry rock for walls, she brought the SUV to a stop and turned toward the back seat. "Andrew, Alissa, come on now, wake up." The children had slept through the ride and their heads swayed, necks bent sorely. They rubbed their puffy faces. "Come on now," she nudged them with her soft, mother's voice, "we're at school." Their heads popped up as they came suddenly awake, blinking toward the playground and the other children.

She climbed down out of the "truck," as Randy called it—too high off the ground for her liking—then rushed the children hand-in-hand through the emptying schoolyard, their baggy jeans swishing, backpacks strapped to slight shoulders, eyes searching out friends. It was a warm summer morning, the last day of school, and their upper lips glistened. Before the heavy wooden door the children stopped and hugged their mom. Seven year-old Alissa asked, "You and Dad are coming to the Last Day Party, right?" .

Their bodies were warm in her arms. "Yes. I work part of the day today, so I won't make it to pick you up right after school, getting out early like you are. Go to daycare and we'll meet you at four o'clock."

"Is Dad coming?" Andrew asked, a slight downward draft in his nine-year-old voice.

"He said he would, remember?"

"Yeah, but—"

"I'll call him today and remind him." She put on a smile.

He studied her with serious little eyes, then smiled too. "Okay."

"Get going to class." She hugged them again and Andrew heaved the thick, wooden door open. Kera watched them as they marched side-by-side down the long school hallway and into their future life. Each thing they did seemed innocent and vulnerable. She watched until they left her sight. As she hurried back to the Excursion her eyes welled-up and her mouth quivered. A tear dropped down onto her cheek like a drip from a worn-out faucet.

Hours later, back where the day had started for the Priven family, at the five-bedroom brownstone house on the corner lot of an upscale neighborhood, Kera parked in her spot along the front curb and hustled across the lawn. She glanced again at their big place that needed a coat of paint and new shingles on the roof. Her head went down as she walked. It dumbfounded her, how much they had paid for the place, which felt twice as big as anything they would ever need. As with the truck, Randy had decided on the neighborhood and the house, but now, it seemed, he could care less. The work needed doing, but only once had Kera summoned the courage to speak to him about it. He had not mentioned it since, nor followed up. He spent all the money they had on his new car, the studio, and dinners with clients.

Kera entered the kitchen and emptied two cans of chopped tomatoes into a pot. She added seasoning, oil and water, then placed the pot on the stove and turned up the heat. Scrubbing furiously at a spot on the stove, her mind wandered. After dropping off the children she had worked four hours at an art supply store, gassed up the monstrosity, returned two calls concerning the children and their friends, and was just now finishing two loads of laundry. She scrubbed so intensely, with upper teeth pressed hard into lower lip, and with such abstraction, that her hand slipped and punched into the pot of now bubbling sauce, which splashed onto her hand.

Kera didn't make a sound, but her face twisted with frustration, with pain. She shifted to the sink, ran cold water over the scalded skin of her trembling fingers. The thin sauce spiraled, blood-like, down the drain and she gazed at it for a long time, lost in worry. She felt desolate and wanted to scream, to swing at something, but she couldn't. All she had wanted was to steal enough time to complete the first home-cooked meal in a week.

Dabbing her hand dry, she glanced at a page length to-do list and crossed off the top three with the slash of a pen. Her hand pulsed with pain, so she climbed creaking stairs to the upper floor, consisting of five bedrooms and two bathrooms. Plucking a tube of salve from the cabinet above the sink she hurried back down the hallway, suddenly paused, then eased open a bedroom door.

This bedroom had four broad windows looking north toward the Bronx and Hutchinson rivers. A skylight above the windows gave variety to the direction of light, softening the room and its shadows. The walls were painted ivory. Alone in the space stood a worn swivel chair and an easel that Kera used for painting.

She stepped in, into the quietness, and closed the door. Leaning against a wall, she squeezed salve absently onto her aching hand, tried desperately to catch her breath, and gazed about, as if feeling the room with her eyes. Finally, she approached the easel. An unfinished canvas displayed a burst of brilliant green background and the beginnings of an ancient rock wall to the front. She slowly ran a finger over the dusty edge of the canvas. Having started the painting nearly a year ago, she had not been able to find the time, or any creative energy, to continue. On her last, brief attempt she had added dark brooding colors and infested the wall with woody vines that separated it, weakened it.

It took a certain amount of time and peace for her to create, no matter how poignant or inspired the original vision. It took positive energy to create beauty, and she had no interest in painting ugliness.

She bent and picked a white sheet from the floor, draped the canvas, left the room.

Planning to vacuum the first floor of the house, she halted in the kitchen and lifted the phone from the wall as if it were a small boulder. She leaned on the counter and pushed the speed dial.

"Hi, Claris, this is Kera. I'm sorry to bother you, but Randy must have his cell phone forwarded to you. Is he there?" Her voice quivered. "Oh, okay, well... what's that? Yes, Andrew and Alissa have a school function this afternoon and I wanted to remind him. Yes. Could you please have him call when he gets back? Okay. Bye."

***

At four in the afternoon Rand sat at a table, drinking espresso in Jergen Balmms, a quaint, big-windowed restaurant in Greenwich Village. Designers, publishers, stars—people in and of The Know—showed themselves here and made contact, kept the pulse of the in-crowd ceaselessly throbbing. He'd completed the morning photography shoot in spite of Marla Pole and what he considered her freakazoid psychoneurotics, and had stopped to rinse his face and comb his hair. He looked fresh.

Two tall models, one blonde, one auburn, came from the rear of the room, past gold trim, black tile, imported tables with lion's claw feet. They spotted Rand and veered his way, one walking lightly, almost erratically, the other straight-on and steady.

"Hi, Randy." The blonde's voice squeaked past glossy, rossa rubino lips.

Rand stood and cleared his throat. "Nadine," he smiled tightly, "it's Rand now. You remember." He turned to the other, "Suzanne, hello."

"You look nice," Nadine continued, rocking back on her splayed heels, but when Rand failed to look back to her, she turned and skittered away.

Suzanne paid no attention to her leaving. "It's been awhile since we worked together, is everything going well for you?"

"Of course," he nodded, marveling at the classic beauty of her face. From her he invariably received the impression of success, and the sense that she would be incredible in the sack. A rare babe she was, especially at age twenty-four. She had obviously known what she wanted, gone out, and seized it. "Never a problem," he said. "How about you, working?"

"The Seychelles, Rio, the Swiss Alps!" Her eyes lit up, blazing green orbs not unlike Rand's own. "I feel so lucky," she said, smiling openly.

He let himself admire her, the way the V of her blouse opened beneath the horizontal line of attentive, unhaltered nipples, and with calm interest she watched him do it. "You're not lucky, you're blessed," he said, and then his eyes held hers.

Her cheeks turned pink. "Thank you." She glanced away for an instant. "So, what do you think of that explosion near San Francisco?"

Rand shifted, surprised by the segue. "Uh, hadn't heard." He felt suddenly bored, except for the way her lips formed the word *explosion*. She could use those lips, no doubt, but Rand now averted his eyes. He could flirt, but he needed her beauty in front of his lens, and wanted to keep their relationship where it mattered most—working toward profit.

"You haven't heard? A military base was blown up. It sounded like the entire—"

At that moment Marla Pole marched through the front door, head and shoulders forward, suit coat buttoned across her chest like body armor, sieging the room. She flipped open her cell phone, as if pulling the pin on a grenade. Blaire was in tow. Rand gestured to them.

Suzanne turned and saw Marla advancing. "Oh, wow! Is she here for you, Rand?"

"Yup." He maintained a cool smile, happy the room would see

Marla here with him. She was a pain, but her magazine top notch. "Maybe we can talk later."

Suzanne's eyes widened at being suddenly dismissed, but she checked her reaction, "Fine," touched his arm briefly with her fingertips, then moved smoothly away.

"Hi." Rand smiled and motioned for Marla and Blaire to have a seat at his table.

Marla closed the phone, "You know, Randy, I really cannot stay." She had come to a halt, right index finger to lips, and gazed into the open rafters of the place.

"Rand. It's Rand now." He forced a smile.

Marla looked right at him, nostrils flared, lips compressed like the edges of a jagged scar. "What I think I'm going to do is this, Randy, I think I'm going to cancel your contract."

Rand reached out casually and placed his hand on her shoulder, "Marla, you don't seriously think you'll find anyone better for—"

She pulled back. "Look, Mr. Twitter, you're good, but not good enough to be fucking off! If you have a problem with this have your attorney call mine." She then performed a literal about-face and marched out. Blaire trotted after her.

Rand found himself staring at the door, slack-jawed, eyebrows arched in amazement. Then he glanced covertly around the restaurant to see if anyone had noticed the incident. Suzanne stood among people absorbed in conversation, but her eyes remained fixed on him, for an instant, then cut away.

Rand smiled weakly, too late, then downed the remaining espresso in his cup. He felt hot around the collar. *One client cancels a shoot, another quits. What the hell is this?* He gathered himself, furtively checked his image in a mirror on the wall, and turned to leave. *Yes, an unfortunate coincidence, but they'll regret it! Anyway, Difficult was Marla's middle name—it will be written on the tag tied to her toe upon departure.*

Moving toward the door, he tapped a shoulder and squeezed a hand as he passed certain key people. Glances of recognition were the toast of two, while one completely disregarded him. *That didn't happen a week ago.* Anyway, there were plenty more where Marla Pole came from. He straightened his shoulders, his spine, walked with his eyes level to the room. He burst out of the place, and into sunlight, determination hot in his eyes. After all, he had a few grenades of his own. Pulling out his cell phone, he poked out a number.

***

Kera handed the checker forty-four dollars and change. He picked through the silver and copper distastefully, grumbled something inaudible, tore off a receipt and thrust it into her bag. Kera hefted the sack of groceries and hurried out the door.

The day had turned grey and the street swarmed with people. She felt they lived in denial. Though they claimed loyalty to the city and its way of life they appeared pallid, blank-faced, like automatons. They dressed in extravagant and varied fashion, but somehow looked like duplicates. Day after day they rushed in frenzied patterns, repeating an exercise they clung to and could not force themselves to question.

What bothered her most was that she was one of them.

As she nosed into traffic five cars beeped and sped past before one slowed enough to let her in. She tromped on the gas pedal and barreled down the boulevard feeling closed-in and surrounded.

A half-hour later she sat with her chin in her hand, elbow propped on a long collapsible table within the crowded school gymnasium. The scent of boiled hot dogs filled the air, but instead of teasing her palate, it made her nauseous. Other parents chatted at tables, children played games and won prizes, but she felt dispirited and small. A dazed expression filled her face, eyes still puffy, mouth downturned, and her insides twisted around wildly, as if she were about to tear into pieces.

She glanced again at the clock on the wall. Randy had not come and she was not the least bit surprised; in fact, she had felt certain he would not make it. *Years ago, when we first met, he would never have been this way. He always had time for "us" and he claimed an interest in raising a family.* Her lip twitched. *Now work keeps him away. But what is all the money and success for, if not the family? Shiny, expensive cars? His car cost enough for us to live on for years. And that gold watch! He's at work so much of the time it feels as if he has some new family.* She sat up, shifted, and tried to find comfort, then noticed her hands, balled-up in tight fists. The look of them startled her, reminded her of wood, twisted and knotted, old and drawn.

Forcing them open, her fingers trembled, and she realized for the first time that they hadn't stopped trembling for weeks. Placing those hands flat on the table, she studied them, how they had grown with her, served her. They were the diary of her experience. She brought them to her face and felt the furrowed recesses of her forehead, the tender skin below her eyes, the pulled corners of her mouth.

She glanced up and forced a smile when she noticed Andrew looking at her questioningly, longingly—a look she now saw not each month, each week, but each day. She knew he was feeling alone also, as if he had no father. He lately showed the signs, little bits of anger surfacing, moments of complete silence and separation. *Distress. My family is in distress.*

Inside she felt cold, like her heart was shivering. She shifted, tapped a foot, wiped a tear from her eye before it fell. *This is not the way!*

Kera had tried in her quiet way to bring Randy home. She shied from confrontation, and though she felt Randy needed to reassess his priorities, she also felt a constant doubt in herself, her judgment, and desires. But in her way she had tried repeatedly over a period of years, and in his way Randy had not responded. *What can I possibly do to change all this, to make it better?*

The strain increased on her face and the pout grew, took control. She stood suddenly, paced to the padded gymnasium wall and turned her tortured face toward it, hid there briefly with those hands clenched together, then looked with a broken heart at her children.

Sweethearts, she thought. *How do I protect such sweet and tender hearts?* She watched them, watched the way their little bodies moved, considered what they must be thinking and feeling. And it was those thoughts of theirs, those innocent feelings, that had always formed her priorities. Priorities which burst into her mind now, as if emblazoned in gold upon the blood red will of motherhood, and they stated clearly that needless pain could not be allowed into the lives of her children—no, not if there remained anything for her to do, not ever.

I have to force a change, and the children must be protected.

She had seen the answer before, but had always batted it away, clear of her consciousness. It came to her now... and it scared her terribly. She had to make Randy speak with her about change, and if he refused, she had to make that change on her own.

But to do this I have to protect the children. If only I could send them away for awhile. Her fingernails pressed deep lines into her palms. And then the idea came to her. She was not certain of herself, and if only for herself she would never do this thing. But it was not for her. She lowered her eyes, took a deep breath, and let it out slowly. Yes, she would have to try. It was the only way to make her family whole again.

Chapter 2

The Ferrari growled up out of the night and the headlights blazed across the brownstone as Rand swung it into the driveway.

He closed the back door too soon and probed in the dark for the light switch. It was near 10 p.m., but he thought a light should have been left on for him. Kera was probably in bed he thought... thought... but then realized he hadn't seen the truck parked out front. He moved hastily through the kitchen, briefcase in hand, and entered the living room, which he had come to dislike. The furniture was sparse, worn, and out of style, and he knew Kera wanted to replace it. Her choices would be modest and inexpensive and he refused to do that. They would wait until they had the money to purchase the best. Right now he didn't have time to think about it.

He noticed the curtains of the front window were pulled open. He had told Kera to keep them closed after dark, always. Peering out into the night, traffic moving past, he saw the truck's empty spot. *That's odd.* He couldn't remember her mentioning errands, anything for the children, anywhere to be, but, well, she must have. He yanked the curtains closed.

As he turned, his toe caught the side of the bucket placed below the trouble spot in the roof. It tipped over and old rainwater ran out onto the carpet. "Damn! Could she have emptied this?" He righted the bucket with his toe, but failed to place it below the leak, left the room feeling perturbed.

Hurrying back to the kitchen, he glanced at a pot on the stove, but opened the refrigerator and instead pulled out some packaged meat, slapped it between two slices of white bread, then climbed the stairs. Quickly passing the bedrooms he went to his office in the back of the house, and keyed open the door. He enjoyed when no one was home to interrupt his thought. A soft glow fell about the room when he clicked on the computer he used to view his photographs. The room held a mahogany desk, soft swivel chair, and large photographic printer. Prints of Rand's work covered nearly every vertical space.

Women were the consistent content of the prints, gorgeous women in every conceivable posture and attire. Most wore clothing of some fashion; a few presented themselves completely, unabashedly, but always as ladies, proud, bold—as his clients wanted their businesses and products represented. In one corner behind the door hung a dusty, tilted photograph of Kera, some ten to twelve years younger, herself modeling a conservative design.

Opening the briefcase while chewing the sandwich, he took out a memory card holding photographic images from his shoot with the *Lady Professional* models. He'd earlier gone to the studio and broke the news about Marla. Claris had responded by renaming Marla "The Bitch", but Rand thought he saw a glint in her worried eyes, as if she wanted most to tell him she had foreseen more trouble coming. He loved Claris, she was a valuable asset to him, but he didn't need anyone telling him I Told You So. He opened the file and looked through the photographs of the day. Marla may have canceled the contract, but he had grounds to be paid for this work, and he planned to treat these photographs with all the usual care. Even more. *If she wants to screw me, we'll see who's the sorest when it's over!*

He opened a file of a previous shoot—more women—and fell to trance-like consideration as he compared images. Lighting, angles, ideas—all seemed excellent, but something bothered him about today's work. He looked for a long while at the subtleties of makeup, hairstyle, wardrobe but couldn't put his finger on it, and decided on coffee.

Downstairs, he reopened the refrigerator, took out the beans. When he went to the grinder he noticed a piece of paper and a photograph lying on the counter. Flipping on the light he read:

Randy, I have taken Alissa and Andrew and gone away.
The children need a father who is there for them.
  Kera.

Rand turned away and poured beans into the grinder. The writing on the note appeared scrawled, erratic. He recognized the photograph. It showed Kera at the age of four, with her mother and father, standing in front of the Old Faithful Inn in Yellowstone National Park, Wyoming. It had been taken on a summer day during a family vacation, just one month before her parents had died in a car crash. Kera had often requested that Rand take her and the children to visit that place, but they had never found the time. At this juncture in their lives there were a million more important things to do.

He forced down the handle of the grinder and its growl filled the room. *I can't believe she did this to me. What a completely lousy time. I have too many things to take care of!* He filled the coffee maker, turned it on with a jab of his finger, then glanced at his watch. It was 10:32. "Kera!" he grumbled.

He heard the sound of sirens on the road out front. Two, maybe three squad cars zoomed by. In his mind he envisioned the truck's empty spot. *I have got to focus on what I'm doing, right now. I'll deal with her later.*

He returned to his office and clicked on a satellite radio tuner, then moved over and stood peering down at his images. A journalist covered late news with a report detailing the bombing incident that had blown apart an Air Force hanger in San Francisco, reportedly destroying two Stealth bombers. Rand, his mind distracted, poked a button on the tuner. The newscast was replaced by the heavy beat of African drums.

Concentrating on improving these latest photographs, he would utilize the computer graphic and printing process to take his most incremental ideas, slight nuances of genius really, and create premier art. He needed to focus for as long as it took to let the ideas evolve. He had his reputation to secure.

***

The next morning Kera knelt, facing Andrew and Alissa, at a gate in LaGuardia airport. A flight attendant waited nearby and a line of people entered the gateway behind them.

"I know," Kera spoke to the children, her voice quivering, "that this is a surprise. But this is a very good place you're going to. They have a lot of fun and there are plenty of children your age." She wore wrinkled jeans and a sleeveless denim top. The children wore sweatshirts and thick-soled basketball shoes. They stared at the floor, sad and a little frightened, with early morning faces and rumpled hair confirming a restless night in a hotel bed. "Megan and Bobby's mom says they have gone there several times and love it." Kera reached out and softly touched their cheeks. "I want you guys to remember to listen to the flight attendant. Don't get off the plane until she comes for you, 'cause you have a stop before you get to Spokane."

"How do we know where to go when we get there?" Andrew, his brow darkly furrowed, took on an air of accountability.

"The flight attendant will take you off the plane and introduce you to a man named Lightner. He's very nice. I talked to him on the phone last night. He's from the Better Way Retreat and plans all the activities for children who live there and for visitors like you."

"How long are we going to stay there?" Alissa's eyes went red, her lower lids forming dams for tears building up.

"Just a couple weeks. It'll be hard only until you get there—"

The flight attendant stepped forward. "I should get them to their seats now, Ma'am."

Kera pulled the children into her arms and forced her fear and sadness deeper. "Everything's going to be great. You guys will love this. I'll call you tonight, and you can call home any time you want." She handed them their daypacks stuffed with books, games, and snacks, and her hands trembled. Everything seemed unreal to her. *I can't be doing this, can I?* Her mind drowned in doubt. "I love you both," she stammered, and her mouth quivered uncontrollably.

"Love you, too," they answered, but their faces sank to the floor again. The attendant placed her hands on their shoulders, steering them away. Andrew suddenly stopped and looked at his mother with narrowed eyes. "Mom, where's Dad?"

Kera felt her stomach squeeze tight and quickly dropped back to her knee. She took hold of his hand and massaged his pudgy fingers and knuckles. "It'll be okay, little man. Mommy's going to see that everything is okay."

He looked about and his expression turned sheepish as he whispered to her, "I'm so scared."

She clasped him to her, turned her face toward the gate area windows. In the glass she glimpsed her reflection and was shocked by the contorted expression staring back at her. Taking a deep breath, she gained control by biting her lip, and looked him in the eye. "It's a safe place. I made sure of that, so don't you worry, Sweetie. Go have fun, okay?"

When she let him go, Alissa stood close, watching them, tears streaming down her cheeks. "Oh, baby girl, it's okay. We need to do this. It's okay. Everything will be fine." She wiped the tears out of Alissa's eyes and Alissa, with doll-sized fingers, wiped the tears out of hers. "This isn't going to be for long, so soon we'll all be back together, and we can talk about all the things you did there, all the adventures you had. Think about that."

"Will it be like that place in the movie, like Jellystone Park?"

"Different, but maybe even better. You'll see how pretty it is there. It's in the middle of the mountains with a forest all around. There'll be flowers growing everywhere!"

Now Alissa dried her own eyes. "Okay. I'll try." The flight attendant stepped forward again. "Okay," Alissa said to the attendant, "I can go now. I've always wanted to go to someplace like Jellystone."

She held the children's hands until their fingers slipped away from her, and the attendant walked them down the ramp where they disappeared. Kera was left alone, kneeling and clutching the railing, staring dazedly at the plane beyond the window, steadfastly avoiding her reflection.

***

At Priven Studios no sign of the *Lady Professional* set remained. The giant studio sat dark and empty and, though surrounded by the churning energy of a megalopolis, quiet. The cameras were put away and strobe lights stood in line near the edge of the main shooting flat. Ancient wood posts reached twenty-four massive feet to the perimeter beam structure. Imported Ryeback arm chairs framed neatly pruned bonsai trees in brightly crafted ceramic pots. A shaft of light stretched out from the office door and cut a narrow swath into this dark interior.

"Yes, I understand." Rand sat at the desk in the office, talked into the phone. "I know it's Saturday, but I also know Mr. Renton is often in the office on weekends. I thought I might try." He listened to the voice on the other end, tapped the tip of a pen on the desk's surface, then traded it for his coffee cup and took a swallow. "I'm sorry to bother you, good luck in catching up. Thank you. Good-bye."

When he hung up the phone he leaned back, wiped his sweaty palms on his trouser legs. He struck the down arrow on the computer keyboard, searched the page full of names and numbers, snatched up the phone again.

"Yes, hello, Rand Priven for Wendell Johns, please."

An aged but steady voice spoke back. "This is Mrs. Johns, Mr. Priven. May I ask the nature of your call?"

"Certainly, Ma'am. I will be working on a project with Wendell next week, for your company, Cosmetica, and I wanted to touch base with him."

"Well, Mr. Priven, Mr. Johns is away. I do think it odd that you would ask for Wendell when inquiring about a project with my company."

Damn! "Uh, well, my people had worked with Mr. Johns on the original contract and such."

"I am unaware of that. Everything is approved through me."

"I am sorry. There's no—"

"I prefer to talk business during the business week, Mr. Priven. I'll have someone call you on Monday."

"Thank you."

"Good-bye." Click.

Silence. Rand glared at the handset, "I could turn Paparazzi on your old saggy ass!" Dropping the phone back on its cradle, he missed, and slammed it down again. He checked his watch. Following some new thought, he rose suddenly and strode into the warehouse, picked up a camera, and turned on the studio's overhead lights.

As he grabbed a tripod and began attaching the camera he noticed movement in the shadows along the wall and started backward a step. A strange, bulky shape rose from the floor. Rand, his heart beating wildly from fright as well as an overdose of caffeine, tripped on a Bonsai tree pot, and fell over backward.

To his further amazement, the apparition spoke. "Are you okay, Mr. Priven?" Rand scrambled to his feet. He knew that voice. Then, the thing shed its skin and Jimmy appeared, rubbing his eyes. Rand now saw that his studio tech had been lying in a mummy-style sleeping bag on the plank floor. He stood there, hair twisted and matted, also looking shocked.

It took Rand a moment... "What, did you sleep here?"

"Yes, sir, uh..." Jimmy stepped from the crumpled bag and picked it up in one quick scoop. "I—uh—I was robbed, sir. And I lost my apartment, because they took all my rent money."

"What? When did this happen?"

"About a week ago. Sorry—I didn't ask if this was okay. I was embarrassed and just needed a place to stay for a little while." He folded the sleeping bag into a tight ball and reached for his shoes.

"Jesus!" Rand had his hands on his hips. "I can't have you living here like a flipping transient! This is a place of business. You understand?"

Jimmy paused and looked at him, blinking.

"Just too many complications and liabilities. I could lose everything!"

Jimmy shifted his gaze to the floor, "Yes, sir, I am sorry, I—"

"You've got to understand that this place is the most important thing in my life. I put down a lot of money to get this building and this equipment. Without this, I have nothing, no future, it's fucking over!" Rand's heart pumped and he felt shocked that Jimmy would have done such a thing, taken such a chance with his life's work.

"I'll get out of here, then, and let you work, sir." He shuffled toward the door with his shoes in hand and the sleeping bag under his arm.

Rand watched him, wiping a bit of sweat from his upper lip. *Damn!* He brushed off the back of his pants and ran his fingers through his hair. *I could have broken my neck.* He looked and saw that Jimmy had nearly reached the office door, dragging his heels as if he had no place to go. Rand spent more time with his crew than anyone and had placed a lot of effort in training them. He knew they worked hard for him, and he needed them. "Hey, Jimmy." Jimmy stopped and turned. "You, uh… you have a place to stay at all?"

Jimmy mumbled, "Oh, I'll find something. I have some friends."

"Okay. Listen, show up early for the shoot Monday."

"Sure," Jimmy said. Then he turned again and shuffled out of the place.

***

At six o'clock that evening, in a house six miles from Rand and Kera's own, Rand's widowed father, his brother and sister, gathered with their families for a Saturday dinner. At seven forty-five, Rand cut the throaty Ferrari into the driveway.

The impressive, sprawling Arts and Crafts house reflected the purple last glow of day created when sunlight is blocked by heavy clouds gathered low on the horizon.

He entered through the back, walked into the kitchen, and saw his father, Harry, seated at the table, sipping iced tea and gazing out the window. His sister, Renee, and his brother's wife, Jamie, were clearing the table and counters. He threw his empty paper coffee cup into the trash.

"There's beer in the refrigerator." His father called out, smiling with his large, removable teeth. "Hot today, huh? It's gonna rain."

Rand pulled out a beer, took a sip, and leaned on the counter across from the women. His sister looked over her shoulder and studied him for something longer than a glance, and Jamie stopped talking long enough to say, "Hi, Randy. Russell's downstairs playing computer games with the boys. Where's Kera and the kids?"

He shook his head—*Why can't anyone get it right? It's Rand!*—and shrugged in reply. He saw that his father watched him from the table. He walked over, tilted the cat from the chair, and sat down across from him.

"Where the hell you been?" his father asked. His black hair had greyed, thinned, and his skin tone resembled the muted colors of winter—but his eyes showed clear and sharp.

"The studio." Rand sipped the beer.

"Going well?"

"Sure." He didn't like to talk with Harry about the studio. His father had never liked his choice of professions, and conversations on the subject often wound up being long dissertations on the folly of Rand's decisions.

Harry looked at Rand's wrist. "Wow. Nice watch."

Rand met his eyes. "Thanks."

Harry eyed him back. "Where's Kera?"

"Busy, she couldn't make it."

"Are the kids with her?"

"I guess."

"You guess?"

"I mean, yes." Rand got up from the chair and walked over, peered into the living room. His father had not been around much when he was growing up and they had never found any comfort ground. But it seemed to Rand that after his father retired he had become bored and turned his energies toward the family, like a new job, something to manage.

George, Rand's brother-in-law, was asleep in a chair in the living room with his fingers twitching at his crotch, commercials blaring on the television. *No class.* George made little money as the manager of a retail sporting goods store. He seldom spoke to any of them, even Renee. But Rand didn't care, he rarely saw him—rarely saw any of them. He was too busy. *Thank God.*

"You hear about those planes?" His father was still watching him. Outside, a bolt of lightning surged outward from a heavy cloud. The windowsill in front of the women flashed with harsh blue light, and they stopped wiping plates to peer intently out through the glass. Everyone paused the way people do on the first few booms of a thunderstorm.

Rand leaned against the wall. A distant thunderclap rolled across the sky. "What planes?" He heard himself mumble.

Russell and the boys, Curtis and William, came noisily up the stairs—the boys arguing about who had won as they disappeared into the back bedrooms. They rushed past Rand as if he wasn't there. Russell grabbed a beer from the refrigerator, saw Rand, and nodded.

"Those fighters from that base in Arizona." Harry remained focused on Rand.

"What about them?" Rand asked. He wasn't looking at his father, his brother, or the women, but stared into his beer can, contemplating the sudden troubles with his client base.

"They were stolen. They have no idea where those planes got off to."

Russell sat in the chair across from Harry. He was four years older than Rand, and for some reason (their mother had always wondered why) his hair had fallen out, starting from the time he was twenty-one. Rand shifted so he didn't have to look exactly at the bald head. Russell had been laid off three times in the last four years, but now worked fifty hours a week as a technician for a communications group, and was thankful to have the job—though his salary and benefits had declined overall. All this was either responsible for, or had failed to prevent, an elephantine gain in his midsection. "They'll find them," Russell said. Another flash lit the windowsill.

"I don't think so," Harry countered.

"What, you think the Russians got them?" Russell donned a facetious smile that appeared more a grimace from some bitter taste in his mouth, and winked up at Rand. Rand thought his brother looked downright disgusting—fat and bald and grimacing like he ate shit for breakfast. Thunder boomed and echoed outside.

"Russians? You ever watch the news, Russell?" Harry glanced from Russell to Rand, then back.

Russell took a couple gulps from his beer, wiped his mouth with his sleeve. "Sure, I watch the news. On the cartoon channel. Mickey Mouse sensationalizes the headlines and Daffy Duck blows the weather forecast." He laughed and laughed and laughed, until it seemed ridiculous.

Harry looked away from him, tilted his head and champed his teeth like he did when he was getting riled, then looked back. "You ought to know that the Russians aren't the scare anymore. I'm more worried about our own."

Russell chuckled and wiggled in his chair. "What you mean?"

"You ever hear of militias and terrorists?"

"Militias? They're out of the picture. The Feds broke them up long ago."

"Those GUYS are still out there, and have been bringing in nerve agents. They aren't outsiders, they're our own, aligned with outsiders. They know the country." Harry's jaws clamped down and he rubbed his tea glass with his thumb, making it squeak. "Do you young people ever pay attention to anything these days?"

"I don't EEEven think those loonies are a real threat." Russell smiled over at the women, who now listened and watched uncertainly as Harry steamed up.

"Come on now, you guys," Renee said. "Don't talk about that stuff. You always argue."

Rand could also see it coming, what always came between those two. They were both opinionated and neither would budge once they'd made their stand. Harry would argue his point loyally, having done the research by watching television and reading the newspapers; Russell would make a joke of it, having no real information at all, but giving his father's opinion no respect.

Rand's attention lapsed and he gazed through the windows, out to the occasional bright bolt that lit the purple and grey yards and the houses lining the street. He started analyzing his business again.

His mother, who had worked a frustrated career as a corporate secretary, had told him early on that he would become an artist—that she could see it in the way he watched light travel across the surfaces of a room as a child. She'd been gone awhile now, dead from breast cancer, but not before using a good portion of her life savings to pay his way through the State University of New York at Stony Brook, so certain, she was, that he would prove exquisitely gifted at creation. His father had said that art added up to a life of leisure, not a career, and had stated that Rand would never make any success of it. He refused to pay anything toward any degree program other than business, since he felt only that field had value and was worthy of a man's dedication. To his mother's mild disappointment, Rand leaned toward photography. Art in general was way too quiet for him (though *boring* was the actual word that had come to his mind). He liked the mystique of cameras, and that attractive women gathered around photographers, and that they rarely minded shedding their clothes. He reveled in captured moments of flesh caressed, teased, slapped by light. He loved the attention he received when he held an expensive camera in his hands.

He studied the occupation and found that top photographers lived high, got what they wanted, held a gold card membership to the platinum palaces of the world. He signed on.

Rand met Kera while in school, though she didn't attend courses there. She had become a promising model with a natural little-girl quality in her face and a supple, proportioned body seemingly created by man's eternal fantasy. Rand immediately thought of David Bailey and Marie Helvin—a noted photographer and model fashion duo from decades earlier—and the two teamed up. Her physical attributes, and Rand's images, had gotten them going with good clients, but then she had suddenly lost any desire she'd had to make a success of it. Regardless of Rand's urging, she let it slip away when they learned of her pregnancy with Andrew.

Rand's desire had grown, but for some time his client list had not, leaving him more than ever yearning to prove his talent, craving for the notoriety that top photographers enjoyed. He focused on becoming the best known, and never doubted he would succeed.

In the last year his creative eye had enjoyed heightened demand. It had been like winning the lottery. Until these latest problems.

Another boom from the sky filled the room. Rand refocused. His father sat alone at the table. Russell was gone from the chair and the women were hanging dishtowels, done with cleanup, appearing uptight, perturbed. Harry had that look, like an argument had taken place—a sort of whipped and vacant expression.

Rand felt frustrated. Wherever he went he ran into the same negative bullshit. *What is wrong with everybody?* Then he noticed how rain made the pane of glass behind Harry look like liquid. He tilted his head back, took a deep gulp, and finished the beer. It dawned on him that if Kera were present, she would go to the refrigerator and get him another.

Chapter 3

Kera sat alone and cross-legged on the bed in the economy class Apristina hotel, six noisy miles from her home. Even at 10:07 p.m. an endless flood of cars roared past on the wet highway outside her window. A shrill siren wailed in the distance. Rain streaked the windowpanes and the yellowish glow of the streetlight modeled the fingerprint smudges missed by the maid. Fast food wrappers littered a table with a worn chair positioned next to it. The place smelled of old smoke.

Kera could feel the jagged edges of dread working away at her, as if slicing her skin from her body, leaving her soul bared and vulnerable. At times she actually writhed on the bed in pain more psychological than physical, but to her indiscernible as such. She felt horrifically afraid and utterly alone. There seemed no one to turn to—cousins in Florida out of touch for years, friends that had become mere acquaintances while she led her harried life.

She had tried several times to call the children, but the lines were endlessly, oddly, busy. The city closed in around her, boxed her in. The sheets were twisted about her bare legs, jeans and denim top lie crumpled in a pile at the foot of the bed. Her hair was a mess. Her eyes looked red, puffy, and sore; but beyond them, her face appeared pale. For the first time in many years her skin had broken out with dry reddish patches under her mouth, though she had hardly noticed and cared not at all. Loud laughing filled the room, emanating from the television set and some late night show, but her mind had turned inward, questioning frantically how it had all come to this.

She had started in Pennsylvania, born to the owners of a small and tidy dairy farm in the countryside outside of Scranton. But at the age of four her parents had been killed in the car crash one wintry evening while returning from a night out together, watching *Man of LaMancha* at a dinner theater in town. Her godparents, brother and wife of her father, lived in New York City, where both worked at a large, expensive hotel. They took her in. Her beauty blossomed and that godfather— having spent much time overhearing the conversations of rich patrons who frequented the hotel—decided using that beauty would not be wrong. (He was, after all, spending large sums of money raising the child.) They had her trained, to walk, talk, and behave like a lady, entered Kera in children's and, later, teenage pageants, pushed her into modeling sessions for product ads.

Sitting now near the edge of the bed, her nose running from crying, Kera recalled those sessions and hated them for the way they had made her feel—something so upsetting that she had never found words for it. But she had lost any ability to say no when her parents had died, her sense of belonging smothered by the shock of being left behind and this godparent who treated her as an opportunity for profit. Now, she was alone again, ravaged by fear, confusion, and pain. Each time she considered her children, a nerve-racking distance away, or her husband, preoccupied by career, neglectful of family, she felt herself losing control.

How she had once desperately longed for her parents, she now longed for Andrew and Alissa. And the intuition that they felt similar anguish tortured her most. Doubt toward her decision to send the children so far away had begun to haunt her mind the moment she had said good-bye to them.

All those years ago there had been nothing to save her from the pain of her parents dying, having her family life ended abruptly and being denied opportunity to understand. This memory is what convinced her to now insulate the children from the arguments, the anger, and the possible total destruction of home life she feared would occur when she met with Randy. She had no family to send them to, and Randy's family would not insulate them in the least; they lived too close and the tension would be too apparent to the children, and she had never trusted the mouth of Randy's brother. Sending them on a "vacation" seemed the best, the only, thing to do.

She thought she would stay in the hotel for a day, to work at getting her thoughts together—but to get hold of them now seemed an impossible feat. She had convinced herself that she could do this, but now the thought of confronting Randy scared her terribly; he was too smart and certain of himself.

The television suddenly flickered, and her eyes went to it. The late night show was gone, replaced by a banner for the Emergency Broadcast System. The laughs had been cut short by the shrill and obnoxious drone warning of some announcement which always turned out to be a test. *My God!* She searched the bed covers for the TV remote.

She found the remote, pushed frantically at the buttons, but every channel repeated the annoying sound. She cocked back her arm in a fit, ready to throw the thing at the TV, but then the drone ended and a voice announced that an emergency message was forthcoming from the broadcasting network. The banner switched to a shot of a news room as a person slipped into the padded chair, hastily pinning on a microphone. Kera recognized him as Richard Creston, news anchor for WRNI-TV, and lowered her arm. He seemed hurried, his tie out of place, jacket unbuttoned, and his face, out of norm for practiced news presenters, showed a hint of alarm.

"Good evening," he said, shuffling papers and organizing himself. "The State Department has released this notification tonight, only moments ago, that a series of bomb blasts has occurred across the country."

Kera dropped the remote in her lap as Creston continued. "Five sites, including the Pentagon; Ft. Meade, Maryland; the National Center for Military Communications in Atlanta; the Strategic Air Command Remote Base in Westlayne, California; and Rival Air Base in Arizona have all been heavily impacted tonight by explosive detonations. No claims of responsibility have thus far been received."

Kera watched intently, her heart thumping loudly in her chest. Creston went on. "At this time, the actual damage to the sites, as well as the implications to the country's intelligence and defense capabilities, are being measured. I assure you that this network will keep you informed of the latest developments." His hand went briefly to his ear and he paused as if listening. Then he continued. "In fact, we have Mary Kay Stevens standing by in the nation's capital. Mary…"

Mary appeared on screen, in somewhat dim light, the immense concrete Pentagon building stood far behind her with powerful emergency lights illuminating it. Fire and rescue crews operated hurriedly in the background. "Richard, this is what we have so far. The Pentagon has in fact received measurable damage to exterior structures…" As she talked, videotaped segments showed the outside of the Pentagon. Entire sections of the building, each some thirty or forty feet long, were in rubble. Military vehicles cluttered the area and numerous cars, civilian in character, had been blown onto their sides or roofs. Smoke poured out of the Pentagon wreckage. "… We have not been informed as to the extent of the damage inside this massive complex, but sources report that communications with remote military sites may have been effected."

Kera raised the remote and clicked frantically to another channel: a different anchor, same subject. Throughout the channel selections every station either broadcast its own report of the incident or had switched to a feed of another station's coverage. Her mind kept leaping to thoughts of the children and their safety. She clicked back to the channel with Richard Creston.

"Repeating that," Creston said, "In addition to the five sites originally reported, we are receiving confirmation now that several military bases around the country have either suffered massive explosions or have in some other way been compromised. In Northern California, Waker Air Base has had three Apache attack helicopters stolen in a situation that has left their main hanger and several adjacent structures in ruins. Aside from the Pentagon, facilities in Maryland, California, and Washington State now seem the heaviest hit."

"Washington State." Kera whispered the words. Creston wasn't saying anything about where in Washington the trouble centered, but that didn't matter. Anywhere in the state was too close to the children. She felt her chest tighten. Deep inside, shrill energy rose, passing through her in a nauseous wave. The faces of her children appeared before her, as if at the end of a long black tunnel. She grabbed the phone—not wanting to, but seeing no option. Before dialing the complete number of her home, however, she heard a busy signal, slammed the handset down, then lifted it and tried again.

***

Rand returned home late. In the upstairs bedroom he left the light off. Illumination filtered into the room from the streetlights outside, and he tried to calm himself by focusing on the subtle yellow hues and soft shadows made even more interesting by the wet exteriors of the windows. It didn't work. He slipped off his pants and dropped them over a ragged Victorian chair, placed his Rolex in a tray on top their 1920's hand-me-down dresser. An eleven-by-fourteen inch photograph hung on the wall, showing Kera, the children, and himself, and he pulled back the covers and climbed into bed with an angry glance at it. He wondered where they were, decided he would find out soon enough. She'd be back. She wasn't strong enough, or right enough, to pull this off.

After leaving his father's house he had driven down puddling streets to the studio, to work on a speculative photograph he had dreamed up. It was an idea having to do with a gorgeous model sitting seductively on the inside of a broken eggshell. He felt certain the National Dairy Council would purchase it for a commercial ad campaign on the benefits of eating eggs. But he couldn't get it right, became frustrated, and left when a strobe light malfunctioned.

The damn rain had slowed and he decided to go to Haggermiers, a bar near Soho known as a hangout for artistic types. He had often overheard the names of potential clients there. Two drinks later a couple gay brothers approached him with the suggestion he do a coffee table book not imaginatively called Gay Brothers. Each time they mentioned it a rude image of his own brother, Russell, leaped into his mind. He took an opportunity to leave and ended up at home.

Lying under the covers, his neck muscles ached. He had labored and yearned too long to lose what he had built up, not over any rumors started by Marla, or by the Gretten Agency about some issue they hadn't even brought to his attention. And why had Wendell John's wife been so flipping prickly?

He tossed listlessly. At a quarter of eleven he fell into an agitated sleep.

***

Kera burst through the front door of their home and ran dripping wet upstairs, slipping in her wet shoes. When she rushed into the bedroom calling Randy's name, he started into a sitting position.

"Jesus Christ! What's going on?" he said, using his hand to shutter his eyes from the bright overhead light that Kera had slapped on.

"Randy!" Kera paced back and forth at the foot of the bed, her voice high, quivering. "I've done something very stupid, Randy."

"Ah, hell, Kera..." He rubbed his eyes and, sounding irritated, asked, "What?"

"I sent Andrew and Alissa away—to Washington—to—to keep them from—from going through this—I—have you—," she whirled to face him, "Have you heard the news?—of course you haven't—you never—"

"What are you saying, Kera?" He shifted out of bed, pulled on his pants.

Kera wiped at her face, her hair, "You've got to see—you've—oh—watch this—" She stepped to the TV and poked the power button, then covered her mouth with the tips of her fingers as she waited what seemed forever for the images to appear. She couldn't stand the crushing grip about her chest, or stop her mind from vaulting wildly from one dreadful thought to another. *I am stupid, just so stupid!*

Richard Creston pitched to a male reporter from the bureau in San Francisco. "Thank you, Richard. It's a scene not unlike a Hollywood film, Ladies and Gentlemen, but here at Westlayne no movie is playing. We've now been told that some of the explosions here were most likely diversions from the real objective. The military's vital communications systems which are housed here have historically been targeted by outside infiltrators, high tech hackers, who have now been successful in making communication between certain military organizations impossible."

Kera let out a whine of frustration. "They said Washington earlier. Now they're not mentioning it!"

The report continued with the theory that the United States had in fact been hit at several key locations by what appeared a swift, effective, and highly organized technological and military attack.

"Oh, come on! That's absurd." Rand looked at Kera, suddenly questioning. "Where are the children?"

Kera felt weak. She bit her knuckles. "In Washington," she muttered.

"What? Washington? Where?"

She twisted her fingers together in front of her. "A little town outside of Spokane."

"Spokane? I've never even heard of that. Is it near the District?"

"No," she said, diverting her eyes from his face. "Not Washington D.C.... Washington State."

He looked at her as if he could not by any means imagine her serious, his eyes wide, a slight mocking up-turn at the corners of his mouth. "You're joking."

She could feel the hot rush of blood in her face, the pressure of it, felt as if it might crack her skull. "I know. I'm so stupid. I felt I had to get them away from us until we settled all this. I didn't want them to see us fighting, to—"

"Fighting about what? So you sent them the entire way across country, without consulting me?"

Her vision blurred with tears. She stared at the television, turning to the words of Richard Creston. "We have information now on the number of casualties at the Pentagon. It will take intense effort for officials to confirm who actually inhabited this immense facility at the time of the blast, but twenty-seven people are now known to have perished. And at Waker Air Base in California seven people are known dead from a blast there. The identity of those victims will be withheld until families can be notified."

***

"Where *exactly* are the kids, Kera?" Rand walked into the bathroom that connected to the bedroom. He wanted a moment to think. From a fitful sleep he had awakened to her, freaking out in the middle of the night. She had taken the children and left him in spite of the fact that he labored to get them everything they wanted. Life had been fine, but now they had issues to settle—all because of her. And now she was back, wanting him to solve her self-inflicted crisis.

He glanced out at her. She kept her eyes on the television. "It's called the Better Way Retreat," she said. "Jennifer Wood has sent her children there for several summers, and they love it. She said the people are very friendly and professional."

Rand rinsed his face in the sink and the cool water sobered him a bit. "You sent our children off to be cared for by people we've never met?"

"It's near Spokane, somewhere on the eastern side of the state, in the mountains," she said.

He ran wet hands through his hair and grabbed a towel, dried his face, looked at her again. She was pacing, looking out the window. "You put them on a plane?"

"Yes."

"That's it?"

"I talked to a man named Lightner on the phone. I called him twice. He said he would meet them when the plane landed. He sounded—he was very nice, very professional, just like Jennifer said."

Rand looked in the mirror and perfected his hair. He came back into the bedroom and pulled on a tee shirt. "You're right. That was mighty stupid."

***

Kera couldn't look at him. His voice had sounded creamy calm, with a thick sentiment of ridicule. He would do this, condescend. She couldn't tell whether he had begun to protect himself for some unknown reason, or if he simply didn't care about anything, or anyone, anymore.

"Where's the number for this retreat?" he asked.

That gave her pause and she thought for a moment. "I think it's down in my purse." She rushed from the room, down the stairs, across the yard, and slipped on the wet door frame of the Excursion, scraping her shin. Her stomach felt like it had turned on its side and she retched up a slimy chunk of fast food chicken. She feared the worst, but kept repeating to herself that the children were safe. *Why would I ever have sent them so far away?*

Back in the room she extended the slip of paper toward Randy. "You call," he said, and plopped into the Victorian chair.

Kera lowered the sound on the television, but before she had completed dialing, the busy tone again interrupted her. "The line's busy, same as when I tried to call them, and you."

"When did you try to call me?"

"Before I came over."

"That's the trouble, everyone's calling each other, panicking...."

Kera turned the TV up again.

"We have not yet heard from the President, but we have received word," Richard Creston stated, "that he may have been whisked away to Air Force One, and is now flying somewhere in the skies above the nation's capital. Our count of lives lost now stands at sixty-three. Penny Winkerton is in Washington D.C., at the Joint Chiefs of Staff Field Office. Penny, what have you learned there?"

"Richard, the overall structure of the massive Pentagon facility appears strong, despite what has occurred, but high level military officials have moved from there, to safer locations. Those locations are currently held secret for obvious reasons, but we have been told that Joint Chiefs of Staff Press Attaché Colonel Gerald Johnson, or The G-Force, as his troops called him years ago, may soon be here at this temporary field office for a press briefing."

"Penny," Richard Creston was visible in a small box within the screen, "have you heard anything on the whereabouts of the President?"

"Some sources say he is still at the White House, while others report that he may have been flown by helicopter to Waverly Air Field, an optional home for Air Force One, and now circles high above the capital. Of course, they maintain two identical Air Force One jets, and although one is currently absent, it's impossible to tell if the President is aboard."

Kera stood there with the phone in her hand. She bent over and turned down the volume on the television and again dialed the number for the retreat. "It's busy. Maybe it's the storm."

"I don't think so." Randy stood up. "The lines will open up after everyone gets their talking done. I'm going to make some coffee. We have to wait and see what happens."

"Wait? We can't wait... can we Randy? I need to know that Alissa and Andrew are all right. They could be hurt and we're sitting here waiting, right?"

He looked at her. "It's Rand now, Kera. I've told you a dozen times, it's Rand." He glared for a second more. "There's nothing to be done until we can reach them on the phone. I'm going to make coffee and then I want you to show me in the atlas where this retreat is."

Kera couldn't believe Randy had worried, at a time like this, about what name she called him. She stared at her notes on the piece of paper. "It's near Latrop, outside of Spokane." But Randy was already gone out of the room. She tucked the paper into her jeans pocket, plopped down onto the edge of the bed, and began to sob.

Randy eventually came back with a cup of coffee, and an atlas, which he threw to her before sitting in the Victorian chair. "What's the name of the town?"

Kera wiped her eyes and picked up the map. "Latrop." She flipped through the pages. There it was, in the smallest lettering, some fifty miles north of Spokane, Washington.

Randy took the atlas and turned to the national map and looked at the distance between New York State and Washington State. "Good job, Kera." He flipped to the table in the rear of the book. "New York to Spokane, almost twenty-five hundred miles." He tossed the book on the bed.

Kera picked it up and opened it to the national map again. Her finger traced a line between the two places, New York City and Latrop. Her tears ran down onto the pages, swelling what was rendered as flat terrain into minuscule contours. She covered her mouth with her hand.

***

From outside came the sound of wet, skidding tires, then colliding metal. Rand got up and went to the window. Off the front corner of their yard, beyond the truck, an older Chevrolet Impala sat bent and smoking under the streetlights. A new Suburban—Rand didn't like them; the Excursions were bigger and more impressive—was run up onto the sidewalk, its rear end battered.

The driver of the Suburban emerged. He looked to be a man around forty, of pretty good size, and he strode through the streaking rain directly toward the Impala. A younger man, maybe twenty-five, rose from the car and when he did the older man grabbed him and shook him angrily. Rand could hear their deep hostile voices, but not exact words. They grappled with each other and fell onto a soggy lawn. The younger man hit the other with fast, hard punches to the face. People began peering out of their house windows, but no one went outside. Pretty soon the older man was on top and he banged the younger man's head on the ground. A motorcycle cop came around the corner, siren screaming, and slid to a stop near them. Ending the fight by getting up, the older man left the younger man lying on the grass. The officer drew his weapon and directed the older man to bend over the Impala, then handcuffed him. Curtains of the neighborhood houses pulled tightly closed.

Rand sat back down in the chair. Kera was still crying on the bed, gazing dumbfoundedly at the TV. Picking up the phone, she dialed with trembling fingers, listened, then threw it down onto the covers and bolted up, pacing again.

A middle-aged man in camouflaged fatigues appeared on screen, and Richard Creston's voice introduced him. "We're going now to the Joint Chiefs of Staff Field Office, where the press attaché Colonel Gerald Johnson is about to give a briefing."

The G-Force wasn't smiling. A well-matured GI Joe, sharply groomed and tailored, he looked dour. "At twenty-two hundred hours tonight several United States military homeland installations were attacked, most usually in the form of, but not limited to, heavy explosives. These attacks have had a minimal and temporary effect upon the tactical capability of the joint military organizations nationwide. In tandem with the physical attacks there have also been computer-based technological assaults on our country's military and civilian communication centers. We don't have a lot of information at this time. We are not yet certain whether the attacks come from external or internal elements. No groups have claimed responsibility for these actions. Currently, we are estimating loss of personnel, equipment, and operations and will give a more complete report when we have additional pertinent information. In the meantime we are asking everyone to stay calm, in their homes, and to understand that all is secure. Thank you." Several reporters in the crowd could be heard firing questions, but Colonel Johnson spun around and was quickly escorted off by two soldiers wearing camouflaged fatigues, berets, and carrying carbines at port arms across their chests.

Rand smiled, it seemed the military was always happiest when they found a way to play hero.

"Oh, God, this is bad!" Kera cried.

Rand felt good that she was upset. She could learn a lesson from this. He got up and went to the window, sipped coffee. Two patrol units had shown up and one fighter sat in the back of each vehicle. A tow truck arrived. Rand went to his office and tried his cell phone. Busy. He walked back into the bedroom, tossed the phone onto the bed. "I don't know why I thought that might work."

Wringing her hands, Kera stood up and implored, "Randy, we've got to do something!"

He glared back at her, her pleading eyes, her little mouth at full pout. "Rand!" He growled. He knew she was doing it on purpose and it irritated him deeply. Everything about the situation did. He had so much to do, so much ahead if he was going to keep things the way he wanted them with his work. If it weren't for her he could be in bed, sleeping, preparing to land a new client on Monday. But now his children were off somewhere in some backwoods joint and he had no choice but to sit here and wait this out.

***

Kera stood looking at him. Her heart raced in her chest. She had loved him more than any love she could ever remember feeling—until the children came. Now, this was love unmatched, unfettered, love as pure as the creation of the world. *That's it, creation....* She had taken part in their creation and it was the most worthy thing she would ever do. They were brought forth from the membrane of her internal mystery, the essence of spirit, and so, the reborn flesh of her lost family. Randy was separate from that. She loved him differently. Still, she loved only the children more than she loved him.

He turned away from her and sat in the chair, faced the window, drank the last of the coffee.

She knew then more than ever that love cannot always comprehend. He was going to sit there and wait—a concept she could not grasp. Her heart thumped. It beat her walls of flesh and bone, pounded on her as if ranting, demanding attention. She had to find a way to get him to help, or she would have some kind of attack. It had taken all her courage to come as far as she had toward leaving him, but trying to handle this new and terrifying situation without him frightened her in a deeper way.

Suddenly, she went to the closet and grabbed a duffel bag, threw it on the bed. From hangers she grabbed a pair of jeans, two tops, a green sweatshirt from the shelf.

"What are you doing?" Randy turned and asked from the chair.

She didn't answer. She felt so emotional she couldn't speak. With two pairs of socks and fresh underwear she pushed the clothing into the duffel, zipped it closed.

"What are you doing?" He sat forward.

She shoved her hand into an old peanut butter jar turned piggy bank. With all the things Randy had bought they never had much cash. It seemed crazy to her, so she had always tried to keep something in the jar and her hand came out now with a handful of change and a couple of one dollar bills. She stuffed it into her pocket, then rushed toward the door.

"What are you doing, Kera?" Randy asked again, but when she didn't answer she saw that he sat back and crossed his legs, looked toward the window again.

She stopped suddenly, remembering the weather, and came back to the closet, grabbed a yellow rain jacket, turned and went through the door again, and down the stairs. *Think. Think! I've got forty dollars in my purse, four or five in my pocket, a credit card with a couple hundred left on it, and a check book with another two hundred deposited there. That will buy a ticket for me, and the children already have return fares charged on the card.* She remembered a small amount they had invested in stock, but that would take too much time to get to, even if Randy would allow it.

In the kitchen she stopped and pulled a used grocery bag from beneath the sink. At the refrigerator, she placed fruit, bread, and cheese into the bag, along with two bottles of fruit drink she'd bought for the children before she had realized she needed to send them away.

She prayed that Randy would come down the stairs and help her.

***

Up in the room Rand considered the situation. He had to admit that these explosions didn't sound good. But this was the United States we were talking about, not some impoverished, upsurgent South American dictatorship. The wackos that did this, like those involved with that Oklahoma thing years ago, and the Trade Towers attacks, would be brought to justice (well, partly anyway), and business would go on the way it always had. In an hour or two the lines of communication would open up and they could call and talk to the children in Lacrotch, or whatever the name of that podunk town was, and have those people send them back.

He heard Kera open the refrigerator. He suspected she was considering flying to Washington to get the children. He shook his head, couldn't help but smile. She'd never pull it off. Big moves like that were beyond her; she lacked courage. He heard the front door slam and got up from the chair, went to the window. Wearing the yellow raincoat, Kera strode across the lawn toward the truck parked at the curb. Street lights shimmered off the rainwater running in the gutters.

She was getting into the truck. Well, he wasn't going to let her do it. She would wreck the Excursion in this weather. He rushed down the stairs and out of the house and suddenly found himself standing behind Kera. She was bent over, staring at the front tire. The front left corner panel was smashed, the tire flat, twisted in at an odd angle.

She turned and looked at him. "I don't know what happened. It wasn't like this earlier." The rain, along with traffic out on busier streets, was so loud that she shouted.

He couldn't believe what he was seeing. "No, no." He should have checked, as close as the accident between the Suburban and Impala had come. He moved in for a closer look, holding a newspaper over his head to thwart the downpour and save his hair from mussing. "Didn't you hear the wreck earlier?"

"No, when?"

"When we were upstairs. There was a wreck and a fight. One of those vehicles must have rammed ours. The cops missed it. I certainly didn't think they'd come this close."

"Can we change the tire?"

"It's not only the tire, the axle's been damaged. The truck's not going anywhere until some work gets done." He felt disgusted. All she ever had to do was pull the truck into the driveway after he had pulled the Ferrari into the garage. "Let's get out of the rain."

Kera stared at the tire, her eyes red, rain running into the creases on her face. She began to weep again, then her hands rose and began pumping up and down next to her head. She sloshed over and sank down onto the curb, her entire body shaking.

Rand watched her, a part of him alarmed at what clearly looked to be a near breakdown, another part of him glad. With the truck wrecked, everything the way it was, she couldn't get mad at herself for not being able to carry through with leaving. This would keep her home, which lessened the chances of his getting caught up further in the whole ordeal. Cars passed and he felt a little foolish, standing there with the broken truck, his wife beside herself on the curb. He had brought the cell phone so he lifted it from his pocket, shielded it from the wet, and started to dial. The busy signal was beginning to piss him off. "Let's go back inside. In a little while everything will settle down."

***

Kera couldn't care less about the vehicle, but it was one thing after another, one thing after another, one thing after another…. Slowly, she tilted her head up and peered at Randy as water ran from her hair, down her nose, and into the flooded gutter at her feet. Then she stood in that manner with which one uprights oneself after being knocked to the ground by a larger entity; that is, wobbly, but willfully. With her saturated sleeve she shakily wiped her eyes and edged toward him. "Let me have your keys, Randy."

"What? You've got the keys. And I told you it's not going anywhere."

"The keys to *your* car."

His eyes got big. "No, no." He shook his head. "I'm going back in." He turned toward the house.

"Come on, Randy. Let me have *the keys*."

He turned back toward her again. "Absolutely not!" he said, and continued away.

She wiped her runny nose with her hand, shifted her weight nervously from leg to leg. "Then you take me. Please, Randy." She heard a car coming and glanced over as it slowed. The driver and passenger surveyed the busted Excursion and looked at her standing in the shadowy, rain glutted street. Kera looked at Randy.

He was watching the car also as he walked away. He turned his head toward her, "No!"

She stomped her foot, spraying water in a wide circle. "Randy, please!"

He stopped and turned, "Damn it, Kera! It's Rand! Okay! It's not Randy anymore!" He angrily waved the car away. It left. "You're not going to the airport on some cross-country wild goose chase. Now let's go inside!" He continued toward the house.

"Please! *Rand*, these are our children. I'm not going to leave them out there, not knowing if they are safe. Rand, please!"

He stopped and turned, stood looking at her, one hand over his head with the paper, the other in his pocket. "This conversation is ridiculous. Considering flying out there is just plain stupid! Everything will be fine."

Kera picked up her bag. "We don't know that." Another car approached and hit her with its headlight beam.

"Let's go in." Rand shouted.

Kera didn't answer. The car was slowing, pulling up to her.

"Come on, Kera." Rand shouted again.

The car came to a stop and Kera looked inside it.

"Kera," he called, "tell them to mind their own business!"

The man on the passenger side of the car rolled down the window.

Rand yelled, "Kera!"

The man asked Kera if she was all right, and Kera thought he looked nice enough. She took a step toward the car.

"Okay, okay!" Rand strode toward them. "I'll take you. I'll take you!"

She looked up. "Do you mean it?"

"Yes. Now, damn it, let's go inside!"

Kera smiled at the person in the car. "Thank you, anyway."

Chapter 4

"I thought they asked everyone to stay home." Rand wove the Ferrari in and out of near gridlocked traffic as he rushed Kera toward the airport. He pressed bumper-to-bumper with the car in front of him and was in turn harried by the car behind. Once again the rain had lightened, but the water that had soaked the ground and collected on limitless pavement helped create the first humid night of the season. Driving along, he was again struck by the senselessness of this feat.

"Maybe these people don't even know," Kera said.

She sat low in the leather seat. He had made her take off the wet raincoat, to protect the car's interior, and it was now tucked into her pack, which she cradled in her lap.

"Or maybe, like us, they're doing the opposite of what was asked." Rand had gone back inside the house, changed into a new pair of khakis, a forest green polo shirt, and lace-up, lug soled shoes he often wore for shooting film. He had brushed his teeth, donned his watch, and filled a travel mug with coffee. At the last moment he had grabbed a camera bag containing his Nikon and a couple of his favorite lenses. After he dropped Kera at the airport he planned to go to the studio and take another approach on that spec image.

He glanced at her, tucked into the seat, fretting, he thought, like a little kid. She looked like she'd been crying for days, her eyes, nose, and mouth swollen. The night's varied-colored lights played onto her. Her hair was still damp and it hung down around her eyes and ears, which were slightly oversized for her slender face and narrow jaw line. Somehow, it all served to make her simple beauty even more opulent. He felt suddenly horny.

Kera picked up the cell phone from its place on the console, dialed it. "I can't believe this is still busy! How do they expect us to communicate at a time like this?" She turned on the radio… "The order came after reports of explosions aboard two airliners little more than an hour ago," a voice said. Kera sat up with her mouth agape. "What?" she asked. "Did you hear that?"

"Not really." *Now what?*

She turned up the volume and the voice continued. "Essential Airlines flight 222 from Washington D.C. to Atlanta, and NationAir flight 1604 from Chicago to Philadelphia have both reportedly crashed after witnesses saw and heard what they described as bright flashes of light and heavy explosions. The order, which originated with Secretary of State Milword, came down through Secretary of Transportation Gunnison's office only fifteen minutes ago, and it has ordered the grounding of all nonmilitary air traffic. At this time, there is no information on the duration of this moratorium on commercial flights."

"Oh, my God!" Kera held her face in her hands, her eyes wide. "Oh, my God! How will I...." Her voice trailed off into silence....

"Now, can we go home?" Rand checked his rearview mirror, signaled in an attempt to ease into the right lane, toward any possible exit.

"Randy—I mean Rand—let me think!"

"There's no thinking that needs to be done, the airport's closed."

She buried her face in her hands.

The jammed traffic came to a dead stop near the highway 95 interchange. Rand hated the delay. He had things to do. Glancing from car to car, he thought again about all he could be accomplishing. Occasionally some bit of light would shine on the faces of drivers near him. On the right, a lady driving a Lasabre stared vacantly ahead. But when Rand turned to the left he saw a black man watching him, angry-eyed and tense. The man nodded and powered down his window. Rand didn't want to follow suit, didn't want to talk to any angry stranger right now, but he had little choice other than to ignore the man, which he thought a definite mistake. He lowered his window and grimaced at the water that dripped onto his arm.

"D'you hear the news?" The man called. A big guy, maybe thirty-five, he wore a black sweatshirt and had short, curly hair, with a little tuft of it under his lower lip.

"About the airlines?"

"Yeah. This is fuckin' crazy! They best be figurin' this out!"

"Yeah. I guess I think they will."

"Better. I was goin' to the airport. Goin' to Charlotte on business."

"Not now."

"No. Not now. They need to end those people that done this and keep that airport open! And put in some more roads, so we can cut this traffic!"

Rand nodded and raised the window. What'd the fucker think, he was the only one not getting work done? It was sounding like things would take awhile to settle down and Rand would much rather have been at the studio, or working on concepts for new clients. He picked up the phone and tried the studio number, thinking he'd check to see if Jimmy was there. "This is ridiculous," he said, dropping the phone onto the console.

They hadn't moved an inch in minutes. People started beeping their horns. Rand punched his with the heel of his hand and held it for a moment. He couldn't get his mind off work, off the fact that he'd had two clients in as many days get angry at him, off the fact that he needed another client to pay their bill so Claris could mail a payment for the studio. It was crap like this that could get out of hand and suddenly you lose everything. It happened all the time. Everyone feared it. One day doing well, lots of stuff, great house, then, overnight, nothing, no toys, no house, no car, no career. Gone. Next thing, you're living in the streets, begging food, wearing dirty clothes, sores running over your body, people pissing on you for fun.

Everything started to close in around him and suddenly Rand began to feel trapped in the tight, stuffy quarters of the sports car. "You're not getting out on any plane. I'm going back. In the morning we can get an estimate for repairing the truck."

Kera looked at him with that watery, bewildered gaze. She started shaking like she had on the curb.

"How do you do this?" she asked in a whisper, her voice quivering. "How do you carry on as usual with our children so far away and all of this tragedy going on?"

"Now wait a minute, damn it! I've already explained that this will pass, and in a few hours we will contact the children and find out they're fine, and in a couple weeks it will be no big thing, the country will be back to order."

"But what if you're wrong? What if the children are in danger, or hurt right this minute?"

"We don't know if any of the attacks took place anywhere near them. Taking the leap that they are in jeopardy is over reacting. There is no reason to believe that anything bad has happened to them, and anyway, you can't get there now, the airlines have been grounded." He lowered the window an inch, trying to get some air.

She held her eyes fixed on him. "Rand, let's drive to our children."

"What?" He couldn't believe it. Her thinking was becoming more and more ludicrous. "Come on, Kera, now you want us to drive three thousand miles across the fricking country?"

"Yes." Her voice had turned shrill, her eyes wild. "To find the children and bring them home!"

Once again, Rand wondered if she was actually losing control, breaking down clinically. She was obviously irrational, and he felt closed in with her. "Kera, that's insane. By the time we get there this whole thing will be blown over and we'll look like a couple of fools. I'm not going to that extreme."

"Look like fools?" she stammered—staring at him with wide-eyed incredulity.

"Oh, my God!" She covered her face and started rocking back-and-forth in the seat, "Oh, my God, my God, I can't believe this."

Rand reached down and turned off the radio, noticing that his fingers trembled. She had never before treated him like this. He turned his eyes away, out the windshield, to the traffic, anything. All he could hear was Kera's rapid breathing, her incessant repeating of, "Oh, my God!" He had never been so close to such callousness, such self-centeredness. He worked so hard for her, for the children. He had given his life to support them. Every waking minute, earning for the house, the cars, the clothes, the food, the heat, the taxes, the college funds! And what did she contribute? She had changed from when they'd met. It had appeared her modeling would bring in a lot of money, and together they would be wealthy. But then she stopped. Just like that. She used the excuse of the pregnancy with Andrew, but her attitude showed she wasn't going back. Finally, he had called her on it and she admitted it no longer interested her. So he had told her that she needed to work on something more than paintings, which brought them nothing. He wanted help paying bills at the time, and now that he had money he still couldn't understand why she wouldn't contribute financially to the security of their family, their future. He tried to answer the problem by spending more time networking, creating, by working more hours, but still she was never happy.

He saw how she grasped the pack in her lap so hard her fingertips and knuckles turned white. "We've got to find my children. Please, take me to my children," she cried.

She said "my" children. They're no longer "ours." She's actually removed me from the equation, negated my part as a father. He yanked the handle and climbed out of the Ferrari, slammed the door, wiped the rainwater from his hands with rigid movements.

There was nothing outside the car to relieve his anxiety—just more cars with horns blaring, the piercing, angry eyes of hundreds of drivers, lights glaring in the night.

Three lanes away, on the opposite side of the concrete wall meridian, traffic raced along in the other direction. He walked over and stepped up to the wall. Vehicles cruised past at sixty miles an hour with less than a car-length between them. Drivers whooshed by within three feet of Rand, fixated on the close view before them. The breeze from the cars buffeted his face.

A couple of those cars suddenly honked and Rand saw that a large dog, a Doberman pincer, had somehow gotten into the middle of traffic. The headlights caught it as it dodged with swift, frantic movements—one car, two—then it went to leap out of the way, but froze when it saw Rand in its path. Fear filled its eyes—fear and something more. A car slammed the dog broadside. It went wood rigid, spinning on its side down under the vehicle. Rand heard it thump heavily along the under-chassis. Rand wondered at the dog's stupidity, wandering onto the deadly highway, not seeing what would happen.

He turned his attention back to the flow of traffic. If only he could get the Ferrari over to that other side, where vehicles rushed by with efficiency, he could get the fuck out of this plight. He turned and looked down the endless line of stilled automobiles behind him. Out of the blinding myriad lights he noticed one as it paralleled traffic along the central meridian, working its way toward him: a motorcycle. It wove between vehicles. About twenty cars away it stopped suddenly and Rand saw two helmeted riders, one of whom straightened his arm out toward a nearby car. A brief flash of light came from the hand. Rand squinted to see better into the rain-misted darkness. The rider jumped off the motorcycle while his driver held it upright. The rider, whose hand had flashed, pulled open the door of the car next to him and yanked its driver from behind the wheel. The driver fell limply onto the pavement, and Rand saw the rider bend down over him and go through his clothing. Nearby motorists jumped from their cars and fled. Rand glanced at the Ferrari. It took no imagination to understand what the thugs would think of him, driving that.

***

Rand jumped into the Ferrari and gunned the engine. "What's going on?" Kera asked, wiping her eyes.

He jerked the wheel and bounced the car roughly up onto the curb. Kera felt the bottom drag on concrete, stopping them. He trounced on the gas and she heard the rear tires spin on wet pavement, then squeal when it became dry with their heat. The car moved forward incrementally.

"Rand, what is it?" she shouted, feeling a strange prickling sensation along her spine. He would never, under any circumstances she could imagine, do this to his car.

Rand looked into the rearview mirror and she saw his face go ashen. He tromped on the pedal again and the car jumped suddenly up onto the shoulder, fishtailing over soggy—and for the low slung, wide-tired sports car—nearly impassable terrain.

"What are you doing?" Kera held onto the door handles and console, but bounced up and hit her head on the low ceiling.

"They murdered him—"

She twisted and looked back into the glaring lights. "What? Who?"

Rand shifted gears. The car bounced along, barely in his control.

"Does someone need our help back there?" she asked.

He didn't answer, instead kept accelerating the car, glancing wildly into his rearview mirror. They approached the connector for highway 95 that would take them across the George Washington Bridge and onto Interstate 80.

Kera saw the signs. She knew enough to understand at that moment that 80 went west. That was the way she so dearly wanted to go. She pointed. "That way, Rand. That's the way to Washington State and the children."

Rand glance fearfully into the rearview mirror again. She turned and saw the jumble of cars backed up on the roadway behind them, but still couldn't see what had scared him.

"They killed a man!" he cried.

His voice trembled; she had never heard it sound that way. He handled every new challenge in turn, proficiently and calmly. But she now saw perspiration forming along his upper lip. His knuckles were white on the wheel. For the first time since she had known him he was not completely in control, and she felt then, in the pit of her stomach, what she needed to say. "Maybe it's too late to help him, but we can still help the children, Rand. Turn there."

He kept glancing into the mirror, fighting to keep control of the car as they swerved and bounced along the shoulder.

"Look!" she said. "There's open highway out there." Interstate 80 was clear, with great gaps of free space between the speeding vehicles.

He did look. He wiped his arm across his mouth. After glancing once more in the rearview mirror he cranked the wheel and turned toward the sign that read West, bounced down off the curb and hit solid pavement.

Part Two

Chapter 5

Kera slumped forward in her seat and buried her face. It was all too overwhelming.   She felt alarmed and saddened that someone had apparently lost their life back there.   Yet, at the same time, she felt relieved, with renewed hope for recovering her children, bolstered by their current direction down the highway.   Strangely, an atrocity had provided a fortuitous turn in events.

Everything had become incomprehensible for her, as if the world had broke free of its axis, tossing her into a great void with nothing solid to hold onto.

For an hour they drove, neither saying a word. Kera listened to the droning of the car's engine, and now focused on the length of the journey before them. Even though Rand was driving nearly seventy-five miles per hour, it seemed the road was alive and simply uncoiling itself endlessly before them. It would take a century to reach Washington.

And to her, Rand felt alien, unreadable, unpredictable, completely uncaring. She found she couldn't look at him, unsure of what might follow. She feared saying the wrong words, even calling him by his real name, and causing him to turn the car around.

"Where's the phone?" he suddenly asked in a flat and hollow voice.

She searched and found that it had bounced onto the floor beneath her seat.

Rand dialed a number.

"Who are you calling? The children?"

"The studio."

"Try the number out west, try the children," she pleaded.

"Be quiet or I'll turn around and go back."

She kept her mouth shut.

Rand began speaking in the abstracted monotone of a man numbed and struggling with multiple complexities. "Jimmy and Claris, this is Rand. I'm going to be—unavailable for a few days. I'll keep you posted. Keep track of all messages. And—Jimmy—stay at the studio while I'm gone, you can keep an eye on things...." He pushed the *end* button and tilted the phone absently toward Kera. "You see, I said the phone lines would be open soon enough...."

She grabbed it, but the busy signal interrupted her before she finished dialing. "Not anymore!" He had used their one chance to reach the children for a call to work. She held the phone in her lap, clasped it between her legs. She worried that since he had gotten through on the phone he would turn the car around.

But Rand drove silently, staring absently at the road ahead.

Sinking down into the seat Kera could feel a chill wash over her. She tried to imagine his thoughts, why he had become so hateful. She knew that leaving him hurt him, could understand his rejection of her, but not the children. Nothing made sense.

She reached down and turned up the radio, wanting to hear any recent news, wanting to ensure against the need for conversation between the two of them. "... We do have word that, in response to reported military type activities by unidentified elements, U.S. military units from Fort Hood, Texas, Fort Polk, Louisiana, and Twenty-nine Palms, California have been deployed in-country, meaning that we now have active duty military personnel at work within our borders, patrolling and apparently seeking out members of what the Pentagon is calling subversive terrorist factions."

"Subversive terrorist factions," Rand sourly mimicked. "That sounds a bit dramatic to me."

Kera looked at him, questioning, "What do you think we should call them?"

Rand answered without lifting his gaze from the road, "I'm not saying I have anything in mind. I really don't give a damn. It's just a little sensational to call them subversive terrorist factions. The military might try concentrating more on protecting innocent people on the streets."

She decided to let it go, to listen to the radio and not be drawn into his discussion. The reporter continued, "Military commanders have confirmed that computer systems within the Pentagon have been damaged and that military leaders are communicating mostly by radio or direct-to-satellite technology. They assure us that, even with this setback, the... ...is well within the scope of handling and... ...which is designed... ...enemies on a global scale."

An electronic clicking followed by a loss of transmission—a dead spot—had intermittently interrupted the radio report. This, added to the complete darkness outside, created an eerie effect for Kera. She shivered, felt weak and overcome. They passed the border sign for Pennsylvania, the state of her parents' death and burial, which they must now travel through without stopping. It had been over ten years since she had visited their graves. She wasn't even certain she could find the cemetery. "Did we forget to bring the map?"

"Forget? I really didn't think I needed it when I left the house!"

Rand was bitterly angry. Kera hesitated, but then asked, "How will we know where we're going?"

A moment passed before he answered. "Right now I know I need Interstate 80 through Pennsylvania. When I stop for gas you can get a map."

Kera didn't want them to stop, at least not until absolutely necessary. "I have some food, are you hungry?"

"No, but I need coffee."

"I have juice."

"Coffee."

***

Rand hit an exit and a QuickMart, filled the tank with gas and his travel mug with tasteless, watery coffee. Kera bought a map, glanced at it, then placed it behind his seat. It appeared to him that looking at the map made her ill.

Back on the highway, Rand felt a spurt of adrenaline burn through him when a car suddenly raced past. He hadn't noticed anything at all behind them, yet it had materialized, a late model Lincoln Town Car, black with black hubcaps, no chrome. A second went by, then a third and fourth, silently, but at an extreme rate of speed, a precise car-length between each. The windows were tinted dark, red filters masking their headlights.

"You see that?" he asked Kera.

"Yes." She watched them disappear into the night.

"They looked like military, or Marshals, or something. I've never seen anything like that," he said, still struck by their sudden appearance, speed and formation.

They cruised a long time through darkness with low hills, and later the mounded tops of the Appalachian Mountains, silhouetted in the moonlight. Rand knew Kera wasn't sleeping, could see her head up, eyes staring into the darkness with her hands together in her lap, still clutching the phone. She was getting what she wanted in her spoiled way and it angered him, all he was going through on account of her. *Well, she'll see what it's like when my business falls apart and we have to give up her truck and move into a smaller house.* But the thought of that made him shudder. *What would people think?*

Finally, he needed to take a leak, so he stopped at a rest area. He washed his hands and face. When he exited the building the eastern sky was beginning to show that first trace of grey light. The idea that he had driven the entire night made his eyes burn. He had rarely covered such ground on the continent, having left the east only once, for a college spring break flight to South Padre Island in Texas. Many changes had occurred in his life since then, and the idea of traveling the country—the few times the idea had arisen—had been quickly buried beneath the desire to build his career.

Kera sat with the door of the car open, her legs to the side, her feet on the pavement. She had put on her green sweatshirt and was looking out toward the horizon, where the sun would eventually rise. He remembered that she had always wanted to again visit the west, as she had with her parents. Now she had found a way.

"I need to shut my eyes for awhile." He walked around to the driver's side door. "Let's take a break."

"I'll drive." She popped up and looked at him over the roof.

"No."

"Then we can keep moving."

"You've never driven this!"

"I can do it. Please!"

"You need sleep, too."

"I'm fine, really." She circled around and edged past him to slip into the car. "Really, I'm fine."

He shook his head, hesitated, and glared at her. But she wouldn't lift her concentration off the controls of the car. He finally thought, *Why not? The sooner we get there, the sooner we get back.* "All right, but stop for breakfast at the next truck stop."

"I have food." She turned the key and the Ferrari let loose a throaty start.

"Kera, I need to take a break and I would like a cooked meal."

She got them back onto the highway and accelerated quickly up to seventy-five miles per hour.

"Don't drive so fast!" Rand demanded.

                              ***

Speed didn't seem like much work for the car. She had never driven it, and it felt sturdy, responsive. She stayed in the left lane and pushed past what seemed a surprising volume of traffic for so early in the morning. She wondered where they all came from, where they were going.

Rand's head came off the headrest. "There—you missed it. I thought we were going to hit the first restaurant!"

"It came up so quick. Let's drive a little further."

"Look, Kera, make the stop! We'll get there soon enough."

Fifteen minutes later they passed the border marker for Ohio and a sign for dining services at the next exit. Kera looked at Rand. His head reclined back, eyes shut. She kept steady pressure on the gas pedal as the exit approached. She again sneaked a look at him. Perspiration from under her arms trickled down her side. She only wanted to drive, to keep going, but then Rand's head came up.

"There's a restaurant at this exit." He didn't look at her, just said the words matter-of-factly, and tilted his head back.

She considered going on. That's what she wanted to do. She was the one who had brought on this trip. If it weren't for her they'd still be back at the house, waiting. Except that Rand would probably be off to work, ignoring the situation. She imagined herself negotiating this journey on her own, all these miles into places she'd never been, all the while the world off-kilter. She decelerated and steered the car onto the off ramp.

It was one of those immense truck stops, with two dozen pumps for diesel and another two dozen for cars. The parking lot held some thirty tractor-trailers. A complex with a store, a restaurant, and a separate hotel plastered with bright, blinking lights that read SHOWERS, GAMES, TELEVISION.

"Pull up to the pumps," Rand said. He dropped his sun visor, opened the mirror, and ran his fingers through his hair, wiped his eyes, looked at his teeth.

As Kera stopped the car she wondered why the most handsome man she had ever known worried so obsessively about his appearance. She had always liked that he took care of himself, but lately his constant primping bothered her. He paid more attention to looks than most models she had known.

"You get us a table," he said, "and I'll fill the tank."

Kera looked at the busy restaurant, all types of strangers coming and going. "I'll wash the windows," she said, not wanting to enter the place alone.

Rand paid for the gas with his charge card, and Kera wondered if he knew how low the available funds had dropped. She carried the map and was surprised when he held the door for her. When the two of them entered the restaurant she felt the rush of cool, conditioned air, heard the clank of dishes. Forty or so customers sat at tables, or a counter that wrapped three quarters of the way around the room. She studied the cross section of people—an older couple dressed in polyester, truckers in greasy baseball caps, a few teenagers drinking cokes. It felt odd to her—all these people sitting in a restaurant, visiting with each other while the country sank into turmoil. But, in another way, it reminded her of New York City: at six o'clock in the morning these people looked to have been up all night.

They sat at a table with streaks of sunrise shining off the leaf-patterned Formica and paper place mats in the shape of Ohio, a little gold star marking the location of the truck stop. Kera saw how far it was to cross the state, and looked desperately out the window. "Sun's coming up," she said, halfheartedly. She took the phone from her pocket and dialed the number for the retreat, frowned, laid it down on the table.

Rand glanced at the phone, then out the window, but didn't comment. A middle-aged waitress, stiff red hair twisted like a frayed rope on top her head, hustled over with menus and a pot of coffee.

"Coffee?"

"I'd like an espresso," Rand said.

"Don't make'um. Reg'lar coffee's all." She waited. Rand turned over the cup that sat in front of him on the table. She filled it, and looked at Kera.

"No, thanks, I'll have water," Kera said. The waitress slid two menus onto the table, then left with a quick silent turn on her gum-soled shoes.

Across the way, two men stared at a television bolted to the ceiling above the counter. Their backs to Kera, shoulders high, elbows levered off the Formica top, they listened intently, round cowboy hats at odds with the square television. She could see that a news report filled the screen, but the place was too busy, too noisy for her to hear.

The waitress returned. "Ready to order?" She flipped open her check pad.

Rand deferred to Kera, waited for her to order, and she wondered how one minute he could be so cold to her, and the next put on an act, as if all were well. "Oatmeal, please," she said.

"Raisins?"

"Yes, please."

"I'll have the steak and eggs, medium rare, over easy," Rand said. The waitress scribbled it down.

"You might want the steak cooked through," Kera added.

"Why?"

Kera could feel the waitress eyeing her. "Just so it's cooked through."

"I like them pink," he said. The waitress turned to leave.

"Excuse me," Kera said. The waitress paused. "Have you heard anything on the news?"

"No time for news." As she said it she arranged a chair under a table, grabbed an armful of plates. "Don't have time for nothin' but work." Then she turned on her heel and strode off.

Rand reached over in front of Kera and swiped the cell phone from the table. She almost grabbed for it, but stopped herself. "Who are you trying to call?"

"James."

"James? You're calling our stockbroker?"

He eyed her with the phone to his ear. "So, when it comes to money you're still talking *Our*?"

"What do you mean by that?"

"Earlier I noticed the children had turned from *ours* to *yours*," he glared at her.

Kera turned her face to the window again, tried to remember saying that, knowing exactly, if she did say it, why.

He put the phone down. "I can't believe this. Nothing's going through, anyway."

She looked toward the cowboys. "Maybe you could go talk to those guys at the counter, see if they've heard anything new."

Rand glanced at the two men. "You can turn on the radio when we get back to the car."

"Please, Rand, they might know something."

"They're not going to know any more than the radio. Let's look at the map."

He opened the atlas to the national map and Kera reached over and rotated it so both could see. Rand pointed to Interstate 80 and traced the route to where they now sat, a couple miles east of the Youngstown, Ohio, turnoff.

"Here's where we are." He ran his finger west along 80: Cleveland, Toledo, Chicago, Des Moines... "Wait. This runs too far south. We need to get on this 94, back here at Chicago. That takes us north toward Washington State." Up past Madison, Minneapolis, and Fargo. He traced the route again.

Kera watched his finger move along the lines. It looked easy—the map was only eighteen inches wide—but she knew it was a long way between her and the children; the amount of map reflecting what they had driven looked insignificant compared to what remained. "How much further do we have to go?"

He looked at the map for a moment, then slid it toward her. "Figure it out."

"So, you'll only be nice when someone's watching...."

Rand sipped his coffee.

She found the mileage chart in the back of the book and indexed Cleveland and Seattle, came up with a figure, then guessed at the differences, since they weren't in Cleveland and wouldn't go all the way to Seattle. She swallowed a mouthful of water and looked out the window, fretting. Cars rushed by on the highway. When she put the children on the plane she had failed to comprehend just how wide this country was, how far away the children would actually be—it was only a few hours by air. "I wish they'd hurry with the food."

"How far?" Rand asked.

"Over two thousand miles." A tear popped out onto her cheek.

Rand stared at her, sipped his coffee, shook his head.

Her voice broke, "I just didn't think how far away it is, when I sent them."

"What *were* you thinking?"

At that time, all that mattered to her was getting Alissa and Andrew away from them, their problems. It would take a real battle to get him to see what he had become and she was afraid he would do things with his new selfish and careless attitude that might forever scar the children. She knew right now that she didn't want to get into that discussion while sitting in this restaurant. She tried to wipe her eyes dry, but tears kept running down her cheeks.

"This is why you failed at modeling," he said, looking at her with a smug expression. "You get too worked up over things."

She wiped at the tears with a napkin from the table. "I didn't fail as a model, *Rand*. I quit because I hated it."

"Why did you hate it?"

"Oh, I don't know. It made me feel—"

"You hated it because you couldn't handle the pressure."

She let out a sigh and her shoulders dropped. She looked out the window again. "I didn't *want* to handle the pressure. I didn't like the people or the way the business worked. The only thing that mattered was the photographs and the money they would bring in. The image."

"Uh, yeah. That's what it's about, photography and generating revenue, profits. And you could have been very good. We'd have made a remarkable team."

"Is that it?" She steadied her hands by taking hold of the table's edge. "Are you still angry with me for leaving modeling?"

"I'm not angry, no." He brought the cup up, sipped, studied her over the rim. "But I thought we had a direction."

The waitress set their plates down in front of them. "Anything else?" she asked. Kera answered no. Rand said, "Real coffee." She left. Rand cut his steak into tiny pieces.

Kera sprinkled a small amount of brown sugar over her oatmeal and raisins. "I'm sorry," she said, sighing, her shoulders sagging. "We did seem to have a direction that was working well for both of us, as far as making money. But one day I realized it wasn't what I wanted at all, always rushing, working such long hours, using myself to sell things I had no interest in. And I knew that I would not be able to raise our children the right way, spending time with them, sharing life. Money just doesn't matter that much."

"But there would have been time for all that, later."

"When?"

"After we had the business going and some investments working."

"No! Don't you see? There are so many things that go into making a good life. Lately we have only been doing one of them. Making money!" She leaned in and glared at him. "Everything else has taken a back seat to making money. It can't be the right way to live, but that's what your parents did, isn't it? Always working. Saving for a time when things would be different...."

He glared back at her. "I'm not my parents, Kera, so don't equate me with them, but remember, some of that savings sent me to school, which in turn provided you a home."

"I know that." Under the table she had begun absently tapping the wall with the side of her foot. She let out a sound part groan and part growl. "You know, I can't always put into words what it is I'm feeling, but I *am* feeling it. This is like a constant stomach ache, only deeper. This just isn't what life is meant to be. We're missing the point. Seems like everyone is missing the point."

She saw that he disagreed with her, his tight-lipped expression one of unyielding impatience. *This really is exactly like bashing my head against a wall.*

She shook her head as if clearing her mind. "But, right now I don't really see any sense in arguing about this while our children are out there alone." She forced a spoonful of oatmeal into her mouth. It tasted like cardboard, but she wanted to finish it, so that, with the food in the car, they could drive for a long period of time.

She looked over at the men still watching the news, and she could see images on the television that showed people carrying other people on stretchers. In the background, buildings emitted great plumes of smoke.

Throughout life, she had caught television and movie images of other countries around the world filled with hate and violence. She had lived never really believing it could happen here. The way most others in the room casually went on with business, it seemed they still didn't believe it.

Rand was now intently eating, so she wiped her mouth and slowly stood, walked quietly over toward the men at the counter, then stopped directly behind them and watched the report. One of them turned and noticed her, touched the brim of his white hat and said, "Howdy."

Chapter 6

"Hello," she said, then turned her eyes back to the screen. He did the same, but then shifted and looked to her again. She glanced back. He smiled. He was in his early thirties, with clear brown eyes and short, thick, black sideburns coming down from under the curl of his hat. A slight swelling appeared under his lower lip. "Can you tell me where this is happening?" she asked.

His eyes appraised the contours of her face. "You mean you and me, or that stuff on the tube?" He smiled again and his dark eyes locked on hers.

Kera felt herself go hot, her face flush. All the men she had worked with, self-assured men, men with money and power, still she never felt comfortable handling their come-ons; in fact, as time went on, she could feel herself getting worse at it. She glanced over toward Rand. Was it because of the way he treated her, or because she had grown up without men in her life?

"I'm sorry," the cowboy said, his face serious and apologetic, "only tryin' for a smile."

Kera pushed herself. "I was asking about the news report." She nodded toward the screen.

"That's in Denver. The courthouse. There've been others." His eyes sparkled until he turned them back toward the images. "Them boys in the White House, they got real trouble here."

Kera glanced again toward Rand. He was chewing steak, sipping coffee with a grimace, and trying the phone—some number, she felt certain, other than the retreat. She asked the cowboy, "Do you feel that this is serious?"

He glanced at his partner who glanced back, sipped coffee, then faced the screen again. Kera noticed this man was older, possibly early fifties, with tightly cropped hair topped by a worn and sharply curved straw cowboy hat. There was a faded tattoo on his beefy right forearm that read simply U.S.M.C.. The younger man with the sideburns pushed his tongue down behind his lower lip, reshaping the lump there. "Well, this'll carry more than a hornet sting, but I'd reckon the boys in green're gonna stomp this out pretty quick." A small, almost imperceptible nod came from the older man as he intently watched the television.

"Have they said who's responsible?" Kera asked.

"No. They haven't been able to catch anyone, or anything like'at."

"What about the phones, are we going to be able to make calls soon?"

"It sounds like these jokers was able to figure a few key points to attack, I don't know, through computers or somethin'. They've jumbled up the technology somehow."

"Are the airports still closed?"

"They been sayin' those'll be shut down for some time. They even shut down the trains and buses 'cause they think those could get hit, or be used to move the wrong people from place to place." He had been looking a great deal at the TV, but now he turned and looked at her the way some men look at beautiful women, eyes full of wonder, a hint of deep sadness. "Where you from?"

"Manhattan."

"City girl, huh?" His eyes sparkled again and his face crinkled.

The man was gentle. He had an old blue bandanna tucked inside the collar of his denim shirt and she could tell from his hands and face that he spent a lot of time in weather. He seemed very different from the white-skinned masses that walked the sunblocked streets of New York. Kera realized the tension had released from her shoulders, felt the tingle of blood draining back into her toes and fingers. She smiled at the man and noticed how nice it felt to do so, and how nice it felt, also, to have him smiling back. "How about you?" she asked.

"South Dakota. Ever been there?"

"No, I haven't."

"It sure is—"

Rand had come over and stood watching Kera, one corner of his mouth turned up, eyes squinted, head tilted slightly back. She noticed the cowboy's shoulders lift and slowly his right foot slid back into a broader stance. Rand spoke curtly to her, "Are you going to finish your meal?"

"I'm really not hungry. I can get it to go."

Rand flashed his Rolex deliberately, studied it. "Then let's get back on the road."

"Okay." She said good-bye to the cowboy and thanked him for the information. He said Yep as she turned away.

They made it to the car and Kera unlocked the driver's side door. "I'll drive. You can get some rest."

"I'll drive," he said, and stood in her way.

She handed him the keys and crossed to the passenger side. Climbing into the seat she glanced over and saw the cowboy watching her through the large windows of the restaurant. He kept the thumb of his right hand tucked into his front pocket, but fanned the fingers out in a subtle wave. Kera looked away.

As Rand signaled to leave the on-ramp and enter the highway, he was forced to slow down and wait as a convoy of fifteen, five-ton army trucks barreled by on stiff solid tires. They dwarfed the Ferrari. Five big jeep-like vehicles bracketed the convoy front and rear, each carrying four soldiers uniformed in camouflage, helmets strapped on tight. Two of the vehicles had five-foot long machine guns attached to their roll bars with a standing soldier manning each.

"This is so scary." Kera gripped the edges of her seat with both hands, peering through the window of the low riding car as the towering trucks thundered by.

"This is what these guys get paid to do. It's covered in our taxes. Let them get out there and shake up whoever is the problem."

Kera realized that was the first time Rand had referred to what was going on as a problem.

The convoy took an exit and Rand accelerated past, hit his cruising speed of seventy-five miles per hour. A compact disk of Eric Clapton blues sat on the console. He opened it and slid it into the player.

Guitar tunes filled the car and Kera sat back and tried to relax, to calm her mind and concentrate on the fact that she would soon find Alissa and Andrew. She watched out the window as they sped past the outskirts of Youngstown and new featureless subdivisions mixed with old neighborhoods of varicolored clapboard houses. Mist later wafted across the highway as they neared the Meander Creek Reservoir and the warm morning light sparkled off the water with mesmerizing effect. In the distance she saw an old farm with a white picket fence surrounding the house, a big red barn that still carried the faded advertisement for John Deere tractors painted on its side, and thick woodlands full of broadleaf trees—blackberry, box elder, Chinkapin Oak. As young as she had been at the time she still could recall her father walking her on the farm, pointing out and telling her the names of trees. For one brief moment she felt calmed, as if his hand again held hers as he coaxed her into admiring the open beauty of the countryside. The guitar music complimented the thought, the feeling, but then she shifted restlessly. "Aren't you going to listen to the news?"

"You heard the news back there."

"How do we know there isn't something new if we aren't listening?"

"What did your cowboy say?"

"Who is my cowboy?"

"You know, Buck, the guy with the greasy hat and the turd stuck behind his lip."

"I doubt his name was Buck and his hat wasn't greasy."

"You're defending him."

"I'm not—"

"Sure. What did he say?"

"That the railroads and bus lines have been stopped and the airports aren't going to open for awhile. They bombed the courthouse in Denver."

"Buck said that? I didn't figure he looked smart enough to remember all those details."

Kera turned her head and looked out the window. She couldn't believe he was jealous, this man who had no time for her. He had to be acting, or half of what had come out of his mouth in the last ten hours would have been completely different.

Just then the cellular phone rang and Kera looked for it. Rand pulled it from his pocket. "Hello? Hey, James, you got through."

"Rand, call the retreat," she said.

"James, you're kidding, right?"

"Rand, please, hang up and call the retreat!"

"Why didn't you sell or something?"

"Rand! Hang up and call the retreat!"

"Listen, James, I—I've got to go. I don't know what to say. Do what you can to protect... James? You there?" He clicked the phone off and jabbed it out toward Kera. "Damn it, Kera. You're going fucking nuts. You understand me? You've gone ballistic here. The guy calls to tell me that we have just lost nearly everything we had in stocks and I can barely hear him because of you screeching at me."

Kera was crying again, "Is that more important than our children, Rand?"

"Of course not, but if I lose my business, we lose our invested money, and then have to sell the house to feed ourselves; I don't want to hear you crying! Okay?"

"We shouldn't be talking to money men instead of trying to reach Andrew and Alissa."

"Then call them!"

She dialed the number—busy—then threw the phone to the floor.

"Oh, great, break it. Then we'll have to find a phone each time we try to reach them."

Kera rocked in her seat. "Why are you being this way? How could he get through?"

"He called me. I don't know how he did it. He got cut off anyway. What can I say?"

"You can start by telling me you're glad you're here, that you love our children and want to do all you can to find them."

"What?"

"You were dead set against this, Rand, still are, and the only reason you came was fear, panic over what you saw on the highway."

He hesitated, his jaw muscles working. "I came because—"

"You didn't come for the children, or for me. You came because you were frightened by that scene on the highway, you panicked."

His hands tightened on the wheel. "You know, I could turn around right now, Kera. I still think this is insane!"

Kera caught herself, said nothing more, only scooted down into the seat, rested her head on her hand, and stared out the window.

***

Rand cruised along at seventy-five miles-per-hour, no change. He knew he wasn't responsible for their conflict, but he also knew that Kera blamed him. Neglect is what he heard her saying. She constantly harped that he neglected his family, did not care. What might a woman want if not a man to provide? He felt good that someday his children would benefit from his hard work, that he would provide a home for all of them to be proud, that one day he and Kera would be recognized by the social elite and treated as one of them. But instead of being appreciative of this, she despised him as some kind of traitor.

And, as if her regard for him weren't faulty enough, she now had the audacity to call him a coward. *I just don't know where this woman gets off! It would be interesting to see how she would react to witnessing a person murdered.* Just thinking of the scene again caused his hands to sweat. He hunkered down in the seat, tried to take comfort from the exquisite profiles of the machine, and forced himself to focus on the road ahead. It went on straight and flat, seemingly forever, shimmering harshly in the midday sun. But the machine failed him. He couldn't keep his mind from tracking over and over through her insults.

An hour and a half later they neared Toledo. Rand spotted smoke on the horizon, rising from the center of what he believed to be downtown, between squat, bronze and black buildings. These towns all seemed insignificant to him, nothing in them like the skyscrapers of a real city. He crossed the Maumee River and took an exit displaying signs for fuel.

Kera rolled down her window, and he could hear sirens squealing, echoing out from the streets in front of him. He spotted a gas station and headed for it. Without a word, he climbed out and pumped gas. The acrid smell of smoke burned his nostrils. It came to him that, except for sirens, the city seemed oddly quiet; not any kind of movement, no traffic, no pedestrians. Glancing nervously around, the only person he could see was inside the station.

The tall, scrawny attendant wore a baseball cap and ponytail, stood behind the counter, his head bobbing in different directions as he kept a jittery watch with wide eyes out the windows. A bell jangled above the door as Rand walked in. The guy took a large swallow of Coca-Cola from a can, clanked it down, and glanced at a shotgun propped against the wall behind him.

"You come from downtown?" the man asked. His greasy fingers trembled when he took the money Rand offered.

"No. The highway."

"Any roadblocks?" he asked, assessing Rand with wild eyes.

"No. Why?"

"There's been a riot. Haven't you heard?" The man handed him back some change.

"No, we're from out of town."

"Started out some chicken joint got robbed. A bunch'a guys caught the fool that did it. They went rough on him, way rough. Well, soon enough he gets joined by some friends of his or something, and that's all she wrote. The whole city started fightin', throwin' stuff and breakin' windows, burnin' places. A cop got killed and then the cops shot a couple people."

"I'm telling you, everyone is overreacting to this whole situation."

"Yeah, it's like all the nutsos was just waiting for an excuse to go off. I just never knew there was so many of 'em, and right here."

"Is the highway west okay to travel?" Rand asked.

"Haven't heard. Radio kept acting up so I shut it off."

Rand turned to leave as Kera flung open the door. "They just said on the radio that a missile was fired into the White House!"

Rand turned her around and strode out the door. "This guy said there's been a riot downtown here. People are getting shot by the police."

They climbed into the car, fastened their seat belts, and Rand keyed the engine, swept the stick shift into gear, accelerated across the road and onto the highway. Kera turned up the radio, but there was only a loud clicking sound. "That's odd; I was just listening to this." She hit the search and it stopped on another station:

"—state that the damage to the White House, though extensive in the area of the missile's penetration... ...limited to that area. It does appear that the President... ...there, but reports of his whereabouts have gone unsubstantiated. The White House is now the scene of much activity as crews work to clean up the debris and secure the area. Units from Fort Bragge, North Carolina, and other... ... ... protective checkpoints along Connecticut and Constitution Avenues.

"Additionally, there have been new reports elsewhere in the country of scattered attacks on government facilities, including communications centers. Nationwide, twenty-three states have placed their National... ...on active duty or standby, and all US Army, Air Force, and Marine Corps units around the country are either on standby or have already gone into action.

"So far, US forces have seen no fighting, mostly due to the lack of any terrorist element confronting... ...responsibility for the acts, or being caught in the process. We earlier interviewed Harlan Rooten, the counter espionage expert and ex-CIA agent. Here are his comments: — The probability is that no one group is singularly responsible for this series of attacks. Quantifiably, that's impro... ...scattered factions willing to perform these acts of outright terrorism against our government are no stronger than one or two hundred members, and restricted, usu... ...very limited area of operation. What has happened here is more likely the act of many guerrilla-profile groups operating together, or within a system of coop... ...again unique, since these factions differ markedly in philosophy and are often led by extremists who would have a difficult time agreeing on methodology and priorities."

As he listened Rand looked down at the speedometer and realized he was traveling at nearly ninety miles-per-hour. He eased off the gas and coasted back down to seventy-five.

Kera's eyes were wide, her face pale. "I am so scared, Rand. I feel like I'm going to have a heart attack."

"Just take it easy, everything's okay." He had his right hand on the gear shifter and Kera reached over and laid her hand on top of it. He considered pulling his hand away, but didn't.

"I'm sorry," she said. "I'm sorry I did this stupid thing."

Rand kept his eyes on the road. *Are you?*

After a moment she continued. "Why haven't you asked me about the note?"

He took his time answering. He relaxed his hand under hers, checked his rearview mirror. "I guess I feel it's up to you to explain."

Kera took a deep breath and looked out her window. "Things are moving so fast. Life, I mean. And we have no time for anything but work and chores and all the stuff it takes to keep a house and family going. But we never do anything fun together. Never go anywhere new together. I can't remember the last time I felt joy. That seems very sad. I mean, really, is this what we're supposed to be doing with our lives, our world?"

Here she goes. "Yes, Kera, it's what everyone is doing."

"I don't want to be like everyone, Rand."

"Well, what is it you want?"

"I want to live more simply. Not like we have been, not chasing some image in our heads, but really living and enjoying our lives. Everything is supposed to be getting easier, more convenient, but it only gets more complicated."

Rand couldn't believe his ears. *This girl is lost because her trip to the playground turned into work.* He snorted and she looked over at him. He sat up straighter, removed his hand from under hers, and took a double hold on the wheel. "You know—I thought—what does that mean, anyway? You want to live—you are living."

***

She could feel it happening, feel him changing. A moment ago he had seemed comforting, willing to talk. Besides taking her children into her arms she wanted nothing more than to talk to him, to have him listen and respect her feelings, for the two of them to come to an understanding. "It means there's got to be a better way of living, where we would have time to watch our children grow, take walks in places where trees grow wild, travel our world once in a while, visit neighbors and family and actually relax on occasion, be creative with our lives. Simplify, instead of running in circles in hopes of raising another dollar. Live where sunshine can reach us and breathe fresh air." She clenched her hands in her lap, closed her eyes tightly; she could see it all in her mind and it made her feel like praying.

***

Rand noticed that his speed had dropped to sixty-five miles-per-hour, so he stepped down on the pedal. He was trying, but he didn't get it—the point of what she was saying. He was thinking that it sounded familiar, that someone must live like that, but not him, not his parents, not really anyone he'd ever run into, certainly not anyone who wanted security, or a stable future. That kind of living was never reality. And if it were, he wouldn't want it; those people had nothing, lived broke, stayed home every night of the week, and died broke. What did they have? He looked over at her with her eyes all scrunched shut like a little girl trying to make her dream come true. "The world's not that way, at least not anymore."

"I know. But we brought about the change. Maybe we can change it back."

"I don't want to change it back."

"Why?"

"Because I don't want to work as a pig farmer. I don't want a dirt floor. I like this car and I want a nicer one. I like having an extra room in a house with central heat. I don't want to cut wood for a fireplace."

"We don't need to farm pigs or have a dirt floor. I'm not asking to go back to a cave, Rand. But what would be wrong with living within our means, working with our hands, raising our children where the air is clean, walking on real dirt once in awhile, instead of pavement?"

"I'm a photographer. The images I create feel *real* to me. It's what I do. And it's the way of the world now, the way we live. You can dream all you want."

"Maybe it's the way of New York, the big cities, but not everywhere, certainly not the world. I've been reading and we can't compare what we do here with what life is in other countries. We are living with our choices here in this country and look what's happening. We've lost the meaning. There must be better options. Society is no longer in control of itself. We've become the mouse, but who's in control of the treadmill?"

"I don't know, I think people who get out and work for it are feeling pretty happy. Aren't we pretty happy? I mean really? I thought we were all pretty happy."

"Rand, I never see you! The children never see you!"

He knew she was exaggerating. They saw each other everyday. Sure there wasn't always time for the niceties, but that's the way it is while a family gets ahead. And that's it. It takes time to get ahead. Then life could and would be different. It amazed him when she looked at things with such a closed mind.

Besides, why should he give up his career? He enjoyed the business and the art of it, enjoyed the money, now that he was making it. Who would he be without it?

***

Kera could tell the conversation was over. Rand's eyes fixed on the horizon in a way that told her his mind had turned inward. She picked up the cell phone and dialed, then noticed four military-green helicopters flying low across the countryside adjacent to the car. They had streamlined profiles and flew fast. It felt odd to her, and terribly frightening, seeing those war craft, knowing they searched for some hostile element, maybe actually fighting, here, within the borders of her homeland.

She felt in the pit of her stomach that the days of peace and tranquility were forever gone, traded foolishly for civil strife from which the country might never rise, to be what it once was—strong, safe, free, honest. She knew that seemed idealistic and romantic, *but the country had once been all that, hadn't it?* Perhaps it was a matter of degree. Maybe the country had never been all strong, all safe, all free, or all honest, but it had possessed a high measure of all those traits. She didn't understand it, but she knew deep within her that everything was linked together. Somehow, the actions of the people living in the country, over time, had brought them all to this. She felt a twinge of shame.

She became conscious of the busy signal blaring in her ear and dropped the phone. "I don't know why I even try." She thought for a second about the conversation she'd had with the cowboy. "I wonder if it's possible that the phones aren't working because of the terrorists?"

"Doubt it. The lines would be dead, not busy."

"Maybe they're blocking them or something—"

"Sounds like fiction to me, like a cheap thriller."

Chapter 7

Somewhere inside Indiana Rand again succumbed to the wear of the road and let Kera drive. He climbed into the passenger seat and fell instantly to sleep.

Kera eased the car's speed up to eighty miles per hour. They were into Indiana. She wondered, *isn't this the Midwest? Aren't we getting close to half the way there?*

As she drove along, looking out at the flat, open farmland, she remembered reading an article not long ago—while waiting for Andrew to finish a dental appointment—about Indiana history and the ancient cultures that had lived there. Spearheads had been found that dated back 10,000 years. She tried to picture in her mind what this land might have looked like all those millennia ago.

The article said one thousand-year-old mounds still existed in the state, remnants of the simple dwellings built by aboriginal peoples long before white settlers arrived in the area. It was now held by many anthropologists that those ancient people had more leisure time than previously thought; that between moments of rigorous struggle came time to eat quietly together, to groom each other, to stare into a sunset and, possibly, contemplate life.

The way Kera saw it, in all those eons of learning humans had little expanded the ability to control their destiny. Ancient man had battled the elements and predators to secure a life of some enjoyment, current man battled prejudice, social complexity, and the constant need for monetary income.

There were answers, Kera thought. Rand might not see the need for change, but she did. She didn't desire a return to the Stone Age, but, then, *what have all our technological advancements done for us if we can spare less time for loved ones than the supposedly simple-minded and "primitive" ancients that came before us? Do we enjoy our time on Earth any more than they did?*

Surfacing from her contemplation she saw a road sign that said Chicago, twenty-five miles. That startled her as she remembered Rand mentioning a change of route near here. He appeared to be sleeping soundly, but she couldn't hardly look at the map and drive at the same time. She brought the car back down to seventy miles-per-hour.

"Rand," she called softly. He opened his eyes. "We're getting close to Chicago. Don't we do something there?"

"Yeah. We need to take Highway 90-94," he answered groggily.

"How do I get there?"

"This takes you. Watch for the signs."

"Which way do I go when I get to it?"

"North." He closed his eyes again. Then they popped open. "Wait!" He sat up and brushed his hands across his face, raked his hair into place with his fingers, reached for the map. "No. I don't want to do that. That would take us directly into Chicago. After seeing what Toledo was like, I don't want to do that."

"Why not?"

"You saw, we need to stay away from cities." He fell silent for a moment, studying the map. Kera glanced over, trying to see the options. "Okay," he continued, "let's stay on 80 until we get to 39, then we go north and it takes us to 90 at Rockford." He traced the line of travel with his finger. "Rockford's large, but a lot smaller and easier to get around than Chicago."

She thought about that. She had traveled so little, had such flimsy experience with these sort of thoughts. "Won't that take us longer?" she asked.

"It'll maybe add an hour."

"Well, we don't want to add time, do we, Rand?"

"I don't want to go through Chicago."

The dread of adding more time to the painful journey crinkled her forehead. "Maybe we could stay on the highway. That would be okay."

"Kera, people are overreacting. I do not want to go into an unfamiliar city the size of Chicago."

"But I don't want a route that will take us an hour longer."

"That's the way we're going. You got us into this. It's my car. And if we get into any more trouble it will be me that has to get us out of it. Just like what happened in Toledo and New York. We're going the way I say. If you hadn't flown into a panic in the first place we wouldn't even be here!"

Kera's dread flared toward anger. Her knuckles squeezed white on the steering wheel. Words screamed for prominence in her mind: *uncaring asshole! He's thinking only of himself. Himself and his stupid car.* She glared at the road but saw none of it. Her thoughts turned to Andrew and Alissa. She saw their little tear-streaked faces and could hear them crying her name, their frail voices trailing off…. Over and over, she silently repeated, *I am with you, my loves. I am sorry for what I have done. I will come for you and take you to safety. Please, believe in me.*

With her silence Rand had again sat back into the seat, and soon his breathing signaled deep sleep. Kera let the speed of the car rise to eighty-five, ninety. The skyscrapers of the Chicago skyline rose in the distance, and passed on the right as she watched the signs for 90-94 fall behind them.

Beyond the city came dense suburbs, compacted together, with snakelike ribbons of congested traffic and mobs nervously milling on sidewalks and parking lots. She sensed the tension of people feeling powerless, uncertain of what to do, and others trying desperately to get away from the area. Flying past them, elevated on the highway's fast track, she watched for police cars, but, oddly, saw none. Finally the suburbs separated, affording space for something other than pavement and buildings, and as the day's last dusky light faded it struck the green fields of newly grown Midwest corn.

She approached Highway 39 and turned on her headlights, slowed for the signs, understood she needed to go north, and left Rand to sleep. She didn't want it any other way right now, the sound of his selfish voice had begun to make her nauseous. There was virtually no traffic, so she made the turn and again brought the car quickly up to speed, taking advantage of this straight flatland highway. Eighty miles per hour. Ninety. The car cruised effortlessly. One hundred. The roadbed became a dark blur. She contemplated how quickly she would reach the children if only she could maintain this pace, but, even for her, with her need, it proved too much. She had never driven this fast and in the narrow beams of light everything outside the car dissolved into an unfocused stream of grey. She eased off the pedal. The purr of the car came a little less mightily. She glanced over to make certain Rand was sleeping—and suddenly movement appeared in the headlight beams—a dog—or—she hit it with a loud *thwack!* She screamed and slammed on the brakes, jerked the wheel—the creature flew up onto the hood and its head exploded on the windshield, cracking it into a thousand brain and blood splattered patterns.

Rand's head snapped up. "What the hell?" he yelled.

Kera forced the wheel again—excessively—and the Ferrari spun around once, twice, tires squealing, then veered off into a muddy ditch filled with brown water—rammed up against the earthen embankment. The front of the car compacted and the hood flew up. The engine died. Everything came to rest.

"What the hell," Rand screamed, "what the hell happened?"

Kera couldn't talk. Her heart pounded so hard it felt as if it blocked air from entering her lungs. She sat with both hands grasping the wheel, the horrifying images of the collision flashing through her mind.

***

Rand undid his seat belt, opened the door, braced himself, then leaped over the mucky water, onto the slippery slope of the ditch, fell to one knee, and stuck his hand into the slimy, stinky mud. He held it shakily up before him as if he had plopped it into a bucket of excrement. "Good God, Kera!" The water wasn't deep enough to enter the car, but with the front tires in the mud and the rear of the car next to him on the sharp decline, he could see immediately that without a tow truck they would go nowhere. He jumped the ditch and edged around the front of his one hundred and fifty thousand dollar sports car, inspecting the damage. "It's fucking totaled!" He stepped backward up onto the grass at the edge of a field of corn and plopped down, wiping his muddy hand onto the green, crushed by the realization that his sleek rod was ruined, and wondering why he had ever trusted her to drive.

***

Kera plopped one foot into the water. It felt cool on her ankle. She smelled the brown earth, humus, which had washed from nearby fields and colored the water something like chocolate milk. For a slight instant in her troubled mind the rich sweet smell flashed forward a long ago past. Stretching the other leg, reaching the slippery embankment, she dug her heel in, stepped up, and climbed to the shoulder of the highway. About fifty yards back a form lie twisted at the dim edge of the pavement. She walked slowly over and peered down at it. Spots marked the fawn, only a couple months old, no bigger than a large dog. Its startled eyes bulged and its dainty baby head was near flat. Its neck angled oddly and one front leg splayed out, while the other had torn away from its shoulder. Kera started to cry.

A 1982 Ford station wagon with mock wood panels along its sides eased up out of the night and pulled over to the edge of the road near her. The illumination of the highway lighting cast a yellowish aura.

Two men and a woman stepped out, and Kera turned to them, holding the back of her hand to her mouth.

"You okay, Hon'?" The woman asked. She was in her mid-forties with a moppish head of grey-streaked black hair and crinkles of worn skin around her eyes. She wore an old brown Windbreaker and faded blue jeans.

"I think so, just so sad for this baby deer."

"Looks like it died quick." One of the men, near sixty years old, squatted down and lifted the fawn by the scruff of skin over its neck and strode over to the wagon, opened the rear gate, threw it inside. He slammed the gate closed again, leaned on it, and looked at Kera, who stood there, eyes wide, shocked by his actions.

The woman smiled, "You best come with us and we'll find you some help."

From the darkness Rand called, "What's the nearest town to here?" He leaped across the ditch and slipped again, stuck his hand back into the mud. "Damn it!" He entered into the peaked light.

The older man eyed him suspiciously, as if Rand had risen from the muck itself, "Mendota. Where ya'll headin'?" He wore a frayed Carhart jacket, stained blue jeans, and an old baseball cap with admiral's leaf trim around the bill; a thick beard lent him the sea captain's appearance, but his slight body appeared malnourished.

Rand sneered at Kera. "A hell of a long ways. Place called Latrop, Washington. But it looks like we'll need to get a room around here for the night." He wiped his hand on a patch of weeds.

"Oh, you will," the woman snickered. "Nobody workin' weekends 'round here."

The younger man, in his mid-forties, had for this entire time been leaning on the side of the station wagon, watching Kera. His eyes looked black and his shoulders were massively broad. He had the thickest wildest dirtiest black hair she had ever seen, and it gave him the look of some cross between man and beast. Kera found that after the first glance she couldn't look at him.

"Well, if you could give us a ride to Mendota, we'd appreciate it," Rand said. The older man turned and headed toward the front of the station wagon.

"Rand," Kera said, "should we get our things and lock the car?"

Rand looked at the car, then her, with an overt expression of disgust.

"Yeah, grab—"

"Rand—" she said in a voice that got his attention "—please, come and help me!"

The two of them walked over and slid down into the ditch, though Rand stopped short of the water and mud. Kera crawled into the car and found her backpack full of food behind her seat. Rand's camera bag was there beside it. "Do you want your camera?"

"Yeah."

She pulled them from the car, along with her sweatshirt, turned toward Rand, and whispered, "I don't feel comfortable about this."

He stood with his hands still soiled and stiff in front of him, looking at the car crinkled into the wall of dirt, and his face tightened. "You mean them," he nodded toward the station wagon, which the older man had idled up near to them, "or the way you wrecked my car?"

"You know I'm sorry about the car, Rand, but I'm talking about them right now. I don't like the looks of that wild-haired man." She handed the camera bag to him and pulled the sweatshirt down over her sleeveless denim top.

"There's nothing to worry about. These are just simple country folk." He said it with that pious tone in his voice and Kera gave him an astonished, disapproving look. His voice rose, "Now what do you think we ought to do, maybe sit and wait for relatives? You've totaled my car, it's late, and we're a hell of a long way from home."

Kera could see the woman standing next to the station wagon little more than thirty feet away as she tilted her head, listening covertly.

Kera shushed him with a subtle movement of her mouth and eyes. "I don't think it's totaled, Rand."

"It's totaled. Are you going to argue with me about that now? I'm beat. I'm going to get a tow truck in Mendota, get my car off the highway, and try and find a decent cup of coffee. I can think of how I want to handle this in the morning." He climbed out of the ditch, hanging the camera bag from his shoulder.

The two men sat in the front seat of the car. The woman opened the rear door and motioned for Rand and Kera to get in, slid in after them. Without looking back the older thin man pulled the shifter into gear and motored out onto the highway.

"Want these?" Kera held out the keys to the Ferrari.

Chapter 8

Rand took the keys and turned to watch his destroyed dream car as they drove away. If that weren't enough of a nightmare, his gaze then met with the lifeless eyes of the dead fawn glaring at him from the rear of the station wagon. Along with the acrid odor of its punctured bowels he could smell musty, oily rags.

I cannot believe how much THIS SUCKS!

It had all started with Claris informing him that Gretten had canceled a badly needed shoot, then Marla Pole had dropped him, Kera had left the note and sent the children away, some morons had decided to play war on a National scale, Kera had maneuvered him into embarking on this goose-chase of a cross-country trip and, finally, had proceeded to destroy the car that represented his success. Now, as he looked past the fawn and watched the Ferrari disappear, he realized he had left his expensive cell phone behind. "Damn!"

The two women turned and looked at him. He was so disgusted with Kera he found himself wanting to be away from her—far away. Now that he thought about it, this nightmare had started much earlier—the day she reneged on their life plans. She had made his climb to the top much harder than it ought to be. He had made it in spite of her. But still she seemed intent on bringing him down.

***

They sat in near total darkness as they drove, with only the slight glow of the dashboard lights and the occasional street lighting that slashed across the sides of their faces and backs of their heads, like searchlights Kera had seen in prison escape movies. She shifted uneasily.

"So where was it again, where you two were headed?" the woman asked.

"Washington State," Kera answered.

"You from New York?"

"Yes. Where are you from?"

There was a moment's pause and the older man lit a cigarette with a silver lighter he pulled from his pocket. Kera could barely make out the woman seated next to her, but in the flicker of the lighter saw up-close that the woman smiled finally and said, "Oh, we're from up the road. But this is all our country, if you know what'a mean."

She could smell that the woman smoked a lot of cigarettes and drank a lot of coffee, yet held no love for toothpaste. And in the closed confines of the car it soon became evident that none of them had taken a bath in some time. "This won't be a problem for you, giving us this ride?"

"No, Hon', we was headed right this way anyhow."

***

In the uncertain glow of the dash lights Rand could see the watery whites of the older man's eyes in the rearview mirror. He could see that, although the man was driving, he watched Rand as smoke from his cigarette wafted up into his face, to the roof of the car, back to Rand who gagged on it and cracked his window. The older man asked, "What you think of this war we got goin' on?"

"Oh, I don't think it's much of a war," Rand smiled. "I think it won't take long for the military and the FBI to find these losers and lock them up. We'll all be back to work in no time." He noticed how the man held his gaze for a moment longer, then without a blink turned his eyes back to the road. The big-shouldered man with the beastly hair sat silent, staring ahead. Rand felt Kera place her hand on his forearm and wanted to pull away from her.

In the bouncing beams of the headlights signs appeared for Mendota and the man turned the car onto Route 92. Rand could see the occasional soft glow from the window of some lonely house, but it suddenly dawned on him that what he saw were candles or lanterns, not lights. An electrified bulb could not be seen. "The power must be off around here."

Rand saw the woman raise her arm and touch her watch. It lit up. Then she peered back out at the dark houses.

Mendota lay shrouded in darkness. There were houses with black windows, a tavern with two pickup trucks out front, and a small grocery store with an OPEN sign in the window. Another sign along the road showed the silhouetted form of a pregnant woman and read CHOOSE LIFE. The front door of a gas station hung open, but the man drove by without slowing. At that point, Rand noticed the woman shift and let out an uneasy sigh. She sat forward and placed her hand on the back of the front seat. The big-shouldered man raised his open left hand silently, like a wave, and the woman sat back.

"Did you have a hotel in mind?" Kera asked the woman. She didn't answer. No one said a word.

Rand felt his stomach tighten. Something seemed to him suddenly and completely odd. He asked, "Did you—" but then the man turned and when he did he pointed a revolver at Rand.

"We know where we're goin', *Loser!*" The last word was exaggerated, to the point—at some other time—of silly humor, but his voice came harsh, strained, and in the dark his eyes were pits of black, blacker somehow than the night that surrounded them, and their depths held unpredictable wrath.

Rand felt Kera's fingers tighten on his arm, felt his chest squeeze inward, and the nerves at the corners of his eyes twitch. Never had any gun been pointed at him; they were foreign things, seen and referred to only by others, or in films at the theater. He had certainly never been in the presence of any person so dangerously hostile. It felt as if his body had been lit on fire, like his eyeballs had somehow strained forward in their sockets. He wanted to leap from the car, but found that he couldn't move.

The older man eyed him in the rearview mirror, and smoke oozed out of him as he spoke, "You're just a part of the fuckin' problem, aren't yuh, rich boy?"

Rand tried to swallow, but his throat closed. He didn't think he could speak if he wanted to. Sweat gathered along his brow. Kera increased the clench on his right arm. Her breathing came in short stutters. It sounded loud to him, as if she were panting into her hands cupped around his ears. Rage consumed the gunman's face.

And then Rand caught a flash of movement as the bulky arm stabbed forward. He felt hard steel connect with the side of his skull. Faintly, behind an onslaught of brain distortions that later reminded him of the feedback used in live rock-and-roll guitar solos, Rand heard Kera screaming his name.

Part Three

Chapter 9

It came to Rand first like a drum beat—slow and rhythmic. Humph. Then, like the sound of a running horse drawing nearer, it grew louder and more urgent. Humph, humph. It reached down into him and brought him out. His eyes opened. The sound continued. Humph, humph, humph.

His backside ached on the hard ground. His brain throbbed like he'd chugged a gallon of clear liquor. His scalp felt like a lip after too much Novocain. Trying to touch it he found he couldn't move his hands, and that scared him. Humph. The sound came again. Rand brought his head up and the back of it struck something hard. He could feel it behind him, rough, like the bark of a tree. Humph. He squinted toward the sound, and the squinting hurt. The quarter moon glowing in the night sky was all he had. Before him he detected motion. Humph. He worked hard at focusing his eyes, caught a blurring back and forth of outlines. Humph. And then it came together. Humph, humph, humph. He saw now how the outline of a large male form had a smaller form pressed downward over the front of the station wagon.

"Stop that!" he heard himself scream. But then, he hadn't screamed at all. Only in his mind, which fear had quickly filled, and forced him to silence.

A metallic click sounded, then a grinding, and the area lit up with a dim glow. The older man's face appeared at the center of the aura. He was on the opposite side of the car, leaning on the hood, a cigarette dangling from his mouth. He lit up, leaving the lighter burn as he appraised the action with a smirk and a chuckle. In front of him were the gunman and Kera. The gunman was behind her, no gun in sight, had his hands up full of her hair, pulled on it as he rammed her with his hips, savagely bending her neck backward. Rand could see Kera's face in profile, hear the humph of air being knocked from her, see her breasts dangling as the man let loose her hair and reached down in front of her.

Rand wanted to shout, but would that help or hinder? Something told him that it was safer to remain quietly there in the dark. He tugged against whatever it was that bound his hands to the trunk of the tree, felt the blood throb anew in his head. Humph. Humph.

That was the only sound that Kera made. Why, he wondered, wasn't she fighting? *Why isn't she rebelling against him the way she rebels against me?* In the glow of the lighter Rand thought he could tell that her eyes were closed. Humph, Humph, Humph! The man's rhythm increased, his head craned backward. Rand could see that the man was nearing an— "Stop!" Rand yelled and the sound of his voice startled him. There was shadowy movement within the car, possibly the woman, and the older man glared at him from across the hood; the younger man paid no attention, but began to thrust harder, deeper, using the full force of his legs like a machine. Humph! Humph! Humph! "Stop! You can't do that!" Rand yelled toward the violence, trembling wildly, stuck there on the ground.

"Damn it, shut that fucker up!"

Rand saw the skyward profile of the man as he spit out the words, continued his thrusting.

The older man turned and strode toward Rand, who felt fear shoot up within him like a rocket. He tried to reason with the man, "Come on, you can't—," but a boot heel whacked him in the temple.

Chapter 10

When Rand opened his eyes it was still night and too dark to see where the drop of water that struck his swollen temple came from. His body weighed on his arms, twisted behind him, and his shoulders throbbed. His neck felt as if it would never again straighten and his hip burned from pressing down on concrete-hard ground. As he sat there he could feel the bark of the tree with his arms, but his hands had gone dead numb, which made him uncertain whether they existed at all below the knots of cord, or, as his harried imagination suggested, had been hacked off by the assailants and tossed away.

He heard a snorting sound and wrenched himself painfully around to face that direction. His heart raced within the dark space of night, now so black he couldn't see his legs before him. More water pitter-pattered onto soggy soil, onto his skull. Nothing else made any sound. He thought it must have rained, or misted so much that the water came from the tree he was tied to.

The car was gone. Somehow he could feel that nothing existed there in front of him, nothing, other than some great unknown. Not a light shined in the night, not a sound from traffic or a subway train, not a voice echoing down familiar streets—only a black and utterly foreign void… and the water pattering. No matter how he turned his head it hit his skull and trickled icily down his neck.

The polo shirt and khaki pants were all he wore, and they were wet, and a chill ran through him. He pulled at the cording around his wrists, felt that hands still existed at the ends of his arms, then panicked with the fear of wondering whether he might lose them after they went without blood long enough, and with the realization that within this black and foreign night he was absolutely defenseless. He struggled violently, yanking frantically at the cording, laboring desperately to stand, to gain some position that felt stronger than sitting, but the tight cords held him, held him down, and the pulling finally scared him too, not knowing whether he tore his own insensate flesh from the tendons, the bone.

He wanted to scream, but screaming might bring the wrong attention. He collapsed back against the tree, his chest heaving, his eyes wide and glaring at the night. His brain searched for options. He could pull at the cords until something of him separated. He could call for help. Those actions could hurt him, or get him killed. To sit shivering and wait for light seemed the only reasonable course of action.

But the darkness increased his confusion, his fear. Adding to the perplexity of it all, unfamiliar sounds came again—rustling, crackling. He had spent not one night outdoors in his entire life. He'd come upon stories of wild dogs, coyotes, even cougars, but he had no idea if they existed here in the Midwest; he had never been here.

There came the sound of a snort, a twig snapping. He felt compelled to call out, to bellow at the blackness swarming around him, but those who had tied him to the tree, kicked him in the head, assaulted Kera, might lurk there.

No, sitting and shivering, waiting for day, was the only damned thing to do. But he hated to do it, stuck and miserable, hurting, knowing full well that it had never been his decision to come anywhere near here. He thought of Kera and the images of the man taking her on the front of the car flashed through his mind. He could again hear the sound of air leaving her body each time the man slammed into her. It made him angry, the memory; it made him angry, that they had come here on this God damned gallivant that made no sense. He felt sick, but wanted to yell, *Didn't she fight them?* He had been knocked out, but had watched for long moments and had not seen her fight.

His body began shaking so violently that he wondered if this was what they talked about, on those hospital shows, the effects of shock. This fear, this anger, this waiting reminded him of the fear and anger and waiting he had known when he'd found that his mother was dying—that feeling of self-depletion, of complete and utter powerlessness. There had been not a thing he could do to save her. There was not a thing to be done now.

Eventually the night passed. The infernal drag before daylight brought a marked dip to colder temperatures. His nose and lips went numb. Dawn came as slowly as every good thing he had ever wanted. But then, he noticed a slight greying of a spot or two on the horizon, which after a time developed into breaks in the density of trees here and there, where the forest around him had thinned enough to let direct light through.

With full light came the proof that he was corded to a tree bordering a clearing, which in turn stood completely surrounded by forest. Where the station wagon had sat, a dirt track started and apparently headed out, though he couldn't see for certain through the trees and brush.

So, it is day. The water had stopped pattering and the temperature seemed to rise. "So the fuck what?" he heard himself say aloud. "What do I do now?" He tugged at the cord, but it hurt his wrists too much to repeat the move. He turned his head and saw that a greasy rope, as thick as his middle finger, wrapped three times around the tree.

So the fuck what? It might have been wire, nylon, chain, it made no difference, tied off masterfully so that his every movement tore flesh. He felt the fear again and it tightened something at the back of his neck, and it grew as fast as the fear had grown when the older man came to silence him. It ached and burned and spread down his spine. He shouldn't be here, but it was too late to do anything about it. He'd come, he'd listened to her. *So the fuck what?*

***

The door busted open and Kera snapped her head up so fast and hard that it bounced off the wall she sat against. She'd been crying for hours and her face felt filthy to her, and somehow not like her own. The word wretched kept coming to mind. *I am wretched.* All of her, every inch, felt defiled. But then, what was all of her? What was her and what wasn't? Where did she end and the rest of the world begin?

Two men came through the door and stared down at her. One of them she recognized without actually looking at him. She would never in all her days—however many that might be—forget him. But the second man was new to her.

In his late thirties, he wore stiff pressed camouflage fatigues and a black beret on his head that covered thick, coarse black hair closely cropped. His narrow face was tight and serious and tanned from the sun. He stood taller, but narrower in the body, than the man with the wild hair. "What's your name?" He said, and his voice sounded much gentler than she expected.

"Kera," she mouthed, looking out the top of her eyes.

He knelt down on one knee, close, and studied her. Then he suddenly popped a small cherry tomato into his mouth and chewed. "Don't be afraid, Kera. We're Patriots. But I need to know, are you a sympathizer, or a nationalist?"

She tried to focus on his words. But the question puzzled her: *What is a sympathizer, a nationalist?* Her head swam. She felt afraid of the answer, afraid of the man standing behind this new man. "I'm from

New York City," she heard herself mumble.

"Are you in favor of the revolution?" he asked softly, with a slight upward crease around the corners of his eyes and mouth.

She had no idea what the "revolution" was. Since this nightmare had started it all seemed blurred, not something of particular detail, except for the consequences to the safety of her children. Toward any purpose, or cause, she had focused little thought. "I'm only trying to reach my children in Washington."

He shifted on his feet, tilted his head, and the upward curve at the corners of his mouth disappeared. His eyes tightened down on her, forced their way deep inside of her, where she felt weak and raw and filthy. She had thought she understood what it felt like to be treated as an object, but what she had known before was nothing compared to this, and men like these, came as a horrible, debilitating surprise. They were physically malicious, and now seemed intent on reaching her internal spaces, on taking what little of herself that remained. She didn't know where she began or ended, but if she let the borders continue to fade, lost the bit of voice within, then little hope of continuing remained—and not continuing meant failing her children. Her face was angled away, but she looked at him out the corner of her eye.

"Now, why would someone be traveling across the country at a time like this?" he asked. "Wouldn't it be safer to leave the children where they are?"

She didn't want to answer, didn't want to give anything more. She looked down at the man's boots; they were shiny, clean, and his fatigues came to a perfect rolled stop at the shin-high tops of them.

The wild-haired man hesitated, then said, "I think I can—"

But this man before her raised his hand, stopped him. "Kera, where were you really going?"

She kept her eyes on his boots, afraid to move.

He stood and looked down at her. "You take some time. But I'm going to need answers. There are government agents out there, and a pretty woman like you would make a perfect spy. I'll not have any infiltrating my command." He turned to leave and said to the wild-haired man, "Outside." They headed out the door, but before leaving, the wild-haired man paused and looked down at her. She couldn't see what expression he wore—her eyes held fast the spot the other man's boots had filled.

***

Rand scrunched his eyes shut, blinked hard three times, and squinted again into the forest across the clearing. The grey of the day and the darkness within the forest made it difficult to see, but Rand felt certain that he had detected a human form, crouched low within the underbrush among the trees. He yearned desperately to crawl around the other side of his tree, to get something substantial between him and whoever, whatever, it was squatting there in the wet dark. But his tightly tied arms prevented him from standing, sliding, doing anything other than sitting there like a decaying corpse.

The eeriness of the form in the trees, the idea that it had lurked there all along, watching him, waiting, kept him from calling out. But, *damn it!*, was this a person who could save him, cut these ropes, free his blood-starved appendages, get him on his feet again? Or was it one of *them*, the sick twisted bastards that had picked them up and treated them like animals? Maybe they had moved the car, pulled Kera into the woods, and were watching him now as he slowly died. Maybe that was their idea of fun.

Across the clearing, movement occurred where the head and face might have been. Rand willed his eyes to focus acutely, and thought the hair looked blonde. He didn't remember any of the abductors having blonde hair. He wasn't certain. It had been night and too dark. He studied it, but the figure refused to move again. It seemed to be facing him, as if the person stared at him as he stared at it. *It is a person, isn't it? What the hell else could it be?*

***

Two windows allowed late afternoon light into the room where Kera sat against the paneled wall, and a single worn couch was the only object for the light to play upon. Kera had been staring at it. Her head hadn't stopped swimming, her heart racing, since the men left the room. Or really, since the station wagon had turned onto that black forest road, Rand's limp body had been yanked out, and she had been wrestled against the hood of the car. She now forced her mind beyond that moment; she could not bear to think of it. She had known, somewhere at the fringes of her consciousness, when the older man went and silenced Rand. But the sounds inside her, the screaming and wailing of her spirit, had prevented her from hearing what took place over there, with Rand, in the dark of the forest. She didn't know if he was still alive. The older man had returned to the car and resumed his watching and his hideous cheering. She saw his face now, in the glowing wafting light of his lighter, those crooked stained teeth, those watery eyes. *Things like this don't happen to people who don't deserve it.*

Fear clawed at her attempts on rational thinking. *They can come to this room at any time!* She forced her mind away again... to Alissa and Andrew. Even then, the pain of her personal horror could not compare to the agony of considering her children's condition.

She stood suddenly, her legs wobbling, and reached for the windowsill, for something to steady her. Her scalp burned where the wild-haired man had pulled her hair. Her back ached and her hips hurt, bringing back the image of his thick claw-like fingers.

Kera now wore only the green sweatshirt and jeans and shoes. The wild-haired man had torn her denim shirt, her bra, and panties away with violent twists that left raw burns on her skin. She ached to squeeze into some invisible crack between the floor boards, except, if she had one wish she would use it to start after her children.

Thoughts ricocheted wildly around in her mind. In one way, fear overwhelmed her—her hands trembled uncontrollably, she wanted to flee—in another, she felt dead.

In the tumult of her daily life, she had completely lost an awareness of her body. She and Rand had not made love in months. That part of her female essence had withdrawn. But now, after the rape of her flesh and femininity, a deep sadness and sense of loss overwhelmed her. That part of her she had failed to cherish... had been murdered. It was gone forever. She mourned over the loss of herself.

All of this was simply too much to withstand. Now, another form of separation began to set in. It reminded her of how she had survived her parents' death; a form of waking-slumber, or of completely... letting... go....

As that separation pulled her toward an almost unconscious state, she peered out the window and saw a grey-painted building, a shed of sorts, and a larger one, possibly a garage. Gravel roads led into the place, surrounded by forest. Under the canopy and within the shaded recesses of trees sat cars, pick-up trucks, and SUVs—some covered with branches or netting the color of earth and foliage, others painted in camouflage. A man dressed in camouflage of blended brown and green held a rifle and stood on the edge of the road about one hundred yards from the building she occupied, watching the distant approaches with concentration. One door of the garage hung open and she could make out movement inside, but the day's light had faded and kept specific actions secret.

Suddenly she heard the sound of many footfalls within her building, doors opening and banging shut, and outside men appeared in considerable numbers. Kera's heart began beating hard against her chest. She jumped back away from the window. She wanted to hide but she also wanted to know what was happening. She could still see, and the men were mostly all dressed in camouflage fatigues, but some had hunting outfits on, or jeans and work jackets. All of them carried rifles or shotguns or long tubes that reminded Kera of the Bazookas she had seen in old war movies.

Now both double doors of the garage were pulled wide and a loud engine started up, rumbled. Kera made out a massive dark green vehicle sitting inside. A jeep pulled up, and she could see the man who had questioned her sitting in the passenger seat, next to a driver wearing fatigues and a black bandanna tied around his head.

The dark green vehicle rumbled out of the garage and Kera thought it looked a little like a tank, maybe smaller, with a man standing on top of it, holding the handles on a big, mounted machine-gun. The vehicle rode on tracks, like a bulldozer, and turned to go down the gravel road, away from her.

She looked and saw that the man in the jeep had spotted her watching through the window. His eyes seemed to glow in the fading light. A shiver ran down her spine and she backed away from the window. Then the man said something to the driver and the driver looked at her, picked up a radio, and spoke into it. Her breath caught and she stumbled backward, sat heavily on the floor behind the couch.

The door of the room flew open and in barged the wild-haired man. His eyes were wide until they found her, then he smiled in a way that made her heart go hard and lodge itself in the bottom of her throat. He shut the door behind him.

"You shouldn't be spying on us." His voice sounded rough, like his vocal cords were stiff, and as he stalked closer to her she could see his nostrils flare and his eyes lock onto her the way a lion's do as it prepares to kill. He had a two-way radio in his hand and he tossed it onto the couch, then worked absently at something on his wrist, and Kera's eyes zoomed in on Rand's Rolex watch.

Her nostrils flared also, from fear and hate, from the unwashed odor of him. Her eyes went to the floor, to his boots with their torn leather and loose soles. She could feel herself drawing in, closing down, like the shell of a clam tightening, sealing, protecting a vulnerable interior. Her sight dimmed and she felt the floor tilt under her.

The boots moved to within a foot and she felt herself rise, then stand on her wobbly legs, and as she tried to step away he grabbed her wrist with a hand that wasn't made of flesh, it seemed, but something with molecules much closer together, lifeless, and from him oozed the indignant energy of a being without conscience.

And then she felt it come into her, like some warm and magic elixir—
Separation.

Chapter 11

"Hello!"   Rand shouted toward the figure in the forest across the clearing.   Some time ago the figure had stood upright, and a dark face had remained turned directly toward him, but it didn't move again.   He'd been too unsure to call out at first, but this clearly was not one of the abductors.   It wouldn't make sense—not that the behavior this person demonstrated made sense either.   "Can you help me?" he yelled.

The figure took a couple slow steps and reached the far edge of the clearing, paused for a moment, then hurried with a hunched and tottering gait to a tree about a hundred feet away from Rand, about halfway to him.   It was a female with long blonde hair and aqua blue, flowing clothing.   Her face seemed oddly dark and indistinguishable as it appeared from behind the tree.   Rand guessed her age for the sixties; a fairly tall and slender woman.

"Can you please help me?"   Rand called again and his head ached from the yelling.   He couldn't understand why she behaved this way, why she hadn't come to help him, what her timidity could be about.   He was tied inescapably to a tree, for God's sake, what harm could he possibly inflict?

She scurried forward then and passed him in a hunched, feathery wave of silken material, coming to a stop behind him, directly on the opposite side of his tree.   Rand stopped breathing.   The tree's large girth prevented him, even when he craned his neck around, from seeing her, but he had a good look as she lurched past, and what he saw shocked him, for her face was full of dark, purple contusions, one massive, horrific wound really, with her left eye swollen shut.

This does not make sense.   What I am experiencing here does not make any damn sense at all.

He could hear her breathing behind him—wheezing really—a soft, rapid, congested sound like a cat with a cold.

"Can you untie me?" he asked.   No new sound came, only the breathing, faster than before.   "Please, I've been beaten.   They've taken my wife.   I need your help."

"I know."   Her voice came strained, as if a hand squeezed her throat, and it was followed by a gurgling cough and then a soft whimper.   "I have nothing to use on the rope."

"Your fingers!   Can't you untie it?   Please, I've been here all night.

My hands have been numb for hours."

"I—" She coughed again, a deep, rattling sound, and then after a moment, "I'll try."

He could hear her move, feel small pulls on the rope. "Hard," she said, "tight." She would work for a bit, then stop with a sigh, a whimper, then start again. Rand couldn't believe how long it was taking her. He shifted and ached at the thought of being free again. He wanted to stand and rip the ropes from his wrists, let the blood flow through his body again. "Can you hurry?"

She didn't answer, but after awhile he could feel the tension release from his shoulders, and the rope went slack. He pulled and his arms came away from the tree. He brought his hands around in front of him and unwound the rope from his chaffed, blood-clotted wrists, threw it to the ground.

The woman had stayed on the opposite side of the tree and Rand stepped around to look at her. She stood with her eyes toward the ground, her shoulders bowed forward, hands held low in front.

My God! Look at her hands.

They were as horribly bruised and swollen as her face, with not an inch of skin its usual color.

"Are you… okay?" he asked. She started weeping, her shoulders and her entire body shaking, her face remaining motionless except for the closing of her good eye and the sucking in of her lips with her sobs. Rand didn't know what to do. He felt shocked over the sight of her. "Can you sit? Can you sit for a moment?" Rand asked.

She crouched stiffly down like an elder woman, but Rand could see now, she was not at all as old as he had assumed. The desire to run his fingers through his hair, to check himself, ran through his mind, but he looked at his damaged hands and knew he couldn't; they ached far too much, too much also for him to consider helping her, and so he stood and watched as she sank down with her back against his tree. Her dress reached her ankles, was torn at the shoulders and soiled. He didn't know the name of the material, if it wasn't silk, but he knew it looked expensive, classy. Among the contusions covering her face deep scrapes had bled and dried hard. Trapped on a swollen finger was a striking, multi-stoned wedding ring. He knelt in front of her. "What happened to you? Is there somewhere we can go for help?"

"No, I—I don't know."

"What happened?"

"Those men. Those men and that woman."

Rand couldn't believe what he had heard. "You mean, the ones who brought me here?"

"Yes."

"In a station wagon?"

"Yes."

"The same men that did this to me?"

"Yes," she said, and started to weep again.

"But, how do you know they were the same people?" Rand cast an angled, focused gaze at her, and she turned her good eye up at him and between sobs said, "Because, I saw from the trees there. I saw in the car lights who it was."

Rand stood and turned and walked a few paces away from her. This woman had watched from the safety of the trees as he was brutalized and his wife raped. He looked at his wrists again and noticed for the first time that his Rolex was gone. "Damn it!"

He turned halfway to the woman. "How could you watch and do nothing?" The blood flowing back into his fingers caused an intense burning, and the pain in his wrists left him holding them out in front of him, protecting them. He glared at her, and couldn't help but see her hands, her face. *My God!* He felt as if he had been mortally wounded, yet knew he must have appeared healthy compared to her.

"They—thought—I was dead."

He wondered about Kera's condition. "Was she alive?" he asked.

The woman wouldn't look at him. She sat with her head down, tears wetting the exposed roots of the tree.

"Kera, my wife, was she alive when they left here?"

The woman's head bobbed upward, "I think so. It was dark. They took her."

He stepped closer. "Do you know where they went? Did they take you somewhere?"

"No. They took my husband."

"When?"

"This is the third morning I have been here."

"You've been hiding in the forest for three days?"

The woman went into silent motionless weeping, her face like a Halloween mask that refused to reveal the true expression within. "I didn't know—what to do."

The ravaged skin on her face looked like it might split open, and Rand sickened at the thought. "How did this happen?" But the woman went further into her weeping, that congested coughing, and made no attempt to answer.

She was too frightened to leave the safety of the trees, but eventually Rand convinced her that they must go for help. With his assistance she stood again and they slowly began to follow the gravel track through the clearing lined by trees, out to the main road.

"What's your name?" he asked.

"Patricia."

"Patricia, I'm Rand." She didn't acknowledge, but instead kept her good eye on the uneven ground before her footfalls. She moved more slowly, more stiffly than she had before, and any little protuberance in the roadbed would catch the toe of her shoe and trip her. And then she would cough until her shoulders sagged again.

Rand noticed something lying in the grass at the edge of the gravel and immediately knew it—his camera bag. As they moved past he steadied Patricia, then bent and picked it up. He could tell by the weight of it that his camera remained inside, and he passed it over his shoulder before again bracing the woman's arm with his own.

Having that camera again, that piece of himself, his world, somehow helped. He would open the case later, when they reached a safe haven.

"What is it?" Patricia asked.

"It's my camera bag. They must have thrown it out of the station wagon as they left. I'm a photographer."

"Don't take my picture."

It was the first strong-minded thing he'd heard her say. He hadn't even thought of taking her picture. "I won't, Patricia."

"Never again. Never." With that she coughed until she bent in half, and Rand held her from falling.

***

There came a knock on the door, but Kera didn't hear it. She continued to lie on her side on the hard floor, shivering, not wanting to see anyone, not wanting to come back to the room, to be inside herself, instead preferring to die.

Still, the door opened. The man who had questioned her entered and shut the door behind him. He carried a plate with food on it, and he stepped neatly toward Kera.

"Here's breakfast for you," he said, and he set it down near her on the floor, then backed up and sat on the couch.

Kera wondered if he knew what the other man did to her. She considered saying it, to see if he would help her, but that could so easily lead to more abuse. They were a band of marauding criminals.

Her eyes eventually focused on the plate, peered over the rim from their low vantage point, saw the food. She didn't want it, until the smell of it came to her. Then she sat up slowly, took the plate in trembling fingers, and used a spoon to eat baked beans, meat, and eggs. It seemed odd to her that she ate the food, though it had no flavor.

The man watched with his hard eyes until she finished, which took no longer than a minute. "I've talked with the soldier that picked you up and judging by the car you drove, and your demeanor, it's doubtful that you're any kind of an agent of the government. We went back to acquire the license plate number of your vehicle, to run a check, but, unfortunately, it had already been stripped down by vandals. They're running wild like packs of hyenas right now. That was some car you were driving."

Kera placed the empty plate back on the floor in front of her and stared at it.

"Was it good?" he asked. She said nothing. "That was venison. Ever had it? It was from a deer brought in same night as you."

Kera remembered the poor fawn lying on the pavement and leaned forward, her stomach twisting. She wanted to wretch, but if she did what would this man do to her? She swallowed hard.

"You can continue this game of silence if you like, but it won't do any of us any good, including your children, if you, in fact, have any."

Her eyes met his, "I have them," then dropped back to the floor again.

After a pause, he said, "Yes, you do. What are their names?" She only stared at the floor. "Okay," he said, then rose and paced with his hands clasped behind his back to the window behind her. "We'll have a little trade-off here. I'll tell you about us, and then, later, you can tell us a little about you. How's that, Kera?" She remained motionless, silent.

"All right, for the time being you can call me Major. I am commander of this state's unit of the Patriots. Have you heard of us?" No answer. "We are a citizen militia whose sole intent is to return the control of this great nation to its people, its citizens. The constitution provides for that. We break no laws set forth by the constitution.

"The United States government is now under siege by numerous organizations such as ours, and, unfortunately, many less honorable entities with fewer legal motives in mind. But our concern must remain focused, and for the betterment of all citizens of this country. We *will* return this land to its rightful overseers.

"In the meantime, it may be a long struggle, with much bloodshed, much sacrifice, from all sides. And we would not be in this situation if the citizens had stayed involved in the matters of their country, if people would have taken an active role in the welfare of this land. It is the people, the citizens, who are truly responsible for the demise of the United States of America. Corporate America and the federal government have run amuck only because the citizens have allowed it.

"And so, we will be taking citizens such as yourself and teaching them how to participate, how to make a difference, how to take back the ownership that is their birthright." He had paced around in front of her and stood only a foot away. His boots again filled Kera's view. "And that's where you come in. We need your help, but we cannot ask your permission for it. You must help. And I believe the more you come to know us, what we do, the more you will want to help. Participating in the history of your country will feel right to you."

He squatted down to her, and she could feel his eyes on her face. But she didn't care. There was nothing, anymore, that he could do to her, nothing left to do anything to.

"This country has been failing for a long time, Kera." He reached his hand out and touched her cheek. Her eyes remained on his boots. "For your children, Kera, for my children, and all the children, we've got to do our part." He remained there for a moment, studying her, then picked up the plate and stood, walked toward the door. "We can start slow with this agreement between us." He stopped and faced her. "But the next time an officer comes through this threshold, you get to your feet." He turned and opened the door briskly, and when he did it revealed the startled wild-haired man standing on the other side, pulling back. The major assayed the other man's presence. "I told you to get her a blanket and a cot, Private." The wild-haired man nodded. "Do it!" the major commanded. "And have Private Remmings escort her to the shower."

***

"No!" Patricia said. Rand knew she meant it, because for the first time in more than an hour she worked to raise her head and look at him when she spoke.

They had followed the gravel track to the main road—no more than a backwoods two-lane blacktop—and turned right, since Patricia thought the car had gone that way when it left the night before. Rand knew it didn't matter which way the car had gone. They stood no chance of finding Kera unaided, and it was obvious that Patricia needed immediate medical care.

They had crept along for half a mile and now stood in dense trees across the road from the first house they came to: a large, two-story, white clapboard farmhouse, probably built seventy or more years ago. The large lawn hadn't been cut for a week or more, and a smooth blacktop driveway led to the house. Some of the building and its windows hid behind trees full of new spring growth. Rand crouched behind the trunk of a tree. "No, what?" he asked.

"Don't go to the house. They might know those men. The men might live there. Too close," she said, and was struck with another fit of coughing.

The skin of her neck, below the contusions, had begun to turn pale, Rand noticed, and her hand, when she touched his, felt cold and clammy. Her good eye seemed glassy, unfocused, and her knees weaker, more wobbly than before. Rand wanted to get her into someone else's care. He didn't know the first thing about emergency aid and her condition scared him.

Also, he couldn't quit thinking of food. He hadn't eaten since that truck stop and his belly rumbled loudly and frequently. And Kera, she kept popping into his mind, forcing him to worry over where they had taken her, what they were doing to her, how he would ever find her. Thinking of her had become confusing. He had questions concerning her safety, but at the same time, anxiety over his present situation, and anger toward her for getting him into it. He wanted her near, not only to know she was all right, but also to let her have it for dragging him into this.

As good as the house looked, he didn't want to approach it, either. There were too many possibilities. "Sit down for a moment," he told Patricia.

"No," she said, and locked her arm around his with strength he didn't know she still possessed. "Don't go! What if the men are there? They'll take you... like they did my husband!" She looked up as she held onto him, and her glassy eye screwed into him, fastened him to her. "I am very wealthy. When this is over I can pay you considerably."

Rand's mouth went dry and his forehead began to leak sweat. *What did she just say?* All the terrible and confusing things having happened the last few days, and now an answer to his prayers dangled before him. It was beginning to look like this situation would take time to remedy, but when ended he would need money, and plenty of it. If the photography business was continuing as usual back in New York City, he would soon be left behind. If it wasn't, it would all be open to the first and best people on the scene when things returned to normal. Since his stock investments were mostly lost, it would take some other form of cash to get him going while he built the business back up, paid the high insurance deductible and purchased a new car, repaid the various and considerable debt he would owe due to Kera's misguided decisions.

Then Patricia's arm fell limply to her side and she withered to a sitting position on the ground.

Without her I am free to go, free to travel away from here before I make contact with anyone. That would be safer, because she's right, there is the chance that even stepping out into the open would draw attention from the wrong parties.

If he left her on the porch of the place there was no telling if she would get care, or further injury. The area might harbor others like those that had picked them up, since the question remained as to what kind of people they actually were—murderous anarchists, opportunists, supremacists, common thugs? On the other hand, if he took her with him she might die under his care. Either way, it appeared unlikely he'd collect any gratuity from her.

The choices bewildered him. He felt as bound now as he had while tied to the tree.

He needed help, not only with Patricia, but also in finding Kera—no matter how or where she was. That was the way to have it all. If he could obtain some official assistance, he might then get Patricia what she required, and be rewarded as she promised, while at the same time using the official resources to relocate Kera. He had to contact the police. Surely the phones would work now. If he could do all this efficiently enough he might return to New York in time to salvage his reputation and business. Come to think of it, saving Patricia might get him some very profitable attention back home.

Suddenly, a branch snapped in the woods behind them. Rand cocked his head and listened. Another crunch of the underbrush sent his heart racing. It could be anyone, with any purpose in mind. He took a step to run....

"Hold yourself right there! Don't move!"

The voice came from behind them, back in the trees, and Rand froze, left his eyes on the house. From down within Patricia came a low, baleful moaning that grew quickly in volume and intensity.

"What's your business here?" called the voice.

Rand knew it was up to him, to give the correct response that might keep them alive.

"We've been attacked," he said, speaking loudly so his voice would carry over the mournful tones of Patricia's wailing. Though he feared the report of a gun firing, the pain of a bullet entering him, he couldn't help turning, to see her as she emitted such a haunting lament.

Patricia sat on the ground, her long thin legs splayed in right angles before her, her destroyed hands useless on her thighs, her broken body in that spread aqua dress giving the impression of a flower wilting, succumbing to the power of the relentless past, present, and future, receding with gravity toward the soil from which it sprang, from which it had wrestled sweet freedom. Her purple-black face, eyes shut and streaming, looking like the rotted disk of the flower, turned to the grey and sunless sky as if seeking one last infusion of light—and the lament rolled out, echoed off the trees and in Rand's ears.

The voice came again, more urgently, "Are you two hurt?"

"Yes." Rand didn't think about doing it, didn't make a decision, but turned his head the rest of the way and looked at the man to the rear, who stood with a shotgun and aged wide frightened eyes aimed at them. "Please, help us," Rand pleaded, and the man lowered the barrel of the gun toward the ground.

Patricia could not stand, but Rand and the other man each draped one of her arms over them, held her around the waist, and slowly walked, dragging her across the road to the house. The camera bag bounced heavily off Rand's hip. His hands ached to the point of making him light-headed. When they reached the porch the front door swung open and a silver-haired woman about the man's age, mid-sixties, held the screen door and said, "Put her in the bed down here, Pa. I'll get some things." The woman wore a welcoming expression, and Rand heard sympathy in her voice when she recognized the condition of Patricia's face. "Lay her down gently, you men."

A single bed covered with a white lacy spread took up a small portion of a bedroom off to the right of the living room. Patricia's arms dangled limply and the two men had to hold her head as they lowered her. With thick, liver-speckled fingers the man pulled a blanket from the closet and unfolded it gently over her legs. Wearing a pair of clean brown coveralls with a white tee-shirt underneath, he moved in a careful, measured way.

"She's lost consciousness," Rand said, and the man looked at him in the way men will when they aren't certain what they need to do, but he took her wrist and held it between his fingers.

"This your wife?" the man asked.

"No," Rand answered. He thought it might be right to tell the man the story, but everything seemed too complicated, too hard to explain, too unreal.

What am I doing here, in this room, with these strangers, with this woman savagely attacked, who seems so close to dying? How could my life have come so immediately, so unexpectedly, to this?

"Her heart's beatin', but it ain't real strong," the man said.

The woman hurried in with a pan of water and some cloth. "Get a couple pillows, Pa, and put them under her knees and feet."

He pulled one from the closet and Rand helped him lift her legs to slide it under her knees. "I'll find another," he said, and left the room.

The woman dipped a bit of cloth into the water and placed it on Patricia's swollen, purple face with a touch so soft that it made something inside Rand twinge, made him wonder. As she gently dabbed the bruises she began cooing softly, like the pigeons, Rand thought, the pigeons that cooed from the eaves of his studio in the morning. It had been a long time since he had paid any attention to their sound. *Are they still there?* He had never liked them because they shat on everything, but now, hearing this woman, he remembered the sound as beautiful. Her face appeared open and innocent, relaxed in such a way that her lips seemed always slightly parted, her eyes filled with a rare mix of awe and wisdom, absent contention.

As he watched her, Rand felt his legs go weak, felt as if every part of him could stop right here and fail.

She looked at him, and he wanted to tell her he had some idea of what happened to that battered face before them, yet he couldn't—being so moved toward silence by her—and only did his best to return her gaze. Her moist eyes were surrounded by the somewhat wrinkled translucent skin of one her age. Rand could tell the woman was nearly weeping, was, in fact, weeping inside, and as he looked at her he recognized motherliness, felt it radiate out from the woman, saw it harbored there in the myriad colored striations of her hazel eyes. She seemed to him somehow not human, but greater, a compassionate lover of all things, and for the first time since he and Kera had been taken, no, for the first time since he had watched his mother die, he felt something inside himself release, and his eyes filled, his vision blurred, and he heard his mother's voice echoing, *"It's okay, my little man. Everything will be okay."*

Chapter 12

Kera was made to get up in the morning with the rest of them, eat with them, participate at least as far as being near them, hearing them, witnessing their in-camp procedures. There were thirty or more adults working around the "compound"—the deserted grange buildings they used as their headquarters.

They seemed a mixed bunch to Kera; a sort of commune with a militaristic mission. A few, like the major, appeared to have extensive military experience and wore not only the uniforms, but the bearings of professional soldiers, had weapons that looked more like what she'd seen in current war movies or the news. They smiled little and moved with precise, efficient focus. Others could have passed for anyone's next door neighbor; they dressed in hunting clothes or work clothes and joked with each other as they passed in the process of errands or mealtimes. There were twelve women of various ages in the group, seven armed as soldiers and five who cooked and cared for the camp. Kera hadn't seen the woman or man accomplice who had picked up Rand and her, and the wild-haired man appeared infrequently, sitting in the shade by himself as if he had no regular duties, or sometimes taking orders from other soldiers.

Eight children lived there also, five boys and three girls. Kera guessed their age spread at three to fourteen. The two oldest boys didn't seem to play a direct part in military life, yet they behaved in that somewhat rigid manner and were schooled in military tactics by the men. Kera had a difficult time keeping her eyes off them, off any or all of the children. She watched them as she helped one of the women pack canned food into a wooden chest bolted to the rear floor of the major's jeep. On the weedy lawn the older children packed tents and other field gear while the younger children played near them. The oldest boy had noticed her watching and returned her gaze. She looked away.

She felt feverishly surprised that he had noticed her, since she now thought of herself as a shadow, nearly invisible and hopefully untouchable; and, though no animosity or hostility burned within his eyes, she felt an immediate pang of guilt, as if that boy somehow knew she should be off, far away, safeguarding her own children. She could not look at him again.

"So, your name's Kera?" the woman abruptly asked, without

turning to her.

The words startled Kera. How was it these people could see her? She had no worth, and knowing that didn't hurt her; it made emptiness easier. She felt more secure in that state of being, let it guide her, let it protect. But now the voice of this woman, directed at her, challenged her ability with shadow, and caused her mind to race.

Please! Do not talk to me. Do not think of me. I am not here.

Only two cans more would fit into the jeep's chest and she quickly placed them inside. The woman closed the wooden lid and slipped the latch into place.

"Help me carry this," the woman said, referring to a crate on the ground that held a few dozen more cans of beans, fruit, vegetables. "We can put the rest into that truck over there." They walked with the crate supported between them. Kera had stolen glances at her as they worked, and the woman seemed stoic, task oriented, almost masculine. She had rough hands with short nails, fingers thick and strong, but her facial skin appeared naturally youthful and soft. Her blond hair was ponytailed and she wore clean jeans, a flannel shirt, work boots.

The woman glanced at her, talked steadily, "I know you're new here and that maybe you don't want to be here, but this is right, what we're doing."

That concept crystallized Kera's depressed and muddled thoughts. *This is right, what we're doing.* The words contrasted completely with her experience since coming to the Patriots, suggested such a foundationless reality, that Kera blinked her eyes and angled her head, as if she'd just seen that proverbial lion give birth to a lamb.

"I know, I know," the woman glanced at her, "but have you ever considered how much this country has changed in the last hundred years, and then asked yourself which changes are good and necessary, and which ones don't make any sense at all?" They sat the crate on the ground and the woman opened the tailgate of the truck, hopped up next to a wooden chest fastened to the bed. "Can you hand me some of those cans?" Kera did and the woman started stacking them in the chest. "It used to be a husband and wife were free to raise a family as they chose. But look now, you have parents losing their children to the state, because a parent spanked a child for doing wrong. There's hundreds of new laws on the books every year and we don't know about most of them until it's too late, and we've lost another freedom.

"And look how so few parents can afford to stay home to raise those kids. No, the big money folks made it so a person can't afford to stay home. They've got us paying top dollar, and even have us paying for things we never had to pay for before, like television! You know, the airwaves are public property, but someone's making a lot of money renting them. Citizens don't see that money though. All the time those folks up there are living high, while everyone down here's got to work harder and harder. The cost of just getting by keeps rising. And this monster of a government we have isn't helping, it's teamed up with the elite. If we had some relief from taxes and fees and permits and all that other stuff, we could raise our own children. Raise'm right, with family. But instead, what we have is federal tax, state tax, city tax. Can you imagine that? Some people are having to pay three income taxes! It's like the government no longer works for us, we work for it. Why, out here, the township just ruled that they are going to charge us for the water we bring up in our wells. We pay a permit fee for approval to put the well in. We pay for the well. Now the township wants us to pay them for the water! The government thinks they own the water in the ground, and there is even talk about selling the water rights to a private company to manage…and make more of a profit!"

The woman looked at Kera apologetically. "I'm sorry. This stuff just makes me so angry. And those are just a few things. The list goes on. We're going to make some changes. The major is an ex-attorney for the state. Did you know that? He's been around and you should hear him recount some of the conversations he's been a part of. No, we're going to make some changes, and we need people to understand and help us."

An attorney? Something about the woman's tone of voice held Kera's attention. She caught words she herself had said not long ago, about the need for change in society, and became surprised that some of the woman's thoughts made sense to her. Still, she started to tremble and mumbled, "But, you're not helping me to help my children." She was shocked by the sound of her voice, the thin threadiness of it—the way it betrayed her, revealed her in the world of seeable, hearable people.

"You have children?" the woman paused with a can in her hand, looked at Kera with a smile. Kera nodded without looking up. "Where are they?" the woman asked.

Kera held out two cans, "Washington State," she mumbled.

"We're a long way from there."

"We were going to them. I—"

"We?"

"Yes, my—my husband and I."

"Where's your husband?"

"He was with me, when they captured us."

The woman cocked her head. "I heard you were alone when he found you with your car crashed. He said he saved you."

Kera's head jerked involuntarily up and she studied the woman's eyes, wondered if anyone, anymore, spoke truth. "No. They hurt my husband—," she felt her throat tighten, "And then they brought me here."

"They? You mean he.... Did your husband do something, attack him or something?"

"No, of course not. They asked if we wanted a ride and we agreed. The next thing we knew they had a gun."

"Who's they?"

"That big wild-haired man and another man and woman."

The woman looked toward the main building, then back again. "Well, the story he's telling sounds a lot different from yours. Something's not right. That Silas is mean and half crazy, I think. I don't understand the need for him; don't trust him. But the major says he knows how to do some things. I hate to picture what that might be."

Kera had heard the name and it banged around in her head. She squeezed her eyes shut and focused her energy. She did not want to know his name, did not want to know anything about him, did not want that name inside her.

The woman looked at a can absently for a moment, then packed the remainder in silence. Kera considered telling the woman more, pointing out Rand's watch as proof, explaining what the wild-haired man was doing to her, but she couldn't. There was no way of trusting anyone, and besides, Kera knew, she wasn't worth helping.

***

Rand sat in the room of the senior couple's home feeling physically and mentally exhausted. Still, frantic thoughts raced through his mind. The memories of his mother, the sound of her voice in his mind, had brought questions concerning the welfare of his family, his father, brother, sister, his wife and children. His emotions coursed in every direction, and he couldn't get a hold on anything. In the single bed in front of him Patricia lay quietly, floating in and out of consciousness.

The elderly couple, Donald and Helen, had left the room moments earlier, after treating the injuries of Patricia and Rand as best they could. Incredibly, the phones still malfunctioned, so no doctor could be reached. Donald reported that television stations had gone off the air, having been destroyed or taken over by pro-radical elements. Electrical power had failed the afternoon before.

Donald used a battery powered radio—an ancient thing—to bring in one station managing to broadcast sporadic news bulletins. The three of them had left Patricia alone momentarily while they crowded around that radio in the living room and listened to reporters describe how the president survived several attempts on his life. Then, from safe refuge, the president gave a short statement in which he denounced the terrorists, promised to bring them to justice, and to return the country to normalcy.

Further reports told of horrifying scenes across the United States. It now appeared that the attacks had not come about as an orchestrated move on the country. With untold numbers of anti-government and anti-U.S. forces constantly cyber attacking military and intelligence information and control systems, one of them finally succeeded. Once a breach occurred, and the nation's defenses faltered, a surprising number of domestic and international factions surfaced and began their attacks. In addition, it took little time for the thin mien of security and uniformity which maintained the national fabric to rip apart. The hate, anger, and disillusionment within society propelled even seemingly decent citizens to perform violent acts. Many major cities were in bedlam as armed groups held portions of municipalities under their control and wreaked havoc with tools as sophisticated as computer viruses and as simple as deadly chemicals poured into water supplies. "Civilization" had pulled apart unbelievably fast. All about the nation, areas now belonged to any person or group strong and corrupt enough to usurp control. It was anarchy, as military and law enforcement agencies became overwhelmed by guerrilla warfare and social upheaval they proved incapable of controlling.

Sitting in the room with Patricia, Rand simply could not grasp how this had happened. He had been wrong: a revolution, if that's what it could be called, an infiltration, was taking place; a country he pictured as vibrant and strong and unified had overnight been brought to its knees. When this passed—if it ever did—their lives would be forever changed.

Donald stepped quietly in and closed the door behind him. A fairly stout man for his age, he stood now in front of Rand with his hands in his pockets and his shoulders hunched humbly forward.

"How is she?" he whispered.

Rand stood slowly, trying to refocus on his immediate surroundings, "The same, I think."

The man placed his hand gently on Rand's shoulder, "I must talk with you." He paused a moment, looked nervously over at Patricia. "I'm in a difficult situation here. This young lady needs help. We all know that." He looked back to Rand with his eyes squared and crinkled. "But I'm not able to help you. I won't leave Helen alone here, and I won't take her out into this trouble. People have gone crazy. It's not safe."

Rand glanced at Patricia, then looked down at his feet. He understood the old man. He himself didn't want to leave the sanctuary of their comforting home. "Yes."

Donald continued, "I've got an old pickup in the barn. It's nothing fancy, but it runs good. It has a cap covering the back and we could make her comfortable in there. Our hospital here shut down about a year back. They couldn't make enough money. So now you must go about forty miles from here, to Conroe. There's a good hospital there, if it is still there. I heard those sonsabitches are burning them to keep our troops from using them."

Donald's words swirled through Rand's mind. Going out again scared him to death.

"What I think," Donald continued, "is that you shouldn't try it at night, not in your condition. Maybe you could stay here, get some rest, and try it at first light."

Rand didn't know what to say, but his heart raced. This had nothing to do with heavy traffic, angry clients, or overdue bills. Going out there could easily lead to getting killed.

After a moment Donald excused himself and left Rand alone with Patricia. He gazed at her, this woman who came into his life like a savior, but also a burden he did not want. Everything had moved too fast, become too complicated. He sat back down and braced himself in the chair. Helen had cleaned his wounds, held ice to his swollen head, but he still hurt all over. In a bowl on a lamp table, the ice now melted, dissolved, just like his world, his life. He had never felt so powerless, so vulnerable and inadequate. Choices had always been black and white for him—crystal clear. Now he felt he had been blind, and still could not see a thing.

The door opened again and Helen came quietly in. She wore a soft, flowered robe, with her silver hair brushed back for the night. Smiling at Rand, she went to the bedside, looked down at Patricia, and touched her purple cheek with gentle fingers. With the movements of an angel granting wishes she again arranged the blankets over Patricia, checked the ice bandages wrapped loosely around the ruined hands.

Rand could not help but stare. When she entered, the rancid world suddenly disappeared, except for the room, the two of them injured, and her. And the energy surrounding him changed, from something so heavy and dark it threatened to suck his life away, to a hopeful, comforting, lightness.

She turned and stepped toward him, whispered. "Can you tell me what happened?"

Rand again felt as if he were about to speak to his mother, or, something more, some great understanding embodiment. "My wife and I were on our way to our children, in Washington State. We had an accident and were picked up by two men and a woman who turned out to be—," he stopped. He had to stop. The emotions came too strongly. Helen reached out without taking her eyes from his, laid her hand on his hand, and Rand felt a debilitating wave of sadness run through him. "They took my wife and tied me to a tree. I was there for the night. The next morning Patricia helped me. I believe the same group ran into them first and took her husband."

Helen looked again at Patricia, keeping a hold of Rand's hand. "I am sick in my heart over what is happening," she said. "I have watched this country change from something to be proud of, to something quite despicable. The hearts and souls of so many of our people have filled with greed and hate."

Rand shook his head as if in a daze. "I don't know—I—missed something—just had no idea what things had come to."

"It would be easy for us to believe that the world is now ending." She squeezed his hand and smiled a little stable smile. "But it's not. I think we're being forced, finally, to state our purpose." She squeezed his hand a final time, and quietly left the room.

Later, Helen and Donald brought in a cot for him, wished him a good night's sleep, and left silently. Rand slowly laid down, tried to stretch out, but his body twisted into a thousand knots.

And though he prayed to fall immediately to sleep, his mind raced over the faces of his family—Kera, Alissa, Andrew, his mother and father. He wished he had found a way to stop briefly at his father's home before leaving New York, to tell him where they were heading. But he had left in such a hurry. He wondered if his father was all right, his brother. Where were they now? Would he ever see them again?

***

Something hit Kera full in the face and she sat bolt upright in a completely dark world. Shocked out of a troubled sleep, fear now gripped her. The silence seemed electrified. She wanted to run, but couldn't see. Her heart raced and her stomach squeezed into a knot. And then, with a realization and a quick stroke of her hand, she snatched some heavy fabric from off her head, uncovering her eyes.

He stood in the doorway of the room, the glare of a hallway light streaming in from behind him: the wild-haired man. She sat rigidly on the cot, holding a pair of camouflage fatigues in her hand. The black boots that had sailed with them across the room lay on the shadowy floor at her feet. Dark blood from her wounded nose dripped onto the floor.

He clicked on the bright overhead light. "Put'em on. You're going into the field today." He shut the door and was gone.

Kera's mind went to Rand. He provided the only shield she ever had; perhaps imperfect, but her mind now tried to recreate him in the shadows. Was he alive? What would he do if here?

An array of noises came from outside, and Kera stood to peer out the window. It was hours before dawn, but the unit of men and women hustled about, pulling vehicles into a single file and loading them with weapons and boxes of ammunition. She didn't know what was happening, but felt the urgency. Whatever event loomed in the future, it was important to these people.

The fatigues. She had been told to put them on, but, even through the numbness now such a part of her, some small objection stirred. To wear these clothes would symbolize partnership with this group warring against the country—*her* country. She would be taking part in civil war. The idea felt alien, wrong. In the past she had felt anger many times toward the government, the direction it was leading the country, the way it seemed to operate of its own volition; but, to wear the uniform of a militant group and move with lethal force against the government seemed to her terribly corrupt, even insane.

The door whipped open again and the wild-haired man glared at her as she stood frowning with the uniform in her hands. His lips tightened and his jaw grew hard. From the other rooms came the sound of people talking, radios squelching, heavy boots pounding across weakened floor boards, metal scraping and clanging. The wild-haired man charged up to her. "God damn it!" he was angry, spitting, fighting to keep his voice low. "You listen... I said put that on! Be ready in one minute!" He turned and slammed the door as he went.

Kera stepped away from the window, used the bed sheet to wipe the blood from her nose, and pulled off her clothes. Nothing mattered. She wanted to hate him, but all she felt with certainty was sinking weight, a lack of sensation. As she pulled on the uniform everything seemed futile and false. She simply could not believe, could not confront, what had happened to her. That ugly beast, the man with wild hair and hate to the core of his heart, had added the final assault needed to finally help her see. All her experiences with so many different men, she should have learned sooner, but she now knew what all women suspected: they were nothing more than a device for the will of men. When men allowed their true nature to break through, and became their savage selves, they exercised complete disdain for the sacred female essence.

Women are pretending. Living is dying. Nothing matters.

She laced the boots, stood with her head hanging, her lips dried and cracked, her brown eyes puffy, red, withdrawn, and waited for the door to open.

***

Rand woke early that morning and noticed first the sound of Patricia's breathing—something about it had changed; it seemed clearer. He sat up and peered at her. She lay with her face toward the ceiling, her arms at her sides, sleeping peacefully.

The soft first light of morning glimmered through the window near her, and outside, the forest of trees and lawn of green gave an interesting contrast to her form lying in bed. Her purple face and battered head rested almost peacefully on a pillow case of cotton and lace. Last evening Helen had cracked the window and the sweet smell of fresh air filled the room.

In the next glance he noticed his camera bag against the wall near the door, had no recollection of how it arrived there. He sat on the cot and opened it. He could not believe it, but the old Nikon appeared undamaged. Lifting it out, it felt heavy, solid, and something about the weight sent energy into him. Photographs he had taken over the years came suddenly, vividly, to mind. He heard laughter. He saw smiles. He raised the camera to his eye and sighted through the viewfinder. Turning the focus ring, the trees outside came into detail, then the drapes of the room, then Patricia's face. Her head was now turned toward him with her good eye open, watching his movements.

Startled, and remembering her request for no photographs, he lowered the camera. Very slowly her face changed, nothing exaggerated, nothing more than a plant slightly parched, then rained upon, but Rand saw it as a full transition of season. Though stiffly, she had smiled, and he had not seen her do that before, not witnessed this potential of her stamina, and it made him smile, and the pleasure of that smile traveled all through him. He wasn't certain why, but at that moment he thought of a New York City coffee shop, a hot syrupy latte, and how nice it would be to sit there and talk with Patricia on such a beautiful morning.

The door opened and Helen stepped quietly in, saw in an instant the transformation, and moved forward, glowing, to take the battered hand of Patricia into her own.

It was there again. Rand saw it in the movements of Helen. He felt it in the flow of living air from the window, the deathlessness of the moment. Confirmation came in the way Patricia's upper body levitated ever so slightly and her good eye openly searched the maternal face gleaming down upon her.

Rand leaned back, brought the camera to his eye, found the two of them silently communicating in the warm and glowing light, and pressed his finger down, easily, purposefully, until the shutter released and the image was etched indelibly.

He felt immediately that with all the beauty he had photographed in his life, he had never, not ever, captured anything as miraculous as this.

Chapter 13

When Donald later explained the plan of using the truck to get to a hospital, Patricia agreed. Rand had remained silent, too embarrassed to reveal his fear. Helen put together a bag of supplies and made a breakfast of warm broth for Patricia, and eggs, ham, potatoes for the men. She also made thin coffee, and though not one of his treasured lattes, Rand thought it was the best thin coffee he had ever tasted, savoring three cups.

Patricia couldn't walk, so Donald brought in a sheet of plywood, Helen wrapped her warmly, and they strapped her to it like an Indian baby on a travois. The three of them carried her out of the house and slid her into the back of the old truck. It came as a hard thing for Rand, his hands and wrists so damaged, and all he could think of was the potential for more bodily harm ahead. He also knew that, in reality, the house and the two elderly people provided little safeguard against the war that raged around them. It was probably no safer there than anywhere.

Rand could see it written all over the faces of Donald and Helen that they wanted to go, to help, and when he eased the truck down the long driveway, they stood somewhat concealed in the partially closed doorway of the house, watching, waving, the air of uncertainty, the element of danger, foremost on everyone's mind.

The morning shone with a clear bright sky, heat rising, and Rand steered the truck down the empty back roads, toward the town of Mendota. When he saw the sign for the town his palms and his forehead began to sweat. He felt nauseous. There was no telling who he might see, or who might see him, as he traveled through this last town of his days before disaster.

Though small, the town was not as small as he had thought. There were old, big two-story farmhouses, small 1950's era ranch styles, and newly constructed models with the garages out front. Most had lawns around them, some quite large, tall trees along the road. But nothing moved. It seemed like everyone had left, left everything in place. Cars sat in driveways and along curbs, bicycles laid in front yards, along with basketballs and barbecues. He saw the placard for a Foreign Legion, but the building was deserted, a For Sale sign posted out front, tilted and ready to topple. A deadly stillness pervaded an eerie desolation that

Rand had never before witnessed. Something had sucked the life out of the place.

Rand wished he'd thought to have Donald draw directions around Mendota, instead of through it. The town could easily provide safe harbor for revolutionaries, or worse. Out of habit he stopped at the stop light in the center of town, but wanted to floor the accelerator, get the hell out of there. The Ferrari, he thought, would have felt better beneath him than the old truck with little power. He remembered the new smell of the sexy car, and noticed how the truck stank like thirty years of hard use.

Suddenly a large black dog rushed out from the corner of a house and charged him, barking savagely. Rand trounced the accelerator, yanked the wheel, and the truck chugged down the road. He looked in the rearview mirror, saw the dog straining at the end of a chain, and realized the panic of his take-off had probably sent Patricia sliding. The cap covering the back of the truck lacked a front window, so he couldn't see her. He thought he should stop and check, but stopping seemed jeopardous, and he wanted to keep progressing toward the hospital, where a greater amount of safety might exist. Rand felt vulnerable in the town and wanted away from it fast, so he urged the truck into a high rate of speed and barreled down the road.

Past the last few houses, he saw open country ahead, looked at the map Donald had drawn, and knew it would be rural and hopefully quiet right through to Conroe. He flexed his hands on the wheel, loosened his grip, and took a deep breath.

He spoke with Donald at breakfast and the old man had already made up his mind to allow Rand use of the truck in his search for Kera. He'd seek police, anyone who would help him track her down, free her from the captors; if they still held her, if she remained alive. He pushed the thought from his mind.

Not long ago finding help would prove a fairly easy job. You have a problem, call 911, they take care of it. But now the normal operations of everyday life were fragmented, disconnected. The stabilizing, comforting effect of the nation's law and order, of, quite literally, common decency, could no longer be taken for granted, even counted on. Still, a starting point must remain. After he dropped Patricia off at the hospital he would check with attendants and locate the local police station—

Rand spotted a large camouflaged vehicle pulling crossways into the road directly in front of him. His body stiffened and he pumped the foot pedal, trying to slow the old truck, with what now proved exceedingly worn brakes. A second, then a third boxy machine pulled forward from dusty side roads right and left and formed a roadblock in front of him. Rand pumped the brake, watched the machines grow closer, pumped the brake, saw an oversized gun barrel swing and point at his truck, pumped the brake, and succeeded in bringing the old Ford to a stop some twenty feet short of the iron behemoths. He sat with sweaty palms clasped to the steering wheel and stared through the dusty windshield. *What now?*

***

When the door again opened Kera responded quickly to the wild-haired man's beckon. She followed him with a frozen heart past a dozen others in the front room—men armed with heavy weapons, with green-and brown-painted faces, fixed stares and solid stances. Kera kept her head down, but she did notice men gathered around a small table, and the major, in control of the conversation, with a map laid out smooth as a tablecloth.

Outside, under a black sky, Kera felt the heat coming, felt the wetness of the humid air on her lips and nostrils. In the shadowy light of a single shuttered bulb attached to the shed, everyone moved fast with serious, straight-lined faces. She heard the growl of the heavy green vehicle inside the shed and smelled its oily exhaust. Drivers dressed in uniform pulled the many smaller vehicles into a single line on the driveway, with camouflaged jeeps and trucks up front, while others loaded military backpacks and wooden boxes of ammunition. Kera could feel something was happening, something other than practice. She glanced around furtively for the children, but saw none.

The doors of the shed were pulled wide and the big boxy green vehicle growled forward; it paused on the gravel before them and rotated in place, as if it were alive and deciding which way to go. Then it belched smoke from a stack and hauled forward so another same vehicle—one that Kera had never seen—could pull out behind it. Two jeeps drove up and one took its place in front of them, the other at the rear, and the four vehicles went down the driveway at a rate of speed faster than Kera thought possible for such heavy machines.

The wild-haired man took her roughly by the elbow and marched her to the front of the vehicle line, to another green jeep. "Get up in there," he growled, and she climbed over the back bumper. "Right there," he motioned where he wanted her to sit; it was on one of the wooden boxes placed behind the driver's seat. Kera read words stenciled on the side of the box: *7.62 mm. 1000 rounds.* As she read, the wild-haired man took hold of her and snapped a pair of handcuffs around her wrist and the roll-bar of the jeep. Kera instinctively tugged, but the look the man engendered brought pause, made her lower her eyes. "You've got no business going along," he spit. "The major's decided to enlist you. But you'll be back." He reached out and cupped her chin in his hand, turned her face toward him. "He shouldn't have you ride back here with no cover," he said. He motioned with a nod toward the handcuffs, "He ordered me to. Keep your head down when the shootin' starts."

He headed toward the door of the house, but stopped some feet away and turned toward her. She had been watching him trudge off, his shoddy boots, torn army pants, drab green shirt with the sleeves sawed-off, and when he looked back at her they met for a moment, eye-to-eye. She saw fear. He seemed concerned, in some odd way, for her safety. She looked away, but not before realizing how the fingers of his hand worked nervously at the Rolex on his opposite wrist. Then the door of the house opened, the men paraded out in a tight band, and the wild-haired man spun around and strode heavily back inside.

Kera wondered again what had happened to the older man and woman who assisted in abducting her and Rand. She had not seen them after that night, but she now remembered, as if from a dream, hearing the woman speak as they drove away from the woods where they left Rand. The woman's voice was questioning, and the wild-haired man's voice came back angrily, telling her to shut up. The older man had defended her, Kera recalled, and that was the last she could remember of them.

The major and his driver climbed into the jeep, sat a cell-phone and a large hand-held radio on the floor between the seats, and watched as the last of the unit loaded themselves into vehicles down the line. There were eleven vehicles, four jeeps of military style, the rest civilian pickup trucks and assorted four-wheel drive standard utility vehicles. All of them had aggressive tires and long radio antennas.

Without looking at the driver, the major said, "Go," and they started down the gravel roadway leading out of the compound. Kera watched the line of vehicles pull out and follow them—for the first time noticing the red filters covering their headlights, which allowed them to emit only the faintest trace of light. Along the half mile stretch to the main road they passed only one house. A man stood in the front picture window with a radio in hand and saluted the major as they drove past. The major saluted in return.

At the main road half the vehicles followed behind the major, the other half turned and proceeded in the opposite direction. There was a jeep on a small hill overlooking the intersection, acting as sentinel, with a tall man in the back leveling a large mounted gun over the road before them.

The major's driver brought their line of vehicles up to forty miles per hour. The wind caused Kera's hair to slap the sides of her face with stinging force; it filled her eyes and made them water. The major twisted toward her, his eyes covering every inch of her face. She looked away from him.

"We have a mission this morning that will call for considerable force," he called out above the noise of wind and whirring tires. "We'll intercept a platoon of national guardsmen patrolling the area and engage them. They have no business here. This is our home, this area.

"I know this feels foreign to you, but understand, we are law abiding citizens of this country who have repeatedly attempted to peacefully alter the course of our political leaders. They have refused to listen to the voice of the people. And so, we are only doing what the constitution calls for. We are a citizen militia, engaged in the business of returning its country to the people."

He steadied his gaze into hers. "I have seen firsthand how America is being run these days and I cannot stand-by and allow it to continue. The common citizen loses each year to the interests of greed, corrupt power mongering, and government deal making with corporations who have more rights than those citizens themselves. We are taxed but not served. Elected officials arrange to send billions of dollars in bailouts to our self-obsessed captains of industry, and for foreign aid to other countries who often become our enemies, while our health standards and way of life erode. They allow millions of foreign citizens to infiltrate our borders, loot our system, and even assign them special privileges. I assure you, we are not a boatload of pirates looking to take advantage of a situation. I hope you will give our cause due thought, witness what happens this morning with an open mind, and consider that we need your help. This militia is connected to a nationwide coalition of militias, but we cannot succeed without the participation of a majority of the citizens. After this, if you do not wish to participate in freeing your country, we will not be able to force you, but we will detain you until the revolution is complete." With that, he stood and turned toward the rear, surveyed the progress of the convoy behind him, then sat and stared forward.

So that was it, Kera thought. They were patriots of their country, civil in their own minds, respectful of citizen rights, but would keep her against her will indefinitely. Kera's stomach knotted and she dropped her head, stared at the floor of the jeep between her feet. She saw in her mind the image of Alissa and Andrew, her babies. Her nostrils flared as her mouth filled with bitter juices. She groaned as if punched in the stomach. This man knew of her children and yet he would keep her from them as if he had some right. *Who do these people think they are?*

She lifted her head and watched the major as the sky turned grey above them. Even in the wind the beret stuck miraculously, perfectly, to the top of his head. The back of his neck was razored clean and his black hair trimmed neatly around the ears. He looked like such an ordinary man, an every-man, an average American citizen; except, of course, for the chrome-plated pistol and leather holster hugging his hip. His fingers were long and thick-knuckled, but clean and softer looking than expected for a soldier's. The seams and creases of his uniform were crisp from starch. She wanted to reach out, to shake him, to wake him, to help him see the wrongs of his actions—to bring him back from whatever *reality* he had gone to.

But she knew it wouldn't work. He clearly believed in his right to hold her against her will, to level his arrogant power against her and anyone who disagreed with him. She lowered her face and swallowed hard, letting the pain, fear, and loneliness numb her once again. She twisted at the handcuffs, but never felt the pain.

They traveled gravel roads for fifteen minutes, then pulled up in a tight line between two rounded, cultivated hilltops. Whoever farmed them had planted corn and some other bushy plant—Kera looked closer and saw what she thought were small green beans starting—and the plants had grown well in the moist early summer air. She watched as the major signaled two men in a jeep behind them and the three of them moved slowly on foot toward the summit of one of the hills.

For the first time she realized that no women soldiers were present.

Two men with rifles ran into the brush near the rear of the vehicles and two more did the same near the front. They quickly became invisible. Another man, wearing a ball cap with two silver bars on it, grouped the other men together, sixteen in all, and she could hear the rasp of his voice as he addressed them. The barrels of their rifles tilted out at odd angles from the group, and with all the movement that had taken place in such a short time they had created surprisingly little sound. A couple of the men had wads of tobacco stuck under their lips; many wore dark green or black baseball caps with camouflage clothing below. The whites of their eyes contrasted with the green and brown grease they had used to paint their faces. They wore heavy belts and packs full of ammunition and whatever else a man needed when he went to confront an enemy he planned to kill. Kera didn't know. But she did know that these men looked like people she had met before. Wipe away the face paint, swap fatigues for suits, and these men could be the same men who walk the avenues of New York City. But she knew in a second the men she saw each day on the city streets, even if they agreed with this cause, would never take the necessary time to participate in a process such as this... they were too busy... in search of money. Money was their cause.

Her reality shifted, and for a moment these men before her appeared as citizens willing to take a great gamble, to strive forward as a matter of their own volition toward something they believed in, something other than material wealth, or image. She watched and yet another perspective emerged, and she wondered if this all wasn't a game— deadly, yes—but a game, even play, aimed at providing activity to testosterone-rich boys. *Couldn't this all just be a game, the winner receiving the power and the fame?*

But as she studied the men, saw the haunting rigidity of their faces, she felt that none of the motivations mattered. There remained no law, no order that might step in and quiet this kind, from the man who opened her and entered her at will, to this major who scented blood and planned to spill it. This rebellion comprised the ultimate priority in their lives, and, excepting some miracle, her involvement seemed assured.

She hoped the army they had come to confront might make such a miracle. But the only miracle Kera ever witnessed was the birth of her children. Beyond that, she had never believed in them. Praying had never brought her parents back, or turned Rand toward her. She had been through too much in her life to count on any dream. She shifted to take some of the pressure off her handcuffed wrist.

The major and two riflemen came down off the hill and gathered with the others. The major spoke. Eight of the men returned to four of the vehicles; two vehicles went slowly, quietly back the way they had come, and two went down the road, eventually disappearing. The remaining men drank coffee or Cokes, checked their rifles, hunkered down at the edge of the road.

The sun came up and the air heated. The men began to wipe sweat from their grease-painted faces. No one spoke. The major kept checking his watch.

Finally, the major, the driver, and a young man in his mid-twenties climbed into the jeep with her. The young man carried a heavy looking rifle, much bigger than most of the others she saw, and sweated heavily under his arms and down his face. His eyes were wide and his jaw muscles flexed repeatedly. He jerked a nod at Kera without speaking. The major picked up the radio he had placed between the seats, checked his watch, then keyed the radio and said, "Patriot Sky, go!"

It might have been one minute, it might have been less, when Kera heard the sound of a helicopter.

***

As Rand squinted nervously through the windshield two soldiers appeared on each side of the truck. They wore full United States National Guard uniforms, with helmets strapped on and M-16s pointed right at his nose.

"Bring your hands up to where I can see them!" shouted the soldier nearest Rand, a man of about forty years, his dark eyes sharp and his shoulders pushed forward into his weapon. Rand raised his hands deliberately, fingers trembling, and the soldier stepped forward, opened the door with a quick pull, backed away with the rifle leveled like a lance. "Step clear of the vehicle. Keep your hands raised, sir!"

Rand turned slowly and slid carefully out of the truck, his eyes darting from the soldier's face to the barrel of the rifle aimed at him. *Please, don't shoot, don't shoot!* The other soldier stepped forward and ran his hands quickly along Rand's chest, his thighs and back.

"There's a woman in the rear," a voice bellowed, and Rand turned slightly to see that two of them had moved to the back of the truck and were peering inside at Patricia.

"She's seriously injured. I'm taking her to a hospital," Rand heard his voice quiver as he spoke to the soldier who had pulled the door open. The man was quite short, Rand now realized, with glossy cocoa-colored skin, taught shoulders, and high cheek bones.

"Do you know," the soldier demanded, "that we are in a state of martial law?"

"No," Rand answered. "Martial law?"

"Can the woman in the truck move on her own, sir?" the soldier went on, the rifle still held level on Rand's nose.

"No. She's terribly hurt."

The soldier's eyes remained locked steadily on Rand. "Lower the gate, Corporal Brent, check her out. Be ready, Johnson!"

"Yes, Sergeant!" the voice again bellowed.

The sergeant asked for identification, and as Rand slowly lifted his wallet from his pocket—the rifle pointed steadily at his heart—the two soldiers lowered the tailgate and one climbed in. Rand could hear Patricia's soft voice in response to the soldier's questions. Corporal Brent popped out—a stocky, barrel-chested kid—and ran to the sergeant checking Rand's identification. "She's—she's in bad shape, Sergeant. She needs a hospital, for sure, and says this guy is her friend." The corporal looked queasy as he glanced at Rand.

"You say that's where you were headed, Mr. Priven?" the sergeant asked.

"Yes," Rand answered. It was starting to feel good, being near friendly force. These guys were the real deal. He wanted to ask them to point the rifles away from him.

The sergeant handed back the drivers license. "Says you're from New York."

"Yes."

"How was she injured?"

"The same way I was." Rand held out his wrists and tilted his head for the sergeant to see his wounds. "I'm not certain who they were, but they've taken my wife and this woman's husband."

"What's your relationship with this woman?"

"I don't have—I really don't know her. But she helped me."

"When did all this occur?"

"Two days ago. Not ten miles back. But look, my wife is out there and Patricia there needs—"

"Mr. Priven, civilians have been ordered off the streets by the President of the United States. You might have been fired on." He turned to the corporal, "Bring up a Humvee and get her off-loaded, over behind an APC. Have Milner call for a medivac." He turned back to Rand. "What we're going to have to do, sir, is have you wait with us until they send a helicopter out, then we'll ship you both into the hospital and the CPC.

"Johnson," he addressed the other soldier at the rear of Rand's truck, "after you get her into the Humvee, get this truck pulled up behind us." He appraised Rand closely, tilted his rifle away, and gestured toward the large green vehicles blocking the road. "You can lower your hands now, Mr. Priven. Let's move over behind those APCs and maybe you can tell us more about the people you ran into."

The APCs with their loud diesel engines reversed and maneuvered back into hiding spots. Rand and the sergeant turned onto the side road and walked over behind one of the large, smoke-sputtering machines as it came to a stop. Four tall and long-limbed elm trees shaded three Humvees. A large company tent stood about ten feet off the road on a bit of flat land backed by a broad cultivated hill full of thick bushy plants. The sun now crested that hill, sending golden shafts of light through hazy, moist air. Four smaller tents stood in formation behind the larger one, and bordering it all a brushy expanse stretched out into a thin line of forest that wrapped around the flanks of the hill. The main tent was open and three soldiers climbed out of the nearest APC and started for it.

"Private Simms," the sergeant commanded one of them, "see if the Lieutenant would like to speak with these folks, and bring this gentleman a cup of coffee. You like coffee, Mr. Priven?" the sergeant asked, a glint in his dark brown eyes.

"Yes. I'd love a cup!" Rand's mouth watered. He looked around. Nine soldiers walked about the camp and more moved within the machines. He guessed they'd been there for some days, the way the edges of the road were marred by the heavy equipment, and large bags of garbage were piled on the opposite side of the road from the tents.

Private Simms sauntered over with a mug of steaming coffee, his rifle hanging at his side from a sling. He was tall as Rand, very young, talked like a southerner. "Lieutenant said he'd be out in a sec'. Here's coffee." He held out both hands to Rand, little containers of cream and sugar in one. "You like this here stuff?"

Rand grabbed the whole of them, took the mug. "Sure, you bet. Thanks."

"Mm, hmm! Got to have Jo!" Simms moved away smiling, sliding his rifle up into the crook of his arm.

A Humvee returned with Patricia wrapped to her plywood sheet in the rear, the corporal driving the pickup truck behind it. They passed Rand and the sergeant, pulled along the road, beyond the tents, then turned around and parked behind the last APC. Rand saw how they situated everything behind the big machines—those APCs, as they called them, formed a shield from whatever approached along the road. Rand stepped over and looked down at Patricia. Her eyes were closed, a pained expression on her face.

"Patricia?" Rand whispered, but she remained still and silent. The glow she held that morning had faded.

The sergeant stepped away. "Have we radioed for that medivac, Corporal Brent?"

"Yes, Sergeant!"

The sergeant came back, produced a notebook. "You say these people took your wife and this woman's husband?"

"Yes."

"You're a long way from home at a time like this."

"Yes, I know. I—well, we—were going, trying to reach our children in a retreat in Washington State—"

"Hold on, now," the sergeant's eyes flashed. "When did all this take place?"

"Two days ago."

"Blessed Jesus! You mentioned two days ago, but I figured you'd been here in this area for awhile." The sergeant's eyes hardened; his voice thickened. "Two days ago. Considering what's happening, you decide to take your wife and drive from one side of the States to the other…I just don't get that."

"Well—" The man's words and manner worked their way into Rand and replaced the relief of being protected by soldiers with the suffocating crush of guilt. Other than maybe his father he had never been questioned by another man about the choices he made with family. The sergeant clearly thought it foolhardy to start across the nation in search of children at such a time; a feeling Rand had shared wholeheartedly.

He nearly defended himself by explaining that it hadn't been his idea, but before he spoke, the recollection that he didn't want to come west in search of Alissa and Andrew, his very own children, stopped him. Goosebumps rose on his skin. He averted his eyes down into the creamy coffee. The sergeant, from his defensive and militaristic view, might think such a move foolish, but wouldn't any father risk danger to save his children? *Did I really not want to come searching for them?* "— Look, uh, there's no doubt that it seems crazy, but, well, I guess I would just like to know what you can do for me, to help me find my wife and children."

"Mr. Priven, we're at war here. The recovery of your wife and children is an urgent matter, and I will certainly notify headquarters of this situation, but what's going to happen is that you'll be sent to the CPC and detained there until conditions allow for your release."

"CPC, you said that before. What is it?"

"The Civilian Protection Center. Anyone effected by the terrorism, evacuated, put out of their home, caught on the streets as you were, they're picked up either by the military or the police and sent there to wait this out in safety. You'll fill out a complete report concerning your family there."

Rand listened and a part of him felt comforted. This had all developed into a tragic nightmare. He'd had enough of venturing through land occupied by murderers and rapists. "And how long will it take to wait this out?" he asked.

The sergeant glanced around at his soldiers, his head nodding imperceptibly. "If it's up to the troops, it won't be long. But there's really no answer to that question. It could be weeks or months."

Rand heard the last three words—*Weeks or Months*—replay in his mind. He thought about waiting in some collection center somewhere for months, while everything he had built in New York disappeared. He thought about not knowing the whereabouts of Kera and the children. "Sergeant, I can't possibly—my wife and children are out there—"

The sergeant glared up at him, tapping the points of his canine teeth together with quick snaps of his jaw. "You know, I don't understand. Civilians never see the signs, never do a thing as far as maintenance on the country. Never prepare. Never pay attention. Not until it's too late. There's always someone else to take care of the problems. With the love of our Jesus, I do understand your wife is out there, but there's not a thing I can do for you now, sir. I have my orders."

Rand turned his head away. Standing there, he felt suddenly and completely diminished, as if shrunk back to the size and abilities of a tiny child. *How could this have happened?* The image of Kera bent and beset over the hood of the station wagon appeared in his mind, stopped his breathing. He couldn't stay locked up in some *Protection Center* while Kera remained in danger, no matter how safe it made him feel. He wrestled his own thoughts. He hadn't wanted to come, because he hadn't felt a real problem existed. He never would have believed that the country would fail, that the infrastructure of such a powerful society could so quickly succumb to what seemed exaggerated foes. And everything with the family happened so quickly, completely out of nowhere, the way Kera had left him and sent the children away.

Then, within the depths of his concentration, the Humph, Humph, Humph of the last sounds he'd heard from his wife turned to Whop, Whop, Whop. His conscious mind came forward and in the distance he heard the sound of a helicopter.

The sergeant commanded, "Johnson! Show those arrogant buzzards where to land. Get a flare on that flat beyond the trees. Corporal Brent, take a man and drive this woman over there, help the chief load her onto the chopper."

The men moved quickly and a female soldier with a radio in her hand jumped out of an APC and jogged over to the sergeant. "Say hello to the Great Gifted Ones," the sergeant said to her, nodding toward the helicopter. "Let'm know we hear them coming." The female spoke into the radio, looked toward the sound of chopping blades. Then the sergeant said to Rand, "Mr. Priven, you come with me," and he started across the road and toward the field beneath the elm trees.

"Sergeant," Rand mumbled. The sergeant turned. "I have a camera in the front seat of the truck. May I get it?" He wanted the camera, but was also stalling for time, searching for an idea that might keep him off the helicopter, away from any CPC.

With a raised hand the sergeant signaled him toward the truck. "You get it. Keep it, and your hands, visible to me."

Rand opened the door and gently removed the camera bag.

"Hold it there," the sergeant called. "Open the bag on the ground and show me the camera."

Rand squatted and pulled out the Nikon. The sergeant moved over and peered into the bag, poked it with his rifle barrel.

"I'm a photographer," Rand held the camera out closer to him.

The sergeant said, "Let's go."

"I—uh—could stay and shoot some photos of—"

"Let's go!" The sergeant motioned toward the field. Rand replaced the camera, grabbed the bag, and followed him. *What can I do?* He knew that once on the helicopter little chance would remain of staying free of the confines of the protection center. They left the cover of the trees and walked into the field of shin-high bushy plants, and Rand turned and saw that Corporal Brent and another soldier were pulling the Humvee with Patricia in it away from the APCs. The heavy whop, whop, whop of the helicopter suddenly doubled in intensity, and Rand looked to see its profile clear the hilltop, black as a raven silhouetted against the rising sun.

He wanted to grab the sergeant, to say Wait, I Am an American Citizen! I Don't Want To Go! But he couldn't. He felt intimidated by the man. The man had knowledge. He knew already how Rand had failed.

"Wait a minute," the sergeant said, and something in his voice made Rand shift his eyes off the helicopter to peer at this man who knew so much. The sergeant stopped in his tracks, eyeing the shadowy bird in the sky with the same hard eyes he had used to see through Rand.

Rand looked back at the helicopter as it soared down low along the contour of the falling hillside, flying in a straight line directly toward them.

Then he looked again at the sergeant and saw the man's face tighten with anger, his head and shoulders inching forward as he concentrated all his energy, his will, on the object catapulting toward them. Then his hand rifled out and he grabbed Rand by the shirt front, yanked him like a rag doll, and screamed, "Get back under those trees, NOW!"

Rand would have stood, too shocked to run, had the sergeant not thrown him with a mighty shove. The force of that shove and the urgency in that voice flooded Rand's veins with adrenaline and he felt himself begin to run, at the same time looking back over his shoulder to see what was the matter.

The sergeant raised his rifle and yelled to Johnson, who had dropped a flare on the flat field and was waving his arms at the helicopter, signaling the spot for landing, and Rand heard the sergeant's voice rise up like thunder over the pounding sound of the blades, "Get BACK! That's NOT OURS! GET BA—" but the last of his words disappeared behind a sound that Rand found familiar, because he had photographed models once long ago in a scene with rockets taking off in the background, and he heard the *WHOOSH* as he ran, and he looked again over his shoulder and saw that a smoking trail of blackness was streaking through the sky toward him, toward the trees, the tents, the APCs.

It struck the front vehicle and caused the same reaction that a balloon has when stuck with a pin. The vehicle rose a few feet in the air and then tore itself apart, landing with a quivering plop more characteristic of rubber than steel. Rand fell and the fall snapped his head back, sent the camera bag flying, but he forgot the wounds on his wrists and tore at the ground with his fingers and climbed to his feet again, grabbed the bag under his arm without thinking. He saw the trees before him, not far, the heavy brush on the other side. And then he heard rifle fire, lots of rifle fire, quick short pops at rapid rate. He ran and the bushy plants pulled at his feet and he couldn't breathe. More rifles fired heavier dull plats, throaty and angry. He heard men yelling but he couldn't decipher the words. He ran as fast as he could and when he reached the brush he dove the way a trained swimmer dives into a clear and familiar lake on a blistering hot summer day. He landed in a heap and felt his vertebrae pop and came to a sudden stop at the base of an old tree stump.

The sound was deafening as the helicopter again fired *WHOOSH*... and the thunder of something bursting apart and the shouts of men, the screams, amidst the heavy reports of the rifles and then the sounds of vehicles, heavy vehicles grinding from the direction the helicopter had come from, firing, overpowering the field. Rand twisted himself deeper into the brush, the adrenaline contorting his heart, fear short-circuiting his brain, trying, he was, to burrow, if he could, down into the ground.

He scrunched his eyes shut, covered the back of his head with his hands, knew that something, someone, was going to find him, blow him to pieces the way of that APC. He sprang to his knees, forgot the camera bag, scrambled forward to hide better, and suddenly as he did the image of that Doberman pincer dodging New York City traffic before it was pummeled by passing cars flashed in his mind. *I am going to die!* He struggled through the thick and tangled brush until he was deeper into the forest and felt the darkness of its cover.

His senses overloaded. His mind froze except for that one thought: *I am going to die!* Then something deep inside Rand, from somewhere indiscernible, flew from within him in the form of a gut-splitting scream.

Eventually he fell into silence, stopped, and laid flat. His chest heaved and his face pressed to the ground as he gulped in the earthy air. *Did I scream? Or am I dead, like that dog on the pavement?* Then he opened his eyes, waited, listened, and the sounds of the battle lessened. The helicopter stopped firing. The rifles popped less frequently.

His heart pounded violently in his throat and he laid there feeling it, hearing it, thinking it would tear apart and squirt his blood into his chest as he lay there dead, alone.

He thought of Kera and the children, saw Andrew and Alissa in his mind; they looked at him with questions on their lips. Questions that made him forget his pounding heart and consider the hollowness of excuses. *Oh, my God!* "What have I done?" he yelled in anger at the ground one inch away.

He struggled himself into silence, flinched at the last sounds of the battle. *BATTLE?* How on earth could it be that he'd been caught in a battle, a war, a scene where people were shooting at each other with missiles? *Isn't this the United States of America?*

He squirmed around the backside of a thick tree and came up again on his knees. Slowly, very slowly, he peered around the tree.

The forest worked its way up the side of the hill, so he now knelt on ground a little higher than the camp he had shortly ago been part of. Trees prevented a clear view, but he saw two unfamiliar APCs and many camouflaged vehicles, pickup trucks and SUVs, racing through the field, through the camp. He could see the APCs of the guard unit still in the spots where they had been parked, completely destroyed, smoking. The tents were in tatters, ablaze.

They have killed them. They have killed those people that I just stood with, spoke with.

Rand dropped to his elbows and crawled to the next tree, closer to the battlefield, his arms and legs trembling. He peered around it, slowly, the muscles of his face twitching. Then a couple more quick shots rang up from the field below. The helicopter swerved and circled toward him. He squirmed down under the brush. *It wasn't me. I didn't shoot!* It flew over the forest he hid within, circled slowly at tree top height. Rand held his breath, burrowed his white face into the dark earth as the brush about him flapped in the wash of the propellers. He tried to pray, but his mind filled with fear and couldn't put the words into order. *Why did I get up? Why did I look? Why didn't I remain still? Now I'm dead, now I'm dead, now I am going to die!*

The helicopter widened its circle and finally the sound of it faded, fell completely away. He heard voices from down in the camp, vehicles powering through the field. He inched his twitching face off the ground and listened. *What happened to Patricia?* He rose up slowly on his knees, trembling, and peered around the tree again.

Men were milling through the camp, lifting things and placing some of them in the vehicles they had parked there. Rand crawled forward to the next tree. The indecipherable, yet powerful, voices of the men echoed up to him through the silent forest. He strained his eyes to see what kind of men these were, what murderers.

They were a mixed lot, some looking like a ragtag third world army, others the same as the well-fitted soldiers he had been with, and a hope arose within him. *Maybe the sergeant and his men have survived.* He crawled a few more feet.

Why am I doing this? Why don't I take this chance to run and hide, for good? And then he saw the camera bag lying where he had left it, now only a few feet away. He stretched out and brought it to him.

The sound of a vehicle grinding down from the top of the hill came to him and he lowered his face, twisted his eyes toward it. It came into view through the foliage, drove down into the center of the camp, and stopped. There were four soldiers in it, two up front, two in back, and three stood up and stepped out onto the ground that Rand had walked moments ago. All the other soldiers—*not soldiers, these aren't soldiers, murderers*—all the other murderers gathered around the man wearing a beret who climbed from the front of the jeep. Except for a few, who continued to walk the perimeters of the camp, they all gathered together—like a huddle at half time.

These are the people who have caused this pain in my life. These are the people responsible for what is happening to all of us.

He bent suddenly and opened the camera bag, lifted the Nikon, twisted off the 50 millimeter lens and pulled out a 300 millimeter telephoto. He hugged the tree, his heart pumping tremors into the viewfinder, and sighted down at the group of men. He focused and could see the faces more clearly, though not in detail. He was simply too far away, but he steadied himself anyway, adjusted the exposure, and pressed the shutter release.

The heavy clunk of the old camera broke the new, tense silence. To Rand it sounded like a rifle shot.

He ducked behind the tree, his eyes scrunched shut. *Oh, no. NO!*

He just knew the sound had carried to the men in the circle and would make them aware of his presence. They had taken no prisoners in the battle, why would they with him? Flying lead would tear him to pieces momentarily.

But he heard no sound that alarmed him further and so shortly edged his face around the tree, until his right eye came clear and he could see them again. They all moved about the camp now, and after a moment he lowered himself on his belly and crawled a few more feet down through the forest, to a spot he determined suitable for a clear shot that would reveal the detail of their faces.

He figured there were at least thirty of them, and, as he had thought, he saw no prisoners being taken. They had outnumbered the guardsmen, and with the advantages of surprise and the helicopter, it had been a short fight. It would seem that at least a few of the guardsmen would have surrendered, considering the odds and the inevitable outcome. Rand recalled the single pops of rifle fire he had heard after the battle had died down.

One of the men now moving through the field stopped, lifted a rifle from the hands of a dead soldier on the ground. Rand clicked the shutter again and this time remained still, watched for a reaction from the man, *the murderer*, through the lens. The man made no sign that he had noticed the sound. No one did. Rand focused on others and clicked off more shots. Then, through the viewfinder, he noticed the man with the beret again. As he watched, the feeling came to him that he had somewhere before seen this man.

The man walked from dead soldier to dead soldier, turning them over, doing something to them that Rand found hard to make out. He clicked off a shot as the man moved from one to another. The man turned the soldier over, not with a callused flop, but gently, and then arranged the soldier on the ground as if he were peacefully sleeping. Rand exposed frame after frame of the man performing this mysterious ritual with the dead soldiers, the smoking hulks of the APCs and tattered remains of the tents in the background.

He had never imagined he would turn his lens on war. There was nothing about war, or bloodshed, that had ever intrigued him. Still, he couldn't help but notice now, that he felt excited by this, that it felt good to capture these people on film. He watched the man walk through the camp and return to his jeep. He stood by it, a perfect pose, with his foot up on the running board, and a soldier in the rear. Rand clicked a shot, refocused, and studied the person in the rear.

The soldier wore camouflage and appeared, in relation to the man with the beret, quite small. Something seemed odd in the way the soldier was sitting: he seemed to look down at the bed of the jeep, but one hand was up, and then, as Rand watched, he lifted his head and gazed past the man with the beret, out at the troops lying in the field. Rand clicked a shot, then inched closer. His heart began racing again. After going another ten feet, he stopped only two trees inside the edge of the forest. A mere fifty yards now separated him from the murderers as they began to return to their vehicles with armfuls of National Guard equipment— rifles, helmets, ammunition, radios. He could see their faces more clearly now, without the telephoto lens, but he brought the camera to his eye again anyhow, focused it immediately on the soldier in the rear of the jeep, and felt his heart leap with joy, with fear, with confusion.

Kera!

She wore a warriors uniform, but he could see her, see the big brown eyes and the pouty mouth, the thick brown hair disheveled upon her head. She was the last thing he had ever expected to see here, in this place, and for a second it froze his mind. Then he fought an impulse to stand and run to her. *Why shouldn't I?* Because he knew he would die instantly, and maybe her with him. He snapped a picture, snapped another and another. It was all he could do, but that wasn't going to her, that wasn't holding her, releasing her from desperation. Unthinkable danger surrounded her. He focused through his lens harder than he had ever focused on anything and he saw that she seemed deflated, limp, and her hand was somehow tied to the jeep. *God, how she must want out of there!*

The rest of the men had all loaded back into their vehicles, had revved the engines—making them sound like hungry animals unwilling to leave fresh kill—and the deadly procession started moving.

Rand yearned to join them, wanted to leap into a vehicle, follow along, but he could think of no way.

Oh, no, NO! Stop! How—How do I free her—Kera—wait!

The jeep turned—all the vehicles turned back toward the top of the hill—and it started away, and as it did Rand noticed that Kera stared back at the field full of dead men. It seemed the others would not give their fallen enemies that respect; she was the only one.

Rand stood and stepped forward from the forest, clear of all but a single tree. His eyes held her as they drove away, and he dared the men, as they became smaller, and he cared nothing for what they could do to him if they did see him.

And then he saw her face shift toward him. He saw that some of the limpness left her features, her shoulders—the way she had drooped disappeared and her body leaned toward him, and he knew that though it was hard to tell, he could tell, their eyes were fixed on each other and she knew who he was. He felt his voice fight for freedom from his chest. He wanted to yell. But he knew he couldn't. So, he raised his hand with the camera. She would know the shiny, silver, bulky camera. A moment passed. Then her mouth moved, moved in exaggerated form, as she silently sent some message to him. He brought the camera down to his face, focused through the telephoto lens, strained his vision. Her mouth moved and her eyes held onto him as tightly as if she were there standing next to him, pressing herself to him as she had a thousand times, and a thousand, it suddenly seemed, years earlier. He tried to read her lips, those lips, but, what?, he couldn't tell. Desperation filled him. He raised the camera high again, stretching his arm. It made no sense, but he knew nothing else to do.

The jeep crested the hill and disappeared. The growl of the engines faded. Not one bird chirped. No wind rustled any leaf. Silence settled over the field, over Rand, like death, he felt certain. *This is the silence of death.* His legs suddenly weakened and he slumped into a pile on the ground beneath the tree.

Chapter 14

Back at the compound, Kera paced along the walls of the small room like a trapped and tormented animal. Her fist would come to her mouth, press her lips into the edges of her teeth, then fly out blindly as if striking some invisible adversary, then pound her hip, or the palm of her other hand. Her face contorted with fear and anger. Her eyes fixed glaringly on the floor.

After the attack on the Guardsmen they had taken a different route back to the compound. The wild-haired man had locked her in the room, and gone with the rest to the shed where the green machines were kept. She could hear them whooping and clapping, and above it all could make out the tones of the major's voice, apparently congratulating, praising them for a job well done.

Kera had covered her eyes during most of the battle. The major had ordered the driver to park at the top of the hill and they had arrived there a moment after the helicopter had opened fire, but in plenty of time to see the government soldiers being shot down with cold-blooded precision.

Death is striking, the way their bodies tore apart, the way the air turned red behind them after a flicker of impact at their chest or throat or head. The way they fell, not like someone protecting themselves, but like an object without life, without consciousness, one instant a spirit alive, the next a vacant inanimate mass.

She had never, in any way, been prepared for the shocking destabilizing horror of seeing life decimated. She had shut her eyes until it was over, until the shooting had stopped. Then she had opened them again and looked out over the field, watched how the revolutionaries had gathered the weapons, anything useful to them as warriors. She watched as they drove away from those that had only moments ago been fathers, sons, brothers, sisters, daughters, and mothers—fellow countrymen, like her, exactly.

And then she had spied Rand at the edge of the woods. She knew nothing of how he might have arrived at that spot beside the forest. The question did not at first enter her mind. She had instinctively pulled away from the jeep, toward her husband, but had quickly met with the restraint of the handcuffs. She had wanted with all her will to go to him and bury her face in his protection, hold him and squeeze him and make certain that he was in fact solid and whole and unharmed.

She wanted to go with him and retrieve their children and never come upon a place or time such as this again.

But she knew if she called out he would be captured, possibly killed, and so she remained silent and watched with her heart tearing into pieces as the distance between them grew again, until finally she lost sight of him. She could only hope he would not follow. Following her would prove a terrible mistake. There would be nothing he could do to free her. The priority was the children. He must make it to the children and save them. She had formed the words repeatedly with her mouth—*the children*—formed them as obviously as she could in her state of numbness and confusion and fear. It was a prayer that he might have understood. He was even then so far from her.

She understood that only the thinnest of prayers maintained the life of her children—if they were alive at all. *Yes, I can will it true, make it true. They are alive! They must be alive!*

She tried to focus on new hope as she paced along the walls of the room, but no matter how she tried to believe in Rand, doubt again filled her. She fought the urge to pull her hair, to tear it from the roots; fought the urge to crumple onto the couch and let the crying begin; fought the urge to pound with her fists until the walls fell away; and she fought the dead soldiers lying back there in that field when, confirming her worst fears, her children's faces began to attach themselves to the desiccated bodies in her mind.

Her eyes went desperately to the window, but she knew the window was a hoax, a false hope. The warriors were gathered inside the shed, not a hundred feet from that window. But then she paused and reconsidered. They were *inside* the shed, and making a lot of noise.

She paced the floor along the walls, but stopped just short of the window frame. She could hear them in the shed, hear their happy voices, hear music from an acoustic guitar. She pressed her face to the wall and peered out through the window, along the flank of the building. Only empty space out there, a few trees, the gravel roadway, the forest beyond.

Rand had stood by a forest, had come from the forest, had found some protection in the forest. She eased toward the glass of the window until she could see the shed. The doors remained closed and the front of the building was void of windows. She ducked down and crossed to the other side of the window, peered out. No human in sight. They were in the shed, celebrating what they had done, though she knew that a few would stand sentinel, out by the main road, on the edges of the compound. Those guards would not hesitate to shoot her.

The images of the dying soldiers came to her again, the faces of her children, and she scrunched her eyes shut. She saw herself dying in the same manner, blood spurting from holes as big as fists. In fact, even if she stayed, but refused to join them, to fight for their cause, it was harder to believe that they would keep her and feed her until the revolution ended, than simply shoot her. They killed easily. If she stayed here her time would be limited. She could stand that... but not the images of her children.

Her heart raced in her chest as she reached out slowly toward the window latch. Her fingers trembled. She felt suddenly exhausted. Anyone exiting the shed would face her window from the other side and immediately see her attempting to unlock it. But if she could... if she could climb out the window while they celebrated inside the shed she might be able to make it to the forest and disappear before anyone realized what had happened.

She pulled her hand back and pressed it to her mouth. She doubted her ability to succeed in any such escape. If she were caught trying to escape they would kill her. She would never see Alissa and Andrew again.

Still, she felt certain now that if she didn't escape she would soon die at the hands of the soldiers or, as the foul smell of him came back to her, at the mercy of the wild-haired man. Her nostrils flared. It was as if he were in the room with her. No, if she was going to die she wanted to die trying to get to her children. She wanted to die knowing she hadn't given up.

She reached out again and gave the release a push. It moved. She pulled her hand back and peered out at the shed door. The party continued. She reached out again and pushed, and the release cleared the latch. Her breath caught.

It dawned on her that they must have somehow fixed the window shut, with nails on the outside, or paint possibly. It could not be so easy. She bent down and got under the window, put her thumbs into the wooden grooves and slowly increased pressure so as not to make sound by forcing it open too quickly. Her arms shook and she could hear her heart beating, drumming in her ears.

The window inched open. The sounds of the celebration grew and echoed around the room. She let off the pressure and drew her arms in. She felt light headed and everything outside her direct field of vision seemed dim and remote. If only she could open the window far enough she could climb through it and run away from here. She could get back onto the road toward her children. *Could that be possible?* A surge of anxiety ran through her. Where would she go? How would she get away? Who would shoot her?

Kera ducked out of sight and bowed her head to her chest. *Dear God, I know I only pray to you when I need something. If you do exist, you know that I'm not even certain of your existence. But if you do watch over us, can you please see that what I am asking for is not for me? Do what you must with me, just let me get away from here long enough to find my children and make certain they are safe and healthy. Please, God!*

She braced her knees against the wall and inched her eyes up to peer out the window. Nothing had changed. She brought her head down and her thumbs up and fitted them into the grooves again. This would be it. One clean push all the way now, all the way open to where she could fit through, jump down, and dash to the forest.

She took a deep breath and pushed. The window slid up easily. When she got it all the way up she stepped to the side, peered out at the shed, saw nothing change, and lifted her right leg and pushed her foot through the opening. She sat on the windowsill and twisted her body through. When she did she looked down at the ground below her and there sat the wild-haired man.

Seated on the ground with his back to the wall of the building, a rifle leaning there and a bottle of beer between his legs, he watched Kera, and in his eyes she saw the same edge as in those of the murderers when they prepared to kill earlier in the day. Without speaking, without thinking, she leaped back in and yanked the window closed.

***

When Rand collapsed on the ground his eyes remained open. He did not lose consciousness, but his mind stopped in the way some people's minds will stop when overloaded with traumatic circumstance. After awhile, and as his body continued to reveal few signs of life, his consciousness began to crawl forward through thought, trying desperately to evaluate the situation.

I am not a soldier, not a cop. I was not even a street tough kid. I am a photographer from a family unused to strife. Okay, I have seen adversity, like a temporary loss of income, or a rise in the interest rates of my credit cards, or a dollar per gallon hike in the price of gasoline. I've struggled, struggled to rise above my peers, make enough to purchase an impressive car, a bigger house.

But now I'm fighting to keep my life for one more moment. I'm praying to find my wife and children safe once more. I'm yearning to see my country and people at peace again.

I'm a member of the greatest—greatest?—well, the most elite— elite? Pampered—yes, that's true—the most pampered society on the face of Earth, and, well, from a segment of that society slightly more pampered than most. Truth is, the men of my family have not had a callous or hard edge in generations. I am a product of the new age—a specialized man. As a man I am supposed to be genetically equipped and responsible for the handling of extremes, but I'm not, for God's sake! I've never had to be! I can't handle this. I have no experience with war or rape or murder.

He might have remained on the ground through the day, the night, until his system processed the shock, had it not been for the sound of Kera's voice. She called his name; the same passionate call he had heard at the edges of his consciousness the night the man clobbered him with the gun barrel. Her voice bounced around in his head and at first he rose slightly and looked in the direction she had last departed, over the hill in the jeep. But as soon as he looked he realized the voice came from within himself, his memory, and his head sank down again. The voice returned, calling him, crying out his name.

There was so much love in that voice, so much concern for his safety. He remembered the feeling of her hand clenching his arm just before his world went black, and the sound of her frightened breathing. And then the image came to him of her sitting in the car next to him that day they had left New York City. *When was that? A hundred years ago?* She had sat there looking like a kid, her mouth, nose, and eyes swollen from crying—so beautiful, so fearful, so innocent.

He had not comforted her. *Why did I not reach out and touch her?* Rand sat up, dirt and weeds clinging to the side of his face. He blinked and looked at the hilltop over which she had disappeared.

He dragged himself to his feet, his eyes vacant, his mind disoriented, and picked up the camera, found the bag, turned and shuffled down onto the trampled field. He saw his truck with the front blown to bits. He didn't blink at the bodies, didn't turn his head away, but went to the middle of the field and stopped and gazed at the carnage, the destroyed APC's, the dead soldiers, the way their heads and bodies separated, the crops growing in the sunshine, the trees, and the way the leaves moved with the breeze, *but is there really any breeze at all?*

He wanted to sit again, sit in the field and rest, collapse, but then he saw a board, it was a large board, his mind grasped it and realized he was looking at the board Patricia had been wrapped to.

He dropped the camera and the bag and shuffled slowly toward it. It must have flown a considerable distance upon concussion of a missile, and a corner of the plywood had stuck into the ground and it was there, standing straight up in the air like a monument to the battle. Rand touched it, came around it with his eyes afraid to see, and did see Patricia lying there in a heap on the ground.

He knelt down beside her. Lying on her side, her neck twisted, her face pushed into the ground. Blood stained her hair.

"Oh, Patricia…." Rand reached down and gently lifted her face from the dirt, laid her head straight. He sat. Her eyes were closed and her face, *that poor face*, looked like a crinkled piece of blackened aluminum foil. Rand's mouth began to water. He couldn't keep up with the gush of saliva, the twist of his stomach, so he spit on the ground off to the side, kept his head turned away, "I am so sorry."

He stood and looked desperately around and saw his camera there and suddenly needed a picture of this horrific scene. This had to be shown to all those who never would see, who never could imagine. He shuffled to the camera and picked it up, weakly dusted it off, pulled the lens shade and pointed the lens at the empty hill.

How can I take a photograph of bodies? How can I point my camera at these people who were just alive, just breathing, but now so—so betrayed and robbed of pride and annihilated by this perverse insanity? He moved the camera uncertainly to include a dead soldier. *Look at them!*

He clicked the shutter.

I am sorry. Click. *I am sorry.* Click, click. *But I must bear witness for those who would not believe. To those like me who would not believe.*

He shuffled and clicked and framed up the bodies and tried to forget the faces as soon as he recognized them there on the ground, tried to forget that he had seen them moving and smiling and breathing... People... Alive... they had been.

He turned and saw the board and paused. She was the victim's victim. He couldn't imagine anything more brutal and woeful. He walked over to Patricia and knelt down again. "I'm sorry," he said, and his voice broke. He looked at her, wiped his mouth absently, framed a shot, and her eye opened. She looked up at him, and he froze. Then he lowered the camera with a jerk and confirmed that her good eye was open and she was looking at him.

"Patricia?" he breathed. *Is there any possible earthly way she can be alive?* Her eye shifted slowly away, then back to his face. He sat the camera on the ground and moved behind her, took her head and hip in his hands and rotated her so that her back was flat on the ground. He carefully brushed her stiff and bloody hair away from her face.

Her lips moved slightly. She stared at him.

What do I do? "Patricia, can you hear me?"

Her lips moved again and he heard, "Yes," gurgle up from her throat.

"What—what can I do?"

Her hand came up off the ground, that blackened, beaten hand, and Rand gently took it. It felt hard, crinkled. It came to him again how badly it must have hurt her to untie him from that tree. Her red watery eye stared at him.

"I don't know what to do," he whispered.

A sound came from her throat, a weak and rattling escape of air, but he heard the word, "Go." Her eye blinked closed with the effort, opened again onto him.

"What?" he whispered. "I—I don't understand."

"Your—w—wi—ife." She blinked again and a tear trickled down her cheek. Her chest rose and she expelled a long rattling breath of air. "My—hus—band—wasn't taken."

Rand could feel her hand tighten weakly around his. She coughed suddenly and the corner of her mouth turned red.

"He—le—ft—me."

For Rand, everything in the world about them went dim. It was her and him, and he understood. There was no mistaking it. Patricia's husband had not been taken by the revolutionaries, he had fled and left her to them.

"I will find her," he whispered, and he meant it, but thought there must have been something more comforting to say to a woman, anyone, who had experienced betrayal in such a way.

He slowly moved so that he could lift her shoulders and place her head in his lap. She continued to watch him with her good eye. He didn't know what to do. He leaned down and whispered in her ear, "I'm so sorry... for what has happened."

She didn't respond, only held her eye fixed on his face, and he realized that was her only way of holding on.

He considered finding her water, possibly a blanket, but he only remained seated there with her head resting on him. He somehow felt that if he walked away to find those things she would be gone from the world when he returned. He didn't want her to have to do this alone. Staring down at her eye which remained open to him, he held her hand and placed his other hand along the side of her face. *Is there not SOMETHING I can do? Is there really NOTHING I can do?*

The sun heated the crown of his head, which threw its shadow luckily across Patricia's head and shoulders. He looked up. It had turned into a warm and bright day. Birds chirped and fluttered in the field; robins and smaller birds he could not identify. He recalled the pigeons again, the way they cooed outside the studio. *I should have learned more about birds, in my life. I should have paid a lot more attention to birds.*

After a time, Rand felt life leave Patricia. At the moment it happened everything went still—the birds in the field, Patricia, himself, the sun, the wind, the trees, the entire Earth, everything, completely quiet and warm in the sun... pausing.

He wondered if she had lived as quietly, as gently, as she had died.

Rand's eyes filled with tears and his head went down over her. Drops fell on her hair like a sudden shower, and he turned his face so as not to get her wet. *Why is everyone going away?* He turned his face back, patted lightly at the moisture in her hair, kissed her battered cheek.

Then he thought about the man who abandoned her to the will of rapists and murderers. *What kind of man, does that? Why did he not protect her? Had he been like that all his life, a man willing to stoop so low? Or had he somehow changed? And how could she, their* relationship, have come to mean so little to him as to deserve such complete disregard?

He suddenly shrank from these questions like a coward told the horrible truth. *How far am I from being him?* Had he not sickened at the sight of Kera after she crashed his car, had even begun to hate her for quitting their life of business together, for leaving him. But now all those animosities seemed childish, foolish, despicable in themselves.

He wondered at the man he had become and how he had given her no choice but to leave him. He had already left her, had he not?

I balked at protesting, when that man assaulted her, balked, and worried mostly about myself!

What he would do to spend one moment now, holding her hand, seeing that face again, that pout, turning that pout to a smile; he could, he knew he could.

He brushed Patricia's hair with his fingers, but his mind now saw the face of Kera and the children...

...Oh Please! What has happened to Alissa and Andrew? There was no way of knowing the quality of the people taking care of them—if anyone was in fact caring for them.

Rand began to tremble, shook his head to clear away the thoughts. But the thoughts progressed and filled his mind with shocking reality.

I had not wanted to go for them! I fought with Kera about it, felt that I needed to work, to keep the business going.

He realized then the reason he had not wanted to venture after the children was not only because he didn't think there was a real problem concerning their safety, but because he had diminished the immediacy of his children's need for safety, and his responsibility for providing it, by prioritizing his own exaggerated needs, his success, his reputation. He could see everything clearly, now. *Can this be true? Could I have become such a man?*

A torrent of guilt and anxiety rushed through him. *It had all come so easily.*

He lifted Patricia's head and placed it gently on the ground, rose and paced off a few steps. The urge to run grew within him. *Run? To where?* He had no idea where Kera was, no idea where the pack of murderers who held her hid.

The idea of presenting himself and his needs to law enforcement or military officials was out of the question—they would detain him just as the sergeant had stated. But he had no vehicle and no direction.

Kera's face returned to his mind. He saw her again in the back of the jeep, saw her looking at him, saw her mouthing words he could not decipher.

He began pacing the field, thinking hard about the way she had worked her mouth, formed the silent words. His mind became focused.

The! That was the first word, the. He could see it easily now that he slowed himself and his thoughts. *The, what?* The second word was longer. It had started with her bringing her jaws together and closing, no, not closing her mouth, like with a "B", but almost, as if she used "T", yes, the "T" sound…or, no, further back… something like a "C". He worked his mouth, popped it apart. Her lips had remained parted. He could even make out in his mind's eye that halfway through the word her tongue had come forward; it had sent a brief reflection of sunlight with its movement, as in "L" …yes!

Children! It came to him suddenly as he saw her forming the word again. *The children.* He stopped pacing, stood there stock still, arms dangling at his sides, eyes held wide on the horizon—*How could I not have known?* There would be no doubt, ever, that the children were her first concern—rightly so.

Rand again felt the draining suck of guilt. Within grasp of the darkest danger Kera still clearly knew her purpose.

Purpose. The word stuck in Rand's mind. Purpose, yes, Helen had said it: *we are being asked to state our purpose.*

Rand knew then what he had to do. He had to find the children. Protect them. It felt like abandoning Kera, but no choice remained. As Kera made clear, the children came first. It was what she wanted most of him now. Only he had the freedom it would take to save Alissa and Andrew.

***

As Kera expected, the door of her confinement room opened. The wild-haired man entered without his usual force, instead exercising controlled and precise movement. She at once saw the change. The anger, animosity, insecurity, all the emotions she had seen flare in him earlier had settled deep into a dark, brooding malignancy.

She stood with her back to the corner, her small hands that had treated her so well through life balled-up in her shirt, her pouty lips compressed, everything trembling like a wet child on a cold day. He came forward slowly, his thick chest expanding with tense, sour lungfuls of air, his face expressionless, his eyes dark and muddy as cesspools.

He pressed upon her with his body, his odor flaring her nostrils, and slowly crushed her against the wall. Her face became buried in the oily filth of his chest. She couldn't breathe. He ground himself into her until her head grew light from lack of air. "Please," she whimpered and choked. He backed off a step, and Kera gasped for air.

Beads of sweat lined his forehead. He breathed fast and hard. The corners of his mouth twisted downward. "Please? You beg? How about how I have begged?"

She looked and for the first time saw some hint of loneliness, or sadness, in his face.

"You were going to leave me," he whispered.

For a moment, under the skin of this unclean, unkempt man, behind the fortified walls of malevolence, she spied the image of a dispirited child.

He struck her so hard that it banged her head against the wall and dropped her into a dazed heap. He grabbed her by the collar, slapped her with a backhand, and the watch he stole from Rand cut her lip.

Her nervous system began to shut down. She could feel him, hear him, smell him, but not see him. The odor came forward, stronger, the sounds reverberated. She went limp as he dragged her away from the wall and laid her flat. He had earlier discarded her bra, so when he ripped open her fatigue shirt her breasts came exposed to his rough, filthy hands.

She felt him yank off her boots, her trousers, and then heard him pull off his pants. He dropped down onto her, his weight again forcing the air from her body, and she felt his tongue on her neck, her face, across her lips. He bit parts of her so hard her eyes teared despite her blinding, shock-induced paralysis.

He forced himself inside her, and she again focused on the desire to withdraw, to separate, to understand more clearly than ever how her life did not matter, could not matter. Nothing was permanent. Holding on too strongly would only cause more pain. Something better waited on the other side, and she began to look toward it.

Maybe man's God did exist; maybe he waited for her with a gentle smile.

She allowed herself to subside. There came a lightening, a lifting, a lessening of heaviness. She imagined herself smiling, felt herself smiling. It wasn't like any smile she had experienced in a long time. It spread not only through the muscles of her face, her head, her chest, but everywhere, down into her toes, her bowels... tingling. She let it go and could feel herself floating into a place where nothing else mattered but the decision to be free.

But then a sound rang into her mind and light came suddenly to the world again. Pain shot through her. She looked up and saw the naked wild-haired man standing over her, straddling her body, his heels grinding down on the backs of her hands, crushing them into the floor. "You are my little child," he said. "I know how to take care of you. I won't do what they did... to me. I won't give you drugs, or leave you."

Like an awakening slap, she had heard the sound again: child. She saw in the eyes of the wild-haired man the frantic belief in what he had said.

Kera filled first with sadness: *What will my children be left to?* Then disgust: *Is this sickness what our world is filled with?* Then rage: *He has no right to do this to us!*

Instinctively, Kera's leg shot upward—her foot came up—she kicked with true force into the dangling sac of the wild-haired man.

He immediately stumbled backward and let loose a deafening bellow. She scrambled to her feet. He made a step toward her, but his face scrunched-up and turned red as he dropped to his knees, hands covering his testicles.

Kera thought little. She grabbed her clothes—not the uniform, but her own clothes that remained in a pile on the floor—then stepped to the window and thrust it open.

The wild-haired man grabbed her arm and spun her around with the hand that wasn't protecting his groin. She banged into the wall and dropped the clothes. "No! Not again!" he growled, and reached for her.

She struck back with her fists in a violent rage. She kicked and her foot struck his knee. She swung her arm wide, brought her fist into the side of his head, caught the temple with lucky knuckles, and dropped him flat onto the floor.

The way he collapsed left her gawking. She stood for a moment with her chest heaving, her mouth agape, staring at the pile of muscled flesh on the floor. He didn't move, the watch reflecting bright light from his wrist. The urge to stomp on him, to drive her heals into the thick of his skull, came over her in a rush.

But she turned and looked out the window. The guitar still played, the voices boomed, the doors of the shed remained closed.

Kera grabbed her clothes and climbed through the window. Just then, a boy exited the shed and stopped when he saw her. Kera froze, clutching her clothes against her. It was the same boy she had locked eyes with when loading the truck. They stared at each other. He turned back toward the shed, but just as quickly stopped, and looked at her again... then he put his head down and walked away from the shed. All at once a vision of beauty and terror, Kera dashed for the forest and never looked back.

***

Rand tried to keep his face expressionless, but as he bent over to lift Patricia the tears flooded from his eyes, ran down his cheeks, seeped through his compressed and rigid lips, and salted his tongue. The muscles of his face reacted against his will.

The way her body gave, her arms flopped, her head rolled, it seemed so innocent, yielding, trusting, like she had resigned herself finally to letting go. He ached with the wish of her opening her eyes again. He knew now that she had placed her trust in him, her complete faith, and he had reacted too slowly, considered her too little, to save her life, as she had saved his.

Rand had never physically buried anyone. In today's world how many people had? He'd even heard that it was now illegal in some places to bury a person without the concrete vault and sealed coffin.

Still, he could not leave Patricia lying out in the open, unprotected as she had been in her last days of light. So he had searched the remains of the camp and come up with a collapsible army shovel. His hands, with wrists still sore from the rope Patricia freed him of, blistered quickly as he dug in the dry hard ground.

Now, as he carried her toward the hole, he could not stop crying and that frustrated him. He continued his efforts at keeping his face straight—because everyone knows the sign of a strong person is the ability to prevent crying, or, at a minimum, mask it.

He worked his way into the hole with her thin body in his arms, laid her on the bottom, and squatted down next to her. The moistness of the cool earth touched the small of his back where his shirt had pulled up. Within the muffled quietness of the hole he could hear his heart beating and he thought: one heart, two people.

He didn't know her last name, didn't know where she came from, didn't know if children awaited her. He did know that she was a rich woman abandoned at the sign of trouble, the time of need, by the man who had promised to protect her. Was it his money or her money, and what did it matter? At that moment the thought of money filled Rand with disgust. What money had afforded her was a pretty dress for her burial, a pretty dress torn and soiled and spattered with blood. What the desire for money had gotten him was a place to squat at the bottom of a grave—no wife, no children, no car, no job, no reputation. No pride.

He remembered how Patricia had offered him the reward for her safe deliverance, and how he had considered the money, like a cold and slimy bloodsucker. For a brief moment, he considered how it might be best if he could fill the hole with himself in it, but just as quickly, precisely, thought of his children, and turned his mind back to his mission.

He climbed out, filled the shovel with dirt, and looked down at her again. *There's a whole lot of time between having nothing, having everything, and having nothing again. What did we do, Patricia, with all that time?*

He went slowly, looking more at the place where the shovel filled with dirt than the place where it emptied, until it came time to cover her head. He knew he must watch as the soil fell upon her tortured face, that to look away would seem disrespectful. So he watched as the earth took ownership of Patricia, and when the hole was again full and mounded, he hoped he had done the saddest most disconcerting duty he would ever do. *Please, for this, allow me no more opportunities.*

As the sun began to fall from the sky he considered hiding in the woods for the night, but instantly knew he had no desire to remain anywhere near all this death. He wanted to get away and forget how humans had come down on their own kind with venom for blood, with hate as keen as a viper's fang, with a partnership unto death that made him weak and lonely and miserable inside.

With the camera bag slung over his shoulder, he turned his back and walked away from the grave, the field, the hill. Then he stopped and looked back. The hill caught the yellow glow of the day's last fading sunshine, and Rand paused. His wife had disappeared over that hill which lay east of him, but he must travel west.

He again saw her riding in the back of the jeep, saw her for a lightning bolt moment bent over the front of the station wagon, and then he turned, shook his head from side to side, shuddered and clenched his fists. *These last days will not be my future, our future!* He focused and a memory returned to him. It was Kera's face the day she had given birth to Andrew. She was in the hospital and the nurse had just placed their newborn baby boy, wrapped like a present, on her breast, and Kera had looked at the glistening little face, and then up at Rand. He had forgotten, long forgotten, the glow that even now helped him understand the emotion of motherhood, of birthing, of selfless devotion. He swore now as he stood on this field of death, as he prepared to walk away from that hill forever, he swore to Kera who could not hear him, that he would never again forget to remember that face—her smiling, beautiful, mother-of-all-creation face.

Part Four

Chapter 15

Kera stood shivering in the rising quiet light of sunrise, stood appraising the horse in the pasture like a thief must consider a car with an open door and keys in the ignition. She knew she had never actually ridden a horse. At the age of four her father had one day sat her on top of a neighbor farmer's pony and walked her in a few small circles around the barnyard. She remembered how safe that seemed, how the soft ears of the pony had felt, how her father's eyes and voice had allowed her the security she needed as her mother had watched with a straight face, more serious than any other watching from beyond the fence.

But her mother and father were not here now.

It had taken some time but she finally stopped her throbbing lip from bleeding. Shivering, she had not weathered the warm night well, and her mind had noticed little, not with the images of Alissa and Andrew fixed there. She had escaped immediate harm, but the only lift it provided came through the knowledge that her children now stood a better chance. For herself, this freedom meant nothing. Kera loved her children, and focused on the fact that she was now free to help them.

She rushed into the pasture, toward the horse one hundred feet away, and crossed into full view of a house sitting on a knoll and overlooking the grassy expanse of openness. The horse spooked and bolted, and Kera froze, realizing she needed to approach more calmly.

The horse had a white patch of a face, and shoulders and haunches sturdy from exercise. It allowed her near as she crept forward, gently murmuring, "Come on, now. I need your help."

Kera focused on the eyes of the animal and after several minutes of gentle persuasion, scratching a spot under its chin, the horse allowed her to drag herself clumsily onto its back, apparently for nothing more than the promise of a good ride. This was a beautifully trained and understanding beast. Kera adjusted to the feel of having mounted it, took handfuls of its mane in her bruised and swollen hands, let it ambled toward a gate in the fence.

She'd forgotten the need to somehow exit the pasture, but the horse approached and flanked the gate, allowing her to lean over and lift the wire looped over the low end of a post.

The road was gravel but the hooves clopped anyway. With her hands buried in the long stiff hair of the mane she leaned toward the forest west of the road, pressed with her leg in that direction, and the horse turned with her, even picked up pace toward a bridle trail leading into the woods. Kera fought to stay seated, her head bouncing like a Bobble Head toy.

She didn't actually trust the horse, but if she were ever to reach her children she needed better transportation than her feet. As slow as this seemed, there was no other avenue for assistance available, even if she would consider it. She felt afraid of everyone and embarrassed by herself. It would either be this horse, or her own two feet that would take her across the remaining country.

She rode through the cool wood, but the wood was soon cut by a road. She stopped the horse just inside the trees and listened for traffic. Birds chirped and crickets cheeped. No automobile sounds.

She held on tightly and touched the horse lightly with her heels, and the heavy shoulders sank as the front hooves trod down into the ditch along the road. The horse eased onto the pavement, went carefully across, and negotiated the ditch on the other side. Soon they were under the cover of forest again.

Kera felt the need to go faster, but at the same time didn't feel ready to handle the horse at anything other than a walk. As they plodded along she watched the woods closely, nervously, and pondered the concept of direction. She knew east and west by where the sun rose and fell, but midday posed a problem. It was easy to lose the direction when the sun moved overhead. In New York City the only time you noticed the sun was when it stood high above. At most times and places buildings blocked the sky, creating a city of shadows and a life with little sunlight.

She decided that from then on she would rise with the dawn, ride until she became uncertain of direction, then rest until it became clear again. The idea of stopping so frequently made her anxious, but it would have to do until she came up with something better. Stopping somewhere and asking directions was out of the question. Besides being harmed, she feared the hunting eyes and minds of everyone, the questions on where she had been, what she had done. The only humans she wanted to talk with were her children. She had no money to buy a map, even if she would stop at a gas station. Also, someone would eventually be looking for the horse, and she knew from watching movies long ago that horse stealing was serious business. With the country in the condition that it was she would probably be hanged if they caught her. The image of her dangling from a rope came to mind and she wondered if she had gone crazy.

She would continue on and hope that Washington State was a big and obvious place.

They came to a narrow, rocky creek and she pulled back on the horse's mane. The water looked only knee deep, but it ran fast and the rocks were large, the footing uncertain. She thought it best to dismount and walk across, but she had nothing with which to lead the horse, and feared she might lose control. Instead, she bent forward and wrapped her arms around the horses thick neck, placed her cheek against its mane, prepared herself, and lightly nudged it with her heels.

The horse stepped forward and placed one hoof into the water, paused, moved another hoof, then another. It felt its way across the creek as gingerly as a mother carrying her young. Kera could feel that the horse had sensed her uncertainty. It was caring for her and this realization caused Kera to bury her face in the thick mane and cry deep wracking releasing sobs.

***

Rand's legs refused to obey his brain. They went off in odd directions, or threatened to quit all together. He couldn't remember ever having walked so far and had little energy remaining. He hadn't stopped moving since turning his back on the hill Kera had disappeared behind, had walked the starry night away, the humid day, had drank no water, eaten no food since leaving Donald and Helen's home. It was now afternoon and he was lost in deep thought, stumbling along a flat, pea-graveled country road.

He considered how, as he walked through the night, he had heard the far-off pop of gunfire and explosions of great magnitude—heavy ground-rumbling eruptions that made him feel as if the earth itself was at war.

No, Earth is not at war. But humans are. He knew he could not blame Earth for what was going on around the globe and in his country right here, right now. Humans might be a product of Earth, but as he had walked through the dark, listening to the gun pops, the explosions that resonated through the ground like the shudderings of some great but dying beast, he saw suddenly and clearly that the children of Earth, at least the human children—blood and bone extensions of the planet— were throwing tantrums, hating with childish greed and fear in ways that only children could.

And so now he wondered: what *is* our purpose? What purpose for all this conflict and death could possibly be justifiable, worthy of what he was having to suffer, not to mention his children, his wife, Patricia, all the Donalds and Helens and soldiers and soldiers' families?

He thought of this war and all the wars he had any awareness of and now saw them as happening in one place, on Earth, and realized they all came together as the dysfunctional behavior of one family—the human family birthed on the planet Earth.

And for Rand, it all came down to his immediate family, citizens of the United States. How could the people of his country, of America, have reached this state of being that now found them murdering members of their immediate own? How was it that any human could murder another, simply over their beliefs? *How could we not have found an honorable way to settle our differences?* Now that he had witnessed murder he understood the dishonor, the horror, the stupidity of it.

He found as he labored along that he lacked the knowledge to address the questions he now asked. As consumed as he had been, so naïvely and narrowly focused, he had become completely uninterested in issues of local, national, and global concern. And as for the more philosophical questions, college had simply not prepared him for what now raced through his mind.

What did college prepare me for? In the dark night of war, where questions became acutely focused on the matter of basic survival, he could see the failure of a system aimed at turning out the next lawyer, computer designer, business manager, technical engineer, or factory worker—the next labor force.

People needed to be taught skills that would keep them alive and prevent them from murdering in situations out of their control, like this. *The basics of living and survival!* Clearly, the most educated minds had not saved them from what they now faced, but those with a basic knowledge of preservation would do best.

Weak, he stumbled and ended up on both knees. The fire of anger and frustration turned into a fever of foolishness passing through him. He now saw himself as a newborn in a race of infants. *There is so much they have failed to comprehend. I mean, We. There is just so damn much I have failed to consider about our society and how well it was working.*

A desire to collapse in the road and give in to exhaustion weighed down on him. He dropped to all fours, stared at the millions of tiny pebbles laid out before him like a foundation of lies. Each one represented a contemporary wisdom—those who work hardest get more out of life; we are a nation built on individualism; owning things is a sign of success—but turn those pebbles of wisdom over and be surprised.

Have I been living in a vacuum? Have I allowed someone to drop the blindfold over my eyes? Is the joke on me?

He had forgotten the sacredness of his marriage, the gift bestowed through his children, the privilege of living in a peaceful and honorable society. He had forgotten how to live, to survive, all, taken for granted, as he had chased through each day—faster, faster—after money, *well,* security, *or, well... after something I don't remember ever seeing, hearing, feeling, knowing or understanding.* It had seemed like something to hold onto, but had gone beyond a roof over their heads, good food in their stomachs; it had gone to an expensive house they could not maintain, an imported car that had left his bank account empty; it had gone to spending more time with the people he worked with than the people at home who loved him.

Anger again rushed forward and pushed him to his feet. He resumed walking. He had failed in too many ways to sit and sleep and let it all go down as his life story—his lack of purpose—his fucking ignorance and naïveté. He would see Kera again, see that face, tell her how he loved her. He would walk until he came to his children, until he could apologize to them for not being what they deserved. He would walk until he made up his mind what he should do with this life, these gifts, these opportunities.

The gravel road approached a paved one still a good distance off. He could see the faint outline of a sign that seemed to indicate a State route. He had not seen a car in hours, but the idea of following a state route made him feel vulnerable. Law enforcement and military would detain

him. Private vehicles might contain terrorists, since no law-abiding
citizens were allowed out. Anyone spotting him meant certain trouble.

He considered hiding in a field or forest until dark and approaching a
farm or small town and stealing a car. He had never done anything like
that, had no idea how to get keys or hot wire a vehicle, and wasn't
interested in doing anything that might cause the police or military to
search him out. Just thinking over all the complexities ushered him
further toward collapse. He knew that if he hid in a field he would sleep
for too long. He had to keep moving.

He approached the wider State route, slipped across, and kept
heading west. Soon he came to a wide, brownish river. The road turned
and went along its bank. Rand skidded his feet down the embankment,
slipped, and landed heavily on his back, the camera bag bouncing hard
on the ground. The fall took the wind out of him, jarred his spine, so he
sat, sucking air back into his lungs, feeling at least comfortable with the
fact that daylight was failing, and trees and brush along the river hid him
from general view.

When he could move again he crawled the remaining feet to the
river's edge and peered into the slowly flowing water. It was brown, not
thick, but certainly not clear. Thirst got the best of him and he cupped
his hand and tasted the river. *Damn good!* It took him several minutes
to get his fill and the water felt right in his stomach. He sat back and
looked across the water, a hundred yards, maybe more. Peering in each
direction he could not see a bridge or any way of crossing. It would be
completely dark soon and he knew he could stumble around for hours
and miles trying to find a bridge. The river flowed slow and tame. He
could feel his pulse quicken at the idea of crossing it in the dark, but
then, that would be a safe time, since no one could pick him out as he
swam across.

Looking around, he saw a piece of log about four feet long and
substantial enough to float the camera bag, but small enough to easily
handle. He waited and watched the light, considered whether he should
wear his shoes, or float them across on top the log. He decided to wear
them, fearing the unknown dangers of the river bottom, and the
possibility that if he took them off he could lose them altogether. He
decided the same with his clothes. He didn't want to become wet and
then possibly chilled. It was bad enough, all he had to go through, how
much of an idiot he had become, but losing his clothes in the river and

wandering about naked for all the world… no, no.

When light faded and he felt invisible to any potential passersby, he floated the log, placed the bag on it, and slipped into the water. It was cold and goose bumps rose immediately on his skin. He hadn't swam that far in many years. Maybe he had never swum that far. He eased in on his belly. *Oh, crap! That's cold.* He slid in all the way and started dog paddling across, one hand on the log, the other propelling him.

Within a minute his optimism dissolved into fatigue. The cold water sucked his body heat, his energy. His hands numbed and he considered again the last time he'd eaten.

It became so dark he couldn't tell how far he had come, how far he had to go. The fact that he could no longer see what lie in front of him filled him with unease. He tried to relax, but the water had stronger currents than he'd thought and it seemed to gain strength around him, while the log became harder to control and the bag bobbed dangerously. Dread filled him. *This is a mistake. I am too tired and too low on energy to do this.* He started to turn around… but… it might be further to return than to push on. His strokes became clumsy and he suddenly heard himself breathing in hoarse rushes. His stomach began to churn.

Suddenly he felt a light on his face, faint, but at the same time distinct in the dark of night. He squinted downstream and saw that it emitted from some high point at what he thought would be the middle of the river. *A boat? Pretty high for a boat.* But soon he could hear the throb of its engine. He tried to swim faster, but he couldn't. The sound grew steadily louder, nearer, and as it did he became certain it was a boat, and terror seized his heart when he realized the thing seemed to stand a good thirty feet above waterline, barging straight at him, sending a deep foreboding vibration through the water.

He paddled with his feet and hand as fast and hard as he could. In the darkness he could feel it more than see it, and the thing felt big as an ocean liner. He had to clear the center of the river so it could pass, but no matter how hard he swam it seemed to head straight for him. The water became alive with the heavy rumble of its engines, and Rand saw in his mind a picture of his body being chopped into thin ribbons by giant propellers the size of those on cargo planes.

As it neared, he heard waves rushing from around the bow like a tidal wave. He glanced up and then gasped for air, seeing the black prow of the steel leviathan rising above him like a whale breaching the sea.

The river grew into a frothing ocean around him and he gave a last desperate thrust of his legs, clawed at the water with his free hand. The wave pushed him high and forced his face through the air. The sound of water surging and of the ship's grinding, forged engines rang in his ears.

But nothing toppled him. He soon sank back and bobbed in the water. The great ship passed and went on in the night, unseeing, uncaring. The log, with his arm wrapped around it, had acted like a stabilizer, increasing his buoyancy. He clung to it as most he could without adding such weight as to sink it. He swam on a crest of adrenaline. The river grew quiet again, and fatigue returned more heavily than before.

A new sound reached him. It wasn't anything he could identify for certain, but he thought it sounded like the trickle of water. With exhausted legs he treaded in place and listened. There came another sound, slight, like the bump of wood against a steel barrel. His heart raced. *Now what?* The sound came from on the river, and it came from nearby, to the front-right.

His arms felt waterlogged and his chest ached. He struggled forward as quietly as he could, had to keep going, but had the sense whatever it was, it was coming nearer.

And then he felt it in the river in front of him, the water moving slightly as if pushed by something in it. He panicked and froze and fought the desire to shout, to scare it away. *What can it be?* Were there living things in these rivers that could harm him? He didn't know. He thought of snakes, of fish, of beaver, but this was bigger and right there next to him. His stomach twisted and he choked on river water and bile, gagged silently. His arms began to refuse directions. His heart felt ready to explode. He lacked the strength to continue and moved to cradle the log, let the camera go.

And then he heard the bump again, faintly, and the tinkle of water. *Could it be some kind of craft? Yes.* It came close, close enough to nearly strike him in the dark. He heard faint movements, much closer and defined, could see in his mind an oar rising, water running off of it and tinkling into the river, and the oar setting softly, bumping onto the sides of whatever the craft. He pulled the log to him. The sounds repeated and this time the water dripped onto his head. The paddle had passed just over him. The wake of the craft bobbed him up and down, slightly. Then he stilled. The sounds faded downstream. The movements of the water returned to normal.

Rand gagged on vomit, went weakly for the other bank, felt strangely hot in the cold water. He figured he was headed in the right direction, feeling the current moving crossways against his body. Within a few strokes his feet touched bottom. Dizziness and exhaustion overcame him. As he pulled himself and the log onto the bank, he vomited a gush of river water. His head kept spinning. Lying down, the world tilted and he vomited again. His ears rang and his muscles tightened involuntarily. Helpless as the newborn he now considered himself, his awareness faded away.

Chapter 16

Kera knew pain intimately. She had experienced childbirth. This war had brought her the latest inflicted horrors of man. And now, this indescribable disemboweling, de-skinning, equine journey. After riding the horse for far too long, no saddle, her entire bottom and gut had gone through many fazes of agony. She felt ruined in yet another way. And still a small smile passed over her face at the utter cruel joke of it all.

And it wasn't the horse, this gallant savior of sorts. To her, it somehow understood its part of the mission and liked being out in new territory, going somewhere special. It seemed to be trying to make the ride as comfortable for her as possible. Still, she had to get off.

They had crossed open and rolling farmland lined with trees and fences and maneuvered along dirt and gravel roads, through forests, past homes and around a town or two. In a late-night stupor, unwilling to stop, she had allowed the horse to calmly negotiate an impressive concrete bridge spanning a broad river. A person had peered at them from the doorway of a house, and they watched from behind trees as a car passed and barreled along a country road. Each time her heart raced. Each time she prepared to flee, to make the horse run and try to hang on. Each time the event passed without incident.

Late afternoon sunshine now fell upon them and honeyed the open rolling hills of corn and, she thought, wheat, through which they traveled. A large white farmhouse beamed yellow a mile down the road. She steered the horse into a field of glowing grain and gazed at the long shoots wafting in a slow breeze as if they were one thing, not a trillion separate entities. For a moment her spirit rose, her heart stopped aching, she recalled beauty. And she had no sooner given thanks for that American scene like a Hallmark card, that she glanced at something catching a ray of brilliant light, lying on the ground at the base of an old wooden fence post. A smile broke across her face. She steered the horse along the fence a few feet and stopped, looking down. There laid a frayed curl of blue nylon cord maybe twelve feet in length.

"Okay. You'll stay here, right? While I get down and get that rope? Okay, Friend?" She ran her hand along the horse's neck. It felt smooth to her, strong. She loved the sweet smell of the animal. It bent its neck and began to pull at the grasses along the fence. Kera swung her leg over, twisted, and dropped to the ground. Her back bent and her hands braced on her knees. She hurt so terribly she wasn't certain she could walk. She flexed muscle, tried to work blood into certain places and out of others.

She squatted like an old woman and picked up the rope, reached it around the horse's neck, and its head came up with a jerk. "It's okay. Okay, Friend." The horse looked straight ahead with its ears turning in different directions, and its big brown eyes a little rounder than before. She tied off the loop, tied the other end to the fence. It made for a tight lead, but the horse seemed content again, and dropped its head, eating away. They had run into river water, and puddles, a few times during the ride so she felt the horse was hydrated, but it hadn't had much to eat. She'd had no water or food.

Kera laid flat, belly up, on the ground and her back released, shoulders loosened. A deep sigh escaped her and diminished into silence. The sky was a dark, pre-dusk blue. Earth felt solid and warm and the scent of the raw dry wheat—*is it wheat?*—opened her nostrils. Everything filled her with such good at that moment that her mind went to it and held it. It took the contrast of horror and rage to now feel, become conscious of, this goodness. Anxiety rushed in and her children's voices called to her. She brought her arms across her body.

Concentrating, Kera shifted her focus to the more immediate: food and, more importantly, the successful continuation of her journey. Her memories of childhood harbored familiarity with farms. *Any farm way out here must have some kind of animals. Maybe chickens or cattle. Maybe eggs or milk.* To go on, she needed food, but couldn't consider asking for it. The thought of talking to anyone filled her with dread. If she could sleep for awhile, go at night to the farm down the road, find some milk or eggs, anything to eat, then she could put in another good many miles. This wasn't the fastest way to travel, but it felt safe, and she was learning to trust the horse. The most important thing was to keep moving.

She fell asleep with the faded sun, listening to the big animal she had named Friend chew grass with its broad teeth.

Her sleep filled with visions of the wild-haired man. She could smell him, feel him hit her again and again, feel his hard hands clasping her hips, feel him savage her, and awoke with a start that caused the horse to pull against the rope and snort. Kera leaped to her feet, raked hair out of her eyes, grasped hold of the nylon. Insect buzzing and chirping filled the air. The scent of rich soil and fields of grasses helped her wake, helped her forget the nightmare—though it would never be only a nightmare. She pushed the images back down inside herself.

Night had settled and offered little moonlight. The horse breathed loudly, bent and pulled another mouthful of grass. Kera's hair had gathered dirt and odd bits of the countryside and she combed her fingers through it as she stood thinking. "It's okay, Friend." Her voice quivered.

She caressed the horse, ran her hands along its back, put her cheek to its shoulder, felt the warmth radiating from its powerful body. Its tawny mane glowed in the night, hung down over the darker, chocolaty, body color. She traced her fingers along its chest, then down to where the muscles bulged around the top of its leg.

The yellow porch light of the farmhouse glowed in the dark. A green yard light illuminated the face of the barn. She cooed to the horse, "I'm going to the farm over there. Please, stay." She backed slowly away, turned, and walked stiffly down the road flanked by a dried and twisted wooden post-and-rail fence.

A shallow drainage ran perpendicular to the road, meandering toward the barn. Kera paused and watched the house, now about fifty yards away. A large pickup truck sat in the drive, and she wondered at the possibility of a person out here leaving keys in the ignition. She could live with going to jail later, after she found her children, but car theft would draw too much attention, and she might get caught before reaching them. Whoever owned the horse had not found her and she had seen no sign of a serious search being conducted. She wanted desperately for it to stay that way. It was true, making this choice to travel slowly would delay her, and might mean the children would be moved to a location unknown to her, even sent back to their now empty home. She was banking on none of that happening, that the people at the retreat would hold them safely until further word from a parent. She couldn't bear to doubt.

Dropping down into the drainage, she moved as quietly as she could toward the barn. Brush snapped under her feet. Fear crept up and counseled her to quit. She stopped and put her hand to her mouth, bit her finger. The house seemed quiet. No lights shined through any window. She needed food.

It was one of those huge red wooden barns, surrounded by a

manicured lawn and gravel driveway, parking area. The buzzing bright green lamp lit the front, so she decided to go around back. She passed through a bit of light, then into shadow. Climbing out of the drainage her feet hit course mown grass, then sharp gravel, as she moved slowly through the dark, fingers first, feeling for the edge of the barn.

She felt a rough metal door, a cold, slide bar latch. She moved it slowly, almost silently.

The door squeaked, but she opened it far enough to squeeze through. It felt colder inside and smelled of oil or gas. She couldn't see a thing. She decided against searching for a light. *I can't do this.* She had not counted on any situation where she couldn't see her fingers held before her face. She thought to give it time and see if her eyes adjusted.

It was no use. The world remained black. So still was the place, she began to wonder if anything lived there. She took a slow step forward with her hands held out, trembling for the possibilities, another step and another. She touched something cold, steely. Running her fingers along it, she guessed it was a large farm tractor or maybe one of those combines. Around the side of it, she went further into the vacuous building. She imagined herself walking in a cave. Then her toe bumped something hard... it felt like a low... half-wall... made of wood. A bag of thick paper scraped along her hand. She felt it again: large, heavy, full. She considered sticking her hand into it, but that scared her. *What might be in there?* She pushed at the outer edges of the bag and it crinkled in the dark. Nothing hissed or flapped or made any other noise than a thick paper bag crinkling at the top. She slowly felt along the inner edges, crept her fingers inside. It felt waxed and contained small hard kernels about the size of raisins. She pinched one between her fingers, brought it up and out of the bag, smelled it. It smelled familiar, like dog food. Then she heard a low, rumbling growl.

***

Rand's eyes opened, but he quickly closed them, afraid they might burn. The sun blazed and sent shafts of white light piercing. *Where am I?* He rolled onto his side and retched.

Opening his eyes again, he appraised the scorched rock and mud bank with a ground level, distorted view, heard water swirling past, near his ears. *The bank of a river, yes, oh yes. I swam the river.* He gagged, like the dry heaves of a tortured drunk. He had, once or twice, been terribly inebriated, but this seemed different to him, like his body and brain were shriveling. His muscles twitched and ached as if they had experienced intense stress. His senses felt dulled, like in a fog. Lying there was all he could do; just the thought of rising made him gag.

Everything faded again, to an uneasy sleep, but in the fitful gyrations of his mind he felt his skin burning. He could hear it sizzling. It smelled like rubber on an open fire. His eyes went wide, he rolled onto his side, felt his face desperately to see if he was burned.

But it was, in fact, night. *Oh, only a nightmare. Only a... what's happening to me?*

***

The urge to flee came as persuasively to Kera as her decision to stand up to Rand. But as her muscles tensed and her conscious mind prepared her to run, something happened. A voice inside her head said, *No. Hold your ground. Don't run.*

Kera froze. Every hair, every inch of skin, every nerve and molecule became a sensor to predict the intention of the beast that growled in the dark before her. Images of yellow fangs and frothy spittle filled her mind.

"It's okay." Her soft voice surprised her. "I am not here to hurt you." She spoke from instinct. "I need your help."

She was rewarded with a savage crescendo of barking—the fang-baring, slavering warning of a certified attack dog. She sensed it stood no more than three feet away, now, though the first growl had been more distant. It had approached silently and stealthily. Kera suddenly realized she could feel its energy on her clothing, like a vibration. Her instincts now defined this as an emergency situation. *Strike*, the voice inside her head said, *strike fast and hard.*

She kicked her foot upward as she had with the wild-haired man. That seemed to be her system's new concept of physical defense. The move carried momentum if not bulk. Her foot smacked something solid. She heard the pop of jaws and teeth coming together, a surprised whimper, then growling—almost more like grumbling—which receded along with soft, hurried footfalls on the floor of the barn. She was again alone.

Well, maybe not a certified attack dog.

Everything quieted. Kera realized that her body, while not tense, stood taught and aware. Her entire being, tuned as an antennae. A feeling of joy permeated her. For a moment she had thought a mauling was inescapable, but that had suddenly turned into victory. With swift, instinctive action, *she* had turned it into victory.

The emotion and image of her attack on the wild-haired man revisited her. The energy that had commanded her then agreed with the energy she now felt. It seemed simultaneously unexplainable and right, true, mysterious.

The dog's bark had been loud, and so she began slowly backing out the way she had come, but stopped, filled the pockets of her jeans with dog food, then continued.

In the drainage the urge to run welled up within her. She forced it down and walked back to the horse. Her hunger pangs had subsided. She felt clear. After untying the horse from the fence post she led it across the road and into a group of trees she had noticed earlier, pulled a few kernels of the dog food from her pocket, smelled them, and stuck one into her mouth.

***

Rand felt better. This time when he awakened the bright light of day beat down with reality. In time he managed to sit up. After rinsing his face and hair in the river, he prepared to drink when it dawned on him that possibly the river water caused his sudden and mysterious illness. He sensed he had experienced a type of seizure, accompanied by nightmares, even hallucinations.

While on his knees, peering into the tempting wetness, he heard the sound of a vehicle approaching. It hadn't dawned on him that a road existed along this shore also, and before he could react, a green pick-up truck appeared above him and not fifty feet away. It looked old, but in good shape, and as it passed he made out a man with a cowboy hat driving. The man looked over, looked down, and his eyes met Rand's. The truck zoomed out of sight.

Rand's pulse quickened, which made his tender stomach gurgle. He stood slowly and wobbled insecurely. The cowboy had looked harmless, but he didn't want any confrontations. Besides, a cowboy could be a law enforcement agent as easily as the next person. Rand shuffled over toward a tree, even as he heard the whining sound of the vehicle returning in reverse gear.

Undernourished, sick, slow moving, he didn't make it to cover, but was caught in full view when the truck ground to a halt on the gravel roadway. The cowboy eyed him through the dust and rolled down the window. "You all right?" he called.

Rand went to speak, but his throat seized and he coughed instead. He saw the cowboy's lips moving, heard him talking quietly, realized that someone sat on the passenger side, but couldn't see that person. Then the passenger door opened and a man came out, dropped his elbows over the edge of the truck bed, and looked down at Rand. "I remember you."

Rand took a moment to recall anything familiar in the cowboy's face, then his memory whirled into gear and he recognized the man that talked with Kera in the restaurant in Ohio; the one he'd spitefully named Buck, with, "The greasy cap and the turd stuck behind his lip." Rand raised one hand in a feeble wave, held his throat with the other, tried desperately to speak. He couldn't. It felt like his throat was burned on the inside.

The driver got out of the truck and side stepped down the bank to Rand. He was a stocky man, thick arms, meaty face. "Can you talk?" he asked.

Rand pointed at his throat, shook his head.

"Come on to the truck. I got some coffee. Wet yer whistle."

Rand nodded. Anything wet sounded great—coffee represented a dream come true. The man held Rand's elbow tightly as they climbed up to the road.

All the while, the other cowboy, Buck, leaned on the truck, watching with a cutting glare. The driver propped Rand up on the opposite side of the truck from Buck, reached into the cab, and brought forth a thermos.

"Say!" Buck said.

Rand looked at him.

"You're a man without a watch!" He had replaced the glare with a grin.

Rand's eyes tightened a notch.

Buck clucked his tongue against the top of his mouth, "Tough loss."

The driver held out a cup of coffee. Rand gulped it down. The warm wetness opened his throat and softened the burning. He nodded and handed the empty cup back to the driver. "More?" the man asked. Rand nodded. The two cowboys stood silently as Rand drank, coughed up some phlegm, spit it out, and said thanks in a scratchy voice.

"We saw you at Byways," the driver said.

"The truck stop," Rand added.

The driver nodded and watched him, standing there with his big hand on the door.   Rand saw the tattoo on his right forearm that read U.S.M.C..   The man's big brown eyes seemed too gentle for a Marine, especially when he said, "You look like you've had a rough time."

"Yeah," Buck chided, "you looked a whole lot cockier awhile back."

Rand lacked the energy to unravel the entire story.   "I drank from the river and I think it made me sick. I nearly drowned coming across."

"You swam that river?" Buck asked.

"Pretty much."

"Damn, Mister, that's the Mississippi!"   The driver chuckled in a rumbling sort of way.

Rand turned and looked at the Big Muddy.   In the bright morning light it seemed wider than it had last night, but still less impressive than its reputation. "They ought to clean the thing up. Whatever's in it damn near killed me."

"Where's yer wife?" Buck asked.

"I wish I knew."   Rand looked at him, but he didn't want to. Buck held his head tilted down, glaring at Rand from just beneath the brim of his hat. Rand felt in no shape to withstand this man's questions. "We were assaulted by some people after... they took her and left me."

With that, Buck came around the rear of the truck.   In a calm but curious voice the driver asked, "Rebels?"

"Yeah, I guess you'd call them that." Rand looked at him. There was no telling who these guys were, or who they sided with.

"Mister," Buck started, "I may not like you, but we aren't going to hurt you."

Rand felt such relief that his body couldn't hold up anymore and he sank down onto the ground, sat there with his head bowed. Both men came down on their haunches.

"I thank you... I didn't know it at first, if they were rebels, but I later saw them wipe out a National Guard unit."

"What do you mean, wipe out?" the driver asked.

"Not a single person left alive."

Rand heard the man growl, and saw his hand squeeze shut. "How many?"

"Twenty, maybe more."

"Fuckin' traitors! This is treason. Line'm up and shoot'm!"   The driver rose and banged his fist on the door.

Buck said to the driver, "We can talk more about this, but we've got to get goin', if we're going to find gas."

"Yeah." The driver clenched his jaw and looked to Rand. "Where yuh trying to get?"

"Washington State."

"Well, yer a long hop from there, but we can get you part way. And from the looks of yuh, yuh ought to take the ride."

"Yes. Of course," Rand said. He saw a look on Buck's face, though, and could tell Buck wanted little of him. Still, any ride, for any length, would help get him closer and make up valuable time. "Oh," Rand looked back down the slope, "I forgot my camera."

The driver headed back down and grabbed the bag.

"Are we still under martial law?" Rand asked.

"Yup." Buck said.

The driver had him slide in between the two of them. "We're long haul drivers, but when we saw this thing getting worse we decided to buy this pickup and make a run back home." They both had thick legs and broad shoulders. Space was limited, but sitting on the soft seat felt good. The driver reached a wide palm out in front of him, "My name's Walt."

"Hi, Walt. I'm Rand."

They shook hands and Walt said, "Pleased to meet you. That's Buck."

Before thinking to check himself, Rand said, "No way!" with a look of delight on his face.

Buck glared. "What the hell?"

"No. I mean, that's great. Great name." Rand looked straight ahead, feeling Buck's eyes on him.

Being in the truck, moving fast down the back roads, two tough-enough hombres aside him, Rand felt better than he had in days. Within five minutes his head tilted and he fell asleep.

Chapter 17

Kera dug her heels into the flanks of the horse. It jumped forward, almost spilling her, then bolted into a run. She grasped the rope, squeezed the barrel-like body with her legs, bent down low and thrust herself forward along the withers and neck of the horse. "Go, Friend! Go!" She wasn't certain she could hold on, but it was a chance she had to take, anything, anything to keep the vehicle from catching them.

It had come suddenly upon her and now barreled down the road in pursuit. Everything happened so fast she hadn't even clearly seen it. She'd been riding along, dozing actually, and suddenly it materialized behind her. Racing along on the horse, she could feel the vehicle gaining, but a fence paralleled the road and prevented her from leaving it.

She glanced back. The vehicle roared to within four or five car lengths. Whoever it was, they could do anything to her. She felt completely vulnerable. Again she looked and saw that it was a dark blue SUV, not unlike the Excursion she had at home. She did a swift double take. The passenger window was down and a person hung out, aiming a large barreled weapon at her.

Kera held herself as low as she could on the horse. Fear tightened her every muscle. *Think, Kera, think!* The ground along the road leveled out. She judged the height of the fence. Little choice remained—try to make the jump, or get shot.

She leaned toward the fence, pulled the rope in that direction. "Jump it, Friend, come on!"

The horse turned toward it, never broke its powerful, machine-like stride. The fence was barbed-wire, about four feet high. She wondered if Friend saw it. Kera held on and closed her eyes. "Jump it, Friend! Go!"

Kera felt the animal gather itself, heard a loud grunt... and everything went soft... like flying... and in her mind Kera pictured the horse with her on top it, sailing into the blue of the sky and never coming to ground again.

But with a heavy jolt they did. There was another grunt and a great exhalation of air. Kera lost her leg hold on the horse. The momentum of the jump carried her body straight forward, into the air, and head first onto the ground. Her neck twisted, the side of her face blazed a trail in the dirt, her shoulders jammed backward, and the heels of her hands scraped along the dry earth. Dust flew as she came to a stop, chest to ground and backside in the air.

She rolled over and laid flat. It felt the same as when the wild-haired man hit her—as if her body somehow catapulted into the future and must now wait for her mind to catch up. Pain blazed along the side of her neck.

Suddenly, she remembered the vehicle. It had stopped along the fence, thirty feet away. Two men watched her, working their door handles.

The open field surrounded them, but the horse stood twenty feet away, eyeing her, with dense trees a distance behind it. She struggled to rise. Friend stepped toward her, and she limped over, grabbed the rope, hauled herself up and on, peered around behind her. The men were out of the big SUV and one had the barrel aimed at her. She turned, squeezed her heels into the responsive, beautiful beast, hunkered down, and prayed that she would never hear a shot, that no bullet would find Friend, her savior.

She heard a shout from behind as they burst into the forest. Kera clung low until they came to an open place where she could straighten, still being protected by trees behind them. The wind brushed her hair back. She raised her bloodied hand upward and it became a fist. She smiled at the sky. "Yes!" she yelled, and it was long and drawn-out and came from a buried, put away place within her. And then she slowed the horse, put her lips to its neck, smelled its sweet smell, and kissed its warm hair.

She didn't know how far the forest ran, but thought they headed more north than northwest, the direction she needed to hold. Still, it didn't concern her to head through the forest and find another country road and swing back on course. She slowed to a walk and let the horse catch its breath. Having nothing to drink since the day before, she wanted to ride until they found a creek or some other source of water.

Very soon, they came to another road. She stopped the horse well inside the trees and peered through branches at the splotches of gravel. She had learned to sit and listen before moving into the open. Other than the chirp of crickets and birds, she heard only silence, so she pressed the horse with her legs and moved forward through the trees. Squeezing through thick branches, they came to the cleared edges of the gravel road. She stopped the horse again and looked up and down the road. The blue vehicle headed toward them. It accelerated, throwing off a plume of dust not two hundred yards away.

Kera squeezed and Friend bolted across the road and into a dense thicket of broadleaf trees. They crashed into a tangle, a maze of heavy fallen branches and collapsed trunks. Hooves churned and slipped on moist ground as the horse drove forward. The whips of tree branches slapped them across their faces and the horse stumbled, lurched, stumbled again, trying desperately to make way through the leg-breaking deadfall and maintain the speed Kera called for.

Through the occasional hole in the wall of vegetation Kera could see the vehicle traveling beside them, off her left shoulder. Fighting to stay mounted, she searched the area for a sign of a clearing, an avenue out and away from the vehicle. Her arms bled as did the skin on the horse's face. She couldn't stand to see Friend injured, but she was catching glimpses of the heavy round barrel aimed at them. *Who are they?*

She dug in her heels and pulled back hard on the rope. The horse halted and quivered, snorted loudly. Kera heard the vehicle passing them, then braking hard on the road. She spotted a clearing off to the right, leaned that way, and squeezed the horse with her legs. It broke in the new direction and plunged through the tangle.

They broke free of the trees and the horse opened its stride in fields of shoulder-high corn. But just as fast, the vehicle raced into view, paralleling her on unseen roads. With the hills and high corn, she could not tell where roads ran and where they did not. They raced straight cross-country, but it was a long way to any cover, or any avenue to sure freedom. Kera could see the SUV would head her off at the end of the field. She slowed the horse, but there seemed no way to turn to give them distance from the vehicle, without running in a futile circle. She felt the heat of panic surge through her veins and stiffen her. Her only choice was to reverse course and head back into the brutal maze of trees.

Her anger grew toward rage. No matter where she ran, someone would come for her, some damned evil would find her, wanting to control her, brutalize her, keep her from her children. And now it would hunt this beautiful creature, this innocent animal that helped her, that somehow sensed her needs and worked selflessly to fulfill them.

Anger burned in Kera and she reined the horse into a jumble of legs and cornstalks and dirt flying. She leaped off and ran toward the fence, toward the road, toward the vehicle as it closed in on them. She took hold of a post and vaulted herself over the fence, landing on her feet as if not an inch of her bled or hurt. Charging into the road, her eyes set hot on the vehicle, the veins in her neck bulged. The vehicle slid to a stop not ten feet from her.

She screamed, "What? What do you want? Do you want me?" She confronted the vehicle with her fists tight in front of her, with blood streaming down her arms and cheeks.

The wide barrel pointed at her out the passenger side window, but she didn't care. Then, she thought, it didn't look much like a barrel at all. It looked like a lens—the sun-shaded lens of a video camera. She saw a man with his eye to the viewfinder. The anger dropped sharply into befuddlement and Kera's stance softened. Her mouth fell open. *What?*

The driver's door opened and a man climbed out. "Hello." He smiled. "We're sorry to bother you. We seem to have startled you."

Kera looked at his hair, his face, his safari-like field shirt, and thought *News Correspondent.* She still hadn't moved, but stood with her chest heaving and hands out before her, trying desperately to understand.

"We saw you back there and wanted to ask a few questions. You know, there aren't many people out riding horses lately. Not with martial law declared. We're not even cleared to roam about as we are." He stepped forward suddenly and approached Kera, raised his hand. "I'm sorry. I'm Garret Hunter. The journalist."

The anger surged back into Kera. "You fool! You chased us like that because you thought we looked interesting and might make a good story?" She was screaming and shaking down to her shoes. They said nothing, but stood there with apologies on their faces.

Kera turned and strode off the road. "We could have been killed!" She took hold of the post, grappled with the fence and fell over it, picked herself up, marched to the horse and prepared to mount. Then she paused. One of the horse's eyelids was cut, it had a knotty bruise on the center of its face, and its muzzle and lips bled in numerous places. It breathed in short, hot blasts. Kera took its face between her hands. It didn't look serious, but the realization that she had caused injury to the horse, that more pain had occurred associated with her, filled her with guilt and sadness. Friend needed a drink and a rest.

She turned to look for a tree or a creek, but saw instead Garret Hunter standing in the road looking sheepish. The cameraman had come silently from the van and was using the fence post as a brace for his camera while he photographed her.

"Turn that camera off!" she yelled.

The cameraman lifted his eye from the viewfinder and lowered the camera. "Sorry."

"Sorry? What is it with you people?" She felt overwhelmed and her hands came up and cradled her face fleetingly, "Don't you understand?" Then one hand covered her mouth as her eyes went wet and wide, staring at the men.

The two men shifted, stood silent.

Kera looked away from them, looked at Friend. "Do you understand that you nearly killed this animal?" She rubbed the sides of the sweating horse, picked a leaf from its hair.

She glared at the men, feeling angry, embarrassed, confused. The two men looked at each other but did not withdraw or speak. Garret Hunter was tanned, with black hair and deep brown eyes. He wasn't as tall as the photographer, who wore a vest with numerous bulging pockets, stood well over six feet, and was nearly bald. Both of them looked tired and a bit haggard. "Look," Garret said, "we didn't mean any harm. As soon as we saw you, you took off, and we just wanted to see what you were up to."

With trembling fingers, Kera wiped at the blood running down her cheek. "I have nothing to say."

"We have a medical kit in the truck," the cameraman said. "That cut on your lip could use some treatment."

"No, I have to get going. I just want to be left alone." She turned to pull herself onto the horse.

"You look like you could use a rest, maybe some food." He just stood there in the road and sounded as if he were pleading with her.

Kera paused and looked at them. "You have food?"

"Yes. Turkey sandwiches, fruit."

Kera's mouth watered. "Really?" she asked.

The photographer added, "Yes, and chocolate chip cookies. Homemade." He grinned and his eyes twinkled. "And I think we have a couple carrots left, for your horse."

***

Rand's eyes opened. He felt lost in time, had no idea where he was. Then he looked up and saw Walt squinting at him. Walt put his finger to his mouth, "Shhhh," and he pointed. Rand turned his head just as a loud BANG went off next to him. He jumped and sat straight up, his heart skipping.

Buck opened the door of the truck and ran out into a field, carrying a long barreled revolver.

"Got'm," Walt said. "Good sized pheasant. We'll stop soon and cook'm up."

Buck grabbed the flopping brightly colored bird off the ground, held it by the head, and spun it around. The bird stilled. Buck raced back to the truck, got in, and slammed the door. "You ever eat pheasant, city boy?"

Rand had it once, cooked with a peach glaze in a New York restaurant, the name of which he could no longer remember. The bird twitched again on the floor of the cab and a drop of blood formed on the tip of its beak. "Sure," he mumbled, rubbing his eyes, thinking of the field full of dead and bloody soldiers.

Buck slipped the revolver under the seat. "I bet you have."

They headed down the blacktop road and Rand gazed at corn and wheat fields as far as he could see. "Where are we?"

"A little north of Cedar Rapids, Iowa," Walt said.

Rand tried to picture the map of the United States. He didn't think he had made it even half way to Washington State. "And where did you guys say you were headed?"

"South Dakota. Our families are there. We're trying to get back home," Walt said.

"And that's moving me straight toward Washington State, right?"

"Pretty much."

"Pretty much? I mean, I'm heading for the northeast part of Washington State. We're going toward that, right?"

"Look," Buck said, "we'll get you as close as we can. You'll be a lot closer than you are right now."

What Buck said came out polite enough, but Rand could hear the obvious edge. Buck was a typical macho country shit kicker. "You don't like me much, do you, Buck?"

Buck shifted his eyes onto Rand. He had the window rolled down, his elbow on the bottom of the frame and his hand clasped about the top.

The dark hair on his arms whipped around in the wind and under it his skin shined, his face too. He had clear dark eyes and rich black hair, and Rand looked at him and realized how he himself must appear dirty and disheveled. He hadn't combed his hair in days, let alone washed it. He was bruised and cut, his clothes despicable, and knew he smelled of body odor and mucky river water. One week ago he would have felt a strong pang of regret that this man looked more together than he did, but, right now, he couldn't have cared less. All he wanted was to find himself in Washington.

"Well," Buck finally answered, "I guess you could say that."

Rand drew himself in. He'd known Buck's answer before he heard it. His first reaction was to say, *I don't like you, either.* But he didn't speak it. Instead, he wondered why? Why did Buck not like him when they had barely shared a word? *Why don't I like Buck?* It made him nervous to consider asking the question, but he found that he really wanted to know. He had met people on this journey that ended up dead moments later, gone forever from the face of Earth, and it seemed to him now a ridiculous frame of mind, not liking each other without knowing each other.

"Why?" Rand asked and almost glanced away, out the window, but stopped himself and peered straight at Buck.

Buck cracked a smile, looked away, ran his hand down along the window frame to the side view mirror. "'Cause I'm tired of you city boys looking down on us country folk, thinkin' you can tell us how to live, as if we ain't figured it out for our own selves."

Rand thought about that. "Well, I'm tired of you country people thinking you're the salt of the earth, like you're something special because you have dirt under your fingernails."

"Special? I would say that you and yer paid-for politicians are the ones who appraise yerselves as special."

"So you're figuring that city folks and politicians are one in the same?"

"City folks tend to have more money, and since money to a politician is like slop to a hog, well, there you are."

"City folks don't tend to have more money."

"I saw that car yer driving. You didn't win that in no quick pick, did you?"

"Well, that car may have been a foolish mistake, but I worked hard for the money to buy that car."

"I am sure a that. City people're always running around in circles. Hell, they run each other over. Shoot each other 'tween cars. Maybe you'd all be better off home sometimes."

Rand thought about that, too. He could not argue. He had come to this same conclusion on his own just a day ago. The time he had spent working for that car he could have spent with Kera and Alissa and Andrew. "You're right, Buck. Now, where is it you're going?"

"Home," Buck said, then he snapped another look at Rand and his face showed how he understood... the truth had just been leveled on him as well. Rand smiled and Buck nodded, "You're right yourself."

"I'll tell you somethin'," Walt started. "I learned in the Corps that it ain't whether you're rich or you're poor, black or white or silver, it's decidin' whose team you're a part of and then holdin' up your end. It's learnin' that what you want, what you think you need, is not as important as what the team needs. That's what the people who started this country understood."

For a few minutes they rode without speaking. Rand thought about what the cowboys had said, thought about the start of a country and all the changes that must have taken place over the decades, the centuries, thought about how the fields of corn and wheat seemed to go on forever around them, like a mirage of sameness and stability. *Maybe these golden fields of grain will never again be part of a United States of America, but they are as lovely and inspiring as anything I can imagine.*

The truck zoomed along one blacktop or gravel road after another and the open fields rarely broke, except for a house here, a pond there, a faded sign for some small town they never saw. *It's big!* This America he barely knew was a giant place full of all sorts of people who had all sorts of considerations. *It's magnificent.*

He reached down on the floorboard and pulled the camera bag onto his lap. "You guys mind if I take a photograph of you?" They both angled a look at him, at the bag. "I'm a photographer. I—I just think I ought to capture some of these images as I go."

"Guess I don't mind."

"Naw, go ahead."

Rand shot their faces as they rode along. He shot their hands and their hats. They threatened to throw him out if he didn't soon stop. He wished he had brought a wide-angle lens, but made the fifty millimeter work. It was a classic old truck, and Walt and Buck, thick jawed, classic men. No matter how he hated to admit it, their workingman breed ran back a long distance further than his. They exemplified a time in American history, owned a block in the foundation of the country. *American men. Men heading home to the people they love.*

"You worried about your wife?" Buck suddenly asked.

Rand lowered the camera. Those five simple words spoken from the lips of another had an unexpected effect on him. His chest sucked in, his shoulders drooped, his eyes turned red. The camera came to rest on the seat. He looked at Buck and wanted to speak, wanted to tell the man all the things he had done wrong and how he prayed to have the chance to change it back around, but he couldn't. It would bring him too close to losing control. And one thing remained certain: though he had all at once realized a love for these countrymen of his, he sure as hell didn't want them to see him crying. He nodded instead.

"I've got a sense," Buck said, "she'll be all right. There's somethin' of a straight shooter in that woman." He thumped a thick knuckle against Rand's knee and Walt added, "That's for damn sure."

***

Kera fed the last of the carrot to the horse and it crunched loudly and flapped its lips, causing her to laugh. It lowered its head and sucked water from a small pond.

When Kera had agreed to eat with the men, she mentioned that Friend needed water and a shady place to rest. The photographer, Nat, had noticed the pond along the road near where she had disappeared into the tangle of trees. They went back and found it, as well as plenty of shade beneath tall cottonwoods.

The men made her nervous and she couldn't help it.

They first insisted on producing a kit with which to treat her wounds. Nat quietly cleaned her face, applied an antibacterial ointment, and lightly touched the puffy purple contusions left by the wild-haired man below her right eye, on her jaw and the backs of her hands. He studied Kera, but didn't ask questions. Then she led the horse to water.

She now returned hesitantly to the truck which the men had pulled off the road and into cool shade. Nat untied a cord holding down the contents of a rooftop luggage rack, and lifted off a small, foldable lawn chair, opened it, set it down. "Have a rest," he said, smiling at Kera.

"Thanks, but I'll stand for a little. I've been sitting quite a lot." She imagined her sore behind red as a beet.

He pulled down another chair and set it up next to the first. Garret had the rear gate swung open and was sitting on the edge of the cargo area, his legs hanging out. From a large cooler he produced turkey, bread, lettuce, and cheese. He set down a knife and held out two bottles, ice water dripping off them. "Kera, would you like orange juice or guava?"

"Wow." Her mouth watered. "Either would be wonderful."

"Your choice."

"I'll take the guava." She opened it, swallowed a couple gulps, and the flavor sprang to life on her dry tongue.

"Cheese and lettuce on the turkey?"

"Please." The sight of the fixings made her stomach growl.

Garret talked as he piled ingredients onto bread, "So, I can't help my curiosity. How is it that we have found you riding your horse through rural Iowa while martial law has been instituted?"

"Martial law? You mean we aren't allowed in the streets?"

He looked at her with surprise. "Exactly, not anyone other than military and police personnel and emergency crews. We're totally beside the law ourselves, Nat and I. At least until, as the President says, the full scope of this fanatical uprising is evaluated."

"Is that what they're calling it, a fanatical uprising?"

"That's what the administration is calling it. Everyone else knows it for what it is: a revolution."

"I haven't heard the latest news. I've been on the move."

"Well, as crazy as it sounds, it may have initially been a coincidence. Certain groups, the Liberty Fighters from the Southeast; the Patriots, pretty much a national group; and the American Liberation Alliance, apparently from the West Coast, all had planned attacks, perhaps to make statements toward change, and, as it turned out, for the same couple days. I won't bore you with details, but suffice it to say, none of the plans would have created a national breakdown on its own. Together they started a chain reaction. It appeared as an immense strike against the government and every person in the country who had harbored grievous thoughts about Uncle Sam came out their back door with gun in hand."

"Is there any sign the Middle East may be involved?" Kera asked.

"That's what was widely considered, but so far it seems like a true inside job. There are rumors floating around that other countries are interested in our problems, which adds a very scary element, but no one knows anything for certain because communications are practically nonexistent in the traditional sense."

"What's the condition of the government? I mean, are we able to fight them off?"

Garret handed her a sandwich wrapped in a paper towel. "Well," he handed another to Nat, who took it and sat on one of the chairs, "we have a real war going on here. The government would seem to have the military strength to overwhelm opposition forces, but that's not what's happening, and it's really not the only issue. This has become, in a very short time, quite a popular movement. There are surprising numbers of Americans siding with the idea of a New Rule, so to speak. And, of course, plenty of people have taken up weapons to assist the government."

"What do you mean, a new rule?"

"Some new form of government. It's too early to see what anyone is really talking about, especially since there has been no collective voice from the revolutionaries, but in general people seem extremely fed up with the way things were being run. No surprise there."

"Are the phones back up?"

"No. That's no use at all. Communication systems were linked together, into large backbones of hardware and software alike. One of the groups employed hackers who figured out how to scramble those backbones and along with a few well placed bombings it has completely frazzled the entire system. The military has figured out how to communicate through their satellites and such, but for the populace they're saying it could take weeks."

Kera took a bite of her sandwich. She had gone less than two days without food, but it felt as if her entire system had become a stomach. She tried to maintain a modicum of manners, but filled her mouth, chewed little, and swallowed the sandwich in short order. She followed it with a final swallow of the guava, and, to her horror, belched loudly. "Oh," she covered her mouth, "Excuse me!"

Both of the men looked at her and smiled. She wiped her mouth with the paper towel and moved slowly over to the chair in stiff-legged, sore-seated fashion, then eased herself into it. "So, what are you two doing out here?" Her mind was turning back to the concept of no communications for weeks.

"Nat and I work freelance. Other journalists seem to be hanging out in DC, or other major points, like the Pentagon. We felt the real story was out here, in the countryside, the small towns."

Kera started to feel drowsy. She sat in the chair, propping herself up with elbows on armrests, fighting to keep alert around the men, to keep thinking. Nat wolfed down his sandwich. She said, "You were hungry too."

He chewed a couple more times on an enormous mouthful, and said, "Yes."

Kera watched him. His eyes looked the same as Rand's. Not in color, not in size, but in something else; the way they seemed to penetrate what they looked at. Photographer's eyes, she thought.

"You look sleepy," he said.

"Yes, I've just been... going and going."

"I know, us too. We stayed in a hotel the other night. Can you believe it? A hard bed with clean sheets. They had portable lights and even a bit of hot water. And armed guards!"

Kera imagined how that would feel, especially a hot soaking bath. A short time ago, she'd been home, with her luxuries, but it seemed like a long, long while and a great distance.

Nat said, "I'm sorry! That's not fair to tell you that. Maybe you haven't had those things in too long."

"No, I haven't. I—"

Nat's mouth curved into a face-filling smile and he held up his hand to stop her. He looked over at Garret. "Garret, what do you think? Does she deserve some special treatment?"

His words increased her anxiety. Kera didn't want any special treatment, didn't know what that meant. She straightened and watched the men closely.

"Most assuredly," Garret answered.

Nat turned back to her. "How would you like a hot shower?"

Kera looked from him to Garret, who stood beaming, chomping on a big bite of sandwich. She asked, "What do you mean?"

"We have a sun shower, one of those black bags that you fill and let the sun heat up. It's been in the luggage rack, getting warm."

"I've never heard of that."

"You just hang it from a tree and open the valve. They're great." Nat was smiling, wiping his mouth, getting up and moving to the truck. "Let me get it down. We both used it yesterday. There's enough water for two people, but you can have it all."

He brought the bag down and Kera saw it as described—a big black bag of water with a tube coming out the bottom. He showed her the valve and how to turn it. "I'll tell you what, we can find a nice private place over there behind the trees and you can take a shower. I have another pair of pants and a T-shirt you can wear. When you come back you can rinse out your clothes in the pond there. It looks pretty clear. In this heat they should dry in an hour."

Kera felt her stomach twist. She had only known the men for an hour. They treated her well so far, but, try as she might, she couldn't feel comfortable with them. Out on her own she started to feel better, stronger, but being within arms reach of strange men had a powerful, undeniable effect.

Still, she hadn't showered since before the final attack of the wild-haired man, since before riding the horse and sweating for days, sleeping on the ground, falling off the horse and scraping her face to a bloody wound. She felt terrible and now, with the option of getting all that filth off her, the offer seemed too wonderful, too necessary to turn down.

"Do you have soap?" She asked.

"I'll give you a fresh bar," Nat answered. His smile sort of folded around his warm face, around those seer's eyes. A lean, fluid body carried him smoothly, easily—a relaxed and comfortable man.

"Thanks!" Kera said, and the anticipation of hot water already had her skin tingling.

Nat found a towel, the extra clothes, and handed them to her with a new bar of soap. He asked her to pick a place and followed her through the dense trees around the pond. Every nerve in her body remained at attention. Out here, away from any town, any people, these men could do whatever they liked and no one would ever know. Except for the camera, she had no proof they were journalists.

She became trapped between seeing the forest as a place of privacy, or molestation. Her mind froze as she continued through the tangle of trees and brush, further and further away from the truck, into the darkness of thick, damp forest, listening to the footfalls of Nat behind her, trying desperately to build courage.

"Well, you certainly want to do this alone," Nat said.

Kera spun around, "Yes," she exclaimed with a wide-eyed glare, "I do!"

Nat's smile shrank. He stood watching her with uncertainty. "Look," he said, slowly, calmly, "I don't know what you've been through. And I'm not asking. But I can tell by looking that it's been a lot. We don't want to cause you any pain. We would like to help."

Kera watched him, listened. His eyes and his words seemed so tranquil.

He continued, "I'm going to hang this bag on that big tree, right there. I want you to enjoy this shower and know that Garret and I will be right over by the truck, waiting for you to come back."

He hung the shower quickly and smiled at her before walking silently away. She watched him go. He never looked back, never paused, just disappeared through the trees.

It grew quiet. She stood surrounded by forest and took a deep breath, let it go. A slow knocking sounded and she looked up and spied a woodpecker the size of a small dog, with white and red markings, working the pulpy flesh of a cottonwood. It banged the tree harder and faster, like a jackhammer, with its beak, with its head, really. Bits of wood rained down. Kera watched, impressed. How tough such birds must be, how persistent to get what they need. The big beautiful bird flew off through the trees with undulating flaps of its broad wings.

It quieted again, became so quiet she felt utterly alone. She had not tied the horse, had decided to let it roam free, believe hopefully that it would not leave her. In that she felt secure. Besides, it had plentiful grass, shade, and water.

She stepped around behind the tree and touched the top button of her blouse—the top *remaining* button. Two buttons had been torn off when....

She looked up at the blue sky above the green leaves of the trees. She leaned back against the trunk, dropped her hands to her side, and worked her fingers into the deep heavy grooves in the bark and squeezed, harder, squeezed. Her head was back and resting against the broad solidity and she looked up at the thick, truly massive branches above her. She wondered how old a tree such as this tree might be. *One hundred years, possibly more? What troubles has it seen? What storms has it weathered?* She turned and faced the body of the forest ancient, wrapped her arms around it, such strength and nobility. She had escaped through a forest, was now cloaked by a forest, since her childhood walks with her father had spent too little time in the company of trees. Looking closer she thought she recognized a type of cedar, a juniper, certainly the cottonwood.

After a few moments Kera opened her blouse, removed it slowly, hung it on a branch, pulled away the jeans all caked with grime, stood and let the air soothe her skin, tickle the hair along her arms, her back, and legs. *Yuck, look at all that hair on my legs!*

She turned the valve and sun-heated water ran over her head, off the edges of her lips, down along her curves, off her nipples, wetted the leafy ground around her feet. It felt as if she would explode with sensation. She grabbed the bar of soap, ripped off the wrapper, ran the bar everywhere around her body, upon her skin, over and through her hair. The soap would not be good for her hair. She couldn't care less. She worked with her fingers, raked at her flesh, rubbed so hard her skin turned red and began to glisten.

She felt amazed at how many places felt sore, bruised, torn. She worked the soap into them, let the pain run its course, focused hot water onto them. She felt the darkness, the disgust, the fear and hate take one step backward, and her old self, some new self, took one bold step to the front.

Chapter 18

With the onset of night Walt pulled the truck around behind an old abandoned barn. Though they all wanted to keep going, they decided a short break for a stretch, some food, and even a little sleep seemed a good idea if they wanted to remain alert. Buck had a small concealed fire of barn boards crackling before Rand finished peeing in a cornfield that ran behind the barn and off into the darkness. The three sat on tractor tires rolled over next to the fire, watched the pheasant and rabbit Buck shot turn brown over the flame.

They had driven all day—left, right, left again, right again— zigzagging along the back roads of Iowa, routes too numerous to count, past towns with names like Dysart, Popejoy, Mallard, and Primghar. Most towns seemed built around a central square anchored by a courthouse. They represented islands in a sea of corn and—as the cowboys told him—bean fields. Rand had never considered so many miniature communities situated along such meandering dusty roads. He had never imagined the endless reaches of farmland, or how quickly he would become accustomed to the constant sweet smell of manure. What he wanted all the sudden was to sit at a few kitchen tables, eat with the locals, listen to their stories. He wanted to get to know these people and what they believed in, to take photographs of them against the broad plain on which they grew the sustenance of the world. It would feel good to gain an understanding of the country, the countrymen, but only if he had his family with him. Together they could rediscover the meaning of the word, America.

As they passed through these seemingly abandoned towns, Rand saw more VFWs and Grange Halls, Foreign Legions, most all dilapidated, for sale. He had never visited such places, but Walt explained their intent: they provided a gathering spot for people to meet, to talk about life, country, society. At one time they enjoyed broad popularity with mainstream citizens who often volunteered in their upkeep and operation. Now most stood neglected and empty. Rand wondered why... but then he knew: as certainly as his life had focused on the pursuit of profit and the attainment of material, so had the lives of countless others. It had become the American way—the ONLY American way. The average citizen would not choose to spend personal time contributing to the upkeep and operation of a gathering place without material payback. Rand could not remember ever volunteering a day in his life.

At one point during the day the men found a pickup parked in a field of growing corn. Buck and Walt had watched the news before TV faltered, and knew that gas stations in cities had become the focal point for violence. Walt siphoned gas out of the truck, while Rand and Buck watched the roads from the top of a knoll, and they drove off in fifteen minutes.

In the firelight behind the barn, Buck poked the sizzling pheasant with a finger. "What I was seeing on the news," he said, "is that it ain't only what the rebels are doing—"

"Traitors," Walt interjected.

"All right," Buck responded. "It's not only the traitors, but everyday folks. Hell, in Columbus, a group of armed citizens stormed the capitol building and pulled some senator out into the street and tarred and feathered him. Tarred and feathered!"

"Why?" Rand asked.

"He wrote a law for gun control that went against the constitution."

"It seems to me that guns are a big part of our problem," Rand said.

Buck looked over at Walt and Walt looked back at Buck. "Whose problem?" Buck asked Rand.

"This country's."

"Guns ain't the problem," Walt said.

Rand rubbed his finger along his head where he had been hit some days ago with the revolver. "I might not be sitting here now if I hadn't been clobbered by a gorilla with a pistol."

Walt poked a stick at the pheasant. "You sure wouldn't be looking at this fine piece a meat here, neither, if it weren't for a gun." He had run some wire through the bird and wrapped the ends of it around two sticks driven into the ground on either side of the fire. "And like you just said, it wasn't the handgun that clobbered you, it was the gorilla. There's some people shouldn't have guns. We have laws that state that and they need to be enforced. But them liberal lawyers and judges keep on making it harder for us law-abiding citizens to keep our law-abiding rights."

Buck added, "And, I'd like to see the faces right now of all those people who said we don't need guns. That's a part of our past, they said. A part we can rise above. Well, I'm wondering how many of them would like to have a gun now, to protect their families."

"Few of them," Rand said. "Guns aren't the answer. You don't stop a crime by committing a crime."

Walt stopped poking the bird and looked at Rand. Quietly he asked, "You mean you wouldn't like to of had a gun when those men took your wife?"

Rand stared at the fire. He had never considered the question, as much as he had come to hate those people. "No," he answered.

"What?"

"I might have shot the wrong person."

Buck looked at him hard. "Oh, come on! Give yourself more credit than that!"

"Really, I have never had any training. I might have made a mistake."

Buck kept on, "Okay, but with training. Knowing that you would have known how to use the gun, would you have liked to have your fingers wrapped around the solid butt of a .44 when it happened?"

Rand thought about it. The moment blazed anew in his mind. "No. I—I don't want to kill anyone. And at least I'm alive. Kera is alive as well. If I had a gun, perhaps shooting would have started, and we would be dead. Guns aren't the answer. We need to get rid of guns."

Buck stood up, his face tightened. Reflecting the fire, his eyes looked like sparklers. "You can't get rid of 'em. There are too many, and there are too many people who understand the importance of 'em."

"You mean mass murderers at schools and drive-by shooters?"

Buck smirked, "You city folks. It is not, as you can now see, unheard of that the government won't be able to protect the citizens. But citizen militias can. And—"

"But citizen—"

"AND, it has never been unreasonable to believe that one day the people would have to take the country back *from* the government!"

"Now wait a minute," Walt said, "Going against the government is not right."

"And I am not sayin' it is, Walt." Buck was angry now, pacing, staring at Rand. "But I am sayin' that to think this country can never be taken over by a corrupt government is nearsighted as hell."

"So whose side are you on right now? And whichever side, is killing each other the answer?" Rand fumed as well. He stood and waved his hand at Buck. "Have you ever seen a battlefield full of bodies?"

"Look, damn it, I'm not sayin' I'm for war. But if it takes a gun to keep our families safe and our government "by-and-for-the-people", then I am okay with that!"

Rand just stood and shook his head, remembering. "Guns kill innocent people. They kill children too."

"Back in the old days a boy was hunting to help support his family by the time he was eight or nine years old. Didn't have too many of those boys killing themselves, or their friends. They had respect for the gun. They had training from their daddies."

"This isn't then, Buck."

"This isn't then because of what people like you are doing to our country, taking our rights away one at a time!"

The two men faced off and stared angrily at each other. Rand could feel that Buck wanted to swing at him and he felt oddly ready himself. Bottled-up rage fueled him. Still, he knew he stood little chance against Buck; the cowboy was too well built and he himself too worn. But after what he had seen, after watching the soldiers, people like himself, murdered, he couldn't accept the other man's argument or demeanor.

"Enough, boys." Walt poked at the sizzling meat. "Going to fists about it ain't settlin' nothin'. That's a big part of the problem, too. People can't seem to disagree about nothin' without fightin' or hatin' over it. Use a little fuckin' decency."

Rand thought Walt a sudden scholar, knew it was true. Still....

Buck wiped his mouth with a quick swipe of his hand and glared at the fire. "I'm fed up is all. I can't stand it no more, the way things have changed, keep changin'. For the worse. People aren't seein' where this is all headin'. It's like the fuckin' Roman Empire about to fall." He glanced at Rand again, then shifted to the side and moved out of the circle of light.

Rand should have felt spooked, not being able to see Buck in the dark, but his mind stayed with the last comment and he smiled agreeably. "Damn, Buck, that was good."

Walt bent down and loosened the wire from one post, slid the pheasant off onto a sheet of cardboard they had found. He had a knife on his belt and cut the bird into pieces. They all sat and started to eat with their fingers.

"Oh, this is good, gentlemen." Rand thought it the best meat he had ever eaten. He thought again about death, looked at the flesh in his hand, then tore off another piece and chewed it.

Buck started without looking up, "Yeah, Walt and me, we tried to eat over an open fire as often as we could in summer, but since we took up drivin' we miss it. See, we grew up together. In South Dakota our families run cattle. Walt's family has the biggest ranch in the southwest counties. We used to spend summers, hell, most of the year, out on horses."

"Horses? I thought ranching was all done with jeeps nowadays."

The two cowboys laughed. Together they said, "That's for pussies."

"Must have been a hard life."

"Naw," Walt said, "it wasn't hard. We was all together. Do you know what I mean, together? It was great. We'd have summer barbecues with over a hundred people." He thrust a piece of the pheasant into his mouth, licked his fingers, smiled as he thought. Then, with a straight face he added, "I think it all changed after 'Nam. I still say people been different ever since. Maybe it was Nixon lyin' like he did. Maybe it was just meant to be. Anyway, the ranchin' sure did change. It's gotten so you can't afford to keep a ranch, taxes and expenses and all. We've sold off good portions of ours, sold off to developers, had to. That's the only way to make a livin' off it."

Buck threw a bone into the fire. "But then, it's gone. Hell, the West is gone, gone to developers and those who lock it up to preserve it, or people who sold their houses in California for a million and came out and bought a section all at once, their own private paradise. It's built-on, locked-up, or bought-up. They've turned it all into a tourist attraction, like that damn Wall Drug tourist trap fiasco! Billboards for a hundred miles, signs everywhere, all for a decrepit dinosaur statue put together in 1960." He licked his fingers, took off his hat, rubbed his forehead in the crook of his arm. "You know, I drive my truck sixty-five hours a week, and most of that time I think. I don't do the speeders. I don't do the pot. I do drink some coffee. And I play a little Merle, or Willie—"

"You been listening to rock-and-roll an awful lot lately, Buck."

"Okay. You got me. It's wild, but I like it sometimes. But I'm sayin' that I do a bit a thinkin', and I can't explain where exactly we've gone wrong, not exactly. But I'll say this. I believe it's got to do with the greenback. We been chasin' it and chasin' it, like a coyote after a jackrabbit. Just like a bunch'a big dummies."

Whether Buck felt he had said too much, or whether his angst got the best of him, he quit, went silent.

Rand said, "I think that too, Buck. I have been realizing the same exact thing." The men finished the meat without saying more.

Walt began speaking in rhyme, rubbing his fingers to work the grease from the cooked meat into his skin, "A lonely ol' cowboy sat by a tree—and wondered what life would be—when the ranges were gone and guns were outlawed—with smog hung as low as the trees. He remembers the fall of the Injun—and in that his kind had a part—but now he feels akin—and knows he can't win—as the Injun died, now his death will start. Don't cry a sad tear my ol' cowboy—don't throw out your worn out ol' boots—for when the last of the dust has settled—and the sun sets no more to ride off—we'll be thinking of you—we'll be pining for you—in some concrete skyscraper's loft." His eyes glowed in the firelight and he rubbed his thick legs with his hands. Buck shifted and kicked dirt on a stray ember.

Rand didn't know, but it came to him that Walt had recited the poem to calm Buck, his friend. Some unspoken communication had passed between them, now silent and staring placidly into the fire.

Rand saw again how they were the last of a breed in this country. In this time of high finance and global technology, what these men stood for, all they had been, would disappear from the land—like a pair of leather chaps disintegrated over time by the sun, wind and rain. And with them, men like them, simple rugged men who knew how to do many things with their hands and their brains and their diligence, well, the country would lose a vast resource, a basic wealth of knowledge and strength and character. The concept of independence sprang from men like these. These were the type that formed the solid backbone of any country—Rand thought—of any specie.

"You write that?" Rand asked.

"Naw. My pa did, about forty years ago. Cowboy poet."

The fire burned down and the dull yellowish glow bounced around on the faces of the men, but not anything else beyond their circle. Rand glanced at Walt and Buck, not wanting to stare, but wondering at the differences between their lives and his. He had obviously missed a lot, couldn't keep the thought from running through his mind how he had lived for many years in a vacuum, as if no other world existed beyond the highly structured society of New York City. The past tragic weeks seemed like a flash of white light from a thunder head—sudden, unforgiving, unsettling, but also intense, focused, transformational.

He had spent his entire adult life chasing a reputation, chasing security, money, material; not only him, but many millions more. Sure, everyone wanted enough security to feel safe from future emergencies, enough money to keep body and soul together, enough material to provide a safe, warm and happy home. *But where does one draw the line? How much of these things do we need? At what point does the striving for more turn into an insecurity threatening the sanity, the survival, of a society?*

Rand knew he had obsessed on those things, to such gross excess, that he had made it the purpose of his existence, and had run right away from living a full life, right away from his family, his community; and now, listening to Buck, he wondered if he, and those like him, had also failed America—eroded the fabric of a society and doomed it to failure.

***

"Can we adjust that lantern down a little?" Kera asked. "It's just so bright I'm afraid someone will see it."

Nat reached over and turned it down so that a faint glow emitted only enough light for them to see each other clearly. "You're right, thanks."

"So," Garret asked, "they took you to a camp of theirs?"

Kera was telling the two men a brief and edited account of how she had come to the point of fleeing on horseback through war-torn countryside.

"Yes," Kera answered. She didn't like the questions. Just talking about it made her feel tense again.

"And how long were you there?"

"A couple days."

"How did they treat you?"

Kera paused, looked from Garret to Nat, to the lantern. "They were—rough."

After her shower she had returned to camp and found Nat dishing out cookies—huge thick chocolatey things made by a woman they met during their travels. As they ate, both men became drowsy and eventually lied down on top their sleeping bags for a nap. Kera sat in the shade, watching the horse, wanting to get back to traveling, but feeling too sore and too worn out. Eventually her clothes had dried and she walked off into the trees and changed back into them. The men awoke when she returned.

"I mean, did they treat you respectfully?" Garrett continued.

The question shocked Kera. It took her a moment to answer. "I was able to, well, escape."

"How?"

As the sun had faded below the horizon they lit a propane camp lantern, had some orange juice Nat pulled from the cooler, and shortly thereafter Garret had started asking these questions. He and Kera sat in the lawn chairs, while Nat sat cross-legged on the ground.

"I managed."

"But how does one manage such a thing, an escape?"

"Through a window. I ran into a forest and kept running, until I found the horse."

"How long did you run?"

"I don't know. I—really—don't—know." She ran her fingers through her hair, squinted into the dark around the camp. "Everything was just a blur."

"I can understand that," Nat said. "So, the last you saw of your husband was in that battlefield?"

"Yes."

"And you still know nothing more about your children in Washington?"

"Hopefully they are at the Better Way Retreat, near Latrop, a small town north of Spokane. That's all I know." Saying this made her feel guilty for sitting there, failing to move on, made her feel like the fool she had proved herself to be by sending them in the first place.

"I have to ask, Kera," Garret cleared his throat, "can we do an interview with you?"

"You just did, didn't you?" She shifted in the seat, still terribly sore from riding the horse.

"I mean, on camera."

"Oh, no, no, I don't want to do that."

"It would sure help us tell the story of all that's going on out here."

"Listen," Kera stood up and stepped away from the men. "I've answered your questions. I don't care to continue."

Nat laid back on his side on the ground and took on a very relaxed air. Garret sipped down the last of his juice. He ran a little water from a two gallon plastic jug into the glass, swirled it around, and poured it on the ground. "Kera, Nat and I are journalists. We do understand that the press has been labeled, and certainly, in some circumstances, deserves to be labeled as exploitative and irresponsible. But for better or worse, the press *is* the public watchdog. It is up to us to improve, yes, but it is also up to the public to remain allied to us, and to demand a free and impartial press. Without the support of the public, the press is nothing, and without the press, the public will be left to the whim and fancy of the world's elite."

Kera turned back to the men, one hand on her hip, the other to the side of her face, her eyes on the ground, considering.

"We could use your story," Garret continued. "We could use it to let people know of the atrocities, to let the government know that they must act, and we could use it to assist in the record keeping of our country's history."

Kera looked at both of them. "I'm sorry. I am a supporter of the press, really I am. But I just can't do it." She took a step away, paused, "I'll let you get back to your work."

She didn't know what she wanted to do at that moment, but she walked up to the animal, stroked its side, wondered if she should mount and ride through the night. She needed sleep, more of a break from the hard back of Friend. It made sense to her that if she pushed herself beyond a certain point physically, stayed endlessly exhausted, she could suffer an accident or an illness that might prevent her from finishing the trip. Still, the urge to keep moving echoed desperately within her and never stopped. Days were going by, adding up to over a week since she had seen the children. This was taking far too long.

"Kera?" Nat had approached quietly in the dark.

Kera turned quickly, "I'm sorry, Nat, I just can't talk about it anymore, especially not on camera."

"No. Don't. I understand completely. Garret pushes. It's his job. I think it's great you made that decision for yourself."

Nat had moved up close to the horse and a loud THWACK! sounded as its tail struck him hard in the back. He stepped away, laughing, with his shoulders arched back. "Packs a pretty good sting."

Kera touched the horse again. "He's so good. He didn't mean to hurt you."

"You never said how you got him."

Kera could barely make out any detail of Nat's face, only a faint form standing in front of her, ringed by the dim light of the lantern behind. She kept a tight hold on the horse's rope, edged back a bit. "I took him. I probably shouldn't have, but I did."

"I understand. With martial law enforced, you've been afraid to go to the authorities, for fear they would detain you and keep you from your children."

She again felt confused. "I didn't know about the law. I only knew I didn't want to deal with anyone."

"I see." There was a pause, a silence, then, "We could drive you to your children, Kera."

Kera yearned to get back into a vehicle and head directly to the children, let these two seemingly trustworthy men assist her. But she quickly reconsidered. Putting herself in the hands of anyone worried her. In the truck... if, just if... she would be powerless. Also, they might, as journalists, find some story more appealing, and lead her astray, or leave her afoot, without so much as a horse. Uncountable things might happen. With the horse she was slower, but certainly independent. And a vehicle had to travel roads, remained more easily seen, and needed gas. "Are you guys able to find gas?"

"It's been difficult. We need some now, as a matter of fact. In the morning we'll look for a gas station, or siphon some from a vehicle."

"Haven't you had a difficult time, keeping out of harm's way?"

"Yes. But you learn what to look for. And I have to tell you, Kera, it's bad out there, very bad. That's part of the reason we are so interested in your story. A strong woman, alone, battling in spite of the odds, riding a horse through a war-torn land. It's almost like we were meant to find you."

Kera wondered about taking people's tragedies and turning them into stories aired for the entertainment and education of strangers. Justification for this did exist, she had watched a hundred of such stories, maybe thousands, but with the tragedy so personal to her, it didn't feel like a story for the telling. "I understand." Friend had gone back to ripping up grass and chewing loudly, breathing in snorts. Insects inhabited the pond en masse and their voices rang out in the night—tweets, rasps and croaks.

Kera felt things now, felt them with her body. Many were subtle, hard for her to figure, but it amazed her how her senses had come so alive. She thought, and she knew. She had known all along. The city closed her off, shut her down. The bombardment of noise and exhaust and rampant unbalanced energy proved too much. But out here, subtleties abounded. Quietness often prevailed. Her senses had come forward, had awakened. She could feel the horse standing next to her, feel Nat's presence, feel the life that went on all around her in the pond and countryside. She was beginning to see bigger, feel bigger, everything seemed so much greater, so much more open and powerful and right. And yet, a moment ago, anxiety had filled her. It was all about survival too. Her body had come alive to survive.

"Are you and Garret going to stay here for the night?"

"Yes, I think so."

"I want to go on, but I think I need a break. Maybe we can talk about it in the morning."

"Yes." A moment of quiet passed. "How will you sleep? You don't have a blanket or anything."

"I'll be okay, in the grass here by Friend."

"Friend?"

"Oh, that's what I've named him." She reached out and placed her hand on the horse's warm back.

"Ah. Well. I'd like to give you a blanket, and we have a tent. We'd like you to take the tent."

"I can't do that."

"Please. We would like that. We can sleep out on the ground or in the truck."

"I'd like to sleep out, by myself."

Silence, then, "Will you at least take a blanket?"

"Yes, a blanket would be nice."

***

Andrew and Alissa, Kera and Rand chased each other through the field of soft golden corn. The soil felt like warm sand under their bare feet. They all laughed as they dodged one another, ran in tireless circles. It felt joyous to again play together. The children had wonderful rich tans and Kera looked radiant, lovelier than Rand had ever seen her. He wanted her. His heart filled with love. This was the meaning of life: forever, together. Nothing would change that, ever.

But then the older man's dark watery eyes searched out Rand in the rear view mirror. Smoke from the man's cigarette filtered back and burned Rand's eyes, his throat and nose. "You're just part of the fucking problem, aren't ya, rich boy?" The man walked circles around Rand, stared at him with hatred.

And the younger, muscular man appeared. He clenched the gun in his burly hand, circled Rand closer and closer, along with the older man, circling, spinning, flying. He emitted growling sounds as he dodged in and out on thick oily wings, growling sounds mixed with those of an angry hornet buzzing. Rand felt pain, felt fear. The younger man drew back his arm, drew back his entire body into one muscular hammer-mass ready to pummel Rand. "Where you think you're goin', Bozo?" he asked in that growling buzzing voice, his eyes full of violence, his mouth lined with foamy spittle.

Lying on the ground, Rand flailed at the night.

Another voice came to him from the dark, "Whoa, hey, it's me, Walt."

Rand's mind cleared, the stars shone above, the outline of the big cowboy standing over him separated from the sky. "Huh? Yeah." Rand's voice quivered.

"We heard some munitions goin' off out there. Don't know for certain where from, but we're goin' to get a move on," Walt said.

It was 3:00 a.m.. Rand felt exhausted, as if his sleep had been no sleep at all. He dragged himself from the ground, stumbled toward the cornfield, or so he thought, and ended up peeing on the road exactly opposite. He then climbed into the truck, in-between Walt and Buck. The other men were silent and Rand soon fell back to sleep.

***

Kera didn't know the time of night. She had lain on the ground for what felt like hours, tossing and turning, unable to sleep for even a moment. She couldn't help herself; the men made her nervous, and she yearned deeply, incomparably for her children.

The moon rose near full, and it created the brightest, clearest night she had seen in a long time. She rose, folded the blanket, thought about sneaking it over to the men, then reconsidered and smoothed it over the horse's back. She felt guilt for this; the kind of guilt a starving person feels for stealing an orange. She must get moving and her butt was brutally sore. She took hold of the nylon cord, mounted, and walked Friend as quietly as she could away from camp. Yes, the blanket helped.

Still, Kera felt desperately lonely and disconsolate. She glanced behind her. The men had seemed nice, but she couldn't dissuade the fear their male presence produced within her. She fought with it, stopped the horse.

Her instincts told her these men were not dangerous, but potentially a considerable benefit. She could choose to stay with them. She could consent to riding along and most likely they would treat her kindly, take her quickly to her children. Her jaw tightened and her mouth pouted with the thought. Her brown eyes reddened. Her recent suffering made her current fear understandable, she knew that. And the other concerns continued to cause doubt—them taking her in a different direction if they found some other, better story, and how visible they were, traveling in the truck. She could go anywhere with the horse.

She touched Friend with her heels and the two started around the woods. In the blue night she knew the right direction in relation to ground they'd already covered, but soon she would enter new ground and lose a sense of heading until the sun rose.

She wondered if the moon followed the sun across the sky, and couldn't believe she didn't remember. Certainly high school had taught her, and so many times in her life had she looked at the moon, but, foolishly, this one simple fact eluded her. Moonbeam glowed upon her face as she rode, staring up at it… all those times she had looked, but never watched. All those places she had lived in the city where moonlight could not reach her. *Well*, she decided, *it must follow the sun*. She determined to let it set her course for an hour or so. Then she would stop again, until dawn, likely only a couple hours away. She needed a map; finding one had become a priority.

Just then, ahead of her, came the pop and boom of armament, flashes of light against the horizon. Friend's ears pricked up and she felt the horse tense. For the sounds to travel such distance, for the light to remain so bright, she reasoned at the number and size of the guns and bombs. Fear bubbled up within her.

Again she stopped the horse, turned and looked behind her. Should she take her chances with the men, or a war full of hate and bloodlust? *Is there a difference between the two? Why is this so confusing? Why can't something seem right? What is it I am supposed to do?*

Another burst went off, closer, and the sky sparked. The horse threw its head back and turned a tight circle. Kera steadied Friend, wiped her eyes, wiped her face with her hands. As hard as she fought to remain strong and positive, the fear and doubt returned. *Damn! I am so tired of crying and faltering and second guessing myself. I need to take control and stay focused!* Immediately, she recognized that as key. If she concentrated on the lengthy distance remaining, and the probability that she couldn't reach her children in time, if she felt incapable each step of the way, then her momentum would slow and her energy would disintegrate in the blaze of emotion. *No! That is not what will happen!*

The pout on Kera's mouth hardened and her eyes tightened down. She pressed Friend with her heels and they trotted off into the night, in the direction they had been traveling, just beyond the edges of the sounds of battle.

Chapter 19

Rand saw a large boulder and wandered over to it, plunked down. The heat of the day had stolen his wind. Never had he experienced such blazing, crackling weather. And, with a great deal of frustration, he still couldn't accept that he had ended up walking again. He took a baby bottle from under the flap of the camera bag, opened it—refusing to use the nipple—and drank sun-heated water.

For three days he had followed the compass and map the cowboys found in the truck they had stolen. His shoe strings had frayed, then broken; the new khakis he started with were torn and filthy, spotted with blood, and the polo shirt no longer appeared green, but black with grime. He stank. Sitting there on that boulder in the middle of a vast undulating plain, he could smell himself, sour, pungent. He felt gaunt. The journey had shaved pounds from his body weight and his self-image had changed from that of a young entrepreneur who once marched brazenly down the cosmopolitan corridors of flash, to a penniless transient shuffling toward free food at some mission.

But no mission existed here, in that sense of the word. Instead, he had spotted numerous jets, fighters of some sort, and convoys of military vehicles on the road. The land he passed through had, he imagined, been beautiful at one point, but now it appeared charred and scarred by the red-hot juggernaut of war. He had come to a tiny town in the middle of night and watched for over an hour as a shadowy line of people, possibly a thousand in all, were marched away in the moonlight, down a narrow roadway across the flat and grass-filled countryside. Either having had their vehicles stolen, or their gasoline, they carried belongings, or rolled them in wheelbarrows. Infantrymen hurried them along, north from the town, toward, Rand imagined, a CPC.

He had pulled his camera from the bag and checked the number of exposures left on the flash card. In the low almost nonexistent light, he had photographed the exodus using a long exposure—knowing the image of the people would appear as one mass of blurred bodies, oozing along the route, like individual molecules in the volume of blood through a vein.

When finally they had disappeared into the night he sneaked up to one of the plain boxy houses, filled his little bottle from an outdoor tap, saw not one person, not one living thing remaining. It was as if he had entered a town emptied by pestilence or war. *Wait, that is what's happening.* No matter how real the current scenario, Rand continued to slip into an eerie state in which everything seemed closer to phantasm than reality—where what happened could not be happening, could not be happening, could not be happening. But he had long ago quit praying for that.

Now, sitting on the boulder, he finished the water and looked around at the thirsty endless land of brown grasses surrounding him. Again, he felt disgusted with himself for being afoot. *What kind of rescue am I performing?* Did this live up to the trust of his wife? He rested his elbows on his knees and his vision sank to the ground.

"Kera." The sound of her name came out of him as a moan, a wish. Her scent followed, like a flower near to his nose... just that wisp, not perfume, not lotion, her. She was silent in his mind. *How long has it been since I have heard her laugh?*

He shook his head and brought his gaze outward again. Walt and Buck had delivered him through the furrowed scabland of South Dakota, across the Cheyenne river, taken him as far as they could, to the border of Wyoming. There they had siphoned a small amount of gas into the truck's tank from a car along the road—a car containing an empty baby bottle—then headed north to their home and their families; northeast really, because they had brought him a little extra distance.

Rand had found it hard to say good-bye. Through their conversations, he had come to like the men and felt they also liked him, city boy or not. They were from different worlds in one way, but the same place, in another; different blood, different people, but dupes, culprits, accomplices, survivors so far, the same.

Upon parting they had shaken hands. Walt said, no matter where you were from in the country, if the country fell, you were part of the reason. And for it to rise again, if it ever did, everyone would have to do their part there too.

Rand felt tortured by the fact, without a doubt he had played a tremendous part in his family's destruction, his country's too; hell, he hadn't voted in years, hadn't studied the news, except the financial channels, couldn't tell you who his councilmen, senators, or representatives were, or how they voted on a single issue.

He focused out into the simmering heat. With the South Dakota Badlands and the Black Hills forest behind, the Wyoming grasses stretched out before him for disheartening distances. To the north stood dirty flattop hills, cut and eroded, laid bare, scarred. Heavy clouds rolled over the prairie and wind caused the knee-high grasses to whisper, to coax and snicker. Like a mirage of the desert, he saw the image of Kera and the children crossing the plain in front of him, heading away.

The heavens rumbled. Wind whipped through his hair. He pushed himself to his feet again.

***

Delirious. Kera felt delirious. For days now she had ridden—*how many?*—refusing to rest more than an hour here, ten minutes there. From fields of grain to forests of strong pine to open and rolling prairie, the horse had responded as if its spirit had been part of some frontier-breaking cattle drive. She had not found a map, couldn't get herself to slow enough to search one out, or even consider getting close enough to anyone to ask. Other than brief rest stops, or delays to negotiate the incredible number of fences across open ground, the countryside had become a blur.

But now what she saw made her laugh, as she rode the trotting horse, bent down along its neck, guts numb and cramping. It made her giggle through her pain.

Shrubs that had covered the landscape moved before her. Patches of grass rose. Trees separated from the ground and walked in her direction.

That's funny. I must really take a break.

But then Friend snorted and straightened its legs, brought itself immediately to an alert stop. Kera hauled drowsily against the cord to keep from falling. *What? Why have you stopped?* The horse never stopped without her request.

Kera squinted and shook her head to clear away the grogginess, then understood. *Camouflage!* Those weren't shrubbery at all, but men wearing camouflage and carrying guns.

She dug in her heels, and the horse bolted forward. The shrubbery grew closer, men with rifles, helmets, holding out their hands, pressing her to stop. She heard their voices, shouting, demanding. She bent low over the horse's head and charged the circle, needed to break through the line. She would not let them stop her. These were those who would….

The men formed in numbers, together, shouting, not retreating, and pointed the guns, made demands in voices indecipherable against the

wind in her ears, the ache in her gut, the pounding of the horse's hooves
into the heavy prairie soil. She heard a sharp *CRACK!* and the horse
stumbled, halted, sending Kera high off the seat, about to fly, pulling the
cord, pulling with her arms and shoulder and legs and groin, pulling, and
the horse turned in a flurry of thousand pound flight and started back the
way they had come.

Soldiers that direction too. Aiming. Aiming at the horse she rode.
Aiming at the horse that brought her further than she could ever have
asked—she pulled again and the horse slowed, caught itself up, stopped,
swung its head, snorted. She glared at a ring of twenty-five men closed
around her, their faces painted, blended with the uniforms they wore.

They questioned her, but she set her jaw, froze steadfastly, fought
fear with anger and silence. With one silent knife swipe they cut the
nylon cord below her grasp, took the horse, rushed her to a ring of
vehicles behind a low rise. United States Infantry. Loaded to the hilt
with weapons and radios. They took her to the back of a big boxy green
vehicle that looked a lot like the ones the revolutionaries, *the murderers*,
had used. The one that identified himself as Captain smelled like Old
Spice, asked her to wait outside, while he entered one through a rear
hatch.

He returned and said the colonel would talk to her in a few minutes
and within a moment seven helicopters broke the silence of the tall
grasses and came down upon them with pounding fists of air and heat.
Kera hated the potent sound of the things, felt their hot breath beat her
face. The soldiers fanned out again and encircled the area, facing out
onto the empty irregular land, becoming one with the infrequent real
vegetation.

A string of heavily outfitted soldiers popped out of the helicopters
like bristling offspring and ran toward her, toward the captain standing
next to her. She wanted to run again. The captain saluted and stepped
toward an older, smaller man in full uniform, grey-black hair, quick dark
eyes, and shouted into his ear. Kera couldn't hear anything with the
whining of the propellers or the engines or whatever it was that was
causing that horrific sound. The two men walked past her and entered
the squatty vehicle. The new arrivals organized into groups of seven and
kneeled or sat on the ground away from the helicopters, pulled their
packs open. The whining went to growling, to the panting whoosh of the
propellers slowing, to nothing but a few clicks and bangs as the pilots

opened hatches, jumped to the ground, and slammed those hatches behind them.

The captain and the other man came back and looked at Kera. Then they studied the far distances in the direction from which the colonel's aircraft had come. Ten more helicopters, some smaller, some larger, passed over and headed north, northwest. Everyone watched. Soon, their pounding sounds faded. Everything got comparatively, eerily, quiet.

"I am Colonel Esparza," the smaller man in uniform said. "What's your name?"

"Please," Kera said, "Let me go to my children." A sense of déjà vu filled her, even as she felt devastated from all the riding.

"We need to know your name and what it is you're doing here."

The colonel had dark skin, dark eyes, a wide nose, full lips. He popped a canteen out of a holster, opened it, and offered it to her.

"You know, there's a law right now, says you can't be out riding your horse."

Kera worried over how long it would take to get past all the questions. She took the water and drank heavily, despite the plastic taste, handed the canteen back, looked at the other men who mostly now watched her, then glared again at the colonel.

He eyed her in return, waiting. But Kera didn't want to talk. She was pissed. This was her country and she felt tired of being set upon by whoever thought they had the right.

The colonel returned the canteen to its place, and stepped away. He seemed to be assessing the soldiers, the area. He glanced at the first soldier. "We'll be right back, Captain. I'll be on the rise there if you need me." He pointed to the top of the bench that overlooked the immediate area. "Young lady," he spoke to Kera, "let's you and me take a walk."

He placed his hand near her shoulder, not quite touching it, and steered her in the direction he had chosen. Her heart quickened with fear and she twisted her body away from his touch. After coming so far she would either be tormented again, or detained and unable to get to Andrew and Alissa. She wondered if Rand could already be with them. It was possible, she thought, that Rand might even have flown them back to New York by now. It was also possible, and she filled with fear just thinking of it, that Rand had not made it to them for any of a hundred reasons, and the children lie in peril, or worse. She wanted to scream in rage, but didn't want to make this situation worse, wanted to speak, but had nothing nice to say that might disarm this man. She found it impossible to formulate a wise tactic on how to handle the situation.

They climbed and reached the top of the grassy bench, and Kera fought to catch her breath. Her mouth went dry again. The colonel breathed heavily also and a slight belly bulged beneath his uniform. Black clouds moved through the sky and lightening struck at the ground what looked to be forty miles away, across a narrow meandering river below them in the valley. The breeze brought the slight smell of rain mixed with the now constant scent of sage—and she had not thought of sage existing in wild places, but in small bottles in her pantry. The view was unobstructed in all directions. She looked below and saw that the soldiers had staked Friend out with a length of rope. It tore hungrily at the grasses. An aluminum bucket of sorts was near Friend and it looked to contain water.

The colonel faced into the mounting breeze, gazed into the distant west, where Kera saw a highway, empty of traffic.

She had developed a sense of direction as she rode, considering the long passing of the sun and the moon, in the same direction, and now noticed far off mountains rising along the southern horizon. She peered into the distances east and knew she had crossed all of it. A meadowlark whistled its flute-like melody and her eyes found its yellow breast in a low bush.

The colonel removed his hat, which revealed a large bald spot at the top of his head. After wiping it with a green handkerchief, he pulled out a pack of cigarettes and lit one, turned and silently offered them to her. She shook her head, and he turned again, puffed, and gazed out at open space. His uniform, and so his body, appeared to sag, but the clothes were well cared for. The two of them stood for a long moment, watching the wind move the grass, the clouds cruise across the broad sky, and lightening strike in that other world away from them. Kera felt herself somehow beginning to relax.

She heard the far off sound of vehicles and saw a long convoy moving along the highway. The colonel watched closely as more than a hundred trucks, tanks, and other military machines passed below them, about two miles away, then rumbled off into the distances west. Four of the helicopters that had landed with the colonel rose and flew out in the same direction.

"What do you think about our country confronting itself?" He spoke without turning and looking at her. Kera remained unwilling to speak. After a pause he went on. "You see, this is the best thing that can happen to us." She glanced at him, wondering if this could be a joke. He took another deep hit of the cigarette and let it out slowly. "We Americans are divided like a poorly managed football team, too much disagreement and infighting, too little sharing of objectives. Can it really be so difficult to agree on a strategy for cooperation?"

Then he turned and walked to the other side of the knoll and looked off toward the north and west. "When this is over," he said, "we will know who we are, what we stand for, where we are going. We're going to finally get some things cleared up."

Ah!, so the football team should all draw weapons and the last man standing makes out the new game plan. Yes, a soldier's idea of sports strategy.

"Do you know where you are, right now?" he asked.

Kera glanced around. She hadn't the vaguest idea.

"I did not think so. You look like you have traveled a long way, and in a hurry. I was thinking you act like a stranger here. And so I know you are not a warrior. A warrior must never allow himself, excuse me, herself, to feel out of place." He turned to her and studied her face. Then he pointed northwest off the bench, toward an area two or three miles away. "That over there is the site of the Battle of the Little Bighorn. Do you know the history?"

Little Bighorn. It sounds familiar. "Not really."

"That's where George Armstrong Custer was defeated by overwhelming forces of the Indian nation." From a leather pouch on his belt he pulled a small pair of binoculars. He looked through them toward the spot, focused, and handed them to Kera.

Custer, of course, who hadn't heard of him? She looked through the binoculars and could see a greenish building, some trees, numerous white markers on the ground, a tall concrete monument. "Are those markers graves?"

"Yes. You can go there and visit them. I did. I have studied every major campaign of the army of the United States." He was standing there smiling at her humbly, and sadly, at the same time. His eyes now looked bloodshot as opposed to clear, and he took a final hit from the cigarette, then twisted it until the burning tobacco fell to the ground. He squashed the smoking bit and slid the butt into his pocket.

He turned again and studied the area of the long ago battle. "I am very concerned. In the 1870s the army of the United States, our army, was given open orders to relocate, and some say annihilate, the Indians. But history has shown that to be a sinful policy. Those Indians were the aboriginal peoples of this land. They had the God-given right to be here. They were the first citizens.   However, we recent arrivals, calling ourselves Americans even though we were from numerous other countries, decided that the Natives were slowing our progress, our manifest destiny. We hunted them down and made certain they could not interfere with our chosen concerns." He looked back to Kera. "And now, not much more than two lifespans later, I have received orders to seek and destroy all members of this revolution." He stood with what now seemed a nauseous smile on his face—watching her—Kera thought—to see if the absurdity of it all had struck her. He took off his hat again and wiped his head with the handkerchief, looking at her the entire time as if he hoped for some comment.

She said, "These so-called revolutionaries are murderers and rapists and should get what they deserve." She could hear that her voice sounded cold and could see that her words gave considerable pause to the colonel.

"All of them?" he asked.

"They are opportunists and predators." Her voice trembled.

"Have you had some personal experience?"

Kera felt herself trembling again and hated it. She worked to regain control.

The colonel continued, "Those who have committed crimes must deal with justice. But I am wondering about a road to peace. Everyone has God-given rights."

"I thought you just said the revolution was good for the country? You're not sounding much like a warrior now."

He nodded slightly, lowered his face to the ground. "Too many battles."

Kera softened toward him. A thought had come to her when riding Friend. "Possibly if we dropped the R."

He raised his eyes and studied her face, questioning.

"Off of revolution," she added.

His eyes widened. "Yes... evolution."

"As in the term Social."

He smiled broadly. "You understand my meaning then."

"But that does not change how I feel about those doing violence."

He became animated, hopeful again. "Very well. But the evolution is good, the questions and concerns productive. I am not in favor of continued bloodshed. This is more than the uproar of a radical and uncompromising few. This is now a movement of the people, of the citizens. For once the apathetic Americans have chosen to pound their fists and demand change. And I feel it is fortuitous for our country, our people, to confront themselves, get the anger out, and reason with our future. But I am feeling like a soldier of the eighteenth century, warring with arms against the rightful owners of the land."

Kera admitted the possibility that the revolutionaries who held her were not a true representation of the citizens now rebelling. It was also true their leader had held some reasonable points of view. "But I saw a group of these revolutionaries murder a group of soldiers."

"When was this? Where?"

"A band of them picked up my husband and me, in Illinois, over a week ago, I guess. They beat my husband and left him for dead. They took me and tried to get me to join. I witnessed the attack and saw the soldiers killed, then I escaped. Our children are in Washington State and that is where I am trying to go."

"Where are you from?"

"New York."

"It has been a long journey for you."

"Yes."

"If you are from New York, why are your children in Washington State?"

Kera didn't know where to start, didn't know if she wanted to start at all. But something about this weary officer, something about her exhaustion and frustration, allowed her to go on. "My husband and I were having problems and it looked like we would separate. I sent them away to save them from the pain of it all."

He nodded his head again. "Tu eres una madre considerada."

Kera looked at him wondering what he had said.

"You are a caring mother."

Kera's eyes welled-up and she covered her mouth with her hand. "It was so stupid!" The colonel watched her, and now she thought he had the saddest eyes of any man she had ever seen. "I put them in grave danger," she whispered.

He spoke in a hush, "You did not know. Not one of us knew."

Her shoulders shook and she squeezed them with her arms, wiped her face, put an end to it.

The colonel watched intently. He didn't offer his handkerchief and Kera felt good about that. "I'm sorry," she said.

"You know, I am afraid just like you," he said. "I am afraid that I will perform unjust deeds during this war. I am afraid that Jesus will frown upon me."

Then Kera noticed his eyes brighten and he tucked his shirt in more neatly, stood a little taller.

"But you," he went on, "you have given me a way to do at least one good thing."

***

Dark heavy clouds had drawn down around Rand. The light of day took on a greenish aura. Everything went suddenly silent and still, so silent in fact that his footfalls began to sound like thunder. He stopped his stumbling and looked about, felt an energy that raised the hair on the back of his neck. A vast openness surrounded him, a grassy plain uninhabited, uncivilized for as far as he could see. He felt alone, fearful, and insignificant. No crowds existed with which to mirror him, to accommodate his mind, no structures pressed close to offer shelter, or to block the ability of his eyes to witness incomprehensible distances that asked continuous disturbing questions. Open space seemed more powerful than he ever imagined, felt bigger than anything had ever felt. Inside, he begged for some way to mark his progress against emptiness.

Then thunder rumbled and shook the ground. Wind drove the thick sharp grasses to whip and rustle.

Rand saw the grey-streaked face of a cloud burst moving across the flat, like a ghostly apparition as immense as a continent. It roared. Driven drops of rain struck and stung him. Then he saw something bounce off the ground. Hail, as big around as a quarter. It pounded the ground, in sheets. He covered his head just in time, as a large one struck his fingers like a sling shot.

There was nowhere for him to go, caught in a deluge of projectiles from above. He found himself sitting, covering as much of his neck and head as he could with his arms and hands, then dropping to the ground in the fetal position as ice bullets pelted him with horrifying power, velocity enough to raise bloody welts on his arms, neck, and back, to possibly crack his skull, his fingers.

At last, he thought to grab the camera bag and cover his head against the hot sharp pain everywhere, in his arms, his body. Fear rushed in. *This is it!* This would kill him. He found himself praying, screaming the prayers over the sound of the bombardment. "Please, God, please! Have I not paid? Do I not see my wrongs? Please, let me live! Let me make it to my family! Please!"

Chapter 20

The helicopters flew low over the contours of the earth, along highways, so low it seemed they would touch the tops of trees and hills. Kera watched out the window as the terrain streaked past below them, and felt as if she were literally flying, without mechanical aid. The ground seemed to lift, build, and mountains loomed in the distance, grew closer by the minute. Progress was made and joy filled her.

Soldiers sat next to her, before her, helmeted, rifles up between their legs. A few of them had microphones attached to their helmets, talked and chuckled at words she could not hear. They had provided her a helmet, but no way to talk with them, or listen in. A couple of the soldiers were dozing, their heads sagging, jerking up, fighting fatigue.

Yes, joy filled Kera's heart, along with trepidation.

The colonel had not waited for a reply when he led her off the bench above Custer's historical nightmare and stated he would fly her to her children. She figured he never imagined she might refuse such a deed. It didn't matter. Though the risks involved in going with them worried her, only a fool would fail to see she had little, if any, choice. Besides, she measured it now as a risk worth taking. Come on, it was a helicopter!

When the word had been given, half the soldiers returned to the aircraft within five minutes. Kera went to say good-bye to Friend. It made her sad, as if everything she ever did added up to a mistake somehow and she realized now the horse would be left alone, a long way from home, to fend for itself. At another time, it may have felt odd, speaking with an animal in such an earnest way, with all those people watching, but she didn't care. This magnificent steed had saved her, simple truth, and if she could take Friend along, she would.

Back at the helicopters, the captain stated it would take them approximately six hours, with a refueling stop, to reach the area she described, but before Kera would step aboard, she asked the Captain to promise her to have a soldier take the horse to the nearest farm, and if no one was there, try to leave it with water, food, and shelter. Without so much as blinking, he agreed, and Kera nearly leaned over to kiss him on the cheek—she could only manage a thank you with a smile and eyes full of tears. Shortly after, three big green birds lifted from the ground and not once changed direction. They flew west-northwest....

In less than six hours she could be arm-in-arm with her children. The possibilities haunted her. After all the worry and wait, after all she had experienced, and imagined them experiencing, it might suddenly end. *If everything will just please be okay.*

She felt a tap on her shoulder and started, looked to see a soldier holding out a clean, green helmet. It had a microphone connected to it. She worked hers off and pulled the new one down over her ears. It fit tightly and pulled her hair, but as soon as she had it on she could hear the sound of static. The soldier reached up and turned a knob on a box mounted on the framework of the helicopter. She saw him speak and heard his voice in her helmet.

"Are you okay, Ma'am?"

Kera looked at him scrunched-up like a big bull in the corner of the crowded troop area. His face was cleanly shaven and his jaw broad, his eyebrows below his helmet, red.

"Okay?" he repeated, forming his face into a question, tapping his helmet with is knuckles.

Kera talked and heard her voice, all tinny and off pitch. "Yes. Thank you." She saw three stripes on the man's jacket, three stripes with a curved stripe connecting them at the bottom. She didn't know what that meant, but it was more stripes than most of the men had.

"How do you like the ride?" He shifted and hung onto a part of the framework near his shoulder. Other soldiers noticed them talking and were intently watching her. She could see the pilot's mouth moving in the cockpit as he talked into his microphone, but she couldn't hear him.

"It's amazing." She smiled. This was an incredible machine that humans had built. Such a different way of flying from the few planes she had flown in while modeling. There was a different feel, a smoothness, almost as if they were gliding. "It's like gliding."

The soldier smiled broadly. "We like it too."

With that and for no apparent reason, all she could see in her mind was soldiers dying, the battlefield, again, the blast of guns, bodies jerking with impact, fragmenting, falling.

She looked around the helicopter. Most of the soldiers appeared eighteen to twenty-five years of age. She had recently gazed into the eyes of death, and one of her many inner-awakenings stated that death instantly and effortlessly humbled everything. This seemed obvious. But once you had witnessed it arrive, like a sudden wind, it left you changed, forever astonished. These men were young and brave and beautiful, but they could easily be reduced to lifeless mass in an instant. Yet, they didn't seem to know, didn't look tense, alert—they weren't watching. They seemed to be waiting. *Waiting for what, a chance to die? A chance to die before anyone has started talking.*

Kera saw her contradiction, how the animosity she now felt toward men in general ran smack into her instinct of being a mother to her own little man. She again felt saddened, frustrated, overcome. Whenever she looked closely nothing made sense. And from the grip of that putrid scum of a wild-haired man the shrunken feeling returned: death might be no worse than life. Death might be an end to doubt and fear.

She turned and directed her gaze out a small distorted window. They rose up over massive mountains, verdant forests, rushing rivers cascading. *No. I am more than that, more than fear. My children will soon be with me again. I am too young to die.*

***

The storm passed and Rand slowly sat up. His skull ached, with bloody knots like halves of Ping-Pong balls sticking up under what was once a well-kempt mane. Several of his fingers were swollen, red, bleeding, possibly fractured. His back and side were numb.

He looked over the camera. It was wet again, but he had nothing with which to dry it. The bag absorbed the onslaught of hail and no damage occurred to the body of the old tough Nikon. Eventually he stood, wearily, and began to walk, shuffle really, looking like a refugee from a nuclear holocaust or one of those idiots at the running of the bulls in Pamplona—he would have chuckled at that thought if he didn't want to cry.

He hurt so badly, felt so tired, he decided he would take any offer of assistance from any person he met, no matter the risks. His stomach gurgled and burned with the juices of hunger, fear and thirst. He had eaten bits of grasses along the way, and now sank to his knees and sucked water out of a pothole brimming from the storm. He refilled his baby bottle. His shoes were like sponges strapped to his feet.

He couldn't get over being angry at himself—angry for being faithless, loveless, self-obsessed, so completely ineffectual. *I have never known a more worthless man!*

He sucked water through the nipple of the bottle. The damn thing kept reminding him of moments in his children's lives. Remembering would be wonderful, except the feelings and images now tortured him.

Something struck Rand hard on the shoulder. Shock and panic dropped him to his knees. A man ran past, stopped a few feet away, and whirled around to face him. Rand couldn't believe his eyes. It was an Indian, dark-skinned with long black hair, braided, wearing the tanned hide pants and boned chest protector of a warrior. Grasped firmly in his hand was a long-handled rock weapon. He whooped fiercely and the sound chilled Rand.

A sharp strike caught Rand on the opposite shoulder, and a second Indian, similarly dressed, ran past him and took a place beside the first.

Rand glanced about—*what the... where are they coming from?*— saw nothing else, and faced them while remaining on his knees. The two dark figures looked at the sky and yipped like wild dogs. Their faces appeared as hostile demons. The second one flexed his grip around the handle of his tomahawk weapon and brandished it menacingly. Rand tried feebly to rise, and they charged him. One hit him with a fist to the stomach, and the other struck the back of his knee with the weapon as he passed by, dropping him hard onto the wet dirt and grass. He urged himself to his hands and knees and turned toward them. They again whooped at the sky, arms outstretched and chests expanded.

Suddenly many men encircled Rand in the tall grass. He couldn't tell how many, maybe six or seven. *Savages!* It seemed so utterly inconceivable. One of them bellowed, "White man, you are trespassing!"

Rand fought to stay calm, to think, but his voice quivered, "I am sorry. I am only trying to find my family."

"Your family is not here, on our land!"

"I understand. I am heading for Washington State. My family is there. I only wanted to pass through your land."

Several men laughed, some rumbled, some cackled. Then the same one spoke, "That's a favorite saying of you white men. You stated the same claim a couple hundred years ago. WE ARE ONLY PASSING THROUGH!"

There was a hush and Rand tried hard to think, but the faces of the savages around him grew dark. He felt a sudden deep pain in his left buttock. When he reached back he found an arrow lodged in him. He pulled at it desperately and it came out with a ripping sound. Adrenaline rushed through his muscles and he jumped up and started to run. The attackers had encircled him and now he saw maybe ten in all, hostile warriors every one.

He tried to run between two, but they closed ranks and shoved hard, sent him sprawling back into the center of the circle. As he laid on the ground the one who had done the talking, a particularly dark-skinned brute wearing a breechcloth below his waist and beadwork across his chest, pulled a knife with a long thick blade from a sheath on his side. Rand recognized the look of murder, the same look as the insane man who had pulled the gun on him in the car with Kera. His heart pounded and he rose weakly to his feet. If he were to die, to not see his children or Kera again, he would at least do so standing.

The man with the knife was maybe thirty and though his shoulders looked hard, his belly stuck out as if he feasted on beer for dinner. Still, Rand knew he stood no chance against any warrior with a knife. Then someone shoved him violently from the rear and as he fell forward the dark brute grabbed him by the shirt collar and stuck the knife deep into his abdomen. Rand felt the pinch of the steel as it went into him, the hardness of it, and he felt his skin, his flesh give way as neatly as material to scissors. An immediate chill ran through his body.

Flailing back and away, the knife edged out as the man held his ground, and Rand gasped in horror at the bloody steel and the gash in his gut.

The man stepped closer. Rand's mind whirled. *This is it. I love you, Kera. I love you, Alissa and Andrew. I am sorry for not being a better father and husband.*

But then Rand saw the attacker stop. His dark head turned and he squinted sideways out at the distances of prairie, and into the eyes of others in his circle. They too became still and looked about suspiciously. A hot wind picked up and swirled around them. Rand felt it against his skin, felt it fill his lungs, felt the chill leave him. The emotion in the eyes of the warriors went from hate to bewilderment. The wind subsided. One by one their eyes settled back on Rand.

He went to his knees and the pain increased. He felt blood trickling from the wound, seeping out between his fingers. He knew he was dying. The brute with the knife reached for him.

"Stop!" a voice sounded and it came from... Rand could not tell where. He felt too confused, too weak.

The Indians pulled back nervously, looking around, as if some mysterious presence was near, yet somehow imperceptible to their vision.

And then Rand flinched, realizing one of the men now stood directly beside him. He feebly reacted, pushed out a hand, then saw how this one faced away, toward the man with the knife. This new one beside him was his age also, built tall and thin. He was bald, but had what looked like a dark tattoo covering his head, wore a black t-shirt, jeans, and moccasins.

The others suddenly noticed this new Indian among them and stepped back, wide-eyed, with arms, hands, weapons out protectively before them. But the leader with the knife did not move. His dark eyes focused on this new Indian, his emotions as undetectable as the hope Rand felt of living another minute.

The one next to Rand spoke first and his voice came bluntly, but calmly. "Why are you attacking this man, huh?"

With a tone as tight as his grip on the knife the dark brute answered, "Because he crosses our ground."

Rand could feel the circle of heavy hate around him. His stomach, his shirt, his pants were soaked through with blood, and his gaze sank to the ground.

"I am aware," said the one beside him, "that you yourself are not on your own ground, huh?"

The other's voice hissed, "We are taking back our land. The whites cannot manage themselves, let alone the sacred ground of our ancestors."

Rand again flinched as the Indian next to him broke out in raucous laughter. He glanced up at the brute's expression, deep furrows of insult and hate. The one next to Rand stopped laughing and said, "Indian, you have one problem still."

The leader stared and waited, but he lost the game of patience and finally spit out, "What is that?"

The other leaned forward slightly and formed the words clearly, excessively with his mouth, "Too—many—cowboys." He smiled at the brute who began to tremble with anger. Then he continued, "They still come and come and come. It is not yet ending. You should go home and care for your family. If you want to take back the land of our fathers by force, go nurture your own people more responsibly, grow your numbers, and come back when our time has returned." Then he shrugged his shoulders and looked at the others in the circle around him, "But you know, this hate crap comes back around in a big way, on all of us, and the cycle will continue forever, huh?"

The leader came quickly forward, and as he did the rest of the circle closed around Rand and the new Indian. They pressed in to where their bodies shaded Rand and he shook with pain, with the fear of waiting to feel the knife again, wondering what it would be like to die on this open and flat and desolate place, this land unknown to his wife and children. *I love you, Kera. I love you, Andrew and Alissa.*

The brute pressed against the new one, glared into his face in a way that let Rand know he would kill them both with pleasure, no remorse of any kind. The sour smell of fear and hate rose up about them. Rand shifted his aching eyeballs over to see what the new man might do and saw him open his mouth: "I'm going to get your father after you, Nukpana. He taught you better," and then he stared steadily, peacefully, back at the one with the knife.

"My father is long dead, Mestee," hissed the leader.

The new man quietly replied, "What does that matter, Indian?"

Rand slid down onto his back, peered up at the faces around him, wondering which would scalp him and cut out his heart.

A couple of the men were young, in their teens; they had clean faces, tight skin, looked like kids off basketball courts, not killing fields. Rand thought of Andrew growing up. Their angry expressions now looked unconvincing to him, like copies of the older warriors present. *These are only—boys, being taught by older—men.* And what was righteous to these older men would one day be righteous to these teens—as if the thistle of hate blossomed from the rosebud of youth.

Rand's eyelids grew heavy and he couldn't feel his body. But he saw the sweat of the Indians glistening in sunlight. Their eyes held mixed emotion. They seemed stalled on the edge of action and uncertainty. He knew this. He had felt this. Maybe all this was happening in a millisecond, but for Rand it moved in slow-motion.

He studied the warrior with the knife. The warrior shifted his glare from the new man, to Rand. His dark eyes were too much to decipher. Rand could not tell what the man would do, or why he waited.

Rand had spent no time around Indians, but back home had heard his father, a time or two, say nigger, his brother too. He had heard a few associates remark, make jokes concerning the shortcomings of minorities around them. Yet, he could not remember any of them ever having a bad experience with a dark-skinned person—they simply passed on what had come before them in the way of stories, jokes, fears.

New York City was filled with people of color. He had existed side-by-side with them, yet knew nothing about them. He lived white. He couldn't remember the last time he had seen an Indian, or Native American, or, well, he felt uncertain of the correct term for them.

All he knew right now, before him here, beyond the paint and feathers, they looked like everyone else.

He wondered what they ate for breakfast, what they talked about in friendly circles, what their mothers taught them as children. What answers might their culture offer for the troubles of the nation?

He felt amazed that he wanted to photograph them. They seemed beautiful. *Look at these men, look at how strongly the story of their people lives within them!*

Rand had a vision, there, next to death. He understood that to this band of Indians he represented a culture with a debt to pay, a punishment to suffer. The wrongs of the ruling society plunged so deeply into the lives of the oppressed that the "sorry" of some government program could never heal the wounds of the skin, let alone of spirit. *POOF!* He could feel all this. Acquittal is what the white race expected; reality made it a remote possibility. And so, what had occurred was a permanent mutual crucifixion—both sides hung by the other—within a country forever willing to build more crosses.

He knew the same kind of hate and anger flaming in the eyes of these older men had for centuries been eating away at the nerves of others as well, all for their own experiences, just like his, now. This revolution provided a way for the angriest, the unhealed, to finally affirm a judgment and sentence of their liking. *When will it end?*

Rand worked hard to hold the glare of the man with the knife and then forced out his words. "You have the power and maybe the right. It is your choice what happens to us, but I am asking you for my freedom and his."

The warrior's jaw flexed. His nostrils flared. His eyes flashed at the new man, then back to Rand. "You think it is that easy?"

Rand wasn't sure, but he thought he might be smiling. "I have no idea anymore, maybe you neither, what the word easy even means."

The warrior studied him, then his shoulder dropped and his hand flicked out and a long bleeding slice appeared below Rand's right eye. Rand lay there, unflinching, and the man hissed, "Perhaps you, yourself, have suffered enough."

He turned and walked off, and with uncertain movements, the others followed. In a group they left and faded into the ravines, washes, and cover of the eastern Wyoming grassland.

Part Five

Chapter 21
The helicopters circled the town of Latrop for several minutes, and the big-jawed, red-haired soldier told Kera they were assessing it for the presence of terrorists. The tiny community sat in a wide and lush valley with a clear blue river running through its center. Kera guessed a hundred homes stood scattered in the flats and along the low, tree-covered mountains to the east, and a central downtown area some two blocks long and two wide contained a few stores and gas stations and restaurants. It looked beautiful and peaceful, but then she spotted a number of military vehicles parked among the buildings. Those vehicles alarmed her. She had prayed unceasingly that the violence had not reached this place.

The helicopter Kera rode in sidled through the trees of a small central park and landed, while the others kept to the air and maintained a circular pattern. The red-haired soldier asked Kera the name of the place her children stayed and then repeated the information into his microphone. She could see the pilots talking, and two soldiers aboard her helicopter undid straps and checked their weapons.

"You're being asked to stay on board, Ma'am," the red-haired soldier smiled. "Those men are going to talk to the locals to try and locate the retreat."

"Why are those military vehicles here?" she asked.

"It sounds as though the Governor of Washington is having his National Guard evacuate some outlying towns and centrally locate citizens in larger areas."

Kera felt an immediate flash of hot blood go to her head. *What if the children have been moved? How will we find them?*

"It's for their protection, Ma'am. If that evacuation happens to include your children, we will find them!" He smiled, and she looked at him, but her mind saw fragile Alissa and Andrew locked in some concentration-like encampment with hundreds of strangers.

Sweat streamed down Kera's forehead and cheeks. With the sun beating down outside, the temperature inside the helicopter rose. The pilots left the engines whirring and the turning propellers sent a hot breeze through the cracks in the partially opened door.

The soldier handed her a paper towel from a roll stuck in a pouch. "It gets warm, but we shouldn't be here long."

Kera thanked him and peered out the window, wiped the towel across her face. The two soldiers, accompanied by one of the pilots, ran across the green lawn of the park and into a gas station on an adjacent corner. Tree branches prevented Kera from seeing what went on inside. A hardware store next to the gas station had one of those old false flat fronts Kera had seen on buildings of western frontier towns in movies. It had many separated windows and the interior looked stacked to the hilt with merchandise. Kera could see boxes on top of boxes, hand tools standing in disarray in a corner, wheelbarrows compressed together.

She watched the soldiers exit the gas station and move quickly a couple doors down the street, a faded and stained brown two-story hotel. They disappeared inside. A painted white sign on the front of the building said Historic Jefferson Hotel. She guessed that many of the buildings in the town were from the early part of the century, possibly the late 1800's. A more modern grocery store stood at the end of the block. Behind the store stood a garage of sorts, white, with swinging wooden doors pulled open. In the doorway, and profiled to Kera, sat a man. He appeared quite old and thin and he sat on a bale of straw with his back rested against the frame of the door. He wore coveralls and a brown cotton shirt. In his hand he held a wide-brimmed hat and appeared to be mending it with slow certain movements of a needle or other instrument. The man looked like a picture of the past, a peaceful one, and Kera found herself mesmerized. In all the country she had covered few had shown themselves and no one sat so relaxed and vulnerable.

Then she saw the soldiers running back to the helicopter. They climbed in and hooked their helmets back into the audio system. Their mouths started moving.

"Can you tell me what they are saying?" Kera asked the red-haired soldier.

He raised his single index finger to quiet her and continued listening. After a moment he looked at her and smiled, stuck his thumb into the air. "They were given directions to the retreat and we're going there now!"

"Has the retreat been evacuated?" she asked.

The soldier talked into the microphone. He nodded as he listened. Kera stared into his eyes and the way they smiled back comforted her. "The National Guard commander here said they approached the retreat concerning evacuation, but leaders there have declined so far."

"Can they do that?"

"I didn't think so...." He smiled and shrugged his shoulders.

Kera felt the helicopter wobble, then lift off. Her heart pounded in her chest. "How far is it?"

"About a three to five minute flight. You're almost there!" Her hand was on her knee and he bent forward and patted it. She grabbed his hand and he squeezed, smiling gently, then slowly let go. His eyes sparkled.

Kera tried to smile in return, but felt faint and frightened. *They will be there, both my children. They will be there, safe and sound!*

She reached out and the soldier again took her hand.

***

Rand jerked awake and immediately felt like hell. He was lying in a dimly lit room. From a short doorway to his left and a small opening in the wall beyond his toes, enough luminance came through to show muted details. Everything appeared earthen, as if in a hole in the ground. Then he remembered the confrontation with the Indians and the man who suddenly appeared beside him.

He moved to rise, but weakness and pain checked him and he paused on his elbows, looked at his abdomen. A thin brown bed sheet covered him and he pulled it back with trembling fingers. Except for another sheet wrapped around his middle like a wide bandage, he was entirely naked. He thought of the ghastly wound and how the knife had gone into him. He pulled the sheet back further and looked at his behind. A makeshift bandage covered his left buttock which screamed with pain as he moved. But then joy flushed through him: *I am alive! I made it!*

I think.

His immediate environment looked surreal to him. The walls of the space consisted of some form of mud and plants mixed, hardened, and to support it all wooden poles made of saplings forming a tightly knit— *what is the word?*—wattle. Crude rough wood framed the window, a single pane of glass. The place smelled of earth and spice—some sweet spice he could not place. He lay on a simple cot made of wood with an animal hide stretched across it. A shadow fell about the room and a dark form hobbled through the doorway.

"Ah, you are alive." The man came in and laid Rand's clothes across his legs. "I washed these for you. They were pretty bad. Huh?" He chuckled.

Rand recognized the man as the same that had come to his aid. He wore no shirt and his dark hairless chest shined. He walked with the aid of a cane grasped in the hand of a thin, tightly knotted forearm. "Where am I?" Rand asked.

"Welcome to my humble abode," the man answered. He moved over to a table made of bare, thickly cut planks. The base was square, about three feet tall, formed from plaster or adobe. The man opened a tin container and pulled out a loaf of bread, cut it with one swift movement of a large knife. With a smile on his face he brought a thick slice to Rand. "Can you eat?"

"Yes." Rand took it. "Thank you." He felt himself staring. The man had not before faced him so squarely, so closely. Rand now saw the full tattoo covering his shaved head. It was done in dark blue and green, a detailed representation of the globe. Below it and across the man's forehead were written the words *One Earth*. Rand looked away, took a bite of the bread, and chewed. The man brought him water in a hollow gourd shell. Rand took it without looking up. *The tattoo, the gourd for a cup, this hovel, what have I gotten into now?*

"How does your side feel?" the man asked.

Rand swallowed. "Sore. But, I'm amazed, I—I thought I was dead." He dared a look at the man.

"It's not bad, huh? Went through skin at the side of your stomach, best I can see. I cleaned it and used a poultice of mud and some very good grasses. We'll watch it, but I think you'll do fine."

Rand felt the hard ridges of dried blood along the cut on his face.

"That was only a scratch. There isn't a hospital for fifty miles. Do you want to go?"

Rand thought about it. Fifty miles. "Is there a vehicle to use?"

"I don't keep one."

Rand felt extremely tired and the thought of fifty miles made him more so. "Do I need to go?"

"My opinion, I don't think so. But I know how some like going to doctors. I've healed more than one wound, though, huh?"

"We'll watch it, then." He took another big bite of the bread. *I could still die here and no one would ever know.* "How long have I been here?"

"Day before yesterday." The man brought Rand a clay plate heaped with dried meat. Then he moved over into the shadow, the corner away from the small window, and sat on a rectangular block very similar to the one that formed the base of the table. It had a course, thickly woven blanket covering part of it.   Next to it and along the wall stood a bookshelf made of limbs and uneven boards, stuffed with books of all sizes and colors.

"I had a camera, have you seen it?" Rand asked urgently.

"It's there, beneath you."

"Is it all right for me to move, do you think?" Rand asked.

"A bit, huh?"

Rand tried to slide up on the cot and rest his back against the wall. The pain in his side was considerable and his head throbbed from the hail-driven lumps.   Before he realized it, the man stood next to him, offering a hand.   "Thanks."   He glanced under the cot and saw the camera bag.

The man returned to the block in the shadow, stood his cane against the wall, sat, stretched his legs out before him.   His feet came into the light and Rand saw moccasins with patches in the soles.

There came a sound and Rand looked to see a large striped animal about the size of a basset hound, but built even lower to the ground, come shuffling in through the open doorway.   It stopped and blinked into the scarce light.

"Hiya, Roger," the man said.   He rose and moved to the table, reached down and handed the thing a slice of bread.   It turned and shuffled back out the door with the bread in its mouth. The man said to Rand, "Badger.   One should never feed the wildlife."   Then he chewed bread and sipped water.

"Where am I?" Rand again asked.

"Where shall I begin?"

"The state."

"Wyoming, the Equality state and Cowboy state."   The man didn't look up from eating.

"What region of the state?"

"Northeast.   Thirty miles west of Newcastle.   On the edge of the

Thunder Basin National Grassland."

Rand chewed a mouthful of dried meat. It was not unlike the jerky he had eaten before, but thicker, moister, much better. His mouth watered. It was cool in the dirt dwelling, but Rand squinted through the window at heat shimmering across bright distances. The tweeting, vibrating sounds of birds and insects filtered in. He stopped chewing. The heat, the sounds, all seemed to get absorbed by the dwelling, which had a solid density to it, as if its walls were alive, part of the surroundings, a womb.

His mind went to his childhood home, the sheltering, nourishing properties a strong home bestowed. He wondered about his father and family, and how a short time ago he thought of them as nuisances.

After finishing the food and water Rand had to urinate, *but how?*
"So, I haven't asked your name."

The man came over and took the plate and gourd. "Most call me Storm." He hobbled out the doorway. Rand could hear water splashing. Then he came back in and sat the dishes on a rough wooden shelf attached to the wall. "My Indian name, Hinun, means Spirit of Storms. Because I enjoy being out in weather."

"Well, Storm, I have a question." Rand fidgeted with the sheet, felt embarrassed.

"Say it."

"Do you have a bathroom?"

Storm was putting the bread and meat away. "Hm, good sign. Both or just one?"

"Just one."

"You should not walk today. I have a can. Can you do it?"

"I think so."

Storm went out and came back with an empty black olive can. "I love those things and you sure can't get'm to grow here." He handed it to Rand, then turned back to his tidying. "What is your name?"

"Rand."

"Okay, Rand, enjoy your pee, huh? Let all the poisons out, all your pain, envision it all going away with your pee. See yourself healing."

Rand couldn't help but stare at this tough looking man talking to him about his urine.

"And make sure you look at the color, huh?"

Rand pulled away the sheet and held the can under his penis, being very careful of the rough cut open edges. He let go and the stream made a powerful sound as the urine filled the can in a circular motion. "It's yellow. Looks normal."

Storm took the can when Rand finished and looked into it, swirled it like one does a fine wine, stuck his nose close and sniffed.

Rand couldn't help but think he was in for a big surprise.

"No blood. But you are dehydrated and also need to eat more vegetables. Drink a little water now, and sleep. When you wake I will have some good things for you to eat."

Chapter 22

When the helicopter pilots found the retreat, Kera peered out the window with heavy anticipation. She needed to see her children now. It felt like years since she had held them at the airport in New York. Her hand still clasped that of the kindly, red-haired soldier who looked through the window alongside her.

What she saw below gave her confidence. Maybe twenty varied dwellings spread out on an open plain along the southern edges of thick coniferous forest. Behind, slowly rising in a broad flank, stood a bald, granite-topped mountain. Many of the buildings looked small and some appeared short, as if built partially into the ground. With their low profiles and earth-toned finishes, she couldn't tell exactly how many buildings existed. An immense fenced garden grew on a flat before the buildings, and flourishing orchards grew alongside it. Kera had seen no road access into the retreat. From Latrop, the pilots had followed a narrow trail meandering through the hills and woods.

Kera's helicopter, and another, descended on the flat beyond the garden. As they landed Kera saw a small group of people exit a larger building central to the rest and intently watch the noisy green machines. There was no sign of Alissa or Andrew.

The soldier said, "They're asking you to wait on board again, Ma'am."

"No!" She shouted. "I have to see. I have to go and find my children." She unhitched the belt that strapped her in.

"Ma'am!" the soldier continued, "it's for your own safety. They will make certain everything is okay here. It will only take a minute." He held out his hand, but this time with a flat palm toward her, firmly signaling her to stay.

She did, but stared out the window, yearning for a glimpse of small and healthy bodies. "Tell them to hurry," she pleaded.

She watched as the colonel and six soldiers walked past the garden, toward the people watching. The people moved toward the soldiers. The blast of the helicopter propellers made a frenzy of hair, dresses and pant legs. The two groups came together and Kera saw that a woman from the retreat stood in the front center of that group, held out her hand to the colonel. He shook it and they talked. After a moment one of the soldiers turned to the helicopters and motioned with his arm.

"Okay," said the red-haired soldier. "They said for you to come out. Follow me away from the helicopters. Stay clear of the tail."

Kera stood too fast and hit her head on the low ceiling with a heavy smack. Then she was out the door, into the noise and blast of the props, and the soldier placed his hand along her back and guided her toward the group.

The colonel turned to her with his sad eyes and smiled. "Kera, this is Mattie. She is the speaker for the community here. She informed me that the people of this community disapprove of any military presence, but I have explained the situation to her."

Mattie said, "Hello, Kera." She was a black woman in her mid-fifties, tall, with round brown eyes and thick black hair that blossomed from her head and fell in long cascades. She held her thin body impeccably straight and her gentle face forward and open to Kera.

"Hello," Kera said. "Are my children here?" Her voice cracked and her hand shook.

Mattie answered, "Yes, I can take you to them now."

"My husband, has he come?"

"You are the first to arrive since the troubles began. Were you expecting him here?"

Kera envisioned Rand standing at the forest edge. Had he failed to come by choice, or consequence? She recalled mouthing the words, *the children*, to him. Possibly, he hadn't made out her communication, but she still hated how he had needed urging in their direction. *What if something terrible has happened to him? If he could come he would be here... wouldn't he?* Thoughts ricocheted around in her mind, but one came leaping to the front. "My children, please!"

Mattie took her in arm and they walked fast, back toward the larger building. Kera saw they covered ground, but she couldn't feel it. She had gone numb, like a circuit blown somewhere in her nervous system, blocking all sensation. She turned her head and in a blur saw the colonel, the red-haired soldier, and more soldiers following closely. The red-haired soldier's eyes were on her, and she saw his kindness, saw, in that second's glance, his deeper interest in her.

A door opened in front of her. Mattie smiled and ushered her in. The place had low ceilings with wooden beams exposed, terra-cotta floors, walls made out of plaster. They marched through the foyer and down a hallway. The place echoed en masse the footfalls around her.

People spoke, in fact, some to her, but she wasn't answering, wasn't really hearing. Her heart pounded and her sweaty hands clenched tightly. Then Mattie opened another door and Kera caught a glimpse of Alissa and Andrew.

Her children sat in a small circle with other children, working with something on the floor before them. In that instant they looked up and saw her. They were healthy and shiny clean, smiling joyfully. Their eyes burst into wide circles and their mouths flew open. "Mommy!" they both cried, and jumped to their feet, ran over the items before them, lunged toward her in excitement so pure that waves of joy rippled through Kera's body.

Kera's senses overloaded. The sweet scent of her children filled her lungs again, made her head light with love. The feel of their little bodies pressed together in her arms, their tiny fingers on her face, each touch landed like that of a supernatural healer. The sound of their voices calling her again and again had the effect of filling her, returning a peace not felt for as long as she could remember. She was on her knees and holding them, squeezing them. Her kisses and her tears made them wet.

"I'm so sorry," she cried, "so sorry!"

"What, Mommy?" Alissa asked. "What's wrong? What happened to you?"

Kera took their faces in her hands, studied them. *Of course. Of course.* Her prayers had been answered, her heart opened, and she heard herself say, "Thank you. THANK YOU!"

"Mom, where's Dad? Is Daddy here? What happened to you?" Andrew studied her with those eyes she had longed to see, but a stabbing pain hit her heart and anger rose within her. The way the children's eyes roamed her face, she knew they could see she'd been through something terrible. A great sorrow confused everything. "I am okay. He's coming, sweetheart." She hoped the words sounded true. "He's on his way." But she felt herself lying.

"What happened to your eye?" he asked.

Kera's hand shot up and touched her right eye. Most of the tenderness had gone, but she felt the cut on her cheek and imagined bruises around it from when the wild-haired man had hit her and from her fall off the horse. "I fell, Sweetie. It's okay."

He buried his face in her bosom again.

After some moments the colonel said, "Kera?"

Kera turned with the children still in her arms.

"I have told Mattie that we must be going."

Kera's heart raced with a sudden sickening fear. She hadn't thought about it, but it appeared the colonel would force them to go with him. There was no way she wanted her children in the company of soldiers. These men seemed capable and protective, but it felt unsafe to Kera, as though sooner or later their luck would run out and fighting would start. Warriors attract warriors. She clutched the children to her with intense determination.

"You are clear to stay," he said. "But I have also told Mattie that we feel the council is making a serious mistake by not evacuating the village to a protected area, and that this village is commanded by martial law to remain closed to inbound and outbound traffic. Residents are to stay in their homes except for emergencies."

Kera stood and pressed a child to each hip. She studied the colonel. "We can stay here?"

"If you like, or we can take you to a protected area."

Kera asked Mattie, "May we stay for... until...?"

"Yes," Mattie answered. "You are welcome here for as long as you like."

Kera turned and looked at the handful of children in the room, at the adult woman with them. She looked down at Alissa and Andrew, "Do you like it here?"

"Yes," they both answered.

"Then we will stay," she said to the colonel.

"This village is not guaranteed protection!" the colonel said, and his eyes showed deep concern.

"I understand."

The colonel nodded and turned to leave the room. The soldiers moved back down the hallway.

"Colonel!" Kera cried out. Everyone paused. Kera ran up to him and hugged him, kissed his cheek. "I can never repay you for such kindness."

"Have you forgotten our talk while overlooking the valley of the Little Bighorn?" he asked, and his eyes steadfastly held her.

"No," she said, "Never."

"Then you know I am already repaid." He smiled and walked away.

Kera took a quick step and reached out and grabbed the sleeve of the red-haired soldier. He turned, and as a woman sees, she saw the light of hope in his eyes. She kissed his cheek and smiled at him, read his name from his shirt patch. "Thank you, Murtaugh!"

"My pleasure, we all needed this," he said. He paused, but when all she returned was a gaze through watery eyes, he turned and marched off down the hallway, rifle in hand, gear packs bouncing off his hips.

***

Rand awoke to a new sweet smell wafting through Storm's earthen home. Lit by the early grey of dawn, the view outside the window showed flatland filled with golden grasses. He turned his head and looked out the door, open as usual, to see more flatland, then a series of eroded and sandy hills caught by the first honey-colored rays. The clarity of the air allowed him to pick out detailed patterns on barren cliff faces and leaves hanging motionless from trees populating a distant wash.

Rand felt rested and stronger.

"Would you like some tea?" Storm asked, from a point beyond Rand's view.

"Yes, please." Rand cleared his throat of the night's phlegm, and the sound of shuffling grew as Storm came near, appeared, and extended an earthen mug in one hand, while holding the cane in the other. Rand took it and the sweet smell grew in his nostrils. "Smells interesting, what is it?"

"Oh, rice grass, wheat grass, other things that grow around here. I won't just tell you, because people hear the names, use the herbs, and use them wrongly. They do not first learn. And so the tradition suffers."

Rand looked close and thought, with the freshness of the morning on the Indian's face, that maybe Storm was not as old as first thought, possibly in his mid-twenties.

He moved out of Rand's view. "If you want to learn, I will teach you, huh?"

Rand sipped the tea. It had a bite, but also a sweetness. "Sweet. Good."

"Oh, I put some honey from my bees in there too. I will pass on your compliment to them."

Rand saw a small ledge built into the wall above his elbow, so he sat the cup there and propped himself up on the cot. The wound in his abdomen felt more stable, less painful. He looked behind and saw Storm sitting on a rug on the hard earthen floor. He had his right jeans' pant leg pulled up and was massaging the leg most favored with the cane. The calf of the leg was missing most of its muscle, leaving only a thin, severely angled bone. The skin looked scarred and purplish.

Rand winced and asked, "Did you have an accident?"

"Oh," Storm rubbed the leg with oil, "no. I was shot. About two years ago."

"By who, if I might ask?"

"A guy trying to protect his family."

Rand thought about that. He didn't like the sound of it. What had Storm been up to?

The Indian finished with the oil and pulled the pant leg down, grabbed the cane and levered himself up off the floor. "So, what were you doing stumbling around the plains, anyhow?"

"It's a long story." Rand sipped the tea.

"I happen to have time, if you're interested in talking."

Rand nodded, smiled. "When the revolution started my wife had just sent our children to Washington State, to a retreat for the summer."

Storm chuckled, "Yeah, you folks like to do that."

"Do what?"

"Send your children away to strangers, whether for their teaching, or just to be away, huh?"

"You folks are different?"

"Not any longer. We were forced to pick up your methods, but in the beginning, yes, we knew the best learning came from elders, our grandfathers and grandmothers. The elders had the responsibility of teaching our young. That created a society of elders with a great sense of self-pride and belonging, and a well mannered, intelligent youth who respected those elders as the keepers of wisdom. We never would have sent our children away to strangers for their education, and break the family circle. Unfortunately, we were forced to, and it *has* broken the circle."

Rand sipped more of the tea. His stomach gurgled with hunger. *The circle.* He tried to see the image of a family in this new way.

"So, your wife had sent your children away."

"And then everything fell apart. We couldn't fly, so we tried to drive, but some lunatics got a hold of us and took my wife, Kera. They beat me and left me for dead." It still made him cringe, each time he told the story.

"And so you are looking for your wife and children?"

"Yes."

"Taking care of your family."

Rand paused, looked at the Indian. Only he knew how poorly he had done. "Well, yes, I am trying." He sipped the tea, fingered his side gingerly.

"It seems we are all trying to take care of our families. That's what I was doing when the fellow shot me."

"What happened?"

Storm handed him more of the thick bread from the day before. It was smeared with a reddish jam, and piled with slices of onion and juicy tomato. Rand took it and thanked him.

"I was in the western part of the state, protesting logging a large corporation wanted to do in an area that had been forever without roads. Logging would open the land, because they need to build roads to log, and this would destroy the natural system, along with the clear-cutting they had planned. We have few of these large roadless areas, these really pristine, sacred places, left in this entire country."

Rand took a bite and chewed. The reddish jam proved thick and a little dry, but it tasted good, and the tomato and onion were excellent.

"The loggers were very angry. We had stopped the logging the year before, in court. But they were able to win their case in the end, and so they began to build the roads. About fifty of us gathered and stood in a line across their path."

"Was this an Indian movement?"

"You mean us?"

"Yes."

"No. Mostly white folks from the cities were there. But there was another Indian from that area too." Storm moved over and dragged the block nearer the window, sat heavily down, chewed on some bread and jam and tomato. The way the hot light cut through the window opening and white-washed the side of his face, the way the subject of discussion hardened his features, the way the radical tattoo covering his head set one's mind to working, Rand thought this was about the most severe looking man he had ever seen, let alone been shut in with. He was right now the image of pure trouble, someone you might imagine in a broken-bottle fight; a man with a hardened mask for a face, a mask about to crack from pressures within, emotions brought on by the telling of this story. His sharply defined jaw muscles clenched against the bread, but the bread had been chewed.

"One of the road builders was using his machine to break our line and he nearly crushed some people. He did not care. I climbed onto his machine, to stop him, and a shot rang out. I was hit."

"Who, who would shoot you?"

"Well, it was never known for certain, huh? All eyes were on me and the bulldozer I tried to stop. But I saw a man with a rifle earlier, as did another man there. Only a working man, a family man afraid of losing his income."

"Was there an investigation?"

"No. The local police don't seem all that interested. I don't know how much you follow these things, but this type of situation arises often, around the world. The Machine, and the people who believe in the Machine, are willing to murder those that do not agree, and the law is unwilling to stop them."

Rand hung his head. "I have seen so much violence." Then he slowly said, "I guess, in this case, they were acting within the law. I mean, I still don't understand why people have to feel guilty for progress. Humans are a part of nature too." As soon as the sound of his voice dissipated Rand felt in his gut the ill timing of his words.

Storm looked at him with wide eyes, a man caught off-guard. His hands clenched the edges of the block he sat on. Rand thought Storm might jump up and grab him. But then the Indian looked at the ground around his feet and blinked several times, then folded his arms around his waist as if protecting his vulnerable core. He rose and moved in his tottering way through the dark shadows of the interior, toward the doorway, and rested his free hand on the door frame. Rand watched, waiting.

Soon, Storm began to speak, turned away, facing open land beyond the doorway. "You are right, we are a part of nature. But everything depends on balance. If bears ruled the planet instead of humans, and populated the face of Earth the way we have, we humans would run in fear, crying out that something must be done, that the bear had become too numerous and prevented us from living safely and freely. But no other creature has such a voice as man. They are crying out in their own way, how we turn their feeding grounds into parking lots, their drinking water to poison, but we choose not to listen. Our egos are the size of pumpkins, our ears walnuts.

"We claim righteousness through survival of the fittest, but we have evolved beyond the war of survival. We are not threatened by anything other than ourselves. We have evolved mentally, which is allowing us to evolve physically, but our spirits have become closed, insecure, selfish.

"We have the ability and so the responsibility of stewarding this planet, but we cannot pretend to rule it, or understand it, and therefore we must be humble and respect all things great and small, because in the end we are simple. Within the great complexity of all things, we know nothing. We must learn humility and compassion.

"It is impossible for me to understand why we violate the sanctity of the land, the water, the air. Look at how many cities we have now, where we cannot drink the water. Do you know the water is filled with chemicals? And how many children will die of cancer before we admit that at least some of it is caused by the poisons we manufacture? How many forests will we clear-cut before we learn they are not ours to destroy!

"Have you ever considered how many living things just one automobile kills in a year? I know, some would laugh. But pay attention sometime. Man has shunned nature, which once sheltered and provided for him. This Earth is our home, it is my home. This universe is my God. And I do not honor it falsely.

"I was willing to fight, even kill, to protect it from the insanity of modern man. I have done things I will never confess, except to the Great Spirit. But the warpath has not conquered my fear. Nor has it changed what is happening. It only created more grief."

Storm's shoulders rose and withdrew, and he sighed loudly within the earthen walls. "Still, to stand by and watch the devastation continue...." His head shook and his free hand wiped at the angles of a face Rand could not see, until the tall man turned and smiled the way a person does after a long illness. His face was furrowed and heavy and older again. He left the doorway and as he did Rand realized Storm had not shown anger, but intense pain. *This man is not hostile; he is torn, tortured. He does not know what to do about something he feels deeply about.*

Storm sat on the block again, looked at Rand for a time, then quietly said, "I am sorry, my friend. I am still searching for a way to serve my

God, to work for what I believe, to assist in changing the temperament of man, my brother, without adding pain and suffering. I fight my desire to crush those who harm my mother, and instead support a peaceful means of moving toward a humble humanity. I fight myself over the anger I feel toward the man who shot me, huh?"

Rand felt a twinge then, felt a new understanding unto himself. He felt the anger Storm spoke of; within him a hot coal glowed, ignited by the men who beat him and assaulted his wife, by the terrorists who murdered Patricia and the soldiers. These were acts of hate and inconceivable ego. It was clear how Storm associated his gunshot violence with the hate and ego violence he saw being waged against the natural world, and Rand now glimpsed a vision of all violence as coming from the same root: a person's belief in their right to harm, subdue, destroy. "I see, my new friend. I believe I understand."

Storm blinked, continued to look at him with his elbows on his knees, his shoulders sagging. "Yes. You understand the hatred of man. The over inflated ego."

"I have seen how some men decide for themselves whether another man will live happily, or with pain and suffering, will live a long life, or die in an instant. It gets inside you once you see it. I feel the cramp of hate myself, toward those men, and it scares me."

"Yes. It is like the fear of some great and unstoppable disease." Storm shook his head. "Hate." He stood with the cane and breathed, made his way to the cot and sat at Rand's side. "It is a rare person who understands the power of ego." He placed his hand on Rand's shoulder and smiled, then reached down, gently touched the bandage around Rand's middle. "Now, may I have a look at these wounds, huh?"

"Yes," Rand said, with a hoarse voice.

Storm smiled at him as he loosed the bandage, "You and me, we will spend tomorrow beneath the open sky."

Chapter 23

Through that first night and half the next day Kera slept with Alissa and Andrew in her arms. Mattie had taken them to a small home used as a visitor's quarters, containing a bedroom, a bathroom, sitting area, and kitchen. She offered Kera a sauna—their main form of bathing—but Kera was wrapped up in her children. She had talked with them for two hours, while the adrenaline wore off, ate a bit of fruit and cheese from a plate brought to them, and drank numerous glasses of cool clear water. Finally, all three fell asleep.

Upon waking she opened her eyes, remained still. Alissa laid in front of her, within her arms, the little face pressed to Kera's chest. Andrew was behind, but she felt his warm body pressed to hers and his arm draped over her neck. The children breathed the heavy vulnerable respiration of easy slumber.

She remained still that way, serene and elated.

The children had told her about the place. She let them talk and felt thankful not to recount her life of the last few weeks.

The retreat housed some twenty families. As she had witnessed from the helicopter, it was a village as much as a camp. From what the children said, the camp seemed to be a product of the village. Many children lived there, and Alissa and Andrew had generally good reports concerning them. At first, they said, it had been hard, because even children had to work in the large community garden. Alissa and Andrew had never dealt with hoes or shovels, or soil, for that matter. They hadn't liked it, but soon learned that adults working with them enjoyed taking plenty of time to play, and even taught them interesting things about bugs and other creatures inhabiting the garden space, as well as the forest around them. They took frequent walks in the forest and Andrew was currently in third place for the most species of trees identified, with twelve.

There came a soft knock on the door of the house. Kera sat up quietly, gently, and touched her face and hair with her hands. She opened the door to find a man and woman in their twenties. The man was blonde, with narrow shoulders and a shy, sharp-toothed grin. The woman was oriental, maybe Chinese, with rosy cheeks and stunningly clear eyes. Kera thought her skin looked as satiny as any she had ever seen and considered again how she herself must look and smell. It had been a long hot time since the shower in the forest, and she was now more conscious of the marks on her face.

They each held a tray full of food and drink. "We thought you might like some tea," the woman said in a hushed voice, smiled at Kera, bowed slightly.

"Oh, yes, thank you, come in." She stood back and allowed them to pass into the room.

They did so quietly, setting the trays on a small table against the wall. The couple wore coarse woolen and cotton clothing, his mostly brown and hers accented with claret. "I am Nee," the woman whispered to Kera, "and this is Lewis." Lewis grinned nervously and his shoulders hunched slightly forward. His hands came together in front of him. Nee continued, "Are Andrew and Alissa sleeping?"

"Yes," Kera nodded toward the bedroom door.

Nee smiled and whispered, "There is juice from our own apples in the glass pitcher, chamomile tea also. There are cereals, some hard-boiled eggs, and plenty of fruit."

"And Nee made some cherry bread for you," Lewis said, his cheeks suddenly crimson, and smiled proudly at Nee.

"It looks wonderful," Kera said quietly.

"Most of the fruit is not this year's, since the harvest has not yet taken place, but it is from our own produce last year," Nee added.

"Thank you." Kera said. "I hope I am not rude, for sleeping in, I was just so tired."

"We are the rude ones," Nee exclaimed. "We only wanted to say hello and offer these things as our welcome. We're sorry if we disturbed you."

Kera reached out and touched Nee's hand. "Thank you for your kindness."

Lewis moved toward the door.

"Your children are precious," Nee whispered.

"Oh, thank you!"

Then Nee bowed and walked through the door with Lewis ahead of her.

"Excuse me," Kera said. The two turned back. "Are the phones working?"

"I don't think so," Nee told her. "There is only one, at the central hall. We don't make a lot of calls."

"I can check later. Thank you."

They nodded and moved along the walkway. Kera closed the door behind them.

She poured a cupful of the tea. It tasted sweet and warm and something inside her soared. She took a slice of the cherry bread and spread a thick layer of butter onto it. It was moist and fresh and filled her mouth with fruity flavor. In the rush to find her children she had often gone days without any food, had even eaten dog food, but it had not bothered her. She had not felt hungry as much as simply wanting nourishment to continue. But, last night she had tasted real food and now her body's yearning for sustenance called with a clear voice. She ate three slices of the bread, followed by an apple, two hard boiled eggs, and more cheese.

At the window she could see several small dwellings painted by the sunshine of a clear day. Some had the course look of adobe, which was more common in the Southwest, according to stories she had read. Still, they blended well with the landscape here, in this northern land. And from this angle she could see other homes with walls full of brownish circles separated by a greyish mortar material. Some of the homes were buried partially into the ground, with the back wall subterranean and the side walls about two-thirds so. They profiled into the side of a low hill, with natural flora growing abundantly around them. Many of the houses had firewood stacked in the rear, and greenhouses connected to the front, facing a southerly direction. She saw only one grassy lawn, of moderate size, which—she noticed when she moved to a window with a fuller view—created a playground next to the garden, at the front and center of the village.

There were four people—three females and one male—working in the garden; the man and one woman appeared elderly, another woman was middle-aged, and the remaining one a child. They all used their hands or hand tools vigorously, even the child. Kera marveled at the size of the fertile space, easily equal to three or four city lots. It was not yet the first day of July, but the plants stood tall and bushy and vibrantly green, with flowers of many colors mixed in.

The children appeared quietly, seemingly asleep as they walked, and Kera took her time holding them. They ate cereal with raisins, drank the apple juice until it was gone. Then Andrew surprised her.

"Mom, you want me to start a sauna for you? So you can get

clean?" He was sitting at the small table, licking his fingers, his grey sweats twisted on his little body.

Kera reached over and combed her fingers through his hair; it had lightened in the time they were apart. His tanned face and hands gave him a healthy look she liked. She had always felt her children spent too much time indoors. "Well, how? Where would you do that?"

"It's easy, Mom." He stood and yanked at his pant legs, straightening them. Even his feet were tanned. "They have little houses under the trees back there. There's one for each big house. You carry water from the pump, or the creek if you're near it, and you fill the pot on the stove. Then you fill the stove with wood and light it. In a little while the water is warm. Then you can use the big spoon to pour the water over you and there's soap in there too."

Kera had not heard Andrew say so many words in a long time. For a moment she only smiled with watery eyes. "Should I ask Mattie and make sure it's okay?"

"Well," he scratched the top of his head, "you could. But we all know the rules and anybody eight or older, who acts responsible (Kera heard how he had to go slow to get the word out, saw how he stood tall and erect when he said it) can take a sauna when they want. As long as you make sure to stopper down the stove and pick up after yourself when you're done."

Kera couldn't get over how he talked so intently about soap and water and rules. She wasn't certain what it all meant, unless she simply smelled as badly as suspected. "It sounds very nice."

"It is. It's fun!" He stood there in front of her with his hair still in a tousle, waiting to take care of her, wanting to show her what he had learned.

"It is nice." Alissa sounded her approval, though busy with bread and jam, her little fingers covered in red. She put down the bread, licked her fingers clean, and opened her box of crayons. Those crayons were one of the few belongings she brought to the retreat. They were kept in a box made of cedar that Kera had given her for a birthday present a year earlier. On a gold plate attached to the top were the initials AP. Kera marveled at how that simple object could give this unfamiliar place the feeling of home.

***

"Slowly." Storm stood in front of Rand, leaning heavily on his cane, offering his free hand as support.

Sitting on the rack, Rand took hold of the hand. He sat up and everything felt pretty good, except his rear, where the arrow had stuck him. Lowering his feet to the ground, tightening his legs, he stood. It seemed easy, but then he caught his breath. "Whoa! Light-headed."

"To be expected, huh?" When Rand steadied and smiled, Storm stepped away and returned with a long narrow piece of wood about five feet long. "I made this cane for you. It's diamond willow." The bark had been shaved off smoothly, the wood clean, vanilla, with darker diamond shaped patches.

"Thank you!" Rand took it and leaned on it. It felt strong.

The Indian motioned toward outside. Rand made his way and rested with his shoulder on the frame of the doorway. The sun washed the land in golden colors. A half hour after sunrise, birds chirped loudly from all directions. The sound of tiny fluttering wings filled the air.

Storm thumped his chest, "It is a good day to be alive." And he chuckled.

Hearing a relaxed, warm tone in his voice, Rand looked at him. In the narrow doorway they stood close, shoulders touching. The gentle light touched the face of the Indian and made him glow. His dark eyes rested on the world with a wide childlike gaze. In contrast from yesterday, the Indian now appeared handsome, in a rugged sort of way. He smiled at Rand, then stepped through the doorway and into the warm dry air. His moccasins absorbed all sound of movement. The cane filled his hand, but flicked easily off the ground.

Rand stepped out gingerly and turned slowly to consider the dwelling. Mud, clay, and dried grasses formed the exterior, with stones of many shapes and sizes pushed into the walls like M&Ms on the face of a cookie. The entire structure stood maybe twenty feet wide and twenty feet long, about seven feet tall. Grasses and brush surrounded it, grew on its roof. It looked like a giant ant hill in the middle of a broad, flat expanse. It was Rand's turn to chuckle. He couldn't believe he was living in such a place. Then he noticed the light on it and its surroundings and wanted to photograph it. What a great location for a fashion shoot. He chuckled again.

"Keep an eye out for rattlers," Storm cautioned.

That brought Rand back to the present and he glanced in different directions about him.

"That's a good snake stick you have there." Storm chuckled again. Both men felt good.

They went slowly to the edge of a tree-filled wash some forty yards from the earthen house. Short cactuses grew among the grasses, and Storm told how he made jam from the fruit. He pointed. "Sage." He picked a piece and held it for Rand to smell. "Good, huh? Sage has taught me much. It's the color of faded envy."

He pointed and named the feathery Eastern Kingbird, the hovering American Kestrel, the Mourning Dove with wings that whistle, and he paused for a moment to watch the movements of each one.

Sitting on the edge of the wash, Storm let his long worried leg hang down into it. It dropped off fifteen feet, spanned twenty yards, ran off to who knew where. The red sandy soil in the bottom formed swirls and pile-ups, evidence of rushing water long gone; only a shallow, slow trickle ran through the center. Trees and shrubs of many types, many shades of green, lined the edges and bottom of the wash, and the thick grass that grew in moist places was greener than what grew up higher where the men now sat.

"Can we sit for five minutes in silence?" Storm asked.

"Sure," Rand answered, but felt a pang from the silence that engulfed him as he crossed the sad lonely country, felt guilt about this terrible, yet necessary delay. He started thinking of continuing his journey. He felt stronger, but believed another couple days of rest were essential. The inhospitable stretches before him brought fear rushing back. Indians or revolutionaries could again attack. He could easily fall prey to the elements. His mood sank as he considered the feeble way in which he made progress. Whatever he tried, he felt like a failure. The chances for his family's safety dwindled while he sat and healed.

"You're not being silent," Storm said.

Rand looked at him. He hadn't spoken a word. The Indian sat with his hands resting on his thighs, the cane laid on the ground next to him. He wore the faded blue jeans, the moccasins, a green tank top, and sat with back and neck straight, eyes half-lidded and directed forward, seemingly unseeing.

"In order to find answers to our questions we must bring peace to our mind, to our soul, huh?" he continued. "This is one reason I value wilderness. Silence by which to search the soul. Some people want to open wilderness, build in it, drive their machines through it. In this country we have only five percent of our land protected as wilderness. Five percent and the rest so fucking noisy I cannot stand it." After a moment he glanced over at Rand with a small humble smile of apology, "Sorry." He shifted himself, but returned to the same posture. "Concentrate on your heart beat and your natural slow breathing. Quiet your mind and open your ears to silence."

Rand had heard of meditation. He knew people back home, some of Kera's friends, who actually practiced it. For him, he thought of it as garbage, a waste of time. But, today, he turned his head back to the front and closed his eyes, put the cane to the side, rested his hands on his thighs. The sounds of birds came back to him, the fluttering of wings, cheeps and chirps, the buzzing of a million insects, his own heart beating in his throat. He took a deep breath, heard it flow from his lungs.

"That's it," Storm whispered. "Let out all the bad—let it out with the air you exhale. Then breathe in the good, fresh air. Wild land can teach you to open your heart, to silence your misery, and consider your actions. It has given me great joy. Before discovering wilderness I had no understanding."

Rand breathed again, as deeply as he could. He let it out. He did it again and his lungs expanded, his shoulders lifted, his wound quit pinching, his scalp tingled. He felt no breeze, but a soft rustling sounded from the nearest tree. He opened his eyes part way and saw tiny round leaves twirling in the air. The sun hit their silvery undersides and made them shimmer like ornaments. The torn hills across the way caught the light and their reddish soils vibrated with intensity and appeared strikingly beautiful. He closed his eyes, breathed. His fingers also tingled, his toes; then came silence, absolutely no sound, for long moments, no sound. It was as if time had stopped. He breathed, and he heard the sound of his own life.

His mother had come to him one day as he sat on a patch of grass in the backyard, crying over some toy his parents refused to buy for him. He saw her walking toward him and the sun splashing off her flowered yellow dress and white sandals. Her hair was tied back in glossy precision and her pink face looked warm. He remembered wanting to be held close by her. She bent down to address him and said with a smile— Randy, my son, you will never have all the things you want in life. That's not what life is for. Life is for beauty. Witnessing beauty and being thankful for it proves our right to be on this earth—and then she reached down and ran her soft fingers along his face, brushed the tears away with her thumb, touched the fine hairs on the edges of his ears, stood tall again and walked off.

His father wore a suit each day to work. Business, you know. And as Rand spread his final college photographs out on the kitchen table his father walked past on his way for coffee and scolded—You will never have anything if you stay with art. Art is not a way to make a living, not a way to support a family, not a way to get anywhere in life. It's child's play!—And then his father had rushed through the door and away to the office that Rand hated to visit.

One day long ago Andrew and Alissa were playing together in the living room in Mt. Vernon. They had plopped themselves down and dressed dolls, made dolls dance and made dolls talk. Funny, how little boys played with dolls, but beautiful and innocent too. The children played as if they would be best friends forever, and Rand felt he must do everything he could to ensure that, to keep them friends and to keep their lives full of playing. Yet, he had walked from the room without a word, or a pause, without a moment for playing along with them.

The warm water had trickled down over Rand's head, his face. He was seated in the bathroom tub, the back of his head in Kera's naked lap as she sat up on the edge, her feet in the water, her legs around his shoulders. She dunked the hand cloth time and time again, let the wet heat sink into his scalp, his shoulders, unwinding him. It was years ago and he had been having a terrible time with work, with family, with children keeping him up all night, and it brought him to bed for days with the flu. She had lifted the world from his shoulders with that water, baptized him against evil, washed away his weaknesses, replenished him, and when he turned he had seen it, how it showed on her face as she ran the warm cloth all over him... Love. In that moment, she nurtured him as he had not been nurtured since his mother nursed him. He had long forgotten that moment in that tub, with Kera's sweet scent and touch, and only now did it come to his mind, to his heart, like fresh air to an ancient tomb—a tomb with walls built of greed, self-absorption, misconception.

His eyes now opened part way. They focused on the silent distances of the dry Wyoming flatlands. The brilliant sun glimmered off grasses and rock. It felt as if he had awakened from a dream, but it was no dream, it was his life, and he glimpsed an understanding and a feeling of acceptance unto himself.   Yet, the razor sharp vision of his failures caused him to ache.

He had to go. He had to find his family, even if it killed him.

Turning his head, he saw that Storm had gone, but then spotted him some yards away, lying flat on the ground, face down. His arms were outstretched, palms to the ground, body flat, cheek pressed to the soil, as if he were hugging a giant balloon. His eyes were open and a euphoric expression filled his face.

Chapter 24

The simple but sturdy sauna stood seven feet tall, ten feet by eight feet in dimension, all wood, ornate touches. When Kera entered she came face-to-face with her image in a mirror mounted on the inside of the door. As she feared, the signs of her tormentor remained obvious: a darkish ring of broken blood vessels encircled her right eye, though it had faded considerably; the cut on her lip had been deep and would leave a scar. She looked the victim. Her children had seen.

Inside, a bench ran the length of one wall. In the corner stood a small but ample wood stove. Heat radiated from its metal exterior with fierce intensity and steam rose from water in a large kettle on top.

A new razor sat on a shelf, next to a fresh bar of soap, unopened shampoo, clean towels, a pair of women's shorts and a short sleeve cotton top. A note tacked to the wall above the towel said—*For you, Kera. You are welcome here.* She felt thankful, to be so well cared for.

She soaped herself so furiously and completely that her eyes stung and her mouth tasted bitter suds. Hot steam turned her skin red and perspiration flowed from her, bringing with it, she prayed, the last of the vile residue from past horrors. She let the swirling steam singe her and then repeatedly ladled near scalding water over herself.

She worked the razor under each arm, then propped each leg in turn on the edge of the bench and shaved the long hair from her legs.

Rand came into her mind and she prayed he was safe, but knew in a second that if he was, he should be here, and a strong animosity welled up. She didn't want to feel it, but with all she had endured, why had he not made it here to be with the children? Where was he now? Had he even tried? Would he ever care for anyone other than himself again?

After dressing she threw her soiled clothes into the stove. She stepped from the hut and closed the door purposefully behind her, headed directly for the small home which contained her children.

When she entered, Andrew and Alissa bombarded her with questions as if she had just arrived. Members of the retreat had earlier made the children aware of conflict occurring within the country, but had gone on to assure them that everything would be okay; everyone was safe, their parents included. Nothing in the retreat had changed and the children continued with chores, games, and outings. But now, with their mother, they expressed a need to better understand the situation.

She explained the big argument going on as well as she could, leaving out all violence, which proved challenging. People were disagreeing, so things like airports simply weren't operating. When she spoke of her and Rand coming for them, she told the children only that she had gone ahead in the car, had an accident and received a ride from the soldiers, and that Rand would soon arrive as well.

"He's not coming," Andrew said, with a hard edge to his mouth and eyes. He had built-up anger toward his father, and Kera couldn't help but understand. The way he looked at her, he knew something more had happened, but didn't ask further questions. Alissa seemed to feel safe and at least outwardly content. She focused on the voice and touch of her mother, and soon went back to making creatures from little wooden beads and cotton string the Retreat had provided.

Kera realized she had used the word "normal" when talking to the children: *everything would soon return to normal*. That particular word repeated itself in her mind. She had absolutely no idea what to expect from anything, what normal would mean in the future.

She asked the children to tell her more about the place. Both of them explained that besides the garden they shared the work of cleaning and organizing the big rooms in which children participating in the retreat lived. They even helped feed and milk the dairy goats, and made cheese from the milk, which they used to top off homemade pizzas full of vegetables from the garden. They played number games, wrote and told stories, sang, danced, and drew pictures with crayons, watercolors and oils. They went for walks into the forest and fields and learned the names of birds and animals, plants, rocks, and, at night, stars.

As they talked, they finished the food on the trays, but were interrupted by a knock on the door. Kera found Mattie and a man waiting outside. The man held a canvass sack in his hand.

"Hello," Kera said as she opened the door.

"Hello," Mattie answered, smiling, and again Kera noticed how the faultless white of her teeth shown brightly against the dark luster of her skin. She was not beautiful in the sense of a cover girl, but the upright and unassuming way she handled herself, and the soft style of her dress, gave her a feminine and benevolent quality that came across as disarming and attractive. "May I introduce you to Lightner?" She nodded toward the hulk of a man standing next to her. "You spoke to him on the phone before sending the children to us."

Kera's heart palpitated.

He stood at least 6'6" tall and weighed possibly two hundred and fifty pounds. His heavy shoulders were stooped a bit, and he wore khaki field pants and a thick grey cotton shirt well worn and half tucked in. Grey had worked most of the way through his thick and unruly hair and bushy sideburns came down to the lobes of his ears. Stubble filled his face and his big brown eyes looked watery, as if plagued by allergies.

"Hello... Mister Lightner," she said. He had a protuberant beefy nose, looked about fifty years old.

"Just Lightner, no Mister," he smiled, holding out his hand.

Kera hesitated—*is it the unruly hair, the massive build?*—then took the hand and judged it the biggest and warmest she had ever felt. He held out the sack.

"Mushrooms for you. We harvest'm from the forest and raise a few out'a season."

Kera accepted the bag and opened it, looked in to find a dozen or more sizable mushrooms. "These look wonderful. Thank you."

"They're morels, quite tasty."

"Have your night and morning been restful?" asked Mattie.

"Yes, they have. Come in."

The two stepped through the door and Andrew ran up to Lightner, took hold of his hand. "Hello, Andrew," the mountain of a man said, his voice a little quieter than a moment before. His manner exuded a certain carefulness.

"Mom, Lightner teaches us stuff in the woods. He keeps track of the tree contest."

"Okay." A smile thawed Kera's face. She glanced up at the big hairy man, thought of the way she had walked the woods as a child, and how she had not taken Andrew into the forest as it appeared Lightner now did. "I see," she said.

Lightner's watery eyes smiled back at her. "This young man is quite a woodsman in the making." He draped his huge paw of a hand over Andrew's head and tousled the hair.

Kera saw that touch, and how comfortable Andrew seemed with the man.

"We were wondering if we might show you around when you're ready?" Mattie asked.

Despite constant regret over her visible injuries, Kera felt a desire to see more of the place. There was something very comfortable about it and she wanted to judge more for herself if it was safe. Besides, she felt intrigued by the people she had seen and met. "Is now a good time?"

"Yes, for me," answered Mattie. "Lightner?"

"Good as any!" he said.

When Mattie saw the condition of Kera's worn tennis shoes she offered to seek replacements later in the day, and with that the five of them left the small house.

"We'll show you the community and give you a bit of our philosophy here at Better Way." Mattie led them down a stone walkway running in front of the houses, which often sat among fingers of trees reaching out from the thicker forest behind them. "We consider ourselves a progressive community, Kera. We strive for solidarity among our citizens. There are seventy-four of us, thirty-two are children." She glanced over and smiled at Kera. "Currently."

They passed rock walls and blooming patches of wild flowers. The air filled with sweet scent. Landscaping had been kept to a minimum, with natural trees, brush, and grasses growing freely. Traditional lawns were rare and small. "We don't like to use this term because it has been so widely misused, but we are about as Earth-friendly here as you can get. All our homes have composting toilets; we use no water to flush our waste. It breaks down and we take the small remaining amounts of ash into the forest where it fertilizes the soil. We could use it on certain plants in the garden but some folks would rather we not." She chuckled lightly. "Our homes are powered by wind and solar energy." She pointed to shiny panels on top of the homes and to a number of windmill-like towers. "We don't use a lot of electricity since our heat is supplied from wood, and our homes are mostly all strawbale or cordwood construction with high thermal capacity. Also, we have only one television, in the central hall, and other electric appliances are used sparingly."

They continued on and came to the central building fronted by the garden, where Kera noticed new people had replaced those working earlier. A number of others walked, or road bicycles, in various directions throughout the community, going about their day. Everyone that came near them smiled and Mattie stopped to introduce each of them to Kera. In turn, they all smiled at the children and called them by name.

Kera felt almost as if she were in a dream. The place existed in complete contrast to the state of the country elsewhere. It felt odd and she found herself working to relate what she saw with what she had experienced over the last weeks. "Everyone is so friendly here," she said.

Mattie smiled proudly. "We are a community, Kera. Commune— another word with a bad rap here in the United States. The idea is for a group of people to live in harmony with themselves and their environment, supporting each other. Each person here works to produce something that is in turn either used by all, or sent out to market, the proceeds from which come back and are distributed. We share. We grow most of what we eat. We make much of what we wear. We create much of what we use. If we can't create it, we try and barter for it. We have one automobile, a truck, parked in Latrop. We have one computer which we use to make a little money, and to teach ourselves and the children this new technology. It's not always easy, living like we do, and it's not perfect, but we work at it, and we have tons of fun too."

They entered the building, the television room, empty of people but furnished with benches, couches, and chairs. They saw the computer room and the large room where small children were day-cared, where Kera had found Andrew and Alissa yesterday. "In here we take turns reading and interacting with children unable to be with parents, or who are guests at the retreat. No child spends more than two hours here each day. Parents choosing to live here agree that children can be with parents for work, play, meals, and education. We even have a few grandparents living here with their children, and they also work, play, and teach. Our children are home-schooled. Public education in this country is directed to provide a workforce for industry, but we teach tools which help develop a realization of self and the natural environment. We think this makes for happier, healthier people who know who they are, what they need out of life, and where they fit in the big picture of the community and universe around them."

Mattie touched on subjects, a way of life, that Kera had given thought to for some time, her whole adult life really. The way she and others had lived deeply troubled her. Life had become endlessly complex. People lost site of any greater purpose and filled their days with constant meaningless consumption and behaviors. Those at the

Retreat seemed to live differently and this intrigued her. But what troubled her more, right here, right now, was a lack of preparation, even an interest, in what was happening across the country.

"Can I ask," she started, "Do you people know what is going on out there?"

***

With the sun still below the horizon, Rand stood outside the front door of the earthen house, camera bag draped from his shoulder, the water bottle poking from it. In his hand he held the cane Storm made him. His clothes were tattered, though still fairly fresh from the washing Storm had given them. The polo shirt looked almost green again, but the hole where the knife entered him had begun to unravel and was surrounded by a dark stain. He had not shaved since leaving home, so a full beard now covered his weathered face, and his hair, bleached from the sun, partially hid his ears and reached halfway down the back of his neck. His pants and shoes had holes in them. Storm provided stiff cording for new shoe strings. Rand said, "I must go. I need to find my family."

Storm had been out in the magical predawn and stood looking steadily at him there, and Rand saw something in the face, the eyes, which he didn't expect. "Wait," the Indian said, tottering quickly past him and inside.

Rand heard the movements of gathering. The rugged red hills began to glow. A robin-sized bird, he now knew it to be a Kingbird, fluttered up onto the edge of the roof and stood staring beady-eyed at him. It flew off in a start, caught a large insect in midair, landed in a bush. A coyote howled off in the distance, and another. Storm came to the door and cocked his head, listened with the glint of admiration in his eye. More of the canines called in an echoing frenzy which grew in loudness and urgency, then stopped short. "Wait," Storm said, and he ducked back in. The sound of his hurried movements returned.

Rand was again ready. He felt prepared to walk the land, though he would rather fly or drive or ride in any damn thing—any damn thing that wouldn't trap him. But the thought of traveling the vast expanses did not worry him as it had. For some reason the land felt less hostile. He had, at this point, lived through more than he ever imagined. *What could stop me now?*

Storm came to the door with a medium-sized nylon backpack in his hand. "Take this with you. I have food in there, water, a sleeping bag, and an extra pair of socks, gloves and a warm hat. Some clean bandage material, too."

Rand considered objecting, but knew he needed it all. He reached out and took hold of the strap. The pack weighed maybe twenty pounds. "Thank you!"

He looked at Storm. No question, here stood a man who selflessly risked his own life in order to save Rand's. The glow of the hills and the softness of the light, the tones of the earthen house at his shoulder, it made for a picture Rand wanted. He set the bag down and took the camera, smiled at Storm, stepped back, looked through the lens. *Yes. Here is a face for all faces to see. Here is a face I must never forget.* The Indian looked easily back, peaceful in the moment. Rand shot a number of photographs and didn't want to stop, each frame told a story. This is a man he would never have known but for adversity, the kind of experience that cuts through unfamiliarity and brings two spirits together to survive, or fail. They had won against the odds, and gone on to share their stories, fears and dreams. Storm no longer presented Rand just a face for photographing, like so many faces from his past. This man—along with Patricia, Buck and Walt—he had connected with them in the brief hot flash of upheaval that melded humanity in a way he had not ever known. They had all saved him and he was now feeling bonded to them, to all such people, unique unto themselves, but also, one.

He put the camera into the pack.

"Was it good?" Storm asked with a smile.

"It was good."

"Take this too?" Storm handed him a scrap of paper with writing on it. It read: Ben G. Hayduke. Box 63. Bill, Wyoming. "I go in to get mail about once a month. Maybe you could keep in touch."

Rand looked at it again. "Ben Hayduke. That's you?"

"Anglo name. My father was a burly white from the Southwest, my mother a teeny-weenie Cheyenne."

Rand put the paper in the pack. It felt odd to him, because he never did this, but he reached out and wrapped his arms around Ben G. Seeker of Storms Hayduke. He squeezed as hard as he could squeeze without applying too much pressure to his middle. He was surprised how good it felt. "I'll keep in touch, Brother," he whispered in the other man's ear. "Thank you for saving my life."

"That was scary shit, huh?" Storm whispered back.

Rand eased the pack onto his back, picked up the cane, and began his walk away. "One thing," He turned back.

Storm cocked his head.

"How did you appear from nowhere when I was stabbed?"

"I was only lying on the ground and you all gathered like a dark cloud. I am sorry I did not stand sooner."

Rand went over the moment in his mind. Before the stabbing, he had been beaten by hail. "What about the hail, were you out in that?"

"Hail?"

From the look on his face, Storm really had no idea of any hail, and it was all not making sense to Rand. He looked at the cane in the Indian's hand, "Well, then, how did you get me back to your house?"

Storm cocked his head and gazed out at the hills as if recalling. "I have been praying a long time for guidance." His eyes settled again on Rand; his arms formed a cradle before him, "How did I get you back to my house? I carried you, like a present."

Chapter 25

"If we are not going to evacuate as the authorities recommend, I guess I am wondering what our plan will be in the event of trouble?" The man was heated, Kera could see that, but he held his frustration at bay. "I would like to hear from Mattie on this."

Kera sat in an old barn with more than forty adults and most of the children from Better Way. The barn stood next to a fifty acre hay field, which spread out between two forest covered foothills far to the rear of the community. It felt to Kera like a secret place, since in order to find it you had to walk a narrow horse and wagon track through an ancient, towering forest. In coming, Andrew proudly identified the furry-needled larch, western red cedar and numerous other trees.

The barn appeared a bit of a skeleton, weathered bare and brown, with pointers of sunlight streaming through the gaps of missing boards, highlighting members of the crowd who sat on long wooden benches.

Kera sat in the middle of the group with Andrew and Alissa to her right, Nee and Lewis on the left. Lightner was there, in the rear, sitting with people Kera had not met, though Mattie introduced her at the start of the meeting. At that moment she had felt vulnerable to the crowd, like some spotlight settled only on her wounds, but when she smiled, the faces before her returned openness and acceptance.

Mattie stood near Kera and began speaking. "As I said, Frank, our plan is why we scheduled time here tonight, to discuss options and possibly hold a vote. As current speaker for the community, I have no opinion, per our charter. I would like to hear from Missy Sanderfield." Mattie sat back down.

A woman in her twenties stood, wearing a long light summer dress, auburn hair braided and hanging nearly to the back of her knees. "Can't we do what we have always done, go about our business and refuse to participate in the insanity of the outside world? We voted not to evacuate because we felt it unnecessary and we should stick by that decision. I would like to hear from Mr. Johnstone, as he is our eldest member and has great wisdom." She sat back down and folded her hands in her lap.

"We must know what we face." A shaky but calm and measured voice came from the rear, as Kera and others turned to watch. One of the grandparents that Mattie had mentioned, a slight man of eight decades, maybe more, with white hair and a white, collared shirt beneath a sweater vest, slowly stood. "To do nothing, to imitate the Jewish community of the 1930s, or the Tibetans even today, that is to embark upon a fatal course for our future. We are confronted with a life-changing decision. If we stoop to violence, violence is what will come of us. If we do not, will we be set upon by lunatics? And another thing: we are here because we disagreed with the direction our government has moved, with the priorities of our society—so therefore, is a revolution not what many of us have known and even hoped would one day occur?" The man glanced toward Kera. "I would like to hear the opinion of the new young lady. I understand she has come a long way. No doubt, she has seen a lot." He lowered himself back to the bench.

Kera's face burned. She felt all eyes turning toward her. She couldn't believe someone requested her thoughts on such a crucial matter. Would they do so if they knew what she had been through, how she had been used and treated more lowly than the most wretched thing on Earth?

No one had ever shown an interest in Kera's ideas or thoughts, from her godparents, to those who led the professional world she took part in, other women she'd known, even her own husband.

Who is it in my past, besides my parents and children, who cared to know what I thought or felt?

The faces turned to her and as she peered back at them, for the first time in her life, she felt strangers were not assessing a beautiful woman who likely had an ego to go with it. The men were not wondering what she'd be like in bed, and the women, what kind of threat she presented. She felt embarrassed at the marks she bore, but with those marks came the story of an ordeal many could never have survived. She had. And she could see their interest in what she had to say.

"You are not obligated to speak when called on," Nee whispered in her ear. "It is fine to say you are not inclined to speak at this time."

Kera looked at Andrew and Alissa. Their eyes focused on her expectantly, proudly. Much of what she might say would be new to them, and that worried her, but she did have information that could help prepare this community for what might happen. And these people had safely guarded her children while she could not.

Kera stood and it felt an awesome task to make her legs work, to push herself up in front of this crowd. "We are from New York. I had decided to send my children here because my husband and I needed some time…" Kera told her story and her hands began to shake. Alissa reached up and placed her hand over her mother's and Kera took hold without looking down

While she did not recount every detail, she did account for every important thing that happened. The rapt eyes of those listening convinced her to remain open and let them decide for themselves.

It came from her and sounded like a confession, a condemnation, a prayer. It compared to lancing a boil, getting all that poison out, away from the aching places inside her. No one stirred or tried to interrupt. All sat and listened, mesmerized, terrified, this gathering of many melded together into one, by such a tale. She gave no opinions: the facts clearly conveyed the potential dangers before them.

When finished, Kera stood there and for a heartbeat silence and stillness filled the room. Then Nee and Mattie came and placed their arms around her.

After another moment Mattie asked, "Is there anyone here that might, considering all we have heard, and in respect to this brave woman, call a recess on tonight's meeting, so we might consider this new information, and come together again tomorrow night with focused and prepared thoughts?"

The room filled with the sound of affirmations. "So moved!" a voice called out and everyone stood and began filing out of the barn. Many paused to touch Kera's hand or shoulder. A number of men gazed upon her openly, and allowed her to feel their sorrow and their anger. A few cried tears.

Mattie and Nee maintained their embrace of her, and with the children they walked to the little house where they stayed with her for the night.

***

Rand marched along and studied the mountains before him. From north to south in an unbroken line they towered into the sky, looking like a barricade, an impediment from hell created to keep him from his family.

At his feet, the grasslands had faded to fields of dry rock and stubble. Ranches dotted the landscape, but it was easy to move around them and the small dusty infrequent towns. He judged that he'd walked well over one hundred miles since leaving Storm.

He stopped and took off the pack, knelt in the dust, drank water from a container Storm had given him, and shifted himself to ease the pinch of the wounds. From the pack he took the remaining portion of jerky, also from Storm. He ripped off a small chunk, replaced the rest, planned to keep it until he desperately needed it—which he hoped wouldn't happen. He pulled the pack straps back over his shoulders, grasped the willow cane, and pushed himself up again.

He wouldn't take the time, but wanted to photograph the country around him, amazed at all he saw, the changes light made across the great expanses. He wondered again how he had spent so much of his life photographing, but not seeing. He felt he wasn't only passing through new lands, but through some new threshold of himself. Apparent to him now were the sounds of living—the birds, the wind, the insects, the faraway cry of coyotes, his own rushing breath in great gullies of silence. Coursing through him now were considerations of a broader world, not only the narrow everyday portion he lived for so long. He felt strong, stronger each day. Everything looked new and wonderful.

Within him, hope blazed. He prayed and worked to convince himself that he would reach his children and one day see his wife. He came closer with each step, felt them wrapped in his arms. *I am coming, Alissa, Andrew. Kera, my love protects you.* He was beginning to believe that if he willed them alive, willed them safe and happy, if he did this well enough, it would prove true.

And so, as he marched along, his mind traveled two lands, moving freely from what he saw before him, and what he saw within. Whichever place it dwelled, it concentrated its full and intense powers.

After several more miles, he again paused. Before him, Rand studied a bulwark of green mountains with imposing diagonal ridges of brown uplifted rock, which sliced through the dry forest covering them. In places, the way the system of massive rock snaked from ridge to ridge reminded him of the Chinese Wall.

Never had he seen anything that compared to this massive work of nature. He'd heard the name, but had never laid eyes on them; the Rocky Mountains. *Must be.* Like the vast and seemingly uncrossable plains behind him, these mountains radiated their own power. He had never understood how rock and soil could present so boldly, or challenge with such energy.

About a mile away a road wound itself high up into the rocky ridges. Rand had hoped to stay away from roads, but now saw this as the only way over such rugged and impassable ground. Night would be the thing. He would rest until sunset and hike the road through the night.

He walked to within a hundred yards of the pavement, not a car in sight, not the sound of one, and took off the pack. Sitting, Rand placed the pack as a pillow for his head, and laid down. He stared at the sky and the faces of his family that resided there, and fell asleep in an instant.

He rose after dark and resumed walking. It felt odd and hard, the pavement beneath his feet. The road cut a drastic angle and Rand felt thankful to have the cane, used it to push himself along. He knew that his legs had grown hard over the past few weeks; his lungs now took air deeper than they had back in the city, this clear, crisp air. He paused and looked out over the moonlit washed lowlands stretching away, back toward where he'd come, noticed the lights of two vehicles moving miles off, but heading toward his mountain. Stars shimmered above. They amazed him, the magnitude of them, opened his mind further and challenged him to wonder, until it all seemed too great and intense and impossible. *Could this universe really go on forever...?* The exhilaration this journey now afforded him felt like a beloved triple shot of espresso. *No, on second thought, different, better really.*

The vehicles wound their way up the mountain and he stepped into the brush along the road and watched them speed past, engines whining. He saw heads silhouetted against headlights after they passed—two pickup trucks with two men each.

Walking... he figured it had been three hours and the road never leveled for more than a step or two. Twice, creatures crashed off through the brush, but he could not see them. He would have liked to observe what lived in such a dramatic place. He came to a creek and filled his bottle, drank heavily. After sitting a few minutes he found his energy depleted, laid back for a rest, and fell asleep.

***

Kera requested a turn in the garden. Along with Andrew and Alissa they had eaten a large amount of foods from their hosts and lodged comfortably in the quaint and pleasant housing. She had prepaid for the children's two week stay at the retreat, but that had passed and it wasn't right for them to take so much and not earn it; they could at least offer labor in return. She went with Nee and weeded, spread manure, learned. The children carried weeds to a series of compost piles outside the fence, and for breaks they sat in the shade of the fruit trees and drank cool apple juice.

With the warm sun on her back Kera's spirits soared. She felt rested for the first time in months, possibly years. Her body healed and the experiences at Better Way gave her a sense of grounding and stability. These people had drawn in around her and her children like a shield— and to be appreciated instantly by strangers who somehow interpreted her innate qualities proved a powerful experience. Her observations, in fact, her instinct, told her she had arrived at a place she'd like to call home. The community possessed all the signs of the healthy, relaxed and purposeful society she sensed might exist, but had never found.

"So, the garden provides most of what the community eats in the way of vegetables, enough variety?" she asked.

"What we need." A slender but solid woman, Nee worked swiftly and precisely, with smooth movements that reflected a comfortable awareness of her body. "Sometimes we want a fruit or vegetable that will not grow here." Her voice offered a touch of accent; her long black hair was braided. She wore a light cotton top open to a smooth bust line and beige shorts that revealed toned calves and thighs. She had left her flip-flop sandals at the gate, worked with her toes in the soft earth. Kera couldn't help but admire her, thought her immaculate. Nee appeared the healthiest woman she had ever seen. Many models needed make-up and soft lighting, but Nee glowed naturally. Kera appreciated her beauty, and also understood her attractiveness rooted itself in something deeper. She behaved with incredible ease and certainty. "Do you understand organics?" she asked. Her voice had a gentle quality.

"Some of it." Kera wiped at a bug on her face and left a track of dirt under her eye. It was a hot day and Nee had given her a straw wide-brimmed hat to keep the sun off her head.

"We don't use chemical fertilizers or insecticides in the garden because we all believe that consuming chemicals is bad for the body and mind. Chemicals retard the immune system and lead to disease, among other things. We prefer our food natural, so we use manure and compost. We also use a lot of heirloom seeds and grow hearty varieties industrial growers ignore and have, in fact, worked to keep from all of us."

"My father was a farmer back east. I was too young to remember but I think he did some organic farming," Kera said.

"The use of chemicals is fairly new. In fact, those of us forty to fifty years of age are likely the first generation of people to eat chemically treated foods all our life. Many of us feel that chemicals are one reason there is so much cancer. They are everywhere. Hormones and antibiotics are used in dairy and beef, pesticides and herbicides and fungicides in produce. And another issue is genetically altered food. It's daunting, if you make a study of it. The best way to get around it is to raise as much of your own food as possible and to buy the rest from organic and local farmers."

"So Lewis feels the same way?"

"Oh, yes," she laughed lightly.

"Are you two married?"

"No, we are friends, and have been together for years and strive for many of the same goals. We eat clean food and drink natural juices and plenty of water. We practice yoga and meditate in the open air daily. We try to enrich our lives through the companionship of like-minded people and spend a lot of time building our relationships."

"Do you have children, Nee?"

"No." Nee stopped pulling weeds from under young corn plants and looked toward Andrew and Alissa playing under a tree.

Kera chopped at the fluffy ground and mixed a small amount of manure into the dark soil. She felt uncomfortable, as if she had forced the conversation onto private ground.

"Your children are very beautiful and behave so well." Nee turned to Kera and smiled. "I have decided not to have children. It's my feeling there are enough children in the world, enough people. As our societies on Earth begin to show signs of wear, as Earth itself shows those signs, I feel the root of most issues is overpopulation. So, as a woman I am making the decision to ignore my biological clock and do my part to control human population. I hope I haven't offended you in any way."

"You haven't. I've thought about that. The growth in our country is so incredible. Yet everyone seems so intent on their right to have children. Living in New York City, it's so congested. It was driving me crazy even if I didn't really understand why. But who am I to point a finger, having had my children already."

"You have two, only two. In many places people talk about the rate of growth, then they have three children, four children, ten children. It seems to me when we talk about issues facing our world most are issues of numbers—too many children in schoolroom classes, too many cars on the roads leading to road rage and air pollution, too little money to expand services in cities bursting with too many citizens. There are many issues, and for me, most issues boil down to too many people."

A moment of silence passed before Nee continued, "Have you seen much of America in your life?"

"No, I'm embarrassed to say I haven't. Mostly the Northeast."

"I have been here many years and have not seen enough myself. As much as I love our community, I would like to travel and experience other areas. There are so many wonderful places I read about as a child."

Kera turned her head and listened, shifted her eyes toward the mountains. First one and then two, three, four helicopters came into distant view, approached, and cruised over the community. Kera had seen no others since she arrived and looked closely, trying to determine if they were the same helicopters, carrying the same men. But she couldn't tell and soon the sound faded and the aircraft pounded out of sight. Kera couldn't keep fear from rising within her. Soldiers had reunited her with her children, but they represented only one thing—violence.

"Last night," Nee asked, "did you hear anything in the distance that sounded like bombs or big guns?"

"Yes."

"I awoke near 1 a.m. and at first I heard nothing, and thought I had come awake for no reason. But then I heard a far off boom, almost like thunder. I think it was soldiers fighting."

"I think so too. Is that the first of that you have heard?"

"Yes. And the last I hope to hear."

It had taken several days, but that evening the community again gathered in the barn. This time Lightner sat next to Andrew, who reached out and took the big quiet man's hand. Lightner looked to Kera with his deep watery eyes searching her face, and she understood he was asking permission to treat the boy with such closeness. She smiled in return. Her mind went to Rand often every day, and her desire for his safety, growing as those days passed, still met instantly with her doubt. Nothing had happened to make her think he had suddenly changed into a father and husband with love in his heart. That love, if any ever really existed, had gone away and he showed no awareness or regret. As hard as she worked to understand him, pain and bitterness remained. And lately Andrew seemed to ask less about his father, as his father had asked so rarely about him. Alissa did ask, and Kera continued to say he would come. With all her mixed emotions, she blocked the image of him lying dead somewhere, but at the same time intuited its truth. He was either dead or gone.

Kera felt deeply thankful for the warm buffer Lightner offered the children.

A number of people proceeded to speak in their turn and each thanked Kera for divulging so openly the dangers she had faced. No television or radio signals reached them in the mountain canyons, no newspapers found a way down their dead-end path. Kera had provided a needed perspective on the condition of the broader society outside. Concern and trepidation tightened several of the voices, but no one spoke with hostility or anger.

"I came here twelve years ago, and many of you came before me," said Jon Farron, a man nearly Lightner's size, dressed in the plaid shirt and torn jeans of a carpenter. His voice boomed throughout the barn and a swath of yellow sunlight shined off his red hair. "I ain't never been so happy anywhere. Never felt like I was home 'til I got here and found Sarah like she'd been waitin' or somethin'. My grandpa was a soldier in World War One, my uncle in World War Two. I heard their stories. And I felt pride in knowing them. Still, I ain't interested in killin'." He looked up at the rafters of the big barn and hooked his thumbs in his belt line. "That there's the question we got to ask ourselves here. Are we willing to kill to protect what we got? I saw what killin' does to a man and I ain't interested. But no, I ain't interested in being killed either. I guess there's a chance this war is going to find us, but I wonder how big the chance is. Big enough maybe, to have a plan. What I'm saying is I ain't going to fight. But I ain't ready to leave neither. I can't see goin' into no city. This is my home. Sarah's too. And I ain't going to go get my shotgun and board up the windows and hide inside. I say we live life and let the Lord take care of us when the time comes. Roger and Wanda Cummins, they have two children and might look at this different."

Roger was short, thin, dark, and Wanda was a little taller, with straight blonde hair. He had come from the south, simple cotton farmer roots; she was the ancestor of a plantation owner. Their two young children sat next to them, quiet, but attentive. Roger stood as straight as a board and smiled at everyone. He held hands with Wanda and looked at her often as he spoke. "We talked about it, Wanda and me. My family, y'all know, they're in Georgia. Wanda's are in South Carolina. We thought about going to one of those areas. But we knew right away that wasn't what we would do. Kera Priven, she told us all what could happen out there. Besides, we've been here only two years, but who are we gonna feel better with than you folks?"

He looked at Wanda and her face was drawn from worry. She spoke with a quiver in her voice. "I am scared for the children. I don't even like them to hear all this, they're so young and all. I don't want them to worry. But we are all stronger together. I think we should form a committee maybe. I just don't want to see anything happen to our children and it sounds like there are some real sick people out there. Nee, would you please tell us what you think?"

Nee rose from her seat next to Kera. Her relaxed hands came together in front of her as she bent forward, a slight bow, and looked at the many faces. "I am thinking of something my grandfather once told me. He said that for each thing we do energy is emitted and that energy travels through the world, through the universe, through time. He said he chose to create only peace and tranquillity for these ever-flowing tides of energy. Doing so would add serenity to the universe as well as assist his spirit on the road to enlightenment. If each person on Earth added only love, then love is what the universe would be."

Nee paused, shifted her stance, and though her countenance held, Kera saw something pass across her face, some trickle of uncertainty that came and went like the shadow of a bird in flight. Her head rocked back slightly and her chest expanded with a long slow breath. "But now I ask my Grandfather, can it truly be right to give my life, to be expected to give my life, for the intention of no negativity? Can it be right to lie down and let criminals lay waste to silent and peaceful souls? Does that sacrifice move this universe toward a more dignified existence, or does it simply allow the violence to grow unimpeded? And also, the question comes to me, who is wrong and who is right in this great fight that now divides our country, who are our friends and our enemies?

"As I stand here before you asking these questions, Grandfather answers me by sending thoughts into my mind. He satisfies my humble doubt and fear by stating that the peaceful war against violence and hate has existed since the beginning of time. It is a war of incomprehensible duration. Each act of violence is answered by another act as wicked, and so the circle continues while we deny ourselves generation upon generation a life in the garden of love." Nee sat and turned her eyes inward, as if reflecting, or gathering.

A bat looped through the open boards of the barn, the place so still Kera heard its wings flap. She herself knew these people too little to understand their motivations and concerns, yet, somehow, she understood Nee had spoken for all of them. Their very purpose opposed violence.

Kera began to realize that she herself had journeyed to this place seeking not only her children but refuge from a lifetime of violence— violence that killed her parents in the collision of high speed glass and steel, that empowered others to disrespect her even as they used her beauty for selfish monetary gain, that manipulated a society into parasitizing its individuals until they had no energy or time or spirit for families that loved them, a society that filled more, everyday, with signs of aggression. She saw more clearly than ever how broken and unbalanced her country had become, how its citizens moved like automatons within a culture so desensitized that few recognized the injustice of what went on around them.

She felt herself overwhelmed, aghast at the immensity of the troubles that lie outside the fragile boundary of the village. All this sincere need for peace and love and yet she knew, from personal experience, that certain violence could only be stopped by using violence against it. *How could I have let that scum dishonor me? Was my violence not necessary?* She sat and stared blankly into space, at a moral dilemma she felt impoverished to answer.

A child fidgeted and she began to focus on faces, these hard working, trusting, loving people who stood for a life of compassion and trust and the idea that one can *be* for all and all can *be* for one. She looked at them and a feeling of pride and power rose within her. She heard a voice inside encourage her, confirm to her, that what she saw in this small community was light, a shining glowing light, like a fresh flame in the hearth of an abandoned house. What was going on in this country was not working, and what was going on here... well, it was working. She couldn't *know*, because she hadn't been here long, but she could *feel*. She felt this place had reason and sanity, with fertile ground for a life of soulful existence, of right living. What they had here, peace and clarity, honoring of Earth and the practice of non-greed, it was right, and it was at least part of an answer.

Nee had spoken a great truth, and Kera knew that what complicated it was fear. Well, she had succumbed to the putrid muck in the bottom of the valley of fear—for a time. If she arrived there again, she'd do what she felt right, but until then, these people had the only answer she had come upon for as long as she could remember. If enough people in enough places held onto that... the good would out-number the bad. It was as simple as that.

As for an immediate plan against violence, she would stay here in this village because this village was the best and safest place. If trouble arrived she would take the children and go into hiding.

A spot must exist where no one would search for them. If others would agree, they could take provisions and hide them in the mountains and secure a refuge where they might all remain safe if violence forced them. Then they could return when it was over and continue to live as they knew they must.

Chapter 26

Rand awoke to a brightening along the horizon and across the vast flatland east of him. He sat quickly upright, angry at himself for letting the rest of the night slip away. In his weariness he had failed to pull the sleeping bag from the pack and a damp shiver now ran through him. He wiped the crust from his eyes with dirty fingers. Opposite of how the rest of him felt cold, the wound in his side burned. He reached into the pack and pulled out the hat and gloves, pulled them on, wobbled unsteadily to his feet. His calves cramped painfully. No way of getting around it, he felt ragged and raw from walking.

He sipped some water, took a mouthful of the disappearing jerky, then stiffly donned the pack and stumbled onto the road. The damn thing continued endlessly UP! The cold of the mountain night had sucked out the goodwill of the day before. He tried hard to let his feet do the walking while training his mind on other things, trying to forget the pain and fatigue. He plodded along for hours, hating the road. Up. *Christ!*

Halting often, he looked over the brown and barren flatland stretched out behind him. Nothing seemed good, except the idea of getting over the top of the mountain. His shoulders sagged and he gazed at the ground. It all seemed so fucking unforgiving—and then his side hurt in a new way and he didn't like that either.

Off in the brush along the road he pulled at the bandage and uncovered the seeping wound. Yellow puss leaked from the edges of skin. He had thought it healing, it looked so good when Storm last inspected it. But now it fought him, like everything. *What, did I feel too good yesterday and need to be reminded of my sins? Can this infliction hold some unseen connection with the dark angel of my guilt and remorse?* A desire welled up to take hold and rip the wound from him, like a giant leech sucking his life away. He saw in his mind the image of himself all dirt and matted hair and raw infected wound, ripping at himself, alone in wilderness. *No!* He poured a bit of the water over it and let it dry in the sun. Then he took the extra bandage from the pack and wrapped himself in it.

Walking. Each time he came to what he thought was the top of the mountain another top showed itself above him. He finished the rest of the jerky and still his belly growled like a bear caught in a trap.

He felt so different yesterday and understood his emotions were running rampant. Wanting to lighten the load he stopped again for the fifth time in an hour and opened the pack. He could leave the water. *No.* The hat and gloves. *But I was so cold this morning.* The sleeping bag. *Absolutely not.* The cane. *I lean on it every step!*

He turned and screamed at the mountain before him. "AH!" And was shocked at how fast the sound disappeared. He swung the cane wildly and beat at the brush, picked up a rock and threw it onto the pavement of the road... then he stopped and stooped, held one hand to the wound in his side, wincing, gasping for air. After a few moments he hoisted the pack and picked up the cane and started plodding upward, staring at the dark pavement with vacant eyes.

Just before sun down Rand saw something lying on the road and stumbled toward it. It was a squashed squirrel, a runty little grey thing. He pulled at the tail, peeled the body up, and walked off the road, sat on a rock and glared at it. Why hadn't he asked Storm for matches? He shouted into the emptiness, "Even a CAVEMAN is smart enough to make a fire!" A fire would make smoke and that wasn't good. *But it could be such a small fire, and who gives a damn anymore anyway, I'm starving to death.* He rose and walked through the brush and gathered a handful of green leaves. He sat back down and chewed on them and looked at the squirrel. It seemed dead less than a day. Maybe the trucks he had seen last night. Something in the leaves was so bitter it numbed his mouth. He poked the squirrel with his finger. *Mostly bone and skin.* He picked it up and pinched the skin under the fir and tore at it suddenly and ripped a piece of hide off, revealed white glistening tendon and pink flesh. He ripped away more of the hide. *I am going to eat, Damn it!,* and anger drove him to pull off all the fur and skin except that around its head and feet and then he filled his mouth with the leaves and took a bite of the squirrel's thin body and chewed with a grimace on his face—as if he wanted to spit food in the face of the cook. *That's right, I'm in a restaurant and the damn dish has arrived a little under done and I'll be a gentleman and live with it but I don't have to like it!* He ate angrily and finished the thing up to its furry head and feet and then he threw it down and wiped his mouth on his sleeve and picked himself and his belongings up and marched out of there. On the road he couldn't stand the mixture of bitter numbness and dank flesh and stopped, took out the bottle and drank, washed the water around in there until his mouth felt clean. *Still a bit numb, but, well, cleaner.*

The meal didn't seem to help so much, but he struggled long into the chill of night and finally had to stop and collapse in the sleeping bag. His legs cramped so painfully that he cried out more than once and finally laid there too exhausted and miserable to sleep. He remembered hearing that bananas had enough potassium to keep away cramping but he couldn't recall the last time he'd had one, couldn't get the sweet taste of banana into his mouth. In the future he would remember whenever he wanted some rich plate of food he would just go eat a fucking banana. He would buy baskets of them. Give them away to children on the streets. He would wear them, drape them over his head, stick his penis in their empty skins. He laughed deliriously.

He could only do all that if he lived. *And frankly this is all becoming too much.* He lay there shivering, leg muscles seizing painfully, his side flaming again like it had when he'd been stabbed. *How many times now have I thought I would die as I fought my way along? Three? Five? Sooner or later it will be true. Don't the odds make it so?* If he couldn't get this journey behind him, if he couldn't reach his children and find his wife, wouldn't it be best to die anyway? *What the hell is anything for?* What the hell would life be like, living and knowing how he had lost everything, *EVERYTHING!*

The sky suddenly filled with stars as he lay there, looking up. *No, they were always there. Always there, like eyes watching. Who's there? What is this? A test? Or are you just killing me? Is this fun for you?*

His eyes stopped jetting about and settled on the vast oneness of the outer spaces. His breathing became deeper and slower as he squinted at the billion little pulses of light above him. *My God. How far is that? I have come farther than I have ever come, but how far is it really, compared to that?* His arms were out at his sides and his body relaxed as he flattened himself on the ground. *I am but a speck.*

The Milky Way shone brightly. The night's silence enveloped him. *Hear that, Rand? There it is again.* It was the same silence he had heard when out with Storm. *Silence, and yet, a living sound.* He tried to grasp it with his mind, but heard Storm say, *quiet your mind.* He opened his mouth and breathed, swallowed silence, let it fill him.

Could pain be an illusion, sadness an untruth, guilt nothing more than a foolish mistake? Could happiness and contentment and love be a choice?

Rand was laying face-up on a humungous ball and the ball was spinning and floating in space, and somehow the ball, this living breathing ball, knew he was riding along and agreed he belonged. Everything felt suddenly peaceful and understood. It was like riding through the endless ocean on the back of a whale—some tremendous and gentle-hearted being—and like a whale in water—the water is the whale as the whale is the water—there was no difference anymore between what was there in space, or within him. *Everything is made of the same thing.*

He recalled Storm lying on the ground as if he were resting in the arms of a lover, or a protective mother. Rand felt it now too. It came into him all warm and strong. *Yes. Everything is made of something, I don't know what, but all the somethings are the same, and all things are one.* His mind quieted and everything became a feeling, smelling, hearing... acceptance. *Wash me. Wash my pain.* His body filled with the energy of everything around him. He felt warm and golden and a part of limitlessness. His cringing had turned to smiling, and sometime later he suddenly realized he had returned to walking, and was absorbed completely in the sounds and images of space.

Chapter 27

At the community meeting Kera had sat and considered her plan until she felt the eyes of Nee upon her. The gentle woman sensed Kera had come to some new understanding, and asked Kera to give her opinion. Kera stood without a moment's pause, but quieted her rushing mind before supporting the points Nee had stated and going on to modestly explain her thoughts and conclusions. They should remain in the village as long as possible, but when certain signs of approaching violence appeared, they must have a hidden place in the mountains in which to seek refuge, a place well stocked and ready for a long stay.

When Kera finished, some follow-up discussion ensued, but at the end of the meeting everyone over fourteen years of age voted by show of hands, and Kera's plan was accepted unanimously. There was only one addition, that upon the first indication of danger, the community would post twenty-four hour watches along the entrance trail of the village, to warn against surprise.

Lightner knew the perfect place for a hideaway. It took three hours of walking a mountain trail through the forest to reach it. A small trout-filled lake sat in a bowl just below a narrow but negotiable pass and would provide an endless source of potable water. The elevation reached only four thousand feet, so even in winter it would not be brutally cold. And the pass beyond the lake provided an exit should trouble come from the direction of the village. The community owned numerous large and heavy canvass tents and the area would provide all the firewood they would need to stay warm. The exact spot for tents lie sheltered and hidden within forest, and air through the pass would most often provide a breeze to prevent campfire smoke from slowly rising and giving them away.

The community went immediately into action. The first two days were used to haul tools needed to begin the process and to familiarize everyone with the route. Caches were established and canned goods stored. Rather than the air of people preparing for war, Kera felt amazed at how cheerfully everyone worked together and supported one another in the thousand decisions needed to complete such an effort. Children paid attention and contributed, and Elders were led to the site by emergency equipped guides moving slowly. By the end of the fourth day enough food for two months was stashed on site, with plans for two months more. They dry stored the tents, and Jon Farron came up with two small but suitable wood burning stoves easily capable of heating four of the tents when erected properly. If the temperatures dictated, everyone could sleep in those tents. The children talked excitedly about the possibility.

On the last evening of preparations Kera left the children to play with friends and walked alone in the cooling woods outside the village. She wore a light sweater and cotton pants made for her by some of the women, and she had more new clothes at the house. She sat on a fallen tree next to the creek that rushed along through heavy forest. Tears fell from eyes filled with calm self-assuredness. A trickle of joy had its way with her heart. It felt almost too good to be true, but she had never been a part of anything so positive and beautiful. The community voted to allow her and the children to stay and even offered her the free dwelling and food until things changed and she became able to produce something in return. She had the answer in her love for the garden and had ideas for expanding the orchard.

The day would come when this warring ended and she would learn what had happened to Rand. He seemed evermore distant from her, but she also knew she would always have some love for him born of a day when they started together. For now, the country would eventually return to some state of normalcy—though she knew for her everything would always be different. There was a cleaner, saner, nobler life and she had found it.

Yes, almost too good to be true. These people knew their humble place and she hadn't seen an episode of ego or selfishness since arriving. Well, okay, there had been a snip or two made out of context, but it remained rare. When she asked, Mattie told her people who could not coexist respectfully were brought to her attention. When someone had three complaints from varied people against them, a meeting of the community was called where the indicated person or family would be notified of the issues and asked their opinion. Usually an agreement took place where those brought into question would agree to change their behavior. Sometimes no agreement could be reached and everyone voted on whether the offenders could stay. Residents had proven stern in this matter. No one brought in front of the community, who then refused to make the requested changes, had been allowed to remain. But in the two instances where this occurred the community offered those people the right to return anytime they reconsidered, and further, they provided them food, money, and other necessary support so they might leave in good stead. It all made such sense. Nothing had happened to make her doubt the community in the least.

It grew dark as Kera sat thinking. It would take a long time before she completely healed inside, but she couldn't remember feeling so good. Her time at the village was lifting her above self-doubt, about what life had brought her, even being molested. She knew now that none of it was deserved. Not the brutal rape, not even the treatment from Rand. It would take time, but she was beginning to feel whole again, and in a new way she had never known.

She thought of paint now as she contemplated the way the day's waning light faded first off the trees, then off the mountain tops across the valley. She would paint no more decayed and crumbling rock walls, such as her last attempt back in New York City. Her art would focus on flourishing gardens now, verdant forests, and smiling children.

The moon's glow turned the trees to silhouettes around her. It had served as guide and delivered her to a new life. One day she would create a special painting for the moon. She rose and walked carefully through the forest, back to the small but sturdy house that had become her home.

***

Rand came face to face with a huge bull moose standing in a wet field. He had come out of some trees, negotiated a stream, and looked up to see it there before him. Its big brown eyes stared as it stood boulder still. Rand backed off and it held its ground, and finally he turned and followed the stream back toward the road—enough of the short cuts.

He was thinking about food again. He had tried slimy grubs, a dusty sparrow, tart leaves, and a bit of porcupine. Through four more days of walking up through mountains Rand had dined at the table of the same questionable chef, not complained, and finally received the reward of reaching the top. The pass had taken him onto a high plateau of sparse forests and wide rich meadows and he felt like a character in the movie *The Sound of Music*. Creeks full of fresh water ran everywhere. Twice a day he stopped and rinsed his seeping wound with cold water, even dared to scour it with clean sand, let it dry easily in warm shade. He had buried the rancid bandage and left the wound open to air, kept his shirt as clean as he could.

He had heard a few vehicles, even an aircraft, but mostly the place was ghostly quiet. As he moved along the roadway he saw numerous signs for backcountry lodges and guiding services. He felt tempted to try one and see what reaction he might receive. Certainly someone out here would be safe to approach and might offer some assistance in reaching his destination. He really had no idea where he was. The names on the signs along the road meant nothing to him.

He had never seen anyplace so beautiful. Even the mountains that sucked his energy were so majestic he had no way to feel angry at them any longer. They were what they were and he the same. No promontory stood in his way, it just stood. Twice he became so moved by the awesomeness of it all that he paused long enough for a photograph.

Rand understood too that his new state of focused endurance could maintain itself only so long without proper nourishment, rest, and possibly medical care for his wound. The sole of one of his shoes had separated from the leather leaving his foot unprotected, swollen and bleeding. The distance covered by each of his steps had shrunk. The only way he could deal with his state of disrepair was to remain focused on his surroundings—the life of the land and universe. He laughed at unfunny things, heard himself talk with no one but the wind. He hoped that as long as he stayed aware of that he would be okay. As long as his feet kept moving forward an end would arrive. He didn't know what that end would be, never had, and who did?

He stopped and looked at a sign that walked up to him. It made him laugh again, even as his mind raced around in his head searching for an answer, searching for truth, and the possibility of such a grand joke. It read: *Yellowstone National Park 1 mile*. He thought of the photograph Kera left on the counter when she took the children and left his life. *THIS is where it all started.*

He didn't know what to think. He felt no anger, only a deep desire to cry. Instead, he simply picked his aching foot from the ground and took another step.

At the end of the day he found it: Old Faithful Inn. The photographs he had seen did little justice to the actual building. Built of logs as round as garbage cans, the brown painted structure stood three stories tall, had several massive wings, and a front entryway large enough for buses, carriages, and kings. Everything looked to be either log, rock, or glass. Dormers reached out above dozens of windows and the steeply angled roof reached an apex aligned with blue sky, leaving rounded mountain peaks diminished in the background. A parking lot the size of a football field stretched out before it, empty. Not a car, not a person in sight. Beyond the pavement and scattered around the tree studded flats which surrounded the building great plumes of cloudy vapor rose from the ground. Everyone knew of the Yellowstone fumeroles, the geysers such as Old Faithful itself. But standing completely alone and seeing the ghost-like dancing plumes, the place exuded an aura of intense mystery. Rand wondered about Rangers who might take him into custody. "Where the fuck is everyone?"

He approached the colossal building. The place had a draw on him and so he staggered up to it and studied its dominance of the landscape.

He moved a little to his left, then back a step, more. Finally he found the place from where he imagined some forgotten photographer—probably another tourist—had taken the photograph of Kera with her parents. A deep sweeping melancholy overtook him. He could see now why she had asked so many times to return. The place, the entire scene, was magnificent.

He wanted to touch it and so approached slowly, putting his hand out finally on one of the logs at shoulder height, leaned on it heavily. He imagined putting his skin to the ancient building would make him feel better; it didn't, but he found himself saying a prayer to the woman he loved, his children, that they all might be alive, as if the ancient thing had talisman power.

He gathered himself after a moment and tried the front door. It was, of course, locked. He peeked in the window and saw a grand entry way, a lobby, everything of wood, here massive and gnarled, there straight and clean, bold. At another window he spied a large dining room full of tables covered with white cloth. *Think of the meals that must have been served in there!* His mouth watered.

He turned and looked around at nothing but parking lots and mountains and forests and boardwalks. He took off the pack and leaned it against the wall, then picked up a garbage can standing next to a support for the roof overhang, and heaved it weakly through the glass. He took a small rock and broke away the remaining shards. He could barely do it, but he climbed through and reached back out and pulled the pack in behind him, sat it against the wall again. The room smelled of food, lovely food. He couldn't separate specific scents; it all blended into one inviting aroma, but shuffled toward the far side of the room and the door looking like a kitchen entrance.

The kitchen was huge, filled with stainless steal everything, including immense refrigerators. Opening one he couldn't believe what he saw: Gallon-sized containers of fruits and vegetables. Tomatoes, cucumbers, celery, lettuce, orange slices, apricots, apples, even bananas, a little dark, but… and he grabbed one immediately. *Ha!*

It seemed everything had been thrown into refrigerators as if the people working left in a hurry only a short time ago. *How can this place have electricity?* He gobbled the banana and took out vegetables, found dressing and slathered the stuff, chunked down all he could for fifteen minutes. He became so full so suddenly he felt sick. And then he found steaks in the freezer. *Oh!* Big frozen tenderloins and T-bones and prime rib, but he couldn't think of eating more, so full now that the wound on his side began to ache.

He needed to get clean and soak the wound, or, better yet, find something to put on it. He walked around the room, searching. *It's a kitchen isn't it? Shouldn't there be a First Aid kit somewhere?* He found it hanging on a wall near the entrance. It might have been better stocked, but he did pick out a tube of antibacterial salve and a roll of fresh bandaging. Now he could heat some water on the stove and— *wait—isn't this an inn? There must be rooms with bathtubs and all the hot water a person could use. Ah, they probably turned off the water heaters when they left*—he went to the sinks and opened the hot water faucet. After a short time, it ran hot. *Good God! This is a miracle!* He left the kitchen and moved as fast as he could for the main lobby, looking for access to the rooms.

He found himself in the heart of the open lobby and paused next to an immense square fireplace. Made of smooth rock the thing looked as wide as a semi-truck, with a separate fireplace and hearth on each of the four sides. It rose above two broad balconies and past another two floors apparently reached by way of log stairways. The roof stood a good hundred feet above him through open air.

He hobbled over to a stairway. A giant half-log step creaked as he climbed and he felt shrunken by the scale of the place, as if inhabiting some immense Tinker Toy set. He could hear Andrew and Alissa running the echoed hallways, giggling from the aura of make-believe.

He checked a couple small rooms, but then found a more luxurious one with a king size bed and claw foot tub. A little bottle of bubble bath sat on the counter and he poured it in as hot water sent steam rising. He chuckled, felt giddy, lucky.

Peeling his grimy clothes off, he could smell the wound. It still oozed but appeared improved from a couple days earlier. He stuck a raw and swollen foot in the water and it scalded, causing him to jerk it out as if a rattlesnake had struck. He ran some cold water and very gradually tried again. It hurt, hurt so good. He wanted the water hot, hot enough, he hoped, to sanitize the wound as well as his stinking self. He cringed when the water touched his testicles, cried out when it rose above the wound. Sweat rolled into his eyes. He shivered as if he stood naked in a snowstorm. Then everything started to tingle. His aching back and legs began to release. Sinking in as far as he could, water came to his nostrils and bubbles tickled and caused him to sneeze. He massaged his face with his hot wet hands. A feeling of ecstasy rose within him as complete as any orgasm he had ever felt. *Well...* Then he thought of Kera and the washcloth, the trickling water, and love. His mind quieted to the sound of water drops around him.

After a time he became groggy and feared falling asleep in the water. He wasn't about to put the clothes back on; in fact, he filled the tub again when he got out, poured in another bubble bath, and threw the clothes in to soak. Then the feeling of exhaustion conquered him and he collapsed under the covers of a real bed.

Chapter 28

Lightner lit the fourth candle, blew out the match in his brawny hand. The candles stood in different spots around the perimeter of his small living room, filling the homey space with warm and, Kera thought, ample light. The place had a hand-hewn look to it. Others in the village had told her the story. Lightner himself had found a man living nearby with acres of Ponderosa Pine, contracted with the man to let him selectively cut four perfect trees per acre, had them delivered to Latrop, used a horse to bring one log at a time up the Better Way trail to his site, and then shaped the logs by hand into a home.

"Your home has such a wonderful feel to it." It was the first log home Kera had entered. She sat on a worn couch situated along a wall opposite a wood burning stove and a hearth of rock. The day had aged, but the summer light refused to die, and the children remained outside to play with Walt, Lightner's goat.

"Thank you," he said. "I have always known I would have a log home. Since first I stepped into one I knew they were for me. I love the forest, and the sheltering energy of these trees is powerful."

"I love it. You really are an artist, the way you built this."

Lightner looked humbly at Kera. "I'm happy you like it." Then he moved his giant frame to the kitchen and asked, "Would you like a glass of wine?"

Kera had not had an alcoholic drink since leaving New York. This was, perhaps, the first time she felt relaxed enough to do so. "Yes, that would be nice."

"I only have Burgundy. Will that do?"

"Yes, thank you."

It was a man's home, Kera could see that. If any woman had ever lived there, she had been erased, at least from the living room. There were photographs on the walls, mostly of birds, some of trees and mountains. "Did you take these photographs?"

He brought the wine in jars left over from jams and such, handed one to Kera and sat in a wooden rocking chair near the wood stove. "Yes, I apologize. I keep trying."

"They're actually quite good." She sipped the wine and it bit, making her cough.

Lightner rose quickly for a big man and handed her a hand towel from an end table near him. "Ah, you shouldn't tell white lies! They catch in your throat." He smiled.

She cleared her throat, recovering her voice. "Sorry. No, that's not it. I haven't had any wine in awhile. The photographs are lovely."

"Do you take pictures?" He leaned back, seeing that she had recovered, and his broad shoulders and back hid the chair from view. One hand held the jar of wine, making it look miniature; the other draped over the arm rest and dangled loosely.

"No, I don't take them. My hus--band does." She felt shocked, the way the word *husband* had sounded foreign on her tongue. As it formed in her mouth it turned hard and nearly impeded her speech. Lightner had caught her slight stumble and distraction, she saw it in his watery eyes, how his right one tightened as he considered her. She added, "He's a fashion and advertising photographer in New York City."

"Well, now there's a pro. He must be very good to work in such an arena."

"He is very good. He puts everything he has into it." It's not that bitterness sharpened her tone, but again, Kera's mouth nearly caught on the words. She realized that, other than the children and her innermost self, she hadn't talked to anyone about Rand other than the telling of her story at the barn. She found herself in trouble, caught up in edgy emotion, but the way Lightner looked at her with such calm interest, his expression so unassuming, encouraged her to go on. "Why does a man do that, Lightner?"

"You mean, putting everything into his work?"

"Yes."

His lips pouched out and he looked at her with contemplation. After a moment he said, "Love." His head rocked back and forth minutely and he took a sip from the jar.

"But it feels like the opposite. It leaves those who love him feeling empty and alone."

Lightner took another sip of the wine, sighed. "I don't have the answer, Kera. Out there, we created a society off-kilter and what you speak of is a common symptom—not the illness, but a symptom. I think it's about love. A man is taught that in order to be loved he must provide. In order to attract love, he must be successful, be an achiever. No one loves a lazy man, or an incompetent. We call them losers. So it gets ingrained in a man, much the same way a woman feels she must keep a tidy house, deliver babies, or cook like a master chef. A man begins to see himself as what he does, the job is him, and lately, how much he makes, because money has become this society's emblem of productivity and worthiness. He loses any sense of self other than the work he does and the money or things he has."

Kera saw the truth in his words, remembered with disdain how many women she knew who were only interested in wealthy men.

Lightner went on, "Everywhere in our society messages are sent which say if a man is not making a lot of money, then he is not much of a man. Well, the average man wants to be the biggest man he can be. Why? Love. Deep down most men really want love, deep loyal love, but they fall into the trap of believing that only a man who has achieved a lot, a lot of distinction, a lot of money, can hold on to love. They become fixated with achieving these things, and before they know it, it's like the army that goes bad, they forget what they are fighting for, other than the blood rush of battle. And like the preeminent soldier who slits his own throat for fear of losing a fight, many a man seeking love, love of a woman, and love of himself I might add, actually drives away the woman, as well as any love he might feel for himself, as a person."

Kera shook her head and gazed into the wine, took a sip, and then looked with bewilderment at Lightner. "So you're saying that a man who refuses to come home after work and be with his family is really out there fighting for the love of his wife and children?"

Lightner chuckled, "I see, I see. Hell, Kera, this process is a long ways down the road, centuries, really. It's a psychosis. But, this surely does not apply to every man who fails to spend time at home."

Kera could see that it made sense. The signs were in the car Rand had bought, the truck for her, the house, the way he seemed so befuddled with her disappointment in him. She sipped the wine, and began feeling more and more anxious; *why is it EVERYTHING seems so complicated?* She turned her head and looked to the photographs on the wall. "What about you? Are you on your own?"

"I am."

"May I ask why?"

He didn't shift, didn't look away, but it took more than a moment for him to answer. "I loved a woman so much once that when she left I behaved poorly and later felt ashamed. Then a woman loved me, and I failed to trust. One day I hope to get another chance, but I lead my life."

"What brought you here?"

"Simplicity. Everywhere else seemed to be sinking into a quagmire of complexity."

"Is that what brings most folks here?"

"We here are abstainers. Is there such a word?"

"I think I understand."

"People come here who don't like what this country is doing, how it's operating. They come to Better Way and go on about their daily business as if nothing odd was happening out there. That was the point of the place anyhow. People come to practice what they feel is a better way of living and try to forget what they could not change. They have separated themselves from the country at large, because they have discovered that there remained nothing they felt they could do to bring the country around to a right direction. Protesting had little effect. Protesters nowadays have to obtain a permit and are even told where to stand and how many people can be present at a time. It's incomprehensible! Voting did no good. The Democrats and Republicans, even with their differences, generally take the country down the same road. Others more radical than us are out there right now fighting the government with arms. Better Way residents don't want to leave their country, don't want to fight the government in war. They feel that the United States is their home, but are deeply against the priorities of those who lead the country. To a one, we all agree that while capitalism has some good elements, the system has bred a people so intent on personal gain they ignore the common ethics that stood this country tall to begin with. Most people out there have forgotten decency, honesty, cooperation. Americans have become known the world over for their obsession of material wealth. The people of Better Way want nothing to do with that.

"We never planned on a violent revolution, Kera. Who'd of thought it could ever happen? So, we have tried to ignore even that. We agree with it no more than we agree with most other movements of this nation. Only after having the army suggest we evacuate, and then hearing your description of the atrocities out there, only then did we go as far as to create a plan of action in case of absolute need; much to your credit. I'll tell you, Better Way is a prayed-for refuge for most of these people. This war approaching has shaken them more than anything I have seen since coming here."

Kera said, "I haven't been sleeping too well these last couple nights. Have you heard them?"

"Yes, we've all heard them. At first, as far off as they were, they sounded like thunderclaps, but they're bombs or missiles all right. They're coming from the west, beyond the mountains."

Kera knew that everyone had continued to work at their professions, bakers, builders, gardeners, woodworkers, accountants, teachers, but she also noticed lately how their faces had changed. In fact, of all the faces there, Kera felt that only Nee and Lightner looked as relaxed as the day she had met them. Before, people went out walking, sat on their porches, talked, but with the sounds the last couple nights, after work no one remained visible. People went inside and stayed there…except Kera.

She went from house to house with the children and talked, took cookies she baked, smiled even when she didn't quite feel like it. This revolution had taken enough. Alissa and Andrew were safe. She had found this remarkable village, these wonderful people. She would do all she could to keep the horrid effects of the violence from ruining what she knew they had created.

***

Rand had never eaten two steaks in one sitting, but he sat at the center table of the great empty Yellowstone dining room and ate a meal of little else, other than a bottle of Red Zinfandel he found in a store room. This wine had always been Kera's favorite, and as he gorged himself on the meat and sipped from a glass, he imagined her sitting there across from him at the white clothed dining table. Her eyes, big and brown and innocent, revealed a little girl at heart. She would always be the loveliest woman he had ever seen. He knew if she were there, she would watch him now with those eyes, that happy twinkle, as if he were the only person in the room. He swallowed wrong and a little wine ran down his chin. Even if he wasn't the only person in the room, which he certainly was at this moment, she would look at him as if nobody else existed. She had always treated him as a very special man.

No, that was before. Now he saw in his mind how the last time they had dined together—*when was that?*—she had not looked at him that way, but down at her plate. *It is incredibly ludicrous, how I did not notice, did not care, at the time.* They had locked eyes little, really, in a very long while. He just could not believe how he had not noticed.

Sitting with the massive wooden structure empty around him, he yearned deeply for her, for their children, for the way they would have loved this place. *I will bring you here, all of you, every year!* He stood and threw his napkin on the table. Breathing in gasps, furious with himself, he turned and strode as fast as he could through the vacuous room, away.

Up the squeaking stairs again, he had to get outside, breathe air open and free, filled with something other than memories. He found a double doorway leading to a veranda and stepped into the late light of day and grasped the wooden railing a story above ground. Looking out at the vast openness about the place, he fought to steady himself.

The sun shone on his face—that calming light that comes with day's repose—and he breathed as deeply as he could. The sun had power, the air too, and he had recently begun to use it. He looked out over the sloped forest, at the trees for miles around, and felt energy there too, energy everywhere.

"Please, if I ever have another hope, if anything good ever again happens to me, let me see my children, let me see my wife, let them know I love them! Let them know how good and important they are, how innocent they are, how much I am aware of what I have done!"

He had not prayed since childhood, had not thought of praying or ever felt the need. He looked at the emerald trees and the undulating land and the silky steam rising from the geysers. He thought of the great unlimited universe, the vast energy-presence that enveloped him, had always enveloped him without his awareness. Big parts of him were changing, and something of it felt empowering, yet bewildering.

He calmed, and then felt inspired to leave. He had needed to bathe, to rest, to eat (a lot) to think, and now he had to get moving.

It took a moment for the sound to register, but it came to him and he cocked his head and listened, then saw. Steam shot from a hole in the ground a hundred yards from where he stood. It came in short bursts maybe ten feet high, then grew in height and in volume until a geyser gush of water and vapor shot forth from the hole and into the sky a hundred feet or more. The great plume caught the tilted sun and turned the water and vapor to a spray of honey.

Beautiful, now that is beautiful!

He watched until the water spout died down and fell silent. Everything around him continued the silence as if all the world had been born of silence. Rand was beginning to love silence.

Then he heard another sound: a racket, a grinding. It echoed from far out in the trees and was unmistakably machine-like.

Rand considered the obvious; rangers were out working in the woods. It might be rangers, or the military. He decided to find them before they found him, and hustled back inside, down the stairs, out the front door—rushed as best he could toward the sound.

He covered a lengthy distance, slowed, and peered through the thick forest. At first he saw only trees and brown, dried grasses beneath them, but then, as he crept as slowly and stealthily as he could, a truck became visible. It was a big red dump truck, with a large trailer attached to the rear. He moved closer and saw a man operating a back-hoe, digging deep into the ground—ground that steamed and sucked at the bucket. The man swung the bucket and dropped a load of sloppy soil into the truck.

The bucket swung wildly back and clawed a fast shovelful. It seemed the man was in a terrible hurry and Rand began to think. He knew little about the west, but Yellowstone had come into his life a time or two in talks, or maybe movies, or was it in classes? He doubted it made sense for anyone, in these times, to dig up the steaming hot pots, or fumaroles—whatever they called them. *What the hell is he doing?*

For the first time in his life Rand felt protective toward land. This was Kera's place, his family's future vacation spot. The man was up to something and he didn't like it. He wanted to confront him, but felt much too weak to get into a tight situation. He had an idea: maybe photographs would be better. He could gather proof and later use it to go after the guy. Kera would appreciate an effort like that. After a moment, he turned and hurried back for his camera.

Rand returned and flanked through the trees, gained a clear view. The operator of the machine appeared average in size, wearing a grey shirt and dark sunglasses. The bill of a black baseball cap came down low over the glasses, and Rand wondered if the guy was trying to conceal his face. In the low light he focused carefully and exposed a frame.

An unidentifiable man on a backhoe would not do. Rand thought of the truck license plates. He worked around to see the back of the truck, but mud rendered the plates unreadable.

Daylight was fading. Rand wanted the right photographs, but also wanted to get going, and started thinking about the truck as transportation. It amazed him how slow his mind was working. But, even if he forgave what the guy was doing, he couldn't risk walking up and asking for a ride. The man sure wasn't working a park project with a revolution going on and everyone else dodging bullets. *The guy's a crook, right? So, if I was to steal a crook's truck, well, that wouldn't be a crime, would it? In a way, I would be disarming a crook, preventing a crime. Yeah.*

The rationale felt right, but Rand's heart pumped furiously. He had never done anything like this. How would he get the truck from the man? If he made a mistake the guy would be on him, and Rand had no illusions about what this character might do to save his transportation and personal property, let alone, possibly, his escape vehicle. It seemed highly risky, but it felt like a sure way to turn a bad situation into a positive one. If Rand worked fast he could sneak into the truck while the guy was still focused on operating the machine.

He didn't want to leave his things behind, but darkness was setting in; the man might leave anytime now. Still, anything could happen and the extra clothing, pack, sleeping bag and cane were necessities. He felt better since he ate and washed and rested, but was far from healed and one-hundred percent. He also knew he couldn't lug that stuff with him when he sneaked up to the truck, so decided to plant everything where he could drive by and grab them before exiting the park; a spot far enough where the guy could not catch him on foot when he stopped.

He returned to the inn and threw everything into the backpack, strapped it all together. While exiting he paused briefly and considered the food in the kitchen. He needed that food. But he needed the truck more, and besides, his belly was full. He looked at the inn one last time, hoping to one day return with his family and recall this as a very temporary time, a terrible time, but a period they might recognize as an impetus for expansive and positive change in their lives.

He moved quickly as he could to the outlet of the road, to where he could most directly drive. As he took off the pack and leaned it against a brown painted fence he heard a rumble and looked up to see the truck approaching through the dusky light.

Rand didn't know what to do. The man might already have seen him. He could hide and try to jump onto the truck as it passed, but doubted he had the energy or agility, and, besides, he had no idea which way the guy would head when leaving the park.

As he stood frozen the headlights of the truck blinked into high, onto him, and back to dim again. It was too late to hide.

The big truck rumbled up, pulling the trailer with the back-hoe. Rand saw the sunglasses, the hat, the face. The driver looked at him, looked rather grim indeed. It appeared he would roll past the stop sign and keep going, but at the very last moment Rand stuck out his thumb. He knew it made no sense, but felt desperate. He had to find his family, and the guy had no idea Rand had watched him digging, would not likely consider a broken down fool any danger at all.

In the dim light, Rand could see the driver look, then ignore him, but Rand stared in distress, waved his thumb more urgently. *Can he even see me in the dark with those glasses on?* His spirits rose when the guy squeaked the truck to a stop and rolled down his window, staring silently down from behind the glasses.

"Hi," Rand said. "What you up to?" *Oh, Jesus, I can't believe I said THAT!*

"Haulin' some stuff for the park." The guy was tightlipped and steady. "You need somethin', or not?"

"I do! Yes. I was wondering, which way you heading?"

"Which way *you* headin'?"

"Well, I'm, uh, probably more flexible than you." Rand felt like an idiot, but he just wanted in the truck.

"Look, I don't have no time for this—" the driver started to roll the window up.

"Please! I need a ride. I've lost my family!"

The guy stopped cranking. "You what?" He pushed the glasses up onto the bridge of his nose and focused harder on Rand.

"It's, well, it's a long story but it's true. I need to get to Washington State to find my family."

The guy just peered at Rand for a long moment. "Well, I'm goin' north a ways. But don't you tell the park service I gave you a ride. I'll lose my contract."

Chapter 29

The night after Kera visited Lightner the sounds of war came closer. She put the children to bed early, because she had come to expect the sounds at a certain time right after dark. *Are wars fought, people killed, according to some schedule?*

A light knock sounded on the door and she stepped over and cracked it open. Lightner stood in the darkness, just a wisp of the light from the house upon him, and smiled. Kera saw instantly how this smile was less stable, less easy than usual. His eyes were as always red and watery, but hints of fear also showed.

"Lightner?" she said softly, opening the door wider.

"Evening, Kera." He held out a big hand and she took hold, felt him gently squeeze. He did not pull her but she ended up on the porch with him and he released her hand and ran his own down into his pockets, rather like a teenage boy about to say Oh Shucks, but without the shoulders raised or the cheeks blushed. He kept looking at her intently. "You know, I have lived alone in my house for a number of years and came to terms long ago with loneliness."

Kera had felt the dampness in his warm palm, sensed vulnerability in him she had not felt before, and it made her like him even more. Still, she cringed inside over what she felt coming.

"After you and the children visited the other night, I have sat around hearing sounds. Just loving the echoes you left there."

Kera smiled. "The children love you," she said.

His eyes lit up and continued to search hers.

Kera had not thought of Lightner, or lately any man, in a romantic way—quite the opposite. Even after meeting seemingly kind men here at the village, she wrestled constantly with what she had come to know of men.

Lightner stepped forward and touched her cheek with his fingers and as he did her breathing stopped, she raised her own hand, and tightened her grip on his arm. Doubt ached and fear bellowed within her; she kept her widened eyes locked on his face.

Lightner paused... but did not pull away. He stay focused on her as well. "I know what you have been through, but I cannot pretend to understand how it feels. I only know the way you speak and handle yourself, the love you show your children, everything about you tells me

I cannot go without expressing how intriqued I am by you." He took his fingers away. "But I don't in any way want to make you feel uncomfortable."

Kera started to breathe again. "Thank you." And she let go of his arm.

"Have I misjudged the possibilities?" he asked, stepping back, a sure smile returning to his face.

"Lightner, I—" Try as she might she could not put her feelings into words. Every thought ran smack into another. As she spoke she realized she did not want to say anything hurtful to this man with such loving energy.

"I do sincerely apologize, Kera..." and with that Lightner turned slowly to go.

"Would you hug me?" she asked.

He turned and looked at her, and for a brief instant there came a flicker of suspicion, like a man who had himself been played or hurt before; but just as fast he peered into her eyes and his look again softened. "Yes, I would."

He stepped nearer with that smile, his massive arms embracing her, the solid chest warm and welcoming. Kera noticed how Lightner smelled fresh and yet, not like soap or cologne, but forest. She closed her eyes and concentrated on relaxing, letting the walls drop, letting herself feel his gentleness. They remained silently locked together for more than a minute.

When they parted Lightner's face looked younger. He smiled, said, "That was nice," and walked quietly off into the night. Kera noticed how quickly the sound of his weighty movements faded.

She moved out into the night looking upward, and the sounds of war punched the not-so-distant sky. Flashes of light streaked far out across the horizon. Throughout life she had seen a hundred times on the news—Film at Eleven—the horrors of war, but it had always been other countries, distant lands. She still could not believe her people had let it come to this, and she wanted desperately to push her arms out and force it all away.

Something touched Kera's shoulder and she spun around in the dark, her heart leaping into her throat, her hands out to defend herself. A form stood near and she stepped backward, away from it, straining to see if it was Lightner.

"Ma'am, don't be afraid, it's me!" The whispered voice sounded familiar. Then a flashlight clicked on, a red beam of faint light, and she saw the helmet, the eyes, the broad jaw of the red-haired soldier from the helicopter that brought her to Better Way.

"Murtaugh! What is it? What are you doing here? Are you hurt?"

"No. I'm—I'm okay." He turned off the light and everything went black again.

"What is it? Are the others here?"

A pause followed, and then, "No. I'm alone. May we go inside?"

"Yes. Come."

As they entered the house, Kera saw that in addition to his usual uniform—the full fatigues in camouflage, the side packs—he wore a camouflage backpack. In contrast to how clean and perfect he had been, his uniform was muddied and ripped on the knees and elbows. His rifle was scraped and dirty. Whiskers filled his face, dirt caked into his pores. Kera looked closer and saw immediately his eyes had changed. "Are you all right?"

"Yes."

But something more was there, on his tongue, she could feel it. "Do you want to take that pack off? Set those things down if you like."

"Yes, yes...." His voice trailed off as he set his rifle flat on the floor, pointing away, and slid the pack off. "Ah, it's dirty, I'll put it outside."

"No, that's okay, on the tile of the kitchen there."

He carried it over and leaned it against a wall, turned and looked to her, wiped his dirty face with his dirty hands, went to the rifle and picked it up again.

"Can I get you some tea, or coffee?"

"Coffee, sure, great."

As she moved past him she could smell a pungent odor and knew it; she had smelled it on herself not long ago. Something had frightened Murtaugh to the very edge of death.

Fixing coffee, she gathered herself and considered how she felt immediately after violence had broken her, how she would want to be treated. Out the corner of her eye she saw him standing, rubbing his arm, fidgeting, not knowing what to do. She felt he might bolt from the place in his distress and again, she knew the feeling. She looked at him and he returned the gaze nervously. "It's okay," she said softly. "It's okay."

His eyes darted about and his chin quivered. "I came—because I wanted to protect you."

At first it didn't ring true, she felt and saw much more, but then, yes, she remembered how he had looked at her during the flight and when they parted, as if he had known how much she hurt and wanted to help. "What has happened, Murtaugh?"

He spun away and paced into the living room, stood in the middle of it and stared at the floor, vigorously rubbing his face and forehead with one dirty hand, the rifle grasped tightly in the other.

Sorrow shot through Kera. *Here it comes. The suffering has found us.*

His shoulders no longer elevated as they had when first they met, but bowed, and his head, angled downward, was turned slightly, revealing the side of his grim expression. The image burned into Kera's mind.

It was like that with trauma to the soul; it left you feeling worthless, gutted, and praying for death. Hating the violence, the very essence of war, how could she convince him that to her a defeated soldier looked every bit the man as a victorious one?

She went to him and stepped around to his front and wrapped her arms around him and brought him up tight and near to her and let him bury his face in the crook of her neck.

***

Darkness had fallen long ago and the guy still wore his sunglasses. Rand worried about how he could see, driving like that; he obviously still wanted to try and hide his features. A couple weeks had passed since Rand's last ride in an automobile and the speed at which they traveled in the oversized truck-with-trailer seemed astounding to him, completely reckless. He thought about the Ferrari and for the first time noticed he felt no sadness over losing it. He couldn't care less about getting the car back—it represented a terrible choice in his life. He now knew what he wanted.

The inside of the truck cab was scratched and worn, the seats dirty, the dashboard dust-layered. Three packs of Camel filters sat up there and left a trail when the driver took a curve too fast—which seemed like all of them. The guy took out a cigarette and lit it, using a lighter molded in the likeness of a miniature woman with a blond bouffant. She was naked, wore high heels, and had really large breasts. When he thumbed back her head her nipples burst into flame.

Rand sat with his feet up on his pack, the cane across his lap, holding the armrest tightly, no seat belt available. Neither of them had said much, which seemed odd to Rand, considering all the circumstances. But for his part he didn't want to blunder again and have the guy kick him out, or worse. He was actually bigger physically, but there was no way of telling what weapon the driver might have within reach. Rand determined to suffer no further physical pain at the hands of strangers.

Besides, maybe he was misjudging the situation, what the guy was up to. He'd softened and offered a ride hadn't he? Rand tried to relax. He had met a lot of people on this journey, now saw people differently than he had before. It had truly come to intrigue him, the different ways of living, the different qualities in people, the experiences they survived.

"In the last few weeks," he began, "I've seen a man shot on the highway—I've been kicked in the head and pistol whipped—my wife has been kidnapped and brutalized—I've seen a platoon of United States soldiers shot down—a woman died in my arms—and I've been stabbed by a Native American ready to take back his homeland."

The man looked straight ahead and drove, then he slipped the sunglasses down his nose, peered over them at Rand, and asked, "You shittin' me?"

"No." Rand looked back at him with the only expression he could—stupefaction. The list of events sounded too incredible even to him.

"What you tryin' to do, pal?" The guy wouldn't keep his eyes on the road, looking at Rand the way one might a movie thriller with an unexpected turn of events.

"I'm trying to find my family, if you can get me closer to Washington. It's a long story, but suffice it to say, I appreciate your help very much."

The guy shook his head, mumbled some expletive, and reached under the seat. Rand waited, uneasy—until he saw a pint of Jack Daniels bourbon. "You need a swig," the guy said.

Rand took the bottle and opened it with a twist, swallowed a bit. "Whoa!" He handed it back, said, "Thanks."

"Well," the guy swallowed too, "as they say, a man's got to do what a man's got to do." He held up the bottle and looked at it, passed it again.

Rand took another, smaller, taste. Those words stuck in his mind: *A man's got to do what a man's got to do.* "Thanks, I mean it, for picking me up."

"It's nothin'. But like I said, keep it a secret. The park won't have us giving nobody a ride. Some insurance thing."

"It'll be our secret." Rand took one final sip. "What you hauling for them?"

The guy took back the bottle, took a swig, cleared his throat, took another swig, cleared his throat again. He wiped his lips on his shirt sleeve. "Oh, just a buncha dirt, you know. The storms the other night flooded a road and I cleared it."

"I see. You mean, you scraped it off a road so people could get through?"

"Exactly, uh huh."

Rand knew there had been no road under the man's shovel. "Where are you taking it?"

"Oh just, well, you know, use it as fill."

"Ah! I see."

"Sure, yeah, a town bought it a ways up the road here." The guy smiled weakly over at him, twitched up around the bridge of his nose, snuffled, smacked his lips, slid the glasses up again. "Ol' Jack sure is good ain't it?"

"Sure is. Sure is. I appreciate it. Hey, what's your name anyway?" Rand looked at the guy and waited.

The driver thumbed his glasses further up his nose. "Hank. My name's Hank. How 'bout you?"

Rand thought, then blurted out, "Dave. My name's Dave. Good to meet you, Hank." And he held out his hand to shake.

"Well, all right," said Hank, and he shook Rand's hand.

"Say, Hank, I guess the government, I mean, the park service being part of the government, you don't have to worry about being out in this martial law thing, huh?"

"Nah." Hank took another drink. "Say, uh, what is it you do, you know, for a livin'?"

"I'm a photographer."

"Hmm." Hank glanced over at him, then back. "You mean like for weddin's?"

"Sure, like that. I photograph models and dresses and magazine covers."

"Ha! Oh!" Hank pulled down the glasses again. "You mean you

take pictures of those girls we see on the front of magazines, like that Madmouzel, and those?" He winked.

"Mademoiselle. Yeah, like those."

"Man! What's that like, doing that kind a work?"

Rand could feel he'd been lied to. Hank was not the guy's name, and he was a crook. But he also knew he may well have used his back and hands to make a living his whole life, and would probably think that someone like Rand really had it made, lived the life of leisure, had nothing to worry about; that a guy like Rand would somehow feel different, maybe better than his blue collar brothers. *In fact, I did feel that way, before being proved the dumbest son-of-a-bitch in the world.* "It has its days."

"Hell, yeah. But, still, you know, you get to meet all those fancy people, go to those places where the girls hang out on the beach in bikinis all day."

"Well, I've done a little of that, sure."

"Yeah, huh, hey, tell me. Tell me about some of them. You ever get lucky with any of them girls?"

Rand saw that the guy meant it. He wanted to hear a story about male conquest, squishy oiled thighs, passionate sex with strangers. He thought back, and he mind could only go in one direction. "Hank, I'll tell you a story I almost forgot."

"Sure, yeah, sure, Dave."

"It was back when I was still in school learning the business."

"Well, okay."

"A number of us in a photography class had lined up models for a shoot, to get photographs for a final grade. I was looking forward to it because I wanted to see if I could end up with a date, you know, I was like any guy that age, ready for some action with a beautiful babe."

"Oh, yeah, I know…" The guy had actually slowed his driving a little and was listening and drinking.

"Well, in walks this one gal and she just sets the room on fire. There are five guys with cameras and we all want to photograph her."

"What'd she look like?"

"At first it was the way she walked. She had this step like, well, I don't know, almost like a wild animal, a deer or something. It was like she walked with care, not like she was afraid, but alert and light. It was a proud walk, like she was noble."

"One a them stuck-up bitches?"

"I thought that, pretty much, but it was sexy too, very different and, well, exotic, in a way. So, I laid back. I acted like I wasn't interested in her and paid more attention to other models. I figured that would work, get a reaction from her."

"I heard about that sort of thing. So what did she do?"

"She didn't do anything. She let the other guys photograph her and did what they asked and one time I did meet eyes with her and she smiled so naturally and beautifully I thought I was going to drop my camera. I tell you, Man, she was something you don't often see ... hell, never."

"So! Did you get'r?"

Rand said, "Yeah." But he wasn't seeing Hank; he was seeing Kera those years back, seeing her eyes how they had first smiled at him. *There was an innocent trust in those eyes. That's what she has always had, a child-like belief in everything. No, that's what she always HAD. Before I proved to her she shouldn't.* "Yeah, I got her. I mean, I married her. She's my wife..."

Rand's voice trailed off and Hank looked over at him. "She's who you're lookin' for?"

"That's right... she and our children... if they'll have me." Rand blinked and looked over at the man, "And if I don't get stopped and held by the police or the military until this thing is over."

Hank shook his head. "This thing, you mean, this revolution! I think it's time myself. They got me so pissed off. Tellin' me I have to stay home! I mean, we got this government always deciding how the rest of us live."

Rand caught how the guy lost interest in his bikini-woman storytelling and felt okay about that—but he didn't like that he really couldn't care less about Rand's family or where ne needed to go to find them.

"And, out here, it's this environmental bullshit. Gets so a company can't operate without worryin' about gettin' shut down or fined into bankruptcy. Those environmentalists got everything locked up. A man can't hardly make a living for all the rules and regulations. It's as if people aren't smart enough to understand, like we're going to do something that might end the world or somethin'. They forget we been out here for a hundred years, more, and the world ain't ended yet!"

The man spoke angrily. Rand listened intently, hearing the beginning of the possible truth about what he was up to. He still wanted to know what they carried behind them, whether *Hank* had the right to be digging up National Park land. He also couldn't help but think of Storm, how this man and he were at opposite ends of the spectrum. Rand now felt pulled in the direction of Storm's beliefs, since he had spent time out in the openness, felt the power and simple truth of everything natural around him. He had never before felt this and what he learned was clearly helping him survive. Besides, National Park land belonged to everyone in the country, it belonged to people like Kera—who had memories of her family and her childhood there. He felt protective of the place now. He wanted to get back there with his family.

Rand found himself getting angry, thinking about what this guy had been doing, but he wanted this ride. And he wanted to try and understand, like he had failed to understand so many things that came before. "So, what would you change, you know, about our country?"

"I'd bring back the day where the common man ran it, took his turn. Seems like we got a bunch of rich people running things now. And we got our public working for the government, instead of the other way around. That whole mess in Washington has gotten too big, we're all laboring to pay for their retirements and their favors."

"But, how do we go about that?"

"Hell, I don't know. I like the idea of state rule. Then you got less power in Washington, and people who live where you do, like you do, they're making the rules."

Rand thought for a moment. "But, take an issue like slavery. Wouldn't local rule have continued slavery?"

The guy looked over and winked, "Maybe."

Rand's forehead furrowed. *Maybe I understand this guy enough...*

The guy continued, "Well, shit, Dave, I say we vote. Not once every couple years, but, like, once every three months." He looked over and laughed. "I mean it, let the people vote on everythin'. Give people back the power, those guys in Washington flubbed their chances, damned hypocrites. Publish one of them pamphlets and put it in all the newspapers, not like a reporter wrote it, 'cause I don't trust them either, but straight forward, just the facts. Tell everybody both sides of every matter, then let them vote. New tax idea. Vote. New laws. Vote. Give people back the control."

"No one would do it," Rand said.

"Huh?"

"The voting thing."

"You wouldn't?"

Rand thought. He knew a month ago he couldn't have answered the same. "Yes, I would."

"Well, me too. Once people got the idea that they was really decidin' what happens in this country, I think they would start votin'."

"And what would you do if more environmental laws were voted into existence?"

The guy took another swig of the bourbon and his jaw muscles knotted. He shook his head. "I wouldn't like it, not a damn bit. We got too many now. Shit, they're tryin' to make it so those laws even control what you do on your own property!" He lit another cigarette with his little flaming beauty. Then he spoke through a cloud of smoke. "It's just trees and dirt, like what I got back here." He pointed to the rear of the truck and glanced over at Rand. "Hell, it's just dirt and the crazy Japanese think it will help them live forever."

Rand swallowed, then smiled big. "Got yourself a business going, huh, Hank?"

"Hell," the guy coughed and laughed out smoke, "I had my eyes on this stuff. Was thinking about how to get it. Now that everything's all fucked up, I'm making more money than I made in all the years I been workin'."

Part Six

Chapter 30

Mattie decided the piles of throwaways and recycling kept in a large shed behind the community hall needed organizing and tidying. Kera understood, the leader of the village wanted people to stay busy and not become incapacitated by fears that war would reach them. They had prepared their plan and felt ready if a need for action arose. Along with Mattie, Lightner, Nee, and Lewis, Kera worked on the project and soon found that people living in Better Way produced almost no garbage. They weren't big consumers and because they created many of the things they used—from food, to clothing, to entertainment—little came into the community with packaging. They recycled nearly everything they got their hands on—paper, plastic bags, bottles, jars, newspapers, wood—things were reused in creative ways and very little was ever used only once. When they made a purchase they chose durable, reusable items with little packaging, manufactured close to home. Additionally, all discarded plant matter from the dinner table or the garden became part of a compost heap that later became fertilizer for the garden, flower beds and orchard.

Mattie had her waterfall hair tied back and wore sweats and an old blue sweatshirt. Kera thought her usual smile seemed diminished, and, for that matter, so did everyone else's—earlier four jets had flown over, very low, followed about five minutes later by six camouflage green helicopters. The appearance of each group soon created copious amounts of gunfire and explosions no more than ten or twenty miles away. No longer was warring relegated to nighttime. Lewis had black circles under his eyes and spoke little.

Kera worked with her head down, thinking. She had not as yet mentioned Murtaugh to the others. The night before, he admitted having gone AWOL from his command. The caliber of soldiers opposing them had come as a shock—men just like himself, Americans, accompanied by others, light and dark-skinned, clearly not American and not speaking English. His unit had realized heavy losses. Most were killed in the first two *terrorist uprisings*, as his superiors continued to call the battles. Colonel Esparza had been lost. Many of the enemy had honed their soldierly skills in Vietnam, Iraq, Afghanistan, and any number of lesser known killing fields, and utilized them here. Every tactic Murtaugh's command used was anticipated and effectively countered.

Murtaugh felt ashamed for leaving his troops, but now considered war horrible. Throughout fighting he had continued to think of Kera, how afraid and innocent she appeared, and how vulnerable the village. He never confessed to running in the heat of battle, but Kera didn't care about that; she had witnessed the terror and felt strongly that man must find a way to never war again. When she explained to him how the community would not want a soldier in their midst, he understood, but pleaded she keep him a secret for the moment, until he had time to think. He slept on the floor of her living room, keeping a low profile during daylight hours, but Kera didn't like deceiving the others, and she wasn't sure the children could keep a secret, even though she had directed them not to tell.

She could see it written on Murtaugh's face, he had fallen in love with her, in the poetic way of the young. Though she actually felt akin to him for not wanting to fight, for helping her, she didn't like that something about her had caused this young and desperate man to put himself in jeopardy and outside the law. And his presence as a soldier gave her no comfort. It made her feel close to trouble and the possibility existed that his arrival would lead the way for others. She felt certain the community would agree, and decided that though she owed him a debt, she couldn't allow much time before she would have to tell Mattie.

Mattie stopped organizing a pile of cardboard and looked with uncharacteristic fluster at the others. "How do you all feel we are doing, as a community?"

This group consisted of people who generally liked to hold their tongues. Everyone waited.

"Nee, I would like your opinion," Mattie said.

Nee wore a pair of leather gloves and she took them off, sat on a pile of newspapers, took a drink of water from a glass bottle. Lewis stood behind her in his rather thin way, and Kera thought he looked ill. She also felt Nee looked tired. Lightner alone seemed unaffected by the growing amounts of turmoil surrounding the community. He propped an elbow against the wall, pulled out a handkerchief, and wiped his forehead.

"What I feel is that people are wearing down with worry." Nee's head tilted and her shoulders hunched in a matter of fact way. "I too am having trouble sleeping."

Lewis let out a sigh, and Kera could see he felt beleaguered by Nee's discomfort. His love for her showed itself in every movement he made.

"Do you all still feel—" Mattie's question was halted by the distant thunder of missiles hitting Earth. They all waited. The world stilled. "Do you all continue to feel that our plan is best?"

Kera knew she had to remain silent. Her idea was being reconsidered and defending it out of turn would be inappropriate. If these leaders wanted to develop another plan and put it before the community, then she had to allow for that with complete humility and understanding, even though she could see no other way.

Nee spoke. "It is the best plan."

Mattie asked, "Lewis?"

"I will do what Nee feels best," he said.

All eyes turned to Lightner, who had listened intently. He rubbed his bushy sideburns. "In a time like this it's hard to stick to the plan, because the plan calls for considerable discipline and courage. But we've thought it out, we've worked it. We're prepared. I say we stick to it."

At that moment the air concussed from a heavy bomb. Kera felt the vibration in her clothes, even though the group stood inside the shed. Mattie and Lewis both jumped, and the rest ducked their heads. Then came echoes of rapid fire. The sounds came from the direction of Latrop, only a few miles away.

"It's time," Mattie said, "for us all to return to our homes and loved ones. Lightner, shall we place watches along the trail tonight?"

"Yes," he said. "I'll notify those first on the list."

Kera could see Mattie and Lewis' faces tighten, see them working to maintain composure. She, in turn, felt a quickening, a narrowing of her vision. She focused on returning to Andrew and Alissa who were drawing with Amber, a girl who often watched children for parents.

As they exited the shed they were confronted by Roy and Molly Shuntz. Kera had only talked with them once, as they lived in a small house on a rise near the rear of the community and kept to themselves more than most. They were the only residents who gave Kera the impression of money, the fashionable way they dressed and their mannerisms. They were quiet and almost overly polite. Roy, a medium-sized, black-haired man, stood in front wearing a backpack, a handcart in tow with their child inside. "We're leaving," he said. "This is too hazardous and we have too much to lose. We are sorry."

Mattie stepped forward. "Roy, Molly, are you certain?" Her voice sounded strained.

"Yes," said Roy.

"It's worse than I'd anticipated," added Molly, bowing her head.

"It sounded as though Latrop might have been hit," Lightner said.

"Further out," Roy answered. "From our home we could see smoke. It was further out, but not much."

There was a moment of hanging silence. Roy forced a smile. "Who knows, we may return. Our place is yours until then."

They turned and started down the trail, but Molly came back and hugged Mattie, Nee and even Kera. She didn't say anything, just squeezed hard and sudden and rushed off after her husband and child.

***

Despite Rand's fatigued condition, and the effects of the bourbon, every sense within him, every nerve, vibrated. A few miles back he'd seen a sign at an intersection that pointed right and read, LATROP, 100 MILES. Rand had not realized how close they were. He wanted to ask the guy if he'd go there, but it was clear he wouldn't. So-called Hank didn't care about anything or anybody other than himself and his dirt-for-profit venture. He saw the irony—now being trapped with a guy as narrowly focused and self-centered as he himself had been for so long. Rand acted calm, as if nothing had changed, but inwardly he plotted.

Hank was pretty tipsy on the whiskey. He hadn't been saying much for some time, just smoking. Rand still felt uncertain about fighting. Whatever he did, he didn't want to increase the risk of getting injured and once again having his progress stopped. He was right there, so close to his children, if, indeed, they were still in Latrop. In his mind he kept Andrew and Alissa healthy, happy, safe.

Beyond the cone of the headlights, Rand could see little of the countryside, but it was apparent from the grade of the road they continued through mountainous terrain. He didn't see struggling with the guy while driving these roads. He had to make a grab for the truck while they were stopped. The idea he needed had actually been nagging him for some time.

"You ever take a leak?" he asked Hank. He tried to make it sound like he was in pain.

The guy refocused, as if he'd been asleep at the wheel. "Hell, yes, I could do that."

In about a mile they spotted a dirt pull-off next to the road. "Let's make it quick," he said to Rand as he steered off the pavement.

Rand fumbled with his pack and then feigned opening his door. The guy hopped out and left the truck running as Rand had hoped. He quickly slid over into the driver's seat and pulled the door closed, slapped the lock down. The guy turned and with a torrent of obscenities jumped onto the side runners and pounded on the window with such force Rand thought it would shatter. "Look you MOTHERFUCKER I will kick in your face now get out of my truck you fuckin' mealy-mouthed punk …"

Rand shifted the big truck into first gear and steered out into the road. It grinded loudly and no matter how far he kept the pedal down it only rolled at about 20 miles per hour. The guy was red-faced from yelling, "I will kill you and everybody you know I swear you will never forgive yourself over this if you don't come to your lame ass senses and get the FUCK out of my truck…"

And then Rand realized he needed to shift to second gear to get the truck to speed up and when he did the guy hopped off. He gave up. He must have feared falling off as the truck picked up speed. Rand looked back in the mirror and saw the guy flip him off and throw his baseball cap down onto the road and kick it and then he faded into the night.

"Hank, my ass." Rand thought that was the easiest thing he'd done in a very long time. He knew it made him a felon and he didn't give a damn.

Chapter 31

Kera woke with a start and stared into the darkness. It felt as if her entire being quivered. Her breathing came in short stutters. Quickly, she reached up and turned on the light. Alissa and Andrew slept soundly beside her.

Her chest rose with the pounding of her heart and she felt a deep and heavy foreboding. She thought to turn off the light, so as not to awaken the children, but she couldn't.

What is it?

A sudden knock on the front door caused her to sit up. She thought of Murtaugh sleeping in the living room. *Who would call at this time of night if it wasn't serious?*

She slipped from bed and pulled on her pants and top, went toward the living room. Murtaugh was up and met her. "Wait in there." She pointed him into the bedroom.

At the front door she called quietly, "Yes?"

Mattie's voice returned, "Kera, we need to speak with you!"

Kera opened the door, not knowing what to expect, and found Mattie and Lightner standing there.

"We're sorry to wake you, may we come in?" asked Mattie.

Kera glanced toward the bedroom, but knew she must let them in. Mattie entered, then Lightner. He had a strange look on his face, his wet eyes were big and sorry and they locked into Kera's. She didn't like the way they looked.

"Roger Cummins had the first watch and he found the Shuntz' handcart empty and pushed off the trail right near Latrop," Mattie said, her voice tight.

Kera tried to calm herself, having made the decision that nothing would bring her to panic. Still, her skin felt like it was crawling and her muscles burned with adrenaline. She felt odd and tried to identify her emotions. "Is that it?" she asked. "Did he find anything else?"

"Some footprints in the dirt," Lightner answered. "Now, Roger is no professional tracker, but he feels there might have been some sort of fight."

Mattie added, "Roger has gone to collect the others. We'll have a meeting in the barn in ten minutes. Everyone is being asked to bring along their essentials."

Lightner's hand settled on Kera's shoulder and squeezed lightly. "May I help you with the children?"

Things were happening too fast. She had Murtaugh hiding. "Let me bring them out," she said. "They're sleeping."

In the room she hustled to pack a bag—toothbrushes, warm clothes, clean underwear—while quietly waking Andrew and Alissa. "You have to go!" She whispered to Murtaugh. "Something's happening. You must go, please!" He stood and watched her with his mouth hanging open.

Kera left the room with the drowsy children, and Lightner stepped forward to assist her.

***

There wasn't a light on in Latrop. As he approached under the blue veil of the moon, it looked to Rand exactly like other towns he had recently traveled past—eerie, deserted, hollow places, where good, hopeful people once lived. But as he crossed a dark, yet shimmering river Rand could see why someone would settle here, the beauty, the—and he could not remember ever having used the word—solitude. Put people in the scene and he imagined a gentle, straightforward place to raise a family.

Then, not far in the distance, the sky lit up, and even within the loud confines of the truck Rand heard rumbling. It frightened him terribly that war had reached the place he hoped to find his children.

When he reached the center of town he brought the truck to a stop. Rand felt stiff from the long drive, but he grabbed his pack and readied himself. When he levered open the door, the cool night air hit him and cleared his brain, washed his nostrils of the acrid cigarette smoke smell. Another bomb sounded in the distance and Rand jerked, looked over his shoulder, but missed the flash of light.

He picked up the backpack and hurriedly crossed the street where he stood gazing at a brown two-story building. Even in the dark, the facade looked old as hell, had a sign on the front that read Historic Jefferson Hotel. He looked up the street, then down the other way. He could tell there wasn't a person within miles, and the hope that filled him only moments before began to trickle away. Latrop was all he knew. The place was near Latrop and it was called Better Way. *Retreat, right?*

Rand hustled down the street. He moved around the block as the sounds came again—rat-a-tat-tat—BOOM! The heavy whir of some machine-like cannon expelling rounds filled the night air and seemed closer than the others. *I have made it across this country, and now what do I do? Where are my children?* He circled the block back to the same place.

He could go off in any direction, but any direction might be wrong. He needed a map. His shoulders shook and he almost laughed and almost cried. *I have needed a map for over two thousand miles.* Across the way sat a gas station, so he left his pack leaning on the wall of the hotel, walked over, and looked through the windows. No maps. The door was locked, but he wondered if there wasn't a map somewhere inside, a drawer possibly. He began to wonder about his new habit: first the inn at Yellowstone, then the truck, now this place. He looked around back, found a small cracked window, took a rock and broke it out. Yanking himself up and through the opening he caught the wound in his stomach and his body filled with a hot flash of pain. He lost his grip and dropped heavily onto the floor and stayed there. The effects of his wounds, fatigue, the long truck ride, frustration, all weighted him down. He lay with his face to the cold floor, but then forced himself slowly up. It seemed crazy to him. All this way and he had forgotten the difficulty of finding the exact location of his children. He calmed himself and peered into the dim light. He shuffled about and checked every drawer, every shelf.

"Ah! Gas stations don't even carry maps anymore!" He barked out in the chilly silence, and saw an image in his mind of his lonely voice haunting through all the empty rooms of Latrop. *Maybe I am dead and only a ghost.* He unlocked the door and stepped back out into the street.

For an hour he searched the town, hoping that someone remained, but finally his thirst drove him back to the gas station where he tried the faucet and was pleased it ran cold. He drank deeply. His side again hurt. Finally, he returned to the hotel and stood over his pack, frantic with worry and frustration. He had to figure this out, now, before the war reached his children ahead of him—if it had not already.

***

The entire community stood assembled in the low shadowy light of the barn. Only the oldest citizens sat. Everyone else stood stone-faced, hiding their anxiety the way a lake hides its life in the frozen depths of winter. With bombs rumbling and gunfire rattling, a battle continued some few miles away.

At the front, Mattie shifted, hesitating—and Kera felt concerned, how uncertain their leader appeared. Silent and introspective, almost meditating, Nee stood next to Kera. Kera had tried to meditate herself, had even asked in her mind for the help of her father and mother long gone, but she sensed no response. She felt only an all-consuming sense of dread, like a gnawing cramp that filled her body cavity, and it seemed out of balance with the facts they had so far gathered. It continued to bewilder her. After all, the Shuntz could easily have decided to abandon their cart in trade for faster travel. Kera had felt brave, had felt sure of her plan, but something had changed and she could not figure it out. She did feel thankful for Lightner's presence, with the children between them.

"Hello, everyone," Mattie spoke with a voice betraying her fears. "Along with the close proximity of the violence, and another occurrence, we felt the circumstances demanded immediate action. I would like to hear from Roger Cummins."

An urgent voice rose quickly from the back, "Let's just do away with the usual formalities and hear the problem so we can figure out what we're going to do!"

Kera couldn't see who had spoken. A number of affirmations were mumbled.

Roger and Wanda were near the front and he let go of Wanda's hand and stepped forward, next to Mattie. His face reflected little of its everyday light, but his steadfast manner showed resolve. He stood straight as a board and spoke slowly. "I had the first watch and I decided to use the moonlight and walk the trail all the way into Latrop. To sort of clear it from the start. I didn't hear anything, or anyone—"

A different voice interrupted, "Come on, Roger, we don't have time for storytelling here!"

And another, "Get to what happened!"

Roger smiled, shifted to glance at Mattie, then went on. "Okay, well, what I found was the Shuntz' handcart. They had decided earlier today to leave until things calmed down. I didn't see them, but the cart had been pushed off the trail and tipped over."

A lot of voices rose; people talked nervously to one another.

"I took a look at the trail there, using my flashlight a little, and saw what I can only think were scuffle marks, like there had been some kind of fight, or struggle. Not a lot, but enough. That's all. I came right back then."

The room broke into a frenzy of tense chatter. The discourse grew so loud that Kera doubted anyone could understand a word. People turned from the broader gathering and smaller groups began to form, some moving closer to the main door of the old barn. Mattie held her hand high and at first she tried to raise her voice above the others, to call for order, but then she quit and stood worrying, looking like a mother dog watching her puppies scatter.

Kera glanced over at Lightner and he watched the crowd with the expression a father might wear while his family is in turmoil.

Kera had assimilated into the community. These were now her people. She had witnessed their strength and assuredness and it had grown within her and fastened her again to Earth. They had become her evidence of a long sought truth, but it seemed they were about to become just another lie—their inner peace, stability, and unity was crumbling. Along with her own sense of haunting, it was all she could do to keep from grabbing the children and bolting out the door.

Then Nee stepped up onto the bench. She stood tall and straight and gazed peacefully out over the crowd. There it was again, Kera thought, *Immaculate.* A breath of hope filled her lungs. Nee's hair shined and hung airily down her back. Her beautiful hands before her touched lightly at the fingertips, and her strong body formed a pedestal for her face, the weariness vanished, the glow resurrected. She gazed out at the group and her steady eyes came across Kera's and they calmed her. *The knowledge anew. Fear only fear. Believe in yourself.*

Slowly everyone noticed Nee, looked *at* her, then *to* her. A hush prevailed. People waited. Kera saw it in their faces. The simple look that Nee gave, it brought faith. It seemed to also say, consider your actions at this moment. Then she stepped quietly down.

Mattie looked as if her lungs had again filled with oxygen. "We need to have a calm, but certainly brief discussion on what it is we choose to do," she said.

At that moment the large door of the barn pulled wide. Everyone turned and refocused their attention to the rear. Gasps and utterances rose as Roy and Molly Shuntz staggered in. Molly carried their child clutched to her bosom.

Everyone went to them and a circle quickly formed around the three timid forms. Because of her position Kera was on the outside, had a hard time seeing, but in that first moment she caught something in Molly's eyes, and it hit her again, that cramp like a white hot hook up under her ribs. She turned to Lightner, pulled the children to him, said, "Stay right with them!" He answered, "Yes."

She pushed herself through the people. Their voices grew shrill in her ears. She could smell fear again and hated it. Then she caught a closer glimpse of Molly's face and saw purplish bruises about her mouth and cheek and ear, saw the emptiness in her eyes. "Let me through!" Kera said. But no one moved for her. She saw Roy's face and he too had bruises and swellings and a horrified vacant expression. "Let me through!" she yelled. And this time a passage formed and Kera found herself next to the couple and she knew, knew it the minute she saw the horrible swollen condition of Molly's hands. "Your hands," she said to her, and it surprised her that her voice came quiet and calm, "did a man do that to you?"

Molly stared at her with that vacuous gaze, then nodded slowly.

"It was my fault," Roy murmured, "my fault. He was too strong... knocked me out. He left our baby alone, but...oh, my poor Molly."

One of the other women tried to take the baby from Molly's arms, but she twisted away and glared.

Kera asked, "Did this man have black, really thick hair, like an animal? Was he very big and strong?"

Molly tilted her head and worked her eyes back to Kera. She again nodded.

Astonishment passed through Kera and she shivered. *How the hell did he find me?* But it quickly dissipated along with any doubt in her mind. *It's him, of course, how could I not have known? And the only reason he's here, is me.* Guilt followed swiftly, accompanied by sorrow, knowing she had somehow led him to these innocent people, and to her children. She felt a calm wash over her, a calm brought on by an immutable wrath.

She thought of Murtaugh hiding in her home, armed and ready to defend them. But she knew he wasn't. She saw in her mind his forlorn features, his battered bravado; a young man needing time to repair. Young beautiful Murtaugh would be no match for the vengeance carried by this man with no conscience. And though she once got the jump on the wild-haired man she couldn't expect it to happen again.

She had pledged nonviolence to herself and to this community, to some great and Universal spirit. At that time she had not imagined this man would come back into her life. Still, when she made the pledge she knew a test might arise that could prove it incredibly difficult to keep.

She stepped up on a bench, looked for Lightner and the children, saw them, and signaled him to bring them to her. "Listen, please!" Everyone quieted and looked to her. Kera's eyes fell on Andrew and Alissa moving toward her. *Dear God, dear Father and Mother, help me now!* She steadied herself and spoke loudly. "I know the man that did this terrible thing to the Shuntz's," she said. "He is the one who did it to me."

Most of the faces before her went blank with confusion. Some of them filled with suspicion and anger. How could she blame them?

"I'm sorry, but we have little time for apologies right now. We must put our plan into action immediately!"

She could see him in her mind, feel him. *I sensed him. I knew he was here.* She wondered if he watched them now. Above all else, she had to keep him away from the children. She wanted deeply to keep him away from all of them. This had to end.

"Is it only one?" someone asked.

"Possibly."

"Then we can face him together!"

"No," she said, but she had to be careful, so they would listen and not vote her down. "He might well have come with an army. He was part of a group. The only thing to do is move to the higher ground and hope they lose our trail." A number of people nodded in approval. Mothers brought children in close around them. "You have what you need with you, along with what we have stored. Let's not delay!"

People started to turn and head out the door. The plan was to allow Lightner to lead, he best knew the path, and no lighting would be allowed along the way. It was good the moon shone brightly. Another bomb or missile went off and lit the horizon with a shudder of brilliance. Still, they moved in silence, just as they all had planned.

Kera again felt proud of them. She felt a sense of knowing, of warm calm. She made her way to the front of the line with Lightner and her children, her babies. She held Andrew's hand and Lightner carried Alissa, and in the moon's blue light she could see his face and eyes and how he worried for her. "It's okay," she said. "Everyone will be okay." His hand came out and she took it, squeezed Andrew's little hand with her other. They started silently up the trail.

She figured if the wild-haired man had found this remote place in search of her, he would soon find her as well, if he hadn't already. Above all others, even her children, he wanted her. What she needed to do was separate herself from her innocent family and friends, to protect them. Sooner than later he would come for her. She stopped abruptly, looked to Lightner. "I forgot. I have something I cannot leave behind."

"Is it crucial?" His voice remained calm, but she heard his doubt.

"Yes. I cannot risk it. I must go back."

"Not alone! I'll go with you."

She took her hand from his and gripped his arm. "No! Please. Stay with my children. Keep going. I'll be all right."

"Mom?" Andrew whined.

She steeled herself, then took Alissa in her arms, bent down to Andrew. "Listen you two. You must do as I ask, for everyone." Inside, she felt herself shutting down. It was the only way.

"But isn't it dangerous to go back?" Andrew asked.

"No. Not really. I crossed this whole country and I made it back to you, didn't I?"

"Yeah."

Alissa squeezed her neck and Kera felt her trembling. *Is this right, Mom, Dad? Is this what I must do?* "It's okay, baby girl. Remember me telling you before, that it would all be okay?"

"Yes," Alissa whispered, her little voice like two reeds rubbing in the wind.

"Then trust me now, Sweetie."

They said nothing more. She kissed their faces, smelled them deeply, and stood, peeled Alissa's arms from around her neck and handed her back to Lightner. It felt to Kera like handing him a part torn from herself. "Go," she said huskily to him, and she turned and walked stiffly back around the line of people.

Many eyes watched her but few said a word. To those who did, she replied only, "Follow Lightner."

Alone, she made her way back through the night.

Chapter 32

Rand was desperate. He had checked the entire perimeter of the downtown area and found that no less than five roads led out. It seemed impossible to tell where they went without following them. He had actually found a phone booth with a phone book—unheard of these days—but no clue to the retreat. All phones he found remained dead.

Sounds of battle continued and worked at his frayed nerves. If he drove down the wrong road in the big red truck he could easily be killed or picked up and detained. And the way the sky lit up each time, he doubted many of those rumblings and pops were more than three miles off.

North. He remembered Kera had said it was north of Latrop. *Right? Or had she only said Latrop was north of Spokane?* There were only two roads that appeared to lead off into the north. He could stay here endlessly wondering, or he could walk one first and then the other, or he could take his chances and drive the loud, very visible, and slow truck. He decided to walk a mile or so up one of the roads and make his next decision from there.

As he labored the pack onto his back, he stopped in place, listening. He heard the sound of a vehicle on one of the nearby roads. He flopped the pack down and listened again, his eyes wide. He hurried to the side of the hotel and peered down a dark street. He still heard it, but it seemed to fade, changing direction. Then he whirled around and caught a glimpse of a dark vehicle as it crossed his street and headed down another two blocks away.

He wanted to yell, but remained too fearful to utter a sound. It seemed to him, no matter what he did he fell back to a gamble that could turn out very badly, even end his ordeal. He grabbed the pack and stood in an entryway where even the moonlight couldn't go.

He heard the sound of the vehicle getting louder and this time it passed only one block away, heading in the opposite direction. It seemed to be cruising the downtown area block-by-block. The vehicle looked to be a large SUV, dark color, maybe official. The thought dawned on him that if it were military or law enforcement surely they would take him to the retreat to retrieve his children, being so close. That's all he wanted. They could take them to any containment camp after that, where they could wait for Kera, if she wasn't already here.

Please, bring my family together.

Then he heard the vehicle and it came into view right at the corner of the building, paused, then began crossing his street, heading away. Rand didn't think anymore, didn't want to think anymore, he just did as he had done when seeing Kera on the back of the Jeep. He stepped out into the moonlight and stood still, watching.

The vehicle continued across his street and headed away. But then it stopped with a flash of bright red lights. It backed up toward him. Rand stood tall and waited, watched.

It pulled over to the edge of the curb, looking blue, or black, eased up next to him and slowed, stopped. Rand squinted, trying to see through the window—then someone powered it down.

"Hello," a voice said.

"Hello."

"Are you okay?"

"Well, no. I could use a little assistance."

"Is this Latrop?"

Rand's eyes adjusted and he could see two featureless heads within the darkness.

"Yeah. It's Latrop. Do you know where Better Way is?"

"No way?" the guy's voice lifted into an ironic tone.

"We're looking for Better Way too," replied the head in the drivers spot.

"You don't know where it is?" Rand asked.

"Nope. We just arrived. So, you aren't from here?"

"No. I am from New York. How about you?"

"Have you seen anyone else?"

Rand felt the pain of the wound again, felt the pain of having come to another dead-end. He felt nauseous and bent down and braced himself.

"You okay?" came the voice of the first.

Rand heard the door on the opposite side open, heard footsteps coming toward him, felt a hand on his back. "You okay, buddy?"

"I'll be fine, sure. Just need to get my wind back." He raised his hand and felt dampness on his forehead. "Tired."

The man helped Rand sit on his pack. All of a sudden he failed to even have the strength to look up.

The man asked, "You alone here? What you doin' anyway?"

"Looking for my family."

"You're not from anywhere around here?"

"No, like I said, New York."

There was a second's pause, then, "New York? That's a long way. You're the second person we've met lately from New York."

Rand looked up. The guy standing with his hand on Rand's back was tall, taller than him, lean, and he wore the type of bulging vest that Rand himself sometimes wore, a photographer's vest. Rand squinted, trying to see him better. The guy smiled and his face sort of wrapped around the smile and warmth radiated from his eyes. "What?" Rand asked. "Who'd you meet from New York?"

"A woman named Kera, she's looking for—"

Rand stood and grabbed the man's arm, faced him, "Kera, that's my wife! When, when did you see her?"

A jet blasted over so low the men ducked. Its roar was deafening as it streaked across the valley and climbed like a missile over the mountains beyond.

Rand screamed above its noise, yanked at the man's sleeve. "My wife! When did you see her?"

Another jet streaked overhead, after the first. The air vibrated and the blaze from the engines glowed in the sky. The other man opened the door of the vehicle and stepped out. The man Rand held onto was smiling ear-to-ear. He shouted, "No way! Your wife? Really! Well, it's been a couple weeks, yeah! We saw her over in Iowa, or, shit, where was it, Garret? Kansas?"

"It was Iowa." Garret called, and smiled too, but to a lesser degree. "She wasn't certain where you were."

Rand looked at him, thought he caught a tone he'd heard before while on this journey, something in the man's voice. "Yeah. That's right. We've been separated. It's really sort of odd..."

"Odd?" Garret returned.

"Oh, just that so many men I've met lately have already met my... ah!... never mind..." Rand was hit with pain and fatigue again, bent over.

"Now, let me ask," the guy with the vest said, "your Kera is about five-foot-seven maybe, brown hair, trim woman, big brown eyes?"

"Yes!" Rand confirmed. "That's her!" He looked from one to the other. "We ran into trouble. Our children are at this Better Way Retreat. Is she okay? Do you know where she is now?"

"No. We're looking for her. We're journalists. Unbelievable!"

"But why are you looking for her?" Rand asked.

Garret answered, "Nat and I helped her a little, and we offered her a ride here, but she declined. Left in the night. We guessed she'd had enough of men for awhile."

Rand looked at Garret and felt himself bristle.

"Listen," Nat started, "you don't look very good. You need to lay down or something?"

"No. No. What I need is to find Better Way. You guys don't have a map?"

"It's not on there. Believe me, we've looked."

"Well, maybe we could drive in your truck. I think it is north of here, not sure. But why'd you want to find her anyway?"

"Well, we—hey, what's your name?"

Rand looked at Nat, then at Garret. He wiped his sleeve across his damp forehead. He looked down at his battered feet and his dried and cracked hands. He heard his mother's voice calling his name. He smiled in a sort of secret, yet proud way. "Randy," he said. "My name is Randy."

"We hoped to do a story with her, Randy. We freelance for network news and documentaries. Garret's a reporter, and I'm the photographer. I heard you're one also."

"Yeah. Foolishness."

"What's that?" Nat asked.

"My entire career, I have focused on foolishness."

"How can a town not be on the map?" Garret interjected, his voice frustrated.

"I believe it's north of here. There looks to be two or three roads heading north. Maybe we could drive out them a mile or so and see what we see?" Randy suggested.

"Let's do it!" said Nat.

As they turned toward the vehicle a dim light suddenly lit up an area down the street. The men looked at each other in disbelief. "This town seemed evacuated. Should we check it out?" Nat asked in a hushed voice.

Randy didn't answer, he started walking toward the light. The others followed.

At the edge of a store they slowed. Randy and Nat peered around the corner. The light came from the top of an old white garage, its wooden doors swung wide. In the frame of the doorway a man sat on a bale of straw. He appeared quite old and thin and he wore faded but crisp dungarees and a green cotton shirt. In one hand he held half a straw hat, in the other a long curved needle.

The three of them stepped around the corner and the old man looked up, studied them briefly, and then went back to his work without a word. They walked up to him, entranced by the illusion the man rendered, of timelessness and tranquility. He continued his work without paying them notice.

Randy couldn't believe what he was seeing, but finally said, "Excuse me, sir."

"How can I help you?" The elder man still did not look at them.

"We're wondering if you might tell us where the Better Way Retreat is?"

"Off the end of Third Street," he nodded toward the north, "there's a trail."

Randy waited. "You mean a road?"

The old man stopped his work and looked up, annoyed. "No, young man, a footpath. You might have to walk a spell. It won't kill you." Then he studied Randy up and down—the worn clothes and battered face—and added, "Er, maybe it could. Take your time, Son." He stuck the hat with the needle and pulled through a length of thread. Two loud booms shook the horizon, but the old man continued his work. The younger men shifted.

"Sir?"

The old man kept working.

"If we follow the trail will we find the town? I mean—is it obvious?"

"Obvious as an eagle at a cockfight."

The three of them stood there a moment, then looked at each other and turned to go.

"One'a you boys wanna buy a hat?"

Randy was about to explain that he had no money when Nat sounded out, "Yes!" and stuck his hand in his back pocket.

The old man pressed himself up and glanced at Nat's head, then reached around the back of the swinging door and produced a finely woven, wide-brimmed straw hat. He flicked his wrist and it landed on Nat's head.

All but the old man smiled. Nat pressed it down and it fit perfectly.

"Twenty bucks," the old man said.

Nat handed him two tens from his wallet. "Say, how far is it on that trail to Better Way?"

"Maybe two miles. A little uphill. You'll do okay, sun's comin' up." He pushed the money into his front pocket and sat back down to his work.

***

Kera ran in and found Murtaugh still in her house, pacing.

"What?" he asked. "What is it?" Apprehension tightened his broad face.

"You have to leave," she said, and tried to keep her voice steady.

He walked his big body over to her and his camouflage uniform and the nearness of his weapon leaning against the wall raised her anxiety. She had to get him away from there. The wild-haired man could be anywhere, and was most certainly near. She could feel him. He would kill Murtaugh in an instant.

"Why? Why must I leave?"

"Because we all voted and they feel you need to go. Now, gather your things. You must hurry."

"Why?" he asked again.

"Because! Don't act like a child!" her voice boomed. She covered her mouth with her hand. His eyes showed pain and he stood silently watching her. "Murtaugh, I know you are here to protect us—"

"Not them so much as you—"

"I know! I know. But there's nothing you can do. You have to believe me."

"But, I can, I—"

"Murtaugh! I'm begging you to go!" She went to the wall and took hold of his rifle and shoved it toward him. "Take this, please, and go."

He snatched it from her as if no one should touch it but himself. Still, his eyes lingered on her face.

Kera rushed to the door and opened it. "Go," she said, waving her arm through the air. "Go. I am begging you..."

With that his eyes tightened and he grabbed his helmet, ammunition pouches, backpack, and strode out the door.

Alone, she gazed about the small place. Already it held memories. But clearly, for her, they were memories that could not last. For the children it would be different. The place marked the beginning of a new life for them. They were now the happiest she had ever seen them. Wanting it to remain that way, she quickly left and headed off through the dark.

Kera approached the barn slowly, wondering if he was there ahead of her. He had found Better Way. Now he would find her. It didn't make sense. Was it something she said, or Rand, or was it simply meant to be?

She saw no one and so stood in the open doorway of the time-honored barn and waited. She watched silently as the light turned from moon blue to steely grey. The chill that preceded dawn came and brought with it a dampness that sent shivers deep into her. She stood in silence, decompressing, and simply watched. *How sweet, I hear no bombs, no guns, no strife.* The sun rose and the sparkling highlights off the dew gave her the impression of a field of gems—gems in the grasses, in the trees, dangling from spider webs. It struck her with melancholy, how rarely she had risen early enough to watch the birth of day, of warmth and light, and how completely rare that she would witness it silently, peacefully, with complete undivided attention. In that other world before Better Way she had rushed blindly through each day, but now that her time neared an end it seemed most crucial to hold peace and make note of the world around her.

The cool night air fell off the mountains in cold wafts, fresh and clear. She heard the buzzing of insects and birds chirping at the dawn. A flock fluttered past and then settled on the grass before her. *Bluebirds. Maybe thirty.* They hopped about and picked at insects and then burst into the air as a flight of some other, dustier bird strafed them and chased them away. Only twenty yards off they landed in a small tree about ten feet tall, *a fir*, she thought, and then, *oh my!*, they spread out upon the branches of the tree and created on their own the image of... *a Christmas tree*... all covered with blue ornaments. *A Christmas tree.* She watched them, clear-eyed and steady, until they flew again.

Out across the fields from the barn, three deer, then two more, came out of the dark forest shadows and stepped into the sunlight of a grassy meadow, searching horizons with their eyes glinting, the tawny hair looking almost golden. How daintily they picked their way, dipped their heads finally, nibbled at the moist grasses.

The world bestowed Kera with these treasures, and raw emotion ran through her like a natural, uncrafted orchestration. She allowed this. She knew she would have to push away all feeling soon, but right now, she wanted to witness life, to feel joy and freedom and beauty in a way she had not felt in a long, long time. Of the few things she owned in life, this moment would be hers. She had learned a lot in these past weeks. She had come in search of her children and found them; she had hoped for a better way of living and those here had offered it. It now seemed clear there was no such reality for her: the injustice in life would find her wherever she went. For her, there would be no perfect life of peace and joy. She felt prepared.

And so, she refused to jump when a scrape sounded on the ground behind her, but instead studied the scene to the front for another long moment, before straightening slowly and turning quietly.

There he stood, his black greasy hair caught by a shaft of light through the openings of the wall. Thick black and green camouflage paint covered his face and neck. And he looked even stronger, larger than she remembered. He was filthy. He wore soiled camouflage pants, not unlike Murtaugh's, and a black sweatshirt, sleeves cut off. Diagonally across his chest hung a belt and cased knife, a really big thing, and he held a rifle in the crook of his arm. Green backpack straps circled his shoulders.

He raised the rifle nonchalantly and sighted it at her forehead.

Kera thought as fast as she could, worked hard to keep her face still, but a loud explosion roared and she jerked involuntarily.

He held the rifle steady—waited, smiled at what the sound had done to her. The blast had come from the battle, apparently renewed, but not from him.

Kera regained her composure and in her mind recited, *I will not continue the violence. I give myself for peace.* Then she asked, "Why would you come all this way just to shoot me?"

He remained silent, held his place, and had that look of angry condescension, as if he felt smug for being there and wanted to say, I Told You So.

Kera moved slowly toward him. "It is incredible that you found me. How did you do it?" and she watched carefully how her words registered. He returned the gaze and she saw more clearly what had barely surfaced those weeks ago: no matter how angry or hateful or pompous he appeared, the flicker of some question, some inner distress, hid there in his dark eyes. She could see his pain, had seen it in her own eyes a thousand times before; in fact, he now looked to her like nothing but pain. She hated him, feared him, but also, now, pitied him. She approached to within a few feet, saw his finger tighten on the trigger. His glare went hard, turned inward. She stopped. "Are you sure? Do you really want to keep living this way?"

The steps had brought her close and she could see his skin all bruised and cut. She could smell him, hiding there behind the rifle.

"I promised to take care of you," he said. It sounded almost like a whine.

I will not continue violence. For my children, my world, for eternity, I give myself for peace.

The sun moved and a bright beam of light shot through the boards and flared in her eyes. She turned her head from him and looked at the glorious shafts streaming in, so bright and warm it seemed the beam could lift her away, take her out of the moment. Perhaps it was her time to go. Perhaps peace meant total surrender.

"I want to make a deal with you," she said.

He still didn't move, but his breathing increased, as if he were under stress, and his eyes cinched down. He slowly edged the rifle barrel toward her head, now only a foot away, an inch, and pressed it there…on her forehead.

He is a man, only a man. I can give myself peacefully—for whatever he would do, so long as it is far from here, from my children, from these people I love…

But then his eyes shifted in his head. He listened.

And Kera heard it too, a small sound, many sounds, and then they appeared, from the door behind her, the doors at the sides, the door opposite, and quickly they came, formed a circle around Kera and him.

The wild-haired man swung the gun from one to the next, spun around as if someone was coming up behind him, but no one was, everyone kept their distance.

Kera searched frantically for her children and saw Lightner and he nodded toward the mountains and she hoped he was saying, saw it in his watery eyes, that the children were safe, far away. She didn't count, but she felt certain most were here, the citizens of Better Way, with her.

Do these people know he will kill them? Kera felt oddly bolstered, proud, yet horrified. Was this a beautiful dream, or a nightmare?

The faces of the people were straight and serious and they focused on the wild-haired man, and though some showed fear, Kera saw no hostility or anger.

"Back away!" the wild-haired man growled. He jabbed the barrel against Kera's head. "I'll shoot you one by one! Slaughter every fucking one of you!" he barked, and against a ray of dawn's sharp light Kera saw spittle eject from his lips.

***

Randy stumbled hurriedly along in the lead, weighted down by his pack, using the cane as a propulsion device, wheezing loudly, yet driven. Carrying the camera gear, Nat and Garret worked hard to keep pace.

Finally, he slowed. They had come at least two miles along the trail without seeing anything. Then a sharp ray of light struck the window of a building hidden among the trees, and Randy lumbered forward. At first, the homes blended so well with their surroundings that he saw few, and only when amongst them did he realize they had found the village.

"It's mighty quiet," Nat said.

Randy turned and realized Nat was photographing him. The camera shook with Nat's breathing. Garrett bent over and placed his hands on the back of his head, tired, huffing. Randy wheezed and felt sharp pain in his side. He noticed a large building in the center of the village and went to it. The doors were open and he entered and called out, but no one answered. He turned and came face-to-face with Nat's lens again. "Really, Nat," he winced, "I'd appreciate you helping me, instead of that!"

Nat lowered the camera.

Garret began, "We're only trying to tell your story—"

"Believe me, I now understand the importance of documenting the condition of our country. But, please…!"

They left the building. Splitting up, they checked the nearest houses. Randy went off in a rush, his face reddened and sweaty, and continued to search for someone, or something that might give him a clue. *They're here! Tell me they are here! Don't let it be that they have evacuated!*

He stumbled from place to place, energized by sheer will, but soon hopelessness dragged him to a halt like a lethal dose of venom. He had no clue how to find his family, but they weren't here, and he had no remaining energy. He felt numb, his legs, his fingertips, even his face.

It was over, unless they came walking toward him from out of nowhere, like some fairy tale, some miracle he had foolishly thought he could earn. He leaned on a tree and gazed at the ground, his head hanging—not seeing anything but the faces of his family in his spent and bewildered mind. He twisted weakly out of the pack and let it drop, sank down to the ground and sat slumped against the tree.

To come all this way, to finally understand how to love my family, and to make something of life, something that matters—for nothing!

"You will succeed, Randy," he heard his mother's voice in his mind. *"You must keep going."*

"I have walked across this country!" he yelled at the ground and his voice sounded hoarse, slurred. "I have done what I needed to do and I have done it as well as I could, so WHY?" he roared.

He glanced over and Nat, crouched on the ground next to a house, wearing that floppy-brimmed hat, had the camera pointed at him again, recording. Randy had looked through enough lenses to know how he appeared and for that moment saw himself there, derelict, a failure, a pitiable picture and a tragic story.

Nat turned the lens away from him and pointed it into the front window of the house.

"Yes! Thank you!" Randy hollered at him, then went back to confronting the dirt and rock. Never before had he felt such a complete lack of strength and desire to live. *Without them I am nothing.*

Slumped over sideways, his face nearly touched the ground. He summoned the energy to raise his head enough to glance over at Nat and check to see that the lens remained trained on the window of the house.

He saw Nat stand with purpose, try the door, and enter the place. Randy watched more closely, but Nat did not reappear. *He must have found something interesting.*

Randy pushed himself to his feet using the cane and tree for support. He had to see what Nat had found. His overworked and undernourished body had quickly stiffened, so it caused intense pain to walk. *How long has it been since I've eaten? Yellowstone. Maybe sixteen hours.* But even then his body had lacked consistent nourishment for weeks. He leaned heavily against the front window of the place and peered in at Nat. The cameraman had his lens aimed at a small object on a table—a wooden box. *Pretty.* It was open and crayons in bright colors spilled from it.

Randy pulled back as if he had put his cheek to a hot plate instead of a window. Then he hobbled around the corner and halted in front of Nat and gaped in wonder at the box. The letters *AP* were engraved on a gold plate attached to the top. "Alissa Priven!" Randy cried out. He picked up the box and rubbed it gently with his dried and cracked hands. "This is my daughter's! Kera gave it to her for a present." He closed it and wrapped his fingers around the box and squeezed it, glanced around the room. He moved quickly into a back bedroom and looked at a bed, a dresser chest. He went to the bed and pulled up the sheets, put his nose to them. "My children have been here!" He turned to wrap his arms around Nat and got a face-full of lens. Nat clicked off the camera. Randy exclaimed, "Thank you! Thank you for finding this!"

"Of course! I thought it made a wonderful image, but I didn't know—"

Garrett came rushing into the house and they showed him what they had found. With this new piece of evidence, Randy again wanted to search and they decided to walk a circle out from the house and look for clues.

"You wait here and Garrett and I will look," Nat suggested. "You need rest." Randy walked away from him without speaking and soon the three had fanned out in a wide circle around the area.

Garrett spotted the path leading out of the village and proudly announced, "I was an Eagle Scout as a boy." The defined and shadowy imprints of shoes, many shoes, marked the trail. "A lot of people have walked this way recently." Randy patted him on the back and the men hurried along the trail as it led them through the hushed morning forest. Randy faltered as he hobbled forward, but his face again appeared eager. His eyes flicked hungrily across the land before him.

Chapter 33

"Is this the man who harmed you, Kera?" asked Nee, her voice loud enough for all to hear.

Kera looked to the group, then the wild-haired man, and feared what he might do next…couldn't figure out why he hadn't already done it. He held his ground but he seemed unable to take charge. She saw hints of angst and confusion in his face. He had reached out and grabbed her with his free hand around the collar, but his eyes kept moving around the crowd. "Yes, this is the man who raped and beat me," she said firmly but quietly, awaiting the rifle report that would end her life. But instead the wild-haired man looked at her with a hint of surprise and confusion.

"Are you okay, Kera?" Nee asked, and Kera looked at her with *Are You Crazy?* written in her eyes. But Nee gazed back at her with love, with steadiness, and Kera understood… Nee was asking permission to continue speaking. Kera nodded a nearly imperceptible, *yes!*

Nee turned and found Roy Shuntz in the crowd. Kera noticed him for the first time, his face tight with rage and terror, his fists balled up before him. "Roy, is this the man who attacked you and Molly?"

"Yes!" he blasted in a high-pitched condemnation. Kera thought the wild-haired man a hulking animal in comparison to young clean Roy. "This man is evil!" Roy cried out.

Many of the men tensed and the wild-haired man's shoulders raised behind the weapon.

Kera saw a ghastly scene in her mind of them rushing him as he began to fire. She spoke softly, "All of you stay where you are. He will shoot you."

The crowd steadied but the wild-haired man remained tensed.

Nee asked, "Would you shoot us?"

The wild-haired man pointed the gun at her. Nee's expression went dry. "No," Kera whispered, and he glanced back at her. She wondered at the expression on his face, filled with hate, anger, yet doubt and apprehension. *Why has he not simply done it?*

"Why?" Nee asked.

He laughed, his shoulders bouncing. *A false laugh*, Kera thought. *He's acting.*

"Can you tell me why you hurt people?" Nee asked. Her voice came more as a purr than a hiss.

The wild-haired man looked back at Nee, his eyes so mixed, his jaw so tight and his grip tightening on Kera's neck. "We could let him go! If he would agree to leave," Kera said. "We could make a deal."

Roy leaned forward, "So that he could do this to someone else down the road, and another after that?" Kera wanted someone to lead Roy away, even if he had as much right as anyone to feel as he did.

The wild-haired man showed a trace of awe in what was taking place before him. He seemed almost entertained.

Nee said, "What if he agreed to lay down his gun? We could feed him and hold him until the war is over and he could get help."

The wild-haired man looked at her as if he had never heard from anyone so stupid, or an idea so ludicrous. He shook his head in disbelief. "Do you all think I'm a fool?" He looked at Kera for a long moment, his eyes, she thought, trying hard to see inside her.

Then he grasped her neck and pushed the barrel harder against her head and started moving toward the door. The crowd closed in around them. The wild-haired man blasted off a round over Kera's head and the group recoiled in unison.

***

At the sound of the rifle shot Nat dropped to his knees and brought the camera up. Garrett jumped behind a tree. Randy stood in place and searched the area before him for the source. It was close. When he couldn't see anything he moved forward with surprisingly deliberate and steady steps, bending and peering around trees.

He hadn't gone but a dozen paces when he caught sight of a red barn, standing tall and tattered in the morning sun. It looked to him like a temple with its high, pointed roof, and the pastoral landscape surrounding it. He pushed forward, leaning on the cane as he ducked around thick, low-hanging pine trees rimmed with orange quaking light. A bluebird flew from a tree and past his head.

The closest trees stood some thirty yards from the barn. Using them as cover, Randy stopped his approach. In a moment Nat, and then Garrett, sneaked up behind him.

"Do you think the gunfire came from in there?" Garrett asked. Nat had the camera up and Randy knew he couldn't stop him. It was his responsibility, not theirs, to find out if his children were here and in harm's way.

"Not sure," he answered, and in that moment he heard a loud voice inside the barn. The ten foot high double doors were open, but with the contrast of bright sun outside and dark interior shadows, he couldn't see in.

In a flurry of violent motion a man barged out of the doorway, his right hand holding a rifle, his left hand grasping a woman around the neck.

Randy's eyes widened—he tensed and straightened—his hand squeezed the head of the cane. "Kera..." And he recognized that man, without question.

"Jesus!" Garrett whispered.

A semi-circle of people exited the barn and closed around Kera and the man, and as a whole they moved like a snake handler trying to confine an escaping cobra— circling, dodging, respecting the deadliness of the viper, but wanting to cut off its escape.

Nat edged up next to Randy, his lens on the scene, and whether his movement betrayed them, or a reflection from the sun, the man with the rifle immediately focused on them hiding behind the trees. He fired a round and both Garrett and Nat fell flat to the ground, the straw hat flopping off Nat's head.

***

Kera felt pain when the wild-haired man shoved her toward the door, felt as if death had finally reached out and grasped her by the throat. *Be at peace.* But try as she might, she couldn't retain any peacefulness inside her. Her plan was not working. They had made no deal, not for the safety of her children or these people. And the fact that they had come and tried so hard to save her, it made her want even more to remain and become a lasting part of them. This felt so different than it had when he had assaulted her alone. She was not alone any longer. She wanted to wrench away, to find some power as she had before and strike him down, but she knew this time he was more than prepared. He turned her with such power and shoved the rifle barrel into her spine so savagely that she felt warm wetness. He yanked back with his other hand buried in her hair and her face turned upward. *It's almost over.*

She thought of her children and felt such love that for an instant she went to them, sat with them high in the mountains and played and ran with them and watched them grow, and their faces came to her and their beauty and charms apparent, and she filled for that instant, filled in a way that only a person on the edge of dying can know.

And then she wondered: in all her life she had never done a mean thing to anyone, not purposefully, always thought of others at least as much as she had thought of herself, always fought to appreciate life, considered the world, respected pretty much everything. She had done the best she could. *So why this?*

And then the pressure in her back subsided and a shadow fell across her face, an explosion rang out next to her ear and deafened her. Her head tilted down and her eyes went to the front and a man stepped out from behind a tree some thirty yards away and stood there still as a pole and looked at her, his eyes so striking. And though his face had grown over with hair, his skin had weathered to a deep russet, his hair had bleached lighter than the wheat in the field behind them, and even as he appeared emaciated, torn, and broken… she knew him.

Kera's mind popped and fizzled. *Randy?* She had given up on him and couldn't grasp him being there.

His face, everything about the way he stood and looked at her, radiated love and desire and repentance. He staggered with a cane, but his other hand came up and the open palm faced them in a show of defenselessness and he moved again, tottered toward them, and part of her wanted to yell for him to stay away, but more of her simply couldn't think, couldn't put him here in any way. All their time apart seemed suddenly like no time. All her nightmares of the past and all her dreams for the future slammed together like two opposing trains on the same track. *Where am I? What is happening?*

***

Randy heard Nat and Garrett hit the ground behind him and hoped neither had been shot. But he couldn't take his eyes off Kera. After finding Alissa's crayon box, unguarded hope had taken hold within him that he would again see his children, but fear blocked the extravagant optimism that Kera—his friend, his lover, his wife—might have made it here, might be here now. He somehow believed that with her here, their children were safe somewhere. He wanted only to hold her, to speak with her and tell her he loved her and now understood all of what she had tried so many times to explain.

Seeing her that first instant in the hands of a man so brutal triggered within Randy the desire to rush forward and free her. The image of Kera bent over the hood of the station wagon returned and clouded his mind. But he knew his attack would never work. He knew from the look on the man's face that any such affront would end the lives of not only Kera, but many others.

Then the answer came to him in one of those brilliant instances in which the mind grasps all: he remembered clearly this very man striking him with a gun a short time ago, but recalled himself in that moment as someone very different; he again saw the helicopter flying in low overhead and annihilating soldiers who showed him how quickly sacred life could end; he buried a woman who had attained what he himself wanted most in life, only to die dejected and abandoned by her loved one; he befriended two cowboys he wouldn't have given spit to a week earlier, people unlike himself, but in so many ways the same; an Indian's ancient hate returned through the hot push of steel into his gut, which in turn allowed another of Indian blood to heal him and so learn what it was to become one with Earth and every other thing.

He focused again on the sight before him. *I know this man. He is a part of me and I am a part of him.*

He stepped forward toward the bridge he knew he must build, hobbled on the cane, but held his free hand out before him, open and unarmed. *I must do this. I must find the common ground. I must set sweet Kera free.*

All others stopped and stood motionless, watching Randy as he inched forward. They wore a variety of expressions: alarm, confusion, disbelief, hope. The gunman squinted, jabbed the point of his rifle barrel into Kera's back. Randy could see he was trying to recall the face before him.

In spite of her situation, Kera looked wonderful to Randy. *She is the most beautiful woman under the sun.* Even though she wore the expressions of incomprehension and fear, he could see all over her face, that adorable and truthful and loving face, that she had changed, had become someone he knew incompletely. He couldn't wait to speak with her.

"Why, it's hubby!" the gunman holding Kera barked, and his face filled with amusement. "Have you been here long, or did you just arrive?"

Randy strengthened his voice, smiled. "I had a little trouble finding the place, but I might ask you the same question."

"You told me... Latrop. I followed the map. You come for your watch or your woman?"

Randy hadn't thought of the watch, but there it was on the man's wrist. He looked to Kera. "I've come for the woman I love."

"Too bad. But you can have the damn watch. It keeps pinchin' me. Hee hee, haw haw haw," he laughed mockingly. "Let's see... the last time I saw you, you were sleepin'."

Randy stopped with a dozen steps remaining between them. "I was unconscious, thanks to your friend with the heavy boot heels."

"He wasn't much of a friend," the man whispered hotly.

Randy looked over the crowd and they scrutinized him in return. To the gunman Randy asked, "So, who are all these people?"

"Sheep."

"Not friends?"

"Fuck you."

"Where are your people?"

"Listen, I'm taking your wife and going away for awhile. Do you mind?"

Randy didn't like the question, didn't like any of the possible answers. He thought of what he wanted to say: *Have you asked her?* But he knew not to make that mistake in this situation. "She's not mine. That's the trouble with us people. We've got to stop trying to possess everything."

The man shifted his feet, his grip on Kera, and glared back. Randy focused on Kera's eyes. "I had her love, had her friendship, had her loyalty, but I wanted more. I wanted everything in the world." He searched her eyes, but her eyes turned away.

"You left her, didn't you? You scum. I know how you people are," the man said, and he moved forward, pushed Kera in front of him. The circle of people flexed, then tightened.

Randy stepped closer. The man's eyes shifted about the crowd. "Listen," Randy said, "we want to live. You want to live. We all have dreams."

The man cackled, "HEY! We've been through all this already, you're late."

"Never dreamed of something you wanted, something you wanted to be?"

"Where I come from you don't make dreams. If you make them, they take them away."

"Who's they?"

"People like you!" He twisted Kera's hair. "And, I guess, people like her!"

Randy continued, "We're all struggling to find some *thing*, any *thing* that makes us feel right inside."

The man shifted again and Kera cringed. Randy let his cane fall, held out both hands openly. "You know what I've learned?"

"I'm just dying to know, OR, maybe you could just shut up!"

"It's not about you getting what I have, or me getting more and more, it's about appreciating what we have... about us all trusting each other, not feeding off each other. And it's about finding purpose. We've all lost that."

"Wow, am I hallucinating? I mean, who are you, Jesus?" The man chuckled and turned his gaze to the people, thinking he had made a good joke. "There are more than one kind of people in this world, hero. There are those who stay and those who don't give a damn." Then he twisted at Kera's hair again and pushed her forward.

Randy felt fear course through him, decided to rush the man, but stopped as a striking oriental woman stepped forward.

"I believe you are like us, and I believe you don't want to kill anymore," she spoke to the gunman.

Randy couldn't believe her, how calm and steady she seemed, thought she couldn't be more perfect, here, this moment. She spoke to the gunman so easily, with such a clear voice of wisdom, that even Randy felt calmer.

The man paused, worked his jaw, his gaze ran across the faces, but returned to Nee's.

Randy felt a weight on his shoulder and looked and there beside him stood a mountain of a man with greying sideburns and watery eyes. The man smiled briefly and squeezed Randy's shoulder reassuringly with a hand the size of a baseball mitt, all the while keeping a close eye on Kera and the gunman.

The oriental woman again stepped lightly forward, further closing the circle. "I am Nee," she said. "I ask, can you save this woman's life and join us?" There remained only eight feet between her and Kera. "Set your gun down. Choose a new beginning for yourself."

The gunman eyed her with bright, amused eyes.

Kera glanced hopefully at Randy and then at the big greying man now standing to the front of him. They all stood close, a tight bundle of explosive tension held together by a thin line of prayerful reasoning.

Randy thought he could see a change in the gunman's face, some trickle of belief, desire, exhaustion, and the relaxing of his grip on Kera. He saw that new hope grow in her eyes as she turned to look at her captor.

A nervous smile spread across the face of the gunman like the jagged rip of an earthquake across barren land. His eyes scanned the faces, searching them hopefully one instant, challenging them the next. Then his eyes went again to Kera's. It seemed like he became locked to her, or something she offered him.

Slowly she spoke, "It's okay, Silas. Here, we take care of each other."

The gunman blinked passively at the sound of Kera saying his name and his entire body seemed to relax. Randy could not believe when he released his thick hand from Kera's hair, and then slowly, nervously stooped to lay the weapon on the ground. He righted himself in a gradual, uncertain motion, and then Randy saw someone move to take hold of the rifle.

Chapter 34

Kera looked through her pain and fear at Randy and could see clearly, now that he stood close, how he had aged in his physical appearance and condition. She thought he needed a hospital. He had lost at least twenty pounds and looked so gaunt that he might fold and fail right before her eyes.

But he had come, and there seemed no question he paid a great price for the journey. She watched him, and he gazed steadily back at her as he had not done in a very long time.

If she were going to die she understood now how important it was for them to again see each other. When, in talking to the wild-haired man, Randy admitted his abuses, something let loose inside her.

And as the people of the village stepped closer and closer to peril, to stand with her, she felt strong love and loyalty. Who would ever risk their own life for another? Now she knew.

She listened to them all and watched their faces and tried to follow what they said. But her attention fractured. She kept thinking of her children.

And she kept a close eye on Murtaugh. She noticed him shortly after Randy appeared, camouflaged and crawling through the trees off to their left, cradling his rifle in front of him. She felt disappointed that he had not left, and afraid that in his distressed condition he might do something unfortunate and irreversible. At first she thought about calling out to him, pleading with him to retreat, but she knew that to live she needed all possibilities left open. Calling out to him could cause catastrophe for those around her as easily as remaining silent. So, when he crouched unnoticed behind a tree and took aim so very close to her head, she prayed in her mind, with all her heart.

She was praying when the hand that clenched her hair and forced her spine to twist around the rifle barrel loosened its hold. Her body quivered as it released. Her mind struggled to understand anything of the moment. Nee and Mattie, Randy, Lewis and Lightner, everyone seemed completely captivated by the wild-haired man.

Kera turned her head, aimed her own consciousness at him, and realized this, right now, was the moment that would save her, or kill her. She again saw in his dark eyes a certain confusion and doubt, and recognized it then, as her own. Life included suffering, we can use it to build, or destroy. Without thinking or fearing more, she spoke his name and opened her heart as far as she could.

She saw the barrel of his rifle passing across her body toward the ground and turned a little more and watched as he stooped and laid it flat. *My God, is he going to try?* Part of her wanted to kill him, part of her wanted to thank him.

Lewis, right there, bent and picked up the rifle, and the wild-haired man watched him intently. Kera saw in his eyes the look of the lost boy, so unsure, and as he studied the crowd, then his weapon, then her, she saw his eyes change, saw the soft insecurity cloud. *He can't do it. He doesn't know how to do it.* She realized she could step away and as she did the wild-haired man shifted and again grabbed hold of her.

"Stop! Release her!"

Kera heard the shout and turned her head, saw Murtaugh, standing near the tree, aiming at the wild-haired man. She felt a twist and a catlike quickness, saw the wild-haired man snatch his rifle from the hands of Lewis. Everyone pulled back in horror, and Kera saw the barrel come down next to her face, heard it ROAR!, saw it spit. Murtaugh's gun fired too, and Murtaugh reeled and fell, and a loud POP! came from the wild-haired man's rifle and it simply disappeared. She heard it rattle on the ground.

She heard a snort come from the wild-haired man and a whooshing sound like two palms rubbing hard and fast together.

She saw Randy's jaw drop open and his eyes grow big.

She caught a movement, or a blur of movement, from where Lightner had stood.

She felt a hand shove down hard on the back of her neck and the point of something very sharp enter her near the spine.

She heard another whoosh, only different, and the sound a water balloon makes when it hits hard ground.

The point left her back and the hand let go and she fell forward.

***

Randy couldn't tell who did it, but he saw the pair of hands reach down and lift the rifle from where the gunman had set it. He saw the gunman's dark eyes turn suspiciously to the faces of the crowd. And Randy watched, frozen in horror, as Kera stepped away only to have the gunman again grab her, heard someone call out, saw the blur of motion as the gunman grabbed back his rifle and snapped off a shot at a soldier who had appeared from nowhere. He saw the soldier fire and then fall and the gunman's rifle splinter and fly from his hands. He saw the gunman pull out his long knife and thrust it toward Kera—so fast, everything, horrific, unstoppable.

And he saw at that instant his cane streak through the air at the end of the giant greying man's magnificent swing and change the shape of the gunman's head.

He saw Kera fall to the ground and as he bolted to her everything went silent. He sank down next to her and took her head in his arms and turned it gently. Her eyes shone up at him and she winced. "Are you okay?" he asked. "Ah, Jesus! Kera, are you okay?"

"I don't know," she said and winced again.

Lightner sank down beside him and the others came in around and Randy said, "Check her back, someone, PLEASE! Help me check to see if her back is hurt."

Nee stepped around and the three of them eased her over. "There's blood," Nee exclaimed, and Lightner held her in place with one hand, searched with the fingers of the other, and they came away bloody, but he said, "It's a scratch, I think."

Then a sound started, a loud whacking, and everyone but Kera turned to see Roy Shuntz kicking with all his might at the body of the gunman, his stiff fingers out like daggers at the ends of his hands, his face contorted, and his long brown hair whipping around his head. Several reached out and pulled him back.

Nat and Garrett came up, camera rolling.

To everyone's surprise and momentary alarm the soldier arrived, looking pale, his rifle dangling from his fingers, a bright red surface spot on the side of his shoulder.

"He's our friend," Kera said.

"The children?" Randy asked, and Lightner answered, "In safe keeping. I can have them here shortly." Randy had Kera's head cradled in his lap, in the palms of his hands, and he bent and kissed her face over and over and spattered her with tears.

Part Seven

Chapter 35

A small group helped Kera and Randy back to the little house she shared with the children. Randy swore he saw the blade enter her, and Lightner feared he moved too late, but somehow the gunman, or Silas, as they had heard Kera say, had failed in his attempt to kill. The knife sliced neatly, but superficially, up her back. They used medical glue and bandages to seal it, gave her a pain killer, and made her comfortable in bed.

After sending men scouting to Latrop and the surrounding area, everyone agreed that with the immediate danger of the gunman now behind them, and signs of war apparently heading away, they could return to their village. They continued a close watch on the trail.

Soon, Lightner arrived with the children, who rushed in and looked wide-eyed about the room and considered faces before settling on Randy's. He sat on the opposite edge of the bed, holding a glass of water for Kera. When he saw them a small gasp could be heard coming from his mouth; he stood and gazed at his beautiful babies. He wanted to rush to them, but from their expressions he could see how his shoddy appearance intimidated them. He slowly approached, but they went to their mother, who pulled them close for kisses.

"I explained to them you were here," Lightner said, with a tentative smile toward Randy. Then he dismissed himself. Kera watched him leave, and Randy caught a certain look in her eye.

He went around the bed and hugged his children. "I am so happy to see you! Are you both okay?" Andrew nodded, but remained silent and leaned back toward his mother. Alissa stayed within his arms and said, "Yes, Daddy. Where were you?"

The place grew quiet. Shoes scraped the floor. Mattie said, "Well, we all need to leave and let this family get reacquainted. We'll get these new gentlemen some food and a place to rest." Nat, Garrett, and Murtaugh said good-bye and everyone crowded out.

Randy turned back to the children. "Your mother and I got separated. I was lost, but I finally made it here." He couldn't believe he was again touching them, looking at them, all of them, right there before him, alive and well. He touched Kera's hand with his fingertips.

"You look so thin. How did you get that cut under your eye? Are you okay?" Kera asked Randy, lying there drowsily with her arms at her sides. Andrew stroked her hair as he leaned against the wall.

Randy hadn't even thought about the cut on his face, but felt his side burning again. "I'll be fine. I'm just so thankful we are all here together."

"Me too," Kera murmured, and her eyelids drooped and she fell asleep. Randy signaled for the children to climb in and lay with Kera, and he sat back in a chair and watched the three of them.

He awoke to the sound of Jon Farron knocking lightly on the door and holding out a bundle of clean clothing. "I thought you might be able to use these." He smiled and Randy thanked him. After mentioning needing a bath, Andrew offered to show him the sauna house, so Randy asked Jon to watch Kera. He left her with a kiss on the cheek, told Alissa to stay with her mother, and walked the short distance with his son. He couldn't take his eyes off the boy.

The two started the fire together and while water heated they sat outside in the grass. Just being with his family was enough for Randy and he could feel he shouldn't talk too much too soon. But Andrew started in nervously and told him how they lived at the retreat, how long Kera had been there, and the plan for hiding in the mountains when trouble came.

Randy went into the sauna alone and sent Andrew back to the house. As the steam worked at him he checked his wound and knew he would have to have someone clean it and bandage it for him. He also knew his feelings were mixed and he searched for an answer. He felt overwhelmed, maybe confused. It had all been so much. He had imagined his family as happy to see him as he was to see them, but a certain coolness existed and it made him feel anxious. Perhaps it was expected; the children had seen so little of him and Kera had become deeply troubled with his past behavior.

He had also noticed a familiarity between Kera and Lightner, a man who had saved her life. He wanted to believe his children only needed time, but Kera's behavior truly worried him. He had failed her, and planned to prove his love, if she would let him.

As he ran a bar of soap around his body and poured steaming water over himself he tried to focus on how wonderful it felt.

***

It took two days for Kera and Randy to rest. When they were awake, he spoke often about his thoughts and feelings, but she went slowly and kept the conversation limited to stories of their ordeal.

When she visited, Randy thanked Nee for what she had done in the face of great danger, and Nee praised his actions in return. Kera asked about Lewis, and Nee confided that he was off on his own, sorting through his feelings on what had happened. She knew the incident had traumatized more than one member of the community, but assured Kera no one felt any bitterness toward her. As she left, she said the community wanted to have a meeting the next morning concerning the gunman and the next action to take. Lightner had wrapped the body and stored it in a root cellar.

***

After Nee departed, Kera laid back on the bed, feeling nervous. She knew Randy would want to talk about the future, but she didn't know what to say. She needed to think things through. He came and sat next to her on the bed and looked at her with questions in his eyes. She glanced at the children playing with a puzzle on the floor, then took Randy's hand and kissed it, pulled him down so that he laid with his back to her, spooned together, and whispered, "Can we talk tomorrow, Randy, after the meeting?"

He answered, "Yes, I would like that," and Kera heard the soft vulnerability there, which at the same time brought love and fear welling up in her.

***

Mattie decided, in spite of the recent horror, they would all meet in the barn. For the first time children were not invited. Mattie explained meeting protocol to Randy, Nat, Garrett and Murtaugh.

The first point of discussion was the lack of any sounds of war for the last two days. It seemed implausible, but soon after the death of the gunman all signs of violence had disappeared from the area. They voted to keep lookouts in place.

Randy recognized the attuned energy present in the big barn, how the people of the community handled themselves so decently. But when the conversation changed to the gunman, he started at what he heard.

"Lightner acted out of context for our community. We choose peace and have settled on this issue many times. He chose to protect Kera at any cost and I want to suggest that we all confirm our support for him, or our disagreement, and decide on our direction forward," Mattie said.

Randy could not imagine any other decision but to support Lightner. He was not sure how much he liked the man, but he had great appreciation for the fact that he saved Kera's life. He must have made some reactive movement as he sat listening because Kera reached over and took his hand.

Mattie continued, "After Kera turned back toward the village that morning a number of us sensed her need and as a group we decided quickly that we would go to support her in whatever the situation. But Lightner chose his actions, and although others acted as well, Lightner is the one most directly responsible for the death of a person, and our village must now live with this." Her eyes traveled steadily to many faces before she added, "I would like to hear Lightner's feelings on this issue."

Lightner stood at his bench near the rear of the barn. Randy sized him up again, wondered about him as a man. "I am not proud of what I have done," Lightner said. "But I feel, given the situation, it was right. Maybe that man thought he was defending himself in that last moment. Shots were fired, and it's murky, and I guess situations such as this always are. I do feel confident he would have gone on to harm any number of us, and though I am a man of peace, I could see no other way to ensure our safety. I just could not take the chance. I leave it for my fellow citizens to decide how we shall handle this from here, and I will respect your decision." He sat down.

"Would you invite someone to speak, Lightner?" Mattie asked.

Lightner rose again and said, "Yes. I would like to hear from Kera." He glanced over toward Kera, and Randy watched. There was no question Lightner cared deeply for Kera, it was in his eyes and even the way he held himself all that distance across the room. Still, Randy could feel no bitterness toward him.

Kera let go of Randy's hand and stood. He saw her fingers trembling as she placed her palms against her chest in self-comfort. "Of course I support Lightner in this. I support all of you. There is no doubt in my mind that I would be gone right now had you all not acted as you did. I thank you from the bottom of my heart, what you did for me and my family. I wanted so much to just keep him from you. I am saddened at how this ended, but I support *all* your actions and feel them just. This has all been very confusing, but I do know what that man was capable of. I do know what he had already done."

In the end several people were given a chance to speak. Many pointed out that the gunman—none of them seemed willing, or able, to call him by the name they all now knew—had no identification on him. They simply did not know who he was, where he had actually come from, or who he knew. They had four trusted testimonies, including Randy, as to the man's brutality without cause. They also agreed that he was a product of a society they all rejected.

He was, nonetheless, a human being, and he was dead by their hand. Plenty of them, especially Nee, felt remorse over having held out a promise to a pitiable man only to break it, and, in fact, end up killing him. Still, none offered any other realistic way to have ended the situation. They voted unanimously that, in consideration of the times and all they knew, he would remain forever a secret of the community, and Lightner would be supported by all if ever needed.

The community also voted that the gunman be buried in their cemetery down by the river. It seemed right. People felt that, though they had sent the darkest energies of his soul away to diffuse, they wanted his innocent elements to rest in peace among them.

With all that accomplished, the people were tired and voted to adjourn.

As they left the barn many reached out and touched Randy. He felt welcomed by them and respected the way the community organized and regarded itself. But, he had not been called to speak, and he wanted to. He didn't think he liked the practice by which speakers were chosen in the meeting. It seemed undemocratic. If your name was never called, you would have no voice.

Also, though he understood the gunman needed to be stopped, the gunman's separateness haunted Randy. *Where do people like... Silas... come from?* He reasoned that the man was a victim of the society he had seen come to waste. The gunman wasn't born a killer, and so something about his environment turned him into one. Perhaps it was the same issue turning school kids into murderers. To some degree, a healthy society needs a unified soul, and Randy now saw how the social structure he had participated in could also divide and turn people against each other.

Chapter 36

After the meeting, Kera arranged to have the children stay with child-care for a little longer and she led Randy into the woods where she sometimes walked.

To her own surprise, Kera turned down a path she had never taken. Randy followed silently behind her, and they came to a level, open grove of large old pines. It was a hazy, damp day. Thinking of what she wanted to say, everything balled up inside her and she turned and wrapped her arms around Randy, put her face in the angle of his neck and shoulder, squeezed him, realized she had not done that in a very long time.

"Are you all right?" he asked.

Where can I begin? I do love him.

"Kera, I am so sorry for what I have done to you and the children—I realize everything now—how I let my career come in between us—how I failed to show each of you the love you deserve."

He eased her head up from his shoulder and she saw how serious and committed he felt. From what he'd been saying since coming together, how he behaved, she believed him. "I can see that, Randy."

"Can you forgive me?"

"Yes," she said. She had forgiven him the moment he came for them. His eyes contained elements she had not seen in him for so long—sadness and humility, desperation, love. Those eyes tore at her and made her want to be someone different. A mother and wife must do all she could to keep her family together.

But absolution and devotion are not the same. She did love him, but that love had changed. You could love someone, hope all the best for them, but not share their dreams and sleep wrapped in their arms and ache for them as part of your everyday life. "I forgive you and I love you Randy, but what are we going to do?"

"We're going to start over. What do you want?"

"I want to stay here. Live a simpler, peaceful life, be close to nature. I want to grow food, build friendships with considerate people who are happy with themselves, be creative with my work and my play. Be with my children and not be torn away from them by an incessant lack of time."

Randy laughed lightly and she knew it was a relieved laugh, a loving laugh. He said, "Well, I can see why you like it here. We can stay for awhile, until it's safe to leave, and see how it goes until then."

She pulled away from him gently but purposefully and quietly said, "I don't need to see how it goes. I have made my decision. I have never been happier than I am here and that goes for the children as well."

The laugh lines dropped from his face. "Okay. Let's talk about it, Kera."

"But you, Randy, how are you going to stay in a place like this?"

"What do you mean?"

"You feed off city life, it's where you get your energy."

"I've done a lot of thinking, Kera. What's most important to me is my family."

She could see the fear growing in his eyes again and it hurt her. "But what would you do here?"

"I don't know, it would take some time to think that through, but it's not a question without an answer."

"You'd go crazy, Randy. You're a man who lives through what you do. And this place is not you."

His eyes scrunched down and he studied her, and she realized he was seeing through her. Still, she couldn't bring herself to say it. "Randy, who are you?"

"A man in love with his wife and his children. A man who feels he has been living blindly for years." He stepped toward her. "I see you, Kera. I'm sorry for the way I was, but I see you now."

"What are you going to do with your life?"

"What? I don't know—I—"

"Randy! A day has never gone by when you did not know what you wanted to do. In these past weeks, with all you have been through, what is it? What do you want to do?"

"Sweetheart, we've both been through a lot. I'm not certain yet. I only know what I don't want to do and that's go back to the way I was."

Kera saw the corner of his mouth twitch ever so slightly. He knew her better than she thought and he wasn't missing anything, not anymore. "Kera, what is the problem here? I mean, what are you really getting at?"

"Don't try and turn it around on me. I am asking you a question." She worked hard to remain calm and brave. Living through what she had, this should come easy, but it felt harder than anything she had ever done. Fear engulfed her and she didn't like it; she felt sick and tired of fear. Kera turned away without his answer and moved through the trees, trying to see clearly what she needed to do, how best to do it.

She had not intended this. She still loved Randy very much. But her heart had gone to Lightner. She felt dishonest in admitting it, in breaking her promises.

But for a long time you tried your best. You did all you could and now it is gone. Move on as you know you must.

She turned and saw his face, realized she could not continue hurting him. She wanted Randy to repair, to live happily, but she could no longer be his nourishment. She needed to concentrate on nourishing herself and their children in the new ways she had discovered. She went to him and stopped just inches away and looked gently into his eyes. "Randy, I'm so sorry. I'm just not in love with you anymore."

At first he didn't move, he only looked at her as if he had frozen in place. She saw the blood drain from his face and she began to cry. His eyes went to the ground. "No," is all he said.

He turned and stumbled, moved toward the house, then stopped. She wanted to go to him and wrap her arms around him, but she couldn't.

Then he turned and trudged back to her and brought his eyes up off the ground and back onto her face, and said, "It's okay… I understand, Kera." He went past her then and walked deeper into the wood.

It was nearly midnight when she heard him return to the home and later watched him sleep on the living room couch.

Chapter 37
One Year Later…

Kera pulled hot muffins from a wood-fired oven and sat them on top. She poked them with a fork: done. She smiled and walked through the living room of the log home and stuck her head out the door. The summer air smelled of moist growth. "Alissa, Andrew, Lightner! They're ready." She went back inside and poured two glasses of goat's milk and two cups of iced herbal tea. The door bounced open and the children ran inside, grabbed a muffin each without comment, and gulped the milk.

Lightner came in slowly, the way he always did, looking about him as if he had never stepped into the place before. He smiled at her and silently picked up the tea and sipped, took a muffin and sank down into the worn couch in the living room.

Kera sat next to him. In the warm home she wore a summer dress the color of pine bark and had a few buttons undone down the front. Her feet were bare. She had let her hair grow long and it reached a good foot down the center of her back. She sipped and nibbled and watched Lightner eat, wondered at the fact that his eyes had cleared up months ago and the allergies never returned. She reached out and scratched at his thick grey sideburn and ran a finger along his jaw.

He stopped and smiled again and, though his eyes had cleared and looked at her now full of playfulness, they sometimes let slip a hint of sorrow. When once she asked, he answered, "I am only wishing you had found me many years earlier."

All she knew is that she trusted Lightner as if she had known him forever. In him she saw the great good of men.

It had been nine months since the revolution ended and Randy left. They had lived with the children in the other little house for awhile, but Kera could not coax love back, made her final decision, and soon Randy eased away. They explained to the children that he would be back again, always near.

Nat, and reluctantly Garrett, had agreed to turn over the videotape and join the community in silence concerning the tragedy. While they soon departed, Murtaugh agreed at the urging of the community to join them in their way of living. They disassembled his rifle and used the pieces in creation and repair of everyday and mostly functional items.

His uniform he washed, folded, and stored.   He was now safety consultant for the village, and also a repairman for most anything technical.

Kera's life story had included intense struggle and she considered the acceptance and analysis of that struggle the most direct route to complete healing.   She went to the grave of the wild-haired man often, alone, and slowly her most personal thoughts held only forgiveness. How else could anything ever be salvaged?

The grave never went unattended or without flowers, and only a week ago Helen Shuntz had been seen sitting down near it.   She and Roy had grown more together than ever.

Kera walked in the forest each day and soon learned the name of every tree.   Her mind would calmly consider life as she walked along, and one day she came to a place within herself where she settled on the fact that understanding everything proved impossible.   Accepting and moving on was her answer.

***

Randy exited Beefy's Foreign Automotive in Flagstaff, Arizona.   At over five thousand feet elevation the spring heat still rose in waves off the pavement of the parking lot.   He sipped an iced double mocha latte decaf and had a camera hanging around his neck and another under an arm.   His beard had not been trimmed in a week and his hair fell over his ears in strands rarely combed.   He'd gained back his natural weight and moved with the fit, easy stride of someone who understood efficiency.

Walking up to the side passenger window of his road-worn 1984 Volkswagen Vanagon camper van, he looked in and smiled at Nee. "The guy says he thinks this is a problem that occurs regularly with older Volkswagens.   He has to go inside it to see for sure and it will cost about a hundred and fifty bucks to start the process."

Nee smiled and sat there with her hands folded in her lap, her legs crossed, and her feet tucked in under them.   Her black hair hung in a long braid and she wore a brown baseball cap, a grey sweatshirt with cutoff sleeves, and a pair of baggy white cotton pants that ended well above the ankles.   Her toenails were painted purple.

Randy sipped the latte and smiled back at her, waiting, thinking, his elbows on the window frame.   "He also said he doesn't think it is serious or that it will break down on us."

Nee smiled again and puckered her lips in thought.   Randy stepped back and snapped a photograph of her.

The pain that had welled up inside and threatened to devour him had finally shrunk down to an occasional and manageable twinge. A year's passing had brought relief.

After the talk with Kera he fought countless emotional duels with himself—days of isolation, nights of bitter contest. Though they never let him see, he knew Kera loved Lightner, and while he came to respect the man, he was not brave enough to watch that love unfold. He began meditating often, photographed everything around the village he could, worked at the disturbing puzzles in his mind and moment by moment rebuilt a bond with his children. He considered leaving and taking them with him, but knew the conflict and pain he would cause. He simply could not rip apart the safe and happy world in which they resided. The facts had changed and there was nothing he could do but accept this and help smooth the way for everyone. He did not want any more anger, pain or violence.

About the time he felt ready to leave Better Way the revolution ended. It had failed in the sense of overturning the government, but the possibility of establishing some new structure, new system, remained under the hopeful and broad umbrella of expanded talks between those in power and those most loudly demanding change. In the end an overwhelming number of citizens supported the goals of the revolution— if not the means—and had become active in peaceful pursuit of those goals. The government had little choice but to listen. Still, the extent of physical damage to the country, and, beyond that, the grievous loss of life, ripped apart the American coverlet and left many people bewildered and uncertain of where the country might begin the process of redirection. It was going to take a lot of time.

Fragmented bus service began operating and Better Way citizens purchased a ticket for Randy. They assured him it was anything but personal. Making his way back to New York City, he saw the countrywide devastation as never before. Entire cities lay in ruin. Millions of people lived on the streets, in tent villages, or abandoned burned-out cars along often impassable roadways. Even with communication partly restored, he couldn't reach his family back east.

But, regardless of war, some things remained eerily unchanged. While feeling deep gratitude in discovering his family safe and healthy in New York City, incredulity elbowed in when, on the day he walked through the door, he found his father and brother locked in one of their antagonistic and pointless arguments at the dining room table. Still, old Ben cried and Russell made an embarrassment of himself, the way he fawned over his returned brother.

The bank was foreclosing on his building, so he made a promise to never again borrow financing. But one day he retrieved his equipment and scrutinized the photographs from his journey. The images and the truth simultaneously appeared before him and a new calling surged through his being as if those photos had been electrified. His country needed him and his abilities. Perhaps he could help his fellow man achieve the great change.

He sent his war photos to a prominent national magazine and a couple newspapers. Two days later they were purchased with interest toward other projects.

Within five days of reaching New York, Randy found Claris and Jimmy and gave them as a farewell fund some of the money he was able to make from selling the studio equipment. He bought the van and prepared it for a journey.

He didn't know where he wanted to go but soon developed a nose for journalism. He rolled mile after mile and photographed real life, not made-for-profit fairy tales, and what he continued to learn about his country and his people filled his heart with excitement and his brain with challenges, if not his wallet with what it took to feed oneself. He wasn't against making a living, but never again would money be his main focus. He found himself pounding his chest and making loud obnoxious sounds on a regular basis. *I have walked through the valley of the shadow of death...and it's sure good living on the other side!*

As he traveled the country, and the country repaired, he began exchanging letters, then phone calls, and finally emails with Kera and the children, and one day Kera mentioned that Nee was hoping to hear from him. They talked and she explained how she had lived at Better Way since coming to America and really hadn't experienced much of the country beyond. He thought that helped to make them perfect road companions. She met him along the way. He intended a platonic arrangement, feeling that he needed more time, but, well, okay, when the hell had that ever worked for anyone?

The two of them had now been traveling together for nearly two months. He felt full of purpose and Nee supported him doing what he did. She had no love of money, or people who coveted too much of it, was proud to live simply and believed completely in Randy's destiny as a communicator of their country's condition.

She was a delight. Everything he had come to realize throughout his march to Better Way had already taken place in her mind, in her spirit. She understood the stories he told of moments along the way and helped him see where he might go with what he learned. She would sing to him as they drove down the road, her oriental songs, and she was teaching him Mandarin as well as bits of other ancient languages. He had watched her in times of frustration or challenge and saw her uncanny ability to relax and feel her way to a proper understanding. In the van she would wrap her arms and legs around him and sleep so soundly and peacefully it made him yearn for her endlessly.

Nee looked at him now and said, "Let's go for it!"

He chuckled. "You don't want to get it repaired?"

"Nah," she shook her head and smiled and her white teeth glowed in the shaded interior. "That's too much money when they don't even know. It might be something very simple."

Randy smiled. He liked the way Nee thought. They might break down in the middle of nowhere, and she knew it, and he'd come to understand... she hoped for that. Bringing up his wrist he glanced at a red, white, and blue Mickey Mouse watch. "Shall we drive for a couple more hours today?"

"I would like to." She nodded vigorously, then reached out and placed her palm on his face, touching her thumb to the slight straight scar beneath his eye.

Randy felt the wonder of the moment. He went around and climbed into the driver's seat, started the engine, got the van rolling. The creaky thing bounced out onto the road. They had one month before heading back to Better Way for a summer break. Both of them looked forward to seeing Kera, the children and Lightner, and had plans to take Andrew and Alissa on the road for two months. Randy wanted his children to see their country, to hear it, smell it, and feel it. He wanted them to try and understand it, what it meant to be American. But before that, there was an Indian in Wyoming he wanted Nee to meet.

****

www.ingramcontent.com/pod-product-compliance
Lightning Source LLC
Chambersburg PA
CBHW062021170626
46813CB00001B/244